How had Juliet [...]
how ripped Ev[...]

His black T-shirt didn't do much to hide the muscles of his biceps, pecs or abs. Thank God.

Evan turned to the fridge for a couple of water bottles.

"You want?" Evan held up a bottle, his dimple showing with his smile.

Looking at him, Juliet realized she did indeed want.

Evan. Right now. Tonight.

She knew he wanted her, too. This wasn't just an undercover op for Evan. *She* wasn't just an undercover op for Evan.

This time she didn't plan to take no for an answer. She had let the attack steal too many months of her life. She didn't plan to let it have even one more day. She wanted Evan and she knew he wanted her.

What was that saying? Leap and the net will appear.

Juliet leaped.

She slid her own jacket off and walked over to him. "Yeah, I want."

UNTRACEABLE

BY
JANIE CROUCH

Printed and bound in Spain
by CPI, Barcelona

Published in Great Britain 2015
by Mills & Boon, an imprint of Harlequin (UK) Limited,
Eton House, 18-24 Paradise Road, Richmond, Surrey, TW9 1SR

© 2015 Janie Crouch

ISBN: 978-0-263-25308-5

46-0615

Janie Crouch has loved to read romance her whole life. She cut her teeth on Mills & Boon® romance novels as a pre-teen, then moved on to a passion for romantic suspense as an adult. Janie lives with her husband and four children overseas. Janie enjoys traveling, long-distance running, movie-watching, knitting and adventure/obstacle racing. You can find out more about her at www.janiecrouch.com.

To my Stephanie: it never ceases to amaze me that you call me your friend. You are a tireless source of support, inspiration and encouragement not just to me but to so many others. Here's some #nofilter for you: you are a treasure, a beauty, and someone who radiates God's love and kindness in everything you do.

I adore you.

Chapter One

Evan Karcz woke up the same way he had almost every day for the past year and a half: with Juliet Branson's terrified sobs echoing through his dreams.

Evan didn't jump out of bed and grab his Glock as he had in the early days. Nor did he have to rush to the bathroom before he lost the contents of his stomach.

Now he just breathed in and out slowly, calming his pounding heart, staring up at the ceiling. He threw the covers off his body in an effort to chill down, even though it was early spring and the temperatures were still cool here in southern Maryland, near Washington, DC. Evan wiped with his arm the small amount of sweat that beaded on his forehead.

He didn't lie there long. It was early, not even close to 5:00 a.m., but the possibility of going back to sleep was pretty much nonexistent. He might as well get up and start moving. He slipped on shorts and sweats and packed a gym bag with clothes for the rest of his day.

He'd head in to Omega Sector Headquarters and get in a workout before work officially started. *Exercise in order to exorcise*, Evan thought, and smiled grimly. Anything would be better than staying in that big bed by himself with nothing surrounding him but his own guilt.

Given the day ahead and all it had in store, he shouldn't

be surprised that the dream had resurfaced with such vividness. Today he'd be unable to avoid seeing the subject of his troubled dreams—his ex-partner, Juliet Branson. Although *avoid* wasn't really accurate. Evan never tried to avoid seeing Juliet; the opposite, in fact. He'd been trying to talk to her for eighteen months, with no real success. Today, Juliet would be unable to avoid seeing *him*.

Evan drove to Omega Headquarters, thankful that the early hour at least helped shorten the notoriously ugly commute. He pulled into the secure parking garage of the nondescript building that housed Omega Sector—a covert interagency task force made up of the best personnel the country had to offer. Evan had worked here for eight years, ever since his recruitment out of the FBI when he was twenty-seven.

The heaviness from this morning's dream lingered as he walked through the doors of Omega's main building. Strange how these halls had once thrilled him, how he had loved everything about his job as an undercover agent. But since Juliet's…incident he couldn't seem to find the same passion he'd once had for the work.

Passionate or not, he was going back under. And he wasn't looking forward to the team meeting that would take place later today, when Juliet would learn the details of the assignment. Evan rubbed a hand over his face. He knew Bob Sinclair, his undercover persona, was a name Juliet would never want to hear again. Nobody blamed her for that.

Omega Headquarters stood largely empty at this hour except for the security personnel. Evan passed through the extensive checks to confirm his identity, then jogged down the stairs into the large gym area. State-of-the-art workout equipment stood side by side with old-school metal weights, a fitting metaphor for Omega: the best blend of new and old techniques, working in unison. There were also rooms for sparring, for yoga, and a full-size track for running. Evan left his gym bag in the locker room and walked into the main workout area.

Sparring definitely topped the agenda for this morning. Evan decided he might as well take his aggression out on the almost-human plastic dummies and leather punching bags, since the individuals he really wanted to take his aggression out on were well beyond his reach.

He grabbed a pair of gloves meant to save his knuckles from the worst of the damage, and was reaching for the doorknob of the sparring room when he heard noises from someone already in there. Who the hell would be up and going at this hour?

Evan let the door shut and walked around the corner so he could see through the small window of the room. Juliet Branson…

Evidently he hadn't been the only one with nightmares this morning.

Evan couldn't help but watch, enthralled, as she danced among the targets with grace and precision. The black tank and tight workout pants she wore gave her the freedom to move as she wanted, stopping sometimes midair and pivoting in a different direction. Her five-foot-four-inch frame was average in height—at six-one Evan was a full head taller than her—but the way she fought belied her smaller stature, the litheness of her muscles evident. Her long blond hair was pulled tightly back in a ponytail, so as not to impede her actions.

The power behind her kicks and punches was impressive. Had these dummies been live people, each would've fallen to the ground, gasping for air. She showed them, and herself, no mercy. Rapid-fire strikes. Over and over, at a punishing speed and rhythm. Sweat dripped and flew with each of her assaults. You'd never be able to tell she'd been out of the field for the past eighteen months.

Evan watched from the shadows of the hallway, where she wouldn't be able to see him. As a trained operative, he recognized and appreciated Juliet's talent in close-quarter fighting like this, although admittedly, fighting dummy targets was completely different than fighting a real opponent.

She attacked the dummies as if she were warding off a demon army from hell. Evan's arms hung at his sides and his shoulders slumped. Fighting demons was probably an apt description for her actions.

He wished he could fight them for her. Or at least with her, but Juliet had no interest in being anywhere near him. Not that he could blame her. A partner was supposed to have your back, to protect you, even in dire circumstances. Evan had failed her in the worst possible way. And Juliet had paid a horrible price for his failure.

He turned and walked the other way, leaving her to her battle. Entering the room would just cause her to tense up and rapidly vacate, anyway. But not before fear and distrust suffused her features when the door first opened. It wasn't just him she distrusted, Evan knew, but he hated the look, anyway.

Plus, he'd be seeing it soon enough, later today in the conference room, when he mentioned Bob Sinclair.

Evan headed up the stairs to the indoor track. It seemed as if he would be trying to outrun his own demons today rather than fighting them. But no matter how fast he ran, he knew they'd still be there when he finished.

JULIET SWUNG HER LEG around in a powerful round-house kick, hitting the target one last time. She took satisfaction in how hard the dummy fell to the ground before its weighted bottom slowly brought it back to a vertical position.

Yeah, she could take down a target dummy like a champ. Too bad that didn't really do anybody much good. In a fight with a real person these days, she was damn near useless.

Of course, Juliet wasn't an active agent anymore, so it wasn't as if she was going to use her hand-to-hand fighting skills anytime soon. But it would be nice to know she'd have them if she needed them, rather than freezing up or cowering in a corner if a real person came at her.

Juliet backhanded the dummy again for good measure.

She grabbed a towel and mopped up her sweat from the past hour of pounding everything in sight. It was now just before 5:00 a.m., and there'd be other people around soon, if not already. Dedicated Omega workers—agents and otherwise—would come in to get a good workout before going upstairs to their jobs.

Juliet would like to think that was what she was doing, too. That she was here at Omega HQ sometimes eighteen or twenty hours a day because of her dedication to an important job and stellar organization. That she worked long hours because she wanted to do her part in keeping her country safe from criminals and terrorists.

Not because of the fear that seemed to pour over her like some sort of suffocating ooze every time she left this place.

It was so much easier to stay here at Omega than to go home alone to her house. Juliet felt safe here, even when she was by herself. There was no chance someone was going to throw a sack over her head and drag her out of a sound sleep in the middle of the night. Of course, there was very little chance that would happen at her home, but Juliet couldn't quite seem to convince her mind of that as she lay awake at night, terrified, remembering. So she stayed here at Omega as much as possible.

It had been eighteen months since her attack. Things should be getting better, not worse. But that wasn't the case.

She glanced down at her phone, which had begun vibrating in her hand as she walked toward the locker room. Her stomach rolled when she saw the screen.

A new email. Not for Juliet Branson, but for Lisa Sinclair, an undercover role Juliet had played in her last mission as an active operative. The one where she'd lost nearly everything.

Sweetheart, I've been thinking about you all night. Soon we'll be together, just the two of us. Sooner than you think.

As usual, no signature or notification of who'd sent it. Juliet leaned against the wall for support and brought her hand up to her suddenly aching head. This email was benign compared to the graphic nature of some of the others. She closed her eyes briefly, pushing those thoughts away. She couldn't let this overwhelm her, not today.

But she knew she'd be thinking about the message all day. And the fact that the emails were starting to come more frequently and become more personal.

Juliet had given the emails to Omega tech support, of course, but they hadn't been able to provide any insight about where or from whom they were coming. Never the same IP address—it seemed to bounce around all over the world.

And she couldn't bring herself to tell anyone about how much the emails upset her. She knew there were people here who cared about her. Two of her three brothers worked at Omega, for goodness' sake; she saw them almost every day. But they were the last people she wanted to talk to about this. Being the only daughter in the family, Juliet had always been surrounded by overprotective, alpha-male testosterone.

Talking to her brothers about residual issues from her attack and rape? Um, no. Not in this lifetime.

Nor did she want to talk to them about creepy emails. Her siblings had work to do, *real* cases to worry about.

"Hey, Jules, you okay?"

Juliet pushed herself away from the wall at the sound of Evan Karcz's voice. He, like her brothers, always called her Jules. She mashed the button to delete the email notification and turn her phone screen black. She didn't want to have to explain it to Evan.

"Um, yeah, I'm fine. Just going in to clean up after my workout. You're here early."

"I was about to run, but I forgot my headphones and was coming back to grab them. You sure you're okay? You look a little pale. And you must have been sparring because you have something in your—"

Evan moved toward her, hand upraised, and before Juliet could stop herself she took a step back, flinching. He froze, then dropped his arm to his side, shoulders drooping.

"Evan, I'm sorry—"

"No, it's okay. Um, you just have some lint or something in your hair." He backed up another step. "I'll see you." He turned and walked off, away from the locker room. So much for getting headphones.

Juliet wanted to hit something, even though she'd just spent over an hour doing just that. She hadn't meant to flinch, especially not from Evan; she'd just been in a particularly vulnerable state of mind because of that email. It didn't take a genius to figure out her reaction had hurt him.

She and Evan had worked together for years. She'd

known him most of her life. He was her brothers' best friend. Hell, he was one of *her* best friends—more, if she was honest. Or had potentially been more. It seemed so long ago that she and Evan used to flirt with each other, secure in the knowledge of *someday*.

But someday never came.

Now whenever she thought of Evan all Juliet could recall was that moment when he'd found her. Of how he'd covered her broken, mostly naked body with his own clothes, actually crying as he had radioed in for an ambulance.

Juliet knew it was unfair to keep Evan frozen in that moment. To keep *herself* frozen there. But she couldn't seem to do anything about it.

So she'd basically avoided him for the past year and a half.

Which hadn't been too difficult, considering her cowardly choice to leave active work and stick herself behind a desk instead. Part handler, part analyst, part strategist. A little too good to be any of them, but not fit to be back out in the field. Juliet couldn't see a time when she would ever be ready for agent work again.

Her job might not be thrilling, but it was safe. And safe was the most important thing to her right now. Although she wished those job changes hadn't hurt Evan.

Juliet made her way to the locker room, showering and changing into her work clothes of black pants and a matching black blazer over a white blouse. The jacket was specially fitted to hold her shoulder holster and firearm. Although Juliet wasn't an agent and wasn't required to be armed at all times, she was rarely without her Glock 9 mm.

Normally she wouldn't be dressed this way. Unlike the FBI, with their daily suits and loafers, Omega tended to be a more casually dressed workforce. But today Juliet had an important operational-specifications meeting. Her boss, Dennis Burgamy, would be there, which made her a little uneasy. Burgamy did not tend to dirty his hands with the day-to-day planning of undercover operations. Thus her more professional suit: armor for battle.

Something was up; she knew it. Juliet was going to need as much armor as she could get.

Chapter Two

Juliet already sat in the conference room between her brothers Cameron and Sawyer, chatting with both, when Evan arrived at the meeting. He wasn't surprised to find the two men flanking Juliet. If Cameron and Sawyer had their way, she'd be wrapped in cotton wool and hidden away somewhere.

The Branson men were brothers to Evan in every way but blood. He'd known them most of his life—Sawyer, Cameron, and their older brother, Dylan, who no longer worked at Omega—and would do anything for any of them. But their overprotectiveness when it came to Juliet frustrated Evan.

Juliet had strength none of the Branson family wanted to admit, including herself. Right now it lay hidden under layers of fear and regret. But the strength resided inside her. He'd seen it multiple times during their tenure as partners in the field. He wished Juliet would trust him to help her find that strength again, but he couldn't force it to happen. Could only wait and hope.

Evan deliberately took the seat directly across from Juliet. She nodded at him and gave him a polite smile before looking away. He decided to engage her brothers instead.

"What's up, Tweedledum and Tweedledummer?"

Neither brother was up to his normal speed. Both were

recovering from gunshot wounds received in action over the past few months, Cameron from an undercover operation gone wrong, and Sawyer from an attempt to fix that. They would recover fully, but were manning desks until they were cleared for field duty.

Not that either seemed to mind desk duty right now. It gave them each more time to spend at home with the loves-of-their-lives, also recently acquired in the cases. Having met Cameron's Sophia and Sawyer's Megan, Evan whole-heartedly supported his friends wanting to stick close to home.

"Watch it there, shorty. I can still kick your butt even with my arm in this sling," Sawyer told him. The "shorty" barb had been around since they were all teenagers and Evan had been the last to hit his growth spurt, so he'd been a head shorter than the Branson boys for a time. Even though they now were all around the same height—each over six feet— Evan still got called shorty from time to time. But it brought the slightest of smiles to Juliet's lips, so he let it slide.

"Yeah, I'd hate to put your other arm in a sling," Evan retorted.

"Why are we having a big powwow with Burgamy?" Cameron cut in, referring to their boss, Dennis Burgamy. "Since when does he sit in on normal op-specification meetings?"

"I was wondering the same thing myself." Juliet glanced briefly at Evan before turning away.

Evan knew he had to tell her about him going back undercover as Sinclair. He didn't want her to hear it for the first time in the middle of the meeting.

"I don't know why Burgamy wants to be in the meeting exactly," Evan said. "But you guys should know that I'm going back under as Bob Sinclair."

Cameron muttered a curse. Sawyer didn't say anything. He'd already been aware that the Sinclair persona had been resurrected a few weeks ago. Evan had posed as Bob Sinclair to help Sawyer out in a case.

The color washed out of Juliet's face and she stood, her chair rolling back from the table forcefully. All three men stood, as well.

"Excuse me," she murmured.

"Jules—" Sawyer reached for her, but stopped when she flinched away.

"No, I'm all right. I'll be back in a minute."

Evan watched as she all but fled from the room. He gave a heavy sigh and sat back down.

"Should one of us go after her?" Cameron asked.

"No, let her go," Evan said. "She just needs to pull herself together."

Sawyer and Cameron looked as though they might argue, but decided against it. Evan knew he was right. Juliet would not want any of them coming after her, crowding her space. She'd be back when she was ready, which would probably be sooner than either of her overprotective brothers suspected.

Evan hated Juliet hearing about the Bob Sinclair situation this way, but knew it would have upset her no matter when or how she heard about it. There was no way around that.

Dennis Burgamy, head of operations at Omega, entered the room along with his assistant, Chantelle DiMuzio, who looked harried. Of course, poor Chantelle always looked harried. Anybody who worked that closely with their boss day in and day out couldn't help it.

Burgamy took the seat at the head of the table, glanced around, and turned to Evan. "Where's Juliet?"

"She had to step out. She'll be back soon."

Burgamy, dressed impeccably in a dark suit, sighed impatiently. Everyone knew there was no love lost between him and the Branson family. Each side tolerated the other, but only barely. Usually Burgamy didn't have much problem with Juliet, however. Why had he even asked about her?

"Well, I don't have much spare time, so we'll need to start without her," Burgamy barked.

"Okay, to get everyone up to speed," Evan began, trying to stall to give Juliet time to return. "In the midst of Sawyer's operation last month with Dr. Megan Fuller and DS-13, we weren't sure if the Ghost Shell hardware system was going to be sold on the black market. Or if we would have the means of stopping it if it was sold."

"A disaster on all counts," Burgamy said.

Everyone nodded. Evan continued. "We were in a time crunch so I put feelers out on the street using some past covers, in case I needed to infiltrate any black market weapons groups."

Evan looked over at Sawyer. "Fortunately, Sawyer was able to acquire Ghost Shell and arrest or eliminate most of DS-13, whom we are considering permanently disbanded."

Sawyer raised an eyebrow. That wasn't exactly how the whole thing had gone down, but whatever. Close enough.

Evan looked up, his attention caught by Juliet coming back through the door.

"Sorry," she murmured to Burgamy, before taking her seat between her brothers once again.

Her features were still a little pinched, but she seemed otherwise well composed. As Evan knew, she was stronger than she thought.

"I was just explaining the situation with Sawyer and DS-13 last month," he said to her. "You already know all of that."

Juliet nodded. She did know it. As a matter of fact, she was the reason Sawyer and his fiancé, Megan Fuller, had gotten out alive at all.

"In the midst of that operation, one of my feelers got a lot of response—Bob Sinclair." Juliet flinched as Evan said it, but he continued. "First, it was DS-13 who expressed interest, but since then someone from Vince Cady's group has made contact."

That got everyone's attention. Vince Cady was a crime boss with his fingers in almost every piece of ugliness you could find: weapons, technology, blackmail. On the surface he looked clean, and did a good job of covering his tracks. Omega had never found anything that could be used to indict Cady, but they knew he was dirty. And even more, he was key to a number of larger groups and sellers. If Omega could get dirt on Cady, they could take down a lot of other bad guys.

Vince Cady was known as a grade-A bastard. Smooth, but with a cruel edge. And very, *very* smart. Which was why he'd never been arrested.

Cady initiating contact with Bob Sinclair provided a huge break for Omega. Having an undercover foothold in his group would be measurable progress, bringing Omega much closer to taking Cady and his network down.

"That's excellent," Cameron said. "It gives Bob Sinclair instant credibility. Cady came to you, not the other way around."

Evan nodded. "Yes, I plan to use that fact to my advantage as much as possible."

"Did he contact you for a specific buy?" Burgamy asked.

Juliet spoke up. "Our most recent intel about Cady suggests that he may have acquired some surface-to-air missiles to sell on the black market. That would be a perfect fit for Bob Sinclair."

Juliet's voice wavered only the slightest bit when she said it.

Evan nodded in encouragement. "I agree," he told the group. "Bob and Lisa Sinclair's reputation is as entrepreneurs. They…" Evan looked over and saw Juliet's pinched features as well as Sawyer and Cameron's thunderous looks, so changed his pronoun choice. "Bob, I mean, is known as a jack-of-all-trades, dabbling in weapons, pharmaceutical drugs, technology, information. He's the type of guy who can help Vince Cady out, so I'm not surprised by the contact."

"Okay, good," Burgamy said. Chantelle, sitting next to him, kept clicking away, taking notes on her tablet the entire time. "What's the timetable for this op?"

Evan still didn't know why Burgamy was even here. Yes, Cady was a pretty big fish and infiltrating his group would be a huge coup, but why the boss would sit in on an early planning meeting like this was beyond Evan.

"I have a meeting scheduled with Cady tomorrow in Baltimore, his base of operation. Since Bob Sinclair is an old cover, I'm just going to pull and use all the old info, IDs, etc. Prep is relatively minimal. I can go under immediately, depending on how the meeting with Cady goes."

"Eighteen months absence isn't going to be a problem?" Burgamy asked.

"Yeah, I'm sure it will come up. I'll make certain I have something to say." Evan didn't know what that would be yet. The truth wasn't an option, and the whole situation with Lisa Sinclair was quite complicated. Evan would have multiple answers rehearsed, depending on exactly what questions were asked, how they were asked, and the climate of the conversation.

That's what a good undercover agent did: constantly took stock of the situation and adapted.

"And what about Lisa Sinclair, Bob's 'wife'?" Burgamy asked.

And there it was, the announcement of the elephant in the room. Evan didn't look over at Juliet to see her reaction. She didn't need anyone gawking at her.

"What about her?" Evan responded, keeping his tone neutral.

"Bob and Lisa Sinclair were a couple. A tight couple." Burgamy leaned more of his weight on his arms, which were folded on the conference table. "The cover worked so well because the criminal groups you infiltrated bought into the whole Bonnie and Clyde, can't-live-without-each-other vibe the two of you gave off."

Evan didn't want to admit it, but Burgamy was right. Going in without Juliet would make this mission more difficult. But the alternative wasn't an option, so Evan wasn't even entertaining it as such. He glanced briefly over at Juliet, who was looking intently down at her notes.

"I'll make it work, as Bob Sinclair alone. I've certainly done my share of undercover work with no partner." Evan could see the Branson brothers nodding, backing him up. Cameron in particular knew about long-term solo undercover work, having recently come off a life-changing operation himself.

But Burgamy wasn't willing to let it go. "Isn't Cady going to wonder about Lisa? Her absence will certainly make suspicions higher, perhaps even jeopardize the entire mission."

Evan sat up straighter in his chair, then leaned toward Burgamy. He could see Juliet's brothers mirroring his actions, tension evident. Evan didn't like where this was going.

"I'm a trained, experienced operative, Burgamy. I'll handle it."

The boss's smile didn't reach his eyes. "I have every confidence in your abilities, Karcz. But the facts are the facts."

Burgamy leaned back in the chair in a relaxed pose that belied the words he'd said. Suddenly the entire meeting became clear to Evan, the purpose of Burgamy's attendance and his endgame. And Evan had played right into his hands. He knew what Burgamy was going to say before his boss even said it, but there was nothing he could do.

Burgamy turned to Juliet. "Juliet needs to go back undercover as Lisa Sinclair to ensure the success of this operation."

Chapter Three

Juliet heard the words that came out of Burgamy's mouth as if from far away. She searched for a response inside herself—knew she should have some sort of explosive negative comment—but could find only silence.

She couldn't go back undercover as Lisa Sinclair. She wasn't ready. It would be a disaster.

It ended up she didn't have to give an answer, anyway. Her brothers took care of the explosive negative comments for her.

"There's no way in hell, Burgamy," Sawyer, her normally laid-back younger brother, said grimly.

The expletive that came from Cameron should've had her smacking his arm or at least telling him to chill out. But Juliet still could find only silence.

Both brothers stood, now in an open argument with Burgamy, listing the reasons Juliet couldn't go back undercover as Lisa Sinclair. She wasn't ready, Burgamy couldn't force her, she hadn't had the needed prep time… Juliet just tuned them out as they continued.

She knew her weaknesses, knew she was a coward. She didn't need to listen to an active discussion of those facts.

Juliet looked up from her folded hands to find Evan staring at her across the table.

She could find no pity in his gaze. Nor disappointment. He actually shrugged and rolled his eyes, gesturing casually with his hand to all the chaos. As if the yelling currently reverberating through the conference room came from preschoolers throwing temper tantrums about sharing their favorite toys, rather than Juliet's boss asking her to do something that would probably get both her and Evan killed.

How could Evan take it so lightly?

Juliet rubbed a hand over her face. There was no point in letting her brothers get in trouble with Burgamy—*again*—over this. The choice belonged to her and she already knew her answer.

She stood up, but didn't try to yell over her brothers, just waited for them to realize she had something to say. Over the years she had perfected that practice.

Eventually everyone grew silent and looked at her.

"No. I won't do it." Juliet said it plainly, not raising her voice in any way.

"Juliet," Burgamy began in his nasally tone, "it's evident that the mission has a greater chance for success if you are part of it."

"I disagree," she said.

Burgamy had no intention of giving up so easily. "But Vince Cady and his people will be expecting you to be with Evan. Bob and Lisa Sinclair are a known couple."

Juliet held up a hand to silence her boss. "My initial presence might be an asset, I concur. But for any longer term I would just be a liability. Evan can't babysit me and successfully complete the mission."

Now it was Evan who spoke up. "Jules—"

She turned to him, could see the anguish in his eyes.

"No, Evan. I'm not of any use to anybody in the field right now. Trust me."

Burgamy was determined to continue his argument. "But—"

Juliet decided to put a stop to it right now and save them all the trouble. "Respectfully, Burgamy, I'm not an agent anymore. You can't force me to do this. So let's not pretend like you can, okay? I'm not going back in the field as Lisa Sinclair." She turned to Evan. "I won't risk your life that way."

Burgamy wisely didn't say anything further. He knew Juliet's words were true. After what had happened to her the last time, no one at Omega would ever try to force her into an undercover assignment. If she ever went under again, it would be her own choice.

Juliet didn't see that happening anytime soon, say, for the next twenty years.

She noticed both her brothers sitting down, evidently accepting the battle was over. Which it was.

"I'll help Evan in any way I can," Juliet said. "I'm willing to be the support team leader, so I can use my experience to assist him."

She spoke to Burgamy as she said it, but saw Evan's surprised look out of the corner of her eye. It was no wonder; for the year that she'd been working as a handler, she'd never volunteered to oversee any of his cases. She'd done some strategy and analysis support for him, but never anything that would keep them in daily contact.

Working as Evan's handler would definitely bring the two of them in regular contact. She'd just have to deal with that. Juliet frowned and rubbed the back of her neck. Maybe she was too much of a coward to go back out in the field, but she could at least help him from the safety of Omega Headquarters. She knew staff support wasn't what Evan really needed from her. Plenty of people were qualified to act as his handler, her two wounded brothers being prime examples. What Evan needed from her was in the field.

Disgust with herself pitted her stomach.

Burgamy, having evidently failed in his purpose for being at the meeting, excused himself and left. His assistant trailed after him. With them gone, some of the tension left the room, and quiet conversations started up.

Juliet looked over at Evan's handsome face as he spoke to Sawyer about Vince Cady. Evan's brown hair, cut short and stylishly, and his beautiful hazel eyes, were in sharp contrast to her brother's darker looks. A small scar marred Evan's cheek, hardly a centimeter from his left eye. He'd gotten it during a case they'd worked on together, three years ago.

Evan had fought the bodyguard of a drug lord they'd been investigating. The huge, muscular guard, having found out the two of them were law enforcement, had decided Evan needed only one eye. The thug would've been successful in that little venture if Juliet hadn't helped wrestle the knife away.

She still smiled a little whenever she thought of that case. Evan had joked a few weeks later, at a Branson family barbecue, that the scar was okay because it finally made him as ugly as her brothers. As if any of them could be called ugly.

It had been a long time since Juliet had been to one of her family's barbecues. She wondered if Evan still went, even without her there for the past year and a half. Probably. Her brothers were his best friends.

The next couple hours were spent discussing details of the case. Evan would meet Vince Cady two days from now, at a place yet to be determined by Cady in Baltimore, which was less than an hour away from DC. There were a lot of unknowns in the case, things Evan would have to figure out on the fly, not unusual in undercover work.

The primary objective of the case wasn't the arrest of Vince Cady. Leaving him in play in order to get information on his other contacts and pipelines took precedence. So, although they'd all like to see him behind bars as soon as possible, that wouldn't happen immediately. Instead, recovery of the surface-to-air missiles—the SAMs— that Cady wanted to sell would be the primary objective. Omega couldn't allow them to be sold to enemies of the United States.

And Evan would be the sole person stopping that from happening.

Juliet ignored the tiny voice inside her that said this mission was too much for one person, even someone as capable as Evan, to handle on his own. Evan would be just fine. And he wouldn't be alone; he'd have plenty of support from the team here at Omega.

Juliet pretended that was enough. Because what else could she do?

Eventually, the meeting wound down as they worked out as many details as they could. The team trickled out one by one, each sure of his or her own assignments. Sawyer and Cameron both hugged her as they left to go back to their own cases, wishing Evan luck, offering their support whenever it was needed.

Juliet grabbed her own items, preparing to go to her office. She had a lot to do before Evan's meeting with Vince Cady.

"Can I walk with you?" Evan asked her.

"Sure." They stepped out of the conference room together and down the hall. It had been a long time since

Juliet had talked to Evan, just the two of them. It felt…
weird. But not as awkward as she would've expected.

"I just wanted to let you know I had no idea Burgamy
was going to say all that junk," Evan told her. Juliet noticed he was careful to keep a distance from her and not
touch or crowd her in any way as they were walking. "I
mean, I knew I would be resuming the role of Bob Sinclair, but I didn't think Burgamy would suggest you go
back under as Lisa."

Juliet swallowed and tried to make light of it. "You
know Burgamy, always willing to do whatever it takes to
get the job done."

"More like, always willing to do whatever it takes to get
credit and recognition from his superior officers."

Juliet nodded. Burgamy definitely had his eye on a position much higher than the one he currently held.

They arrived at Juliet's office, one of the few perks of
working as an analyst was having an office rather than
just a desk like active operatives, and she entered. She
thought Evan would say his goodbyes and head out, but
he followed her in. She placed the case files on her desk
and turned to him.

"You look very nice today," Evan said, leaning against
the wall near the door. "Professional."

Compared to the jeans and sweater she normally wore,
that was probably true. "Thanks." Juliet half smiled. "I
wanted to put in an effort, since Burgamy was attending
the meeting. Although if I had known why, I wouldn't
have bothered."

Evan grimaced. "I don't blame you."

"So you feel ready to take on Bob Sinclair again?" As
soon as Juliet uttered the words she wished she could take
them back. She didn't want to talk about Evan's feelings

regarding Sinclair any more than she would want to talk about hers if she was resuming the role of Lisa.

"Yeah, sure." Evan shrugged. "Can't miss an opportunity like this with someone like Vince Cady."

"Good." Juliet didn't know what else to say.

"Look, Jules…" Evan took a step from the wall. "I just wanted you to know, *make sure* you know, that nobody, even Burgamy, expects you to resume Lisa Sinclair. Burgamy wanted to try, had to try just in case, but he didn't really expect you to do it."

Juliet appreciated the sentiment from Evan, although she wasn't sure if he was correct.

"I know your brothers want to protect you, which is why they were so adamant in there this morning," he continued. "They love you and don't want anything bad to happen to you again."

"Thanks, Evan." Juliet was tentative, not sure what his point was.

"And, of course, I *never*…" Evan ran his hands through his hair, seeming to need a moment to gather himself. "I never want you to go through anything like that again."

Anguish was evident in his face. Juliet hurt for him. Ironic, since he was hurting for her.

"Evan—"

"But I want you to know something, Jules," he added. "Although I would never try to talk you into going undercover against your will, you are capable of much more than you give yourself credit for. You can be a good agent again, if you decide to be."

He said it with so much conviction that, somewhere deep inside, Juliet wished it were true.

Thought maybe, just for a second, that it could be.

But then she thought of this morning, how she'd gotten another of those stupid emails and had let it completely derail her *again*. How she arrived every day at Omega Headquarters at 4:00 a.m. because she was too scared to stay in her own house alone. She thought of the over-whelming panic that occurred whenever someone, how-ever innocently, touched her from behind. She thought of all the ways she had screwed up the last mission, and the price she had paid for it.

And she thought of Evan and how *he* would be the one to suffer, or worse, if she went back out in the field and couldn't perform her duties.

Evan wanted to support her, and Juliet appreciated his kind words, but he didn't know all the facts. No matter what he said, Juliet would never again be a good agent.

"I'm sorry I'm sending you out there alone, Evan. I know it's a sucky thing to do."

"No." He shook his head. "This isn't about me or Bob Sinclair or this case at all. I'll be fine. The case will be fine. I just wanted you to know that I think—that I *know*—you can do it. When you're ready."

Chapter Four

Evan watched as Juliet shuffled some papers, made a flimsy excuse about needing to be somewhere, and all but fled out the door. She didn't make eye contact with him the entire time. Of course, she didn't have to, for him to know what she was thinking.

That there was no way she'd ever be a good agent again.

Evan walked out of Juliet's now empty office and down the hall to his own desk. There was no point going after her to convince her of his opinion, even if he knew he was right. Juliet still wasn't ready to hear or accept the truth—that she could still do this job if she'd just give herself a chance.

Not that Evan expected her to do it immediately. She wasn't ready to take those first steps back into active field-work, and that was fine. She should take all the time she needed to recover from what had happened to her.

He sat at his desk, pushing away the thoughts attempting to crowd into his mind. Images of Juliet lying bleeding on a warehouse floor, feebly trying to fend Evan off before she realized it was him and not the man who had attacked her.

In the middle of an undercover buy, the leader of a rival group, who didn't like that Bob and Lisa Sinclair were cutting in on his share of black-market profits, had forcefully taken Juliet in the middle of the night. Before Evan even knew what had happened, and could get to her, she had been horribly beaten and raped.

Every muscle in his body tensed. Even now, eighteen months later, Evan had a hard time just forming the words in his mind.

And that was part of the problem, wasn't it? They all—Evan, the Branson brothers, even Juliet herself—just tip-toed around it. Nobody ever really talked about it. He knew Juliet saw a shrink every once in a while, and was glad she did, but she never talked to anyone else about what had happened. Even though things didn't seem to be getting better for her, and maybe getting worse.

Evan sighed and leaned back in his chair. In order to make things easier for Juliet, they'd all agreed to her un-spoken request not to talk about the attack. To give her time. But now, a year and a half later, they were doing the same thing: just agreeing and protecting and sheltering her. For example, supporting her in the choice to leave active field duty and embrace a desk job.

Honestly, that just made Evan mad, because he'd never known people less suited for a desk job than any member of the Branson family, Juliet included.

Juliet especially.

Evan had worked with her for years in the field and knew her instincts were unparalleled. She could read an undercover situation and formulate a plan—sometimes multiple plans—almost instantaneously. She could pin-point the weakness of an organization or a person's indi-vidual psyche with frightening speed and accuracy.

More than once while undercover with her, Evan had been thankful she was a good guy, on his team, rather than vice versa. To say she was wasted as an analyst/handler wasn't exactly true; she was good at that, too. But she could be so much more.

Evan had no problem with Juliet taking the time she needed to heal from the physical and psychological wounds she had suffered last time she'd been undercover. As far as he was concerned she could take the rest of her life, if that's what she needed, and never set foot in the field again. He would be the first one to back her up in that decision. To hold her hand. To do more if she'd let him.

But what Evan couldn't stomach was that Juliet thought of herself as a *failure* as an undercover operative because of what had happened to her. That because she hadn't been able to escape her attacker, she'd failed.

Evan had tried multiple times to tell her what he had written in his official report of the incident. Even under the worst of possible circumstances, Juliet hadn't broken cover.

She'd saved multiple lives, his included, because of that. No one could've asked for more from her. Seasoned agents had broken under much less duress than Juliet had endured. But despite everything that happened to her even through the rape, Juliet hadn't told anyone she was law enforcement.

She was the furthest thing from a failure as an agent as possible. Evan wished he could make her understand that.

But Juliet no longer trusted herself. No longer considered becoming reinstated even a possibility. Because she believed she was—and always would be—a failure as an agent.

Evan knew he walked a fine line. He didn't want to push her for more than she was ready to take on, but knew that without some sort of push she might never move forward at all. Either way, it didn't matter. She wasn't ready right now, despite what he or anybody else said. Evan would just keep encouraging her, and hopefully, they'd find some way to ease her back in a few months from now.

Baby steps.

He needed to try to get Juliet to open up and talk about what was going on in her head, see if he could figure out a way to help her make some progress.

Of course, Evan couldn't throw stones too far while sitting in his glass house. He hadn't told anybody about the dreams that had been plaguing him for the past year and a half. Hadn't told anyone about how he sometimes sat in his car in front of Juliet's house at night, just to make sure she was safe.

In case she needed him to protect her. The way he hadn't been able to do on that last mission. The way that had haunted him ever since.

So maybe Juliet wasn't the only one who needed to make forward progress. Baby steps for him, too.

But right now he needed to get ready for his meeting with Vince Cady. He flipped through the files on his desk one more time.

Cady was a vicious bastard. Evan was delighted at the opportunity to slip inside his organization and wreak as much havoc as possible. He was a little mad that arresting Cady wasn't a priority for this operation, but understood why it wasn't. Omega always kept the big picture in mind.

A chair creaking at the desk across from his drew Evan's focus. Sawyer Branson winced a little as he took his arm out of the sling it had resided in for the past few weeks, and stretched it gently. "Ready for everything with Cady tomorrow?" he asked, rotating his shoulder.

Evan closed the files. "Yep. As much as I can be with this sort of thing. How's the arm?"

His friend grimaced. "Let's just say I don't recommend

getting shot. Even a flesh wound hurts like hell and takes a long time to heal. But it could've been much worse."

"And with pretty Dr. Megan now working right upstairs, I'll bet you're not even itching to get back out in the field." Evan tried not to snicker as he said it, but wasn't entirely successful.

Sawyer got that goofy smile at the mention of Megan Fuller, the same smile his brother Cameron got at the mention of his fiancée, Sophia Reardon.

Branson men were falling like flies around here. Evan couldn't help but grin.

"I'm not rushing the healing process, let's just say that," Sawyer said, stretching his arm out again. "Wouldn't want to have any permanent damage."

"Well, don't worry. I'll handle all the heavy lifting out in the field while you and Cameron play lover boys to your respective ladies."

Sawyer got serious. "You sure you feel all right about going in with Cady? Cam and I both feel we've left you on your own. Especially without Juliet available in this situation."

"I'll be fine. I've been doing most ops on my own for the past year now."

Neither of them mentioned why. Neither had to.

"Where are you meeting Cady tomorrow?" Sawyer asked after a moment's pause that held a novel's worth of unsaid words.

"Undetermined as of yet. I'm going to try to get him somewhere neutral. We'll see how it plays out."

"All right." Sawyer got up and put his arm back into the sling. "Keep us all posted."

"Yeah, it will be good to have Juliet as team leader on this one. She sees things nobody else does, sometimes."

Her brother nodded hesitantly. "Yeah, maybe. I hope so."

"She'll be fine, Sawyer. Safe here at Omega, as always."

Sawyer looked as if he might say something else, but didn't. He just nodded again, then began walking down the hall. "Hey, family barbecue next weekend. My mom says you better be there for this one or she's coming after you personally," he called over his shoulder.

"Yeah, okay, tell her I'll be there unless this case dictates otherwise." And the case would dictate otherwise; Evan would make sure of that. He loved the Branson family and their get-togethers. But until things were more comfortable between him and Juliet, he wouldn't be going. Juliet needed to know that her family was hers. Evan would never want to take that from her.

Evan read through the files one more time, familiarizing himself with every part of Vince Cady's operation. He would never let the drug lord know he had this sort of knowledge, of course. To Cady, Bob Sinclair would be a midlevel criminal: smart, but not too clever; industrious, but still a little lazy. Someone useful and nonthreatening.

Evan could admit it was easier when he'd had Juliet playing his wife. He'd just pretended to be in awe of her and head over heels in love. Nobody had ever had any difficulty buying that cover. Bob and Lisa Sinclair had made a good team. Everybody had accepted that Lisa was the brains of the couple and Bob was willing to do anything she asked. It made them seem appealing and adept, but not threatening.

Not threatening except to Robert Avilo, another midlevel criminal who didn't like how successful the Sinclairs had become in black-market buying and selling on what he considered to be his turf. In an attempt to get rid of the competition, to scare off the Sinclairs, Avilo had attacked Juliet.

Such a pity Avilo had died a few days after the attack

while resisting arrest. An arrest made based on an "anonymous" tip. Evan wished he could've killed the bastard himself. But he still took a little comfort knowing the man was dead and that Juliet would never have to see his face again.

And though she never broke cover even when raped by Avilo, Evan and Juliet had completely pulled out of the case after the attack. Juliet had been in the hospital and Evan had refused to leave her side. He had no idea what the word was on the street about why the Sinclairs hadn't been around for the past year and a half. Their disappearance had been pretty abrupt. But Evan took comfort in knowing that rumors floating about the Sinclairs would not be whispers that they were law enforcement.

Juliet, in her bravery and her silence, had seen to that.

But DS-13, the crime syndicate group, hadn't had any problems with Bob Sinclair's sudden reappearance when they'd contacted him last month. Neither had Vince Cady. Evan just hoped it stayed that way tomorrow, but knew he'd have to be ready for some questions.

He dumped onto his desk the contents of a large envelope he'd gotten from his filing cabinet earlier today. It contained items that had belonged to Bob Sinclair, and would help reestablish Evan's cover. A driver's license, of course. It had to be a real one that linked back to Bob Sinclair. There were too many online sites that, for a reasonable fee, could let Cady know if an ID was fake. So Bob Sinclair's license was real, complete with links to several unpaid parking tickets, and even arrests, when Bob had been younger. If a local cop ran his license or social security number—and it wasn't unreasonable to think that someone of Vince Cady's criminal caliber would have at least one police officer on his payroll—it would look real.

So would the credit cards in Sinclair's name, another way a cover could be easily blown if an operative wasn't careful. In today's technologically savvy world, credit cards that had never been used, or a social security number that could be traced back only a couple of years, were easily found and red-flagged. Bob Sinclair's credit cards had purchases and statements dating back ten years. It was some analyst's job at Omega to make sure all these electronically trackable items looked as real as possible. Whoever that person was did a damn good job.

The other items from the envelope included business cards for exporting companies and banks around the Baltimore and DC area. Even Sinclair's library card, randomly placed in his wallet. Plus two photographs. The first was of Bob and Lisa's wedding day. Evan and Juliet had posed outside a church, in wedding garb, hand in hand and smiling. Rice showered them in the picture, the perfect way to make it look as if a large crowd of people surrounded them. In actuality it had just been a few other agents, who had enjoyed pelting them with rice from every angle.

Evan picked up the other picture and studied it longer. He remembered that day from two years ago with crystal clarity. The photo had been taken in front of the Cape Henry Lighthouse on Chesapeake Bay in Virginia, during the winter. He and Juliet had driven there for the express purpose of getting this memento from the Sinclairs' secluded "honeymoon" so they could both have a copy in their wallet. A couple who posed as being in love with each other as much as Bob and Lisa did would definitely have pictures of each other with them at all times. Plus, it gave them added history, a more firm timeline.

Details like that could be the difference between life and death in an undercover operation.

For the photo, Evan had scooped Juliet up and cradled her in his arms. They'd asked a stranger to take their picture with their little disposable camera, explaining they were on their honeymoon. The stranger had gladly obliged, but had insisted Evan and Juliet seal the moment with a kiss.

The kiss had started out brief, just a staged moment for a picture. But then Evan had found he hadn't wanted to stop kissing Juliet. And judging by the way she clung to him, she hadn't wanted to stop, either. Her soft lips and warm mouth had been so different from the cold air that had surrounded them.

They had both totally forgotten about the stranger taking their picture, who evidently at some point had just left the camera on a nearby step and walked away, giving the "newlyweds" their privacy. When Evan and Juliet had finally broken apart, they'd both been breathing heavily. And had been confused as hell about what had just happened between them—so unexpected, but so perfectly right at the same time.

They'd been about to go undercover on a critical operation, however, so both of them had pushed whatever had just happened between them aside. Something to deal with later.

Of course, if Evan had known what would happen later, he would've made very different choices that day. He would have driven to the nearest hotel and made love with Juliet until neither of them could walk.

Evan took the credit cards and pictures and put them back into the wallet. Maybe it would've changed everything, maybe it would've changed nothing. He'd never know.

He took Bob Sinclair's wedding ring and slipped it on his finger. He might as well start getting used to its weight. He picked up the Saint Christopher necklace—Bob and Lisa had matching ones—and placed the chain around his neck. He kissed the medallion as Bob Sinclair had always done.

Evan stood and began packing everything away, straightening up his desk a little. If everything went the way they hoped, he wouldn't be here in Omega HQ very often over the next few days, for it would be too dangerous. He had done all he could do here at the office. He grabbed the keys to the SUV he'd be driving until the case was over.

It was time to slip on the Bob Sinclair persona. To think like him, walk like him, become him.

Chapter Five

Juliet found herself back at Omega Headquarters the next morning, early again. But for once her early arrival wasn't due to unreasonable fears and memories driving her from her home. Today she was in because she wanted to be, in order to provide Evan with any support he would need while meeting with Vince Cady.

She didn't expect there would be a whole lot she could do. Evan wouldn't be wearing a wire or transmitting device. No agent would take something like that to a first meeting with a perpetrator when he or she was sure to be searched; it would be a quick way to get killed. But if Evan needed any info, or advice Juliet could provide, she wanted to be there for his call.

She felt guilty enough for sending him in alone, but determined not to rehash all that again today. She would just do what she could from this end.

She stopped at the coffee shop down the block from Omega, ordered a cup of her favorite brew and made her way to the nondescript front doors of Sector Headquarters. The lobby of Omega could be mistaken for any financial or business building on the outskirts of Washington, DC. A security desk sat in front of the elevators. Everyone had to show their badges to get by. Nothing unusual.

But it was inside the elevators where the true security

started. A retinal and fingerprint scan, as well as an individualized code, were required before a passenger was taken to any secure floor. Nobody just walked off the streets and got into Omega.

It was the reason Juliet felt safe here, when she didn't anywhere else.

The morning ended up being as uneventful as she had hoped. She sat at her desk, monitoring all calls and electronic submissions that might be coming from Evan. But except for a brief text stating the meeting was confirmed for 11:00 a.m. near the Baltimore Pier, they hadn't heard anything from him. No news wasn't necessarily good news in this business, but it wasn't necessarily bad news, either.

Juliet forced herself to relax. She'd feel better once Evan's initial meeting with Vince Cady was complete. So much rode on this one event.

Her brother Sawyer stuck his head in the door. "Heard from Karcz?"

"A couple of hours ago. Everything seemed good. Meeting scheduled for eleven." Juliet looked down at the clock on one of the computer screens she had open. Five minutes to eleven. Moment of truth.

"Cam and I are headed into DC proper. Bomb threat issue and the Bureau needs some extra hands. All available agents are headed in."

Juliet nodded. "Okay. Well, I've definitely got it covered here. Just waiting for Evan to check in after the meeting. Nothing I can really do except wait. But in case he needs any emergency info I want to be standing by."

"Okay, sis. We'll be on cell phone silence because of the bomb threat. FBI on the scene is concerned that the perps might be using a cell to detonate, so they're jamming all frequencies."

"I'll figure something out if I need you. I'm expecting a boring day."

Sawyer left and Juliet went back to her work. One computer actively monitored the Baltimore Police Department. They had no idea what was going on with this case, so could actually stumble in and do harm if she wasn't careful. She'd give them info on a need-to-know basis, if it looked as if they might interfere with the case somehow. She'd also been reading through the files of Vince Cady's known associates all morning. Nothing terribly interesting there, either, but Juliet wanted to make sure she was up to speed on all the names and faces.

She almost missed it. Amid the chaos of the monitors and files, hypervigilant in her effort to make sure she could provide any support Evan might need—overcompensating for guilt much?—Juliet almost missed the single communiqué that could bring the entire operation crashing down.

It was an automated email from the Omega system. It had filtered through the Virginia courts and correction system, and provided a list of three people who had been released from a Richmond jail on bond this morning at eight o'clock. Omega's system only red-flagged info concerning criminals or suspects in their database—people Omega had caught, were currently trying to catch, or planned to catch in the future.

The system listed one of the releases, a low-level hired thug named Mark Bolick, because of the agent who had apprehended the suspect: Evan Karcz. At first Juliet didn't pay the communiqué any attention. As an analyst, she had multiple lists like this come across her computer screen every day.

Mark Bolick had been arrested last month during an altercation between the crime group DS-13 and some Omega agents, a situation that had almost left her brother Sawyer dead. Most of the members of DS-13, including the dirty ex-FBI agent running the crime ring, had been killed. But some had been arrested, including Bolick. Evan had been undercover, not directly involved in the case. But because Sawyer, the agent in charge, had been in critical condition, Evan had arrested the remaining bad guys. Not common practice in undercover work.

Mark Bolick in and of himself wasn't much of a problem. Juliet didn't know why he was getting out on bail so early and didn't really care. The problem was Bolick had ties to Vince Cady, based on information she'd read in the files this morning. Although he didn't seem to be a big part of Cady's organization, he was dating Cady's niece.

It didn't take a genius to figure out that Bolick, after sitting in jail for over a month, would be heading up to Baltimore as soon as possible, probably to see his girlfriend. But it wasn't a stretch to think he might check in with Cady immediately.

And he'd be sure to remember the man posing as Bob Sinclair as the one who had arrested him just a few weeks before. That would mean the end of the case for Evan.

And probably his life, especially if they'd already discussed any details about anything. Or maybe just because Cady or one of his men would see it as an opportunity to get rid of an undercover cop.

Juliet immediately speed dialed Evan's phone. A call was risky, but at least produced immediate communication. Evan would be able to talk his way out of it, make up some excuse to Cady about why he was taking the call.

But he didn't answer.

Juliet immediately sent a text from her computer to the

same number. Aunt Suzie had a heart attack. Mom needs you to come home right away.

Aunt Suzie was the signal for general emergency. Come home right away meant to get out of there now. Evan wouldn't have any details, but he would know what the message meant.

Juliet sat staring at her computer, waiting for the screen to give a received message. All Omega-issued phones had the capacity to show if a message had been received. Helpful, but not foolproof, since it couldn't notify the handler if the *agent* was the one who had actually read the text. Just that it had been accessed.

Juliet didn't necessarily expect Evan to respond, depending on what was going on in the meeting with Cady, but she did want to know the warning had been received.

But nothing. She sent the text again, just to be sure. Still nothing.

Multiple scenarios ran through her head ranging from the benign—Evan was in a momentary situation where he couldn't access his phone or didn't have a signal—to the catastrophic—he had already been exposed as an undercover agent and executed by Vince Cady.

Juliet gave it five more minutes, sending the message three more times.

Nothing.

She looked at her watch and did some quick calculations. Eleven-fifteen. Evan should definitely already be meeting with Cady by now. And it was a hundred fifty miles from Richmond to Baltimore, so it was conceivable that Mark Bolick could've already made it there, too. She needed to find out where Evan was and get in touch with him.

Juliet opened the program that allowed her to use

Evan's phone as a tracker. She entered in the code for it and waited.

Device not found.

Juliet entered in the code one more time to be sure. Nothing again. Now she really began to worry. There were too many unknowns in this situation. She had to make a decision. She didn't want to blow the operation for nothing, but neither was she willing to risk Evan's life.

She called the contact number she had for the Baltimore PD. Quickly she explained the situation to a ranking officer there, asking him to send out a unit to check the location of Evan's meeting with Cady near the Baltimore Pier, explaining the need for speed but also stealth, if possible. The officer assured her of their cooperation and that he would call back shortly.

It didn't take long, about fifteen minutes—although it felt much longer—for the officer to call her back. His response had Juliet immediately running down the hall to Burgamy's office.

"Dennis, we have a problem with Evan in the undercover op," she told her supervisor, without any preamble. She explained about Mark Bolick.

"Have you contacted Baltimore PD and GPS for his phone?"

"Yes, for both. I'm not getting any GPS location reading for his phone at all. BPD sent a unit to the location I provided, where Evan reported the meeting with Vince Cady would be held, but no one was there. They said it was completely empty, with no sign of any sort of struggle or foul play."

Burgamy stood. "Okay, that's both good and bad."

Juliet knew what he meant. Evan wasn't lying in a pool

of blood somewhere, so that was good. But they had no idea where he was, and no way of contacting him. That was bad.

Very bad.

"It's just a matter of time before Mark Bolick shows up while Evan is there." Juliet tried not to pace around Burgamy's office, but it was difficult.

"Have Baltimore put out an APB on Bolick. Maybe we can catch him before he meets up with Cady and Evan. If he's in Baltimore, he's breaking his bond agreement, anyway, by being out of state."

Juliet had her phone out to make the call.

Burgamy stopped her. "Juliet, you worked with Evan as this persona before. Do you know of any places he might have suggested to Cady? Neutral places that would make the guy more comfortable? Obviously, the meeting wasn't going as well as Evan hoped if they aren't at the location they agreed to, and his phone is completely offline."

This probably wouldn't have happened if you'd gone undercover with him.

Burgamy didn't say the words out loud, and may not have even been thinking them. But Juliet could feel them floating in the air. Maybe it was just her own guilt talking.

"I don't know. Yeah. Maybe a couple of places." Juliet could picture a few.

"I don't have any agents to send out. Everybody has gone into DC to help with this bomb issue. Until we know for sure Evan is in trouble, the bomb has to be my priority."

Juliet nodded. Burgamy was right; he couldn't pull men off a known crisis for something that was only a possible one. "Okay, I'll work with Baltimore PD. Hopefully this is just some sort of fluke thing and Evan will be in touch soon."

But her gut told her the opposite.

Chapter Six

From the very beginning this meeting with Vince Cady hadn't gone the way Evan had hoped. It had started okay, a call with an agreed meeting time and place at an empty office building near the Baltimore Pier. The location allowed for privacy, but also a measure of safety for Cady. It would be easy to disappear into the nearby crowds if a quick getaway was needed.

Evan had reported the meeting location to Omega, then had shown up, ready for Bob Sinclair to be anything and everything the drug lord needed him to be. But Cady wasn't there. Evan had waited fifteen minutes, wondering with each minute that passed if the entire operation was a failure before it even began, before two thugs had shown up.

"Where's Cady?" he had asked.

Neither had answered, just walked up to him and began frisking him. Thank God he wasn't wearing a wire.

"I don't have a weapon," Evan had told them during the pat-down. That had been a conscious decision. In some undercover ops he did carry a weapon, because that's what the persona would do. But Bob Sinclair was a buyer and seller, not muscle for hire. In most situations, he wouldn't have a weapon.

Although Evan sort of wished Bob had one now.

The thugs took his cell phone from his pocket and one walked outside with it. Then the other guy, still not saying a word, pulled out his own phone and dialed a number.

He handed the device to Evan.

"Um, hello?"

"Mr. Sinclair, this is Vince Cady."

"I thought we were meeting here at the pier, Mr. Cady." Evan tried to put just the right amount of annoyance into his tone. Bob Sinclair would want Vince Cady's business, but would not be desperate for it.

"Yes, well, we've had a slight change in plans for security purposes. I felt this was necessary, since we have never actually met."

"Okay, so what's the new plan?"

"Now that I know we are talking on a secure line and that no one else can hear us, I was hoping we could come up with a new meeting location."

This wasn't totally unreasonable. It seemed as if Cady was a suspicious bastard, but that was probably why he was still in business.

Evan thought fast. Juliet could still use his phone to track him, but if he could suggest somewhere he was familiar with, that would at least give Evan a slight advantage. Being outnumbered and unarmed was disadvantage enough.

"Fine. There's a group of warehouses near the Francis Scott Key Bridge." Evan gave Cady the address. "It's neutral and private. Let's meet there."

"Sounds fine, Mr. Sinclair. My associates will escort you. And I will gladly replace your phone. Sorry for the inconvenience."

Evan was about to ask what he meant, but Cady had already disconnected.

"I guess we're going to the Francis Scott Key Bridge," Evan told the man putting the phone away.

"Mr. Cady said there would be two of you."

Evan didn't blink an eye. "Not today. The wife couldn't make it."

The other thug walked in from outside. "Okay, it's done. Are we ready?"

"Can I get my phone back now?" Evan asked him.

"No. It's on its way to the bottom of the harbor. Sorry." The man didn't look a bit sorry.

Damn. This meant Evan was totally on his own. Unless Omega had developed some super tracking software in the past six hours, his only contact with them was now a plaything for fishes.

The ride to the warehouse near the Francis Scott Key Bridge was uneventful. Less than uneventful, almost completely silent.

"I left my Jeep in hourly parking. Between my cell phone in the harbor and our little field trip, this is turning into an expensive day."

Nothing. Evan gave up on trying to engage them.

The warehouses were what Evan remembered. A large area of identical buildings, almost all empty, surrounded by industrial structures. It would be easy to get lost, or end up in the wrong warehouse if you didn't know exactly where you were going. Multiple ways leading in and out. Helpful for people who didn't like being hemmed in. He and Juliet had done business at this very location as Bob and Lisa Sinclair.

A door to one of the empty warehouses stood open and they drove straight in. There stood Vince Cady, leaning casually against his SUV, surrounded by four of his closest buddies. Evan got out of the car as it stopped.

"Mr. Sinclair." Cady walked toward him and shook his

hand. The man was in his midfifties, with salt-and-pepper hair, short and trim. "It is good to finally meet you. I am sorry for all the subterfuge and drama of switching locations."

"You've got to have security measures. I understand."

"And where is the lovely Mrs. Sinclair I've heard so much about?"

Evan hadn't expected Cady to start asking about Juliet this early. "She's not here."

"I can see that. *Why* is she not here with you?"

"Lisa and I don't do business together anymore." Evan tried to keep it as broad and simple as possible.

Cady stared at him for a long moment, one eyebrow raised. "I don't like unexpected changes, Mr. Sinclair. I was told you and Mrs. Sinclair always worked together. That you were the brawn and she was the brains of your partnership, no offense intended."

Evan gave his most easygoing smile. "Well, now I'm both the brawn and the brains of the operation. Nothing has to go through a committee."

But Cady didn't seem interested in Evan's friendly demeanor. "From what I understand, Mrs. Sinclair has not been seen for quite a long time. Over a year in fact."

Evan shrugged. Cady knew more than Omega had thought. Evan didn't want to give away any info by blabbering. "We went our separate ways. So what?"

"I had heard such good things about you, Mr. Sinclair. About you and Mrs. Sinclair as a team." Cady turned and walked back toward his men, who were standing by the car a few feet away. Evan was very well aware that he was in the middle of a warehouse surrounded by Vince Cady's thugs. Highly armed ones.

And he had no weapon and no backup coming.

"But I'd also heard a few rumors, too. Rumors that

you might be law enforcement and that Mrs. Sinclair was no longer with you because she'd found out that fact and left." Now surrounded safely by his men, Cady turned back and faced Evan. "I so hoped she'd be with you today so that those rumors could be put to rest. But she isn't, and I have no choice but to believe that you aren't who you say you are."

So much for not worrying about any rumors surrounding the Sinclairs' absence. Suddenly Evan found six weapons pointed directly at him.

"That makes you a loose end. Unfortunately, I don't allow any loose ends."

JULIET HADN'T BEEN SURE exactly where she was going in Baltimore when she jumped into her car not long after talking with Burgamy; she just knew she couldn't stay in the office. The Baltimore PD was being less than helpful, although, in their defense, Juliet wasn't sure exactly what she was asking them to do.

Look for someone, somewhere in your city, who may be in danger, but may be perfectly fine.

Baltimore law enforcement had their own problems, and right now Evan Karcz wasn't one of them.

They had put out the APB on Mark Bolick. And thanks to some cameras she'd accessed showing Bolick leaving the courthouse that morning, she knew what he was driving and his license plate.

Given all that information, the chances of Bolick getting picked up by the police were pretty good. But the chances of that happening before he blew Evan's cover were much slimmer.

She would start at the pier. Maybe there was something the officers had missed. Northern DC to Baltimore was only forty-five minutes. Juliet was already halfway there.

But the call came in before she ever reached the pier. Juliet's heart stopped just for a moment when she saw it was her contact at the Baltimore PD. She put the phone on speaker and answered it, still driving.

"Agent Branson—"

Juliet didn't bother to correct him about the incorrect agent title.

"—the vehicle from the APB you had us put out has been spotted. A uniform radioed it in, but then was called to a nearby emergency and so wasn't able to pursue."

Damn it. "Okay. Was the vehicle seen near the pier?"

"No, near the Francis Scott Key Bridge."

As soon as Juliet heard the words she swerved across two lanes to reach the exit from the highway, ignoring the angry honks from other drivers.

She was just a few minutes from the FSK Bridge, southeast of Baltimore. The officer gave her the last known whereabouts of Bolick's car. Not far from the warehouses she and Evan had used for some buys when they'd worked together.

Had he moved the meeting out here? If so, why hadn't he let them know? Of course, it was possible that Mark Bolick was in this area for an entirely different reason that had nothing to do with Vince Cady or Evan. Or that the car the officer saw was the wrong one or no longer held Bolick.

Juliet's familiarity with the roads near the warehouses helped her as she navigated. But the area was large and there were lots of places to stay hidden if someone was trying to. That was one of the reasons she and Evan had chosen it for use in their undercover work.

She spotted Bolick's car, with him still driving it, thank goodness, as it pulled up in front of one of the warehouses. Juliet cursed under her breath. Vince Cady must be around here somewhere and Bolick was about to walk in on his meeting with Evan. It was too late to call for any sort of backup, and if she tried to arrest Bolick right here, he might yell and tip Cady off. She needed to do something more drastic.

Juliet pulled in behind Bolick as he was getting out of his vehicle, glad that the relaxed dress code at Omega made her look less like law enforcement. She didn't let herself think about what she was doing, just threw her car keys under the floor mat, grabbed her Glock 9 mm out of the glove compartment and slid it into the back waistband of her jeans as she quickly opened her own door. She grabbed some papers resting on the passenger seat.

Bolick wasn't a big guy, thank goodness.

"Hi. Excuse me? Sir?" Juliet ruffled through the papers as she got out of her car. "I'm so sorry. I'm completely lost."

"I can't help you, lady." Bolick made no move toward her, didn't even look at her, but Juliet didn't let that deter her. She kept walking.

"I just need to figure out where I am, based on this address. My phone died—"

"Sorry. I don't know anything about this area." Bolick turned away and began heading for the warehouse door. Juliet rushed to catch up with him.

"Can you just look at this?" She touched him on the arm and he turned, scowling. Juliet didn't wait to see what he would do next. She hit him in the chin with a brisk uppercut, putting her weight behind the punch, before he could get a good look at her.

She caught Bolick as he crumpled to the ground, just as she had expected.

Juliet could feel her entire body shaking as she dragged him the few feet to the trunk of his car. She got the keys out of his pocket and unlocked it, using all her strength to heft his unconscious form and roll him in. She knew he wouldn't be out forever, so grabbed some duct tape from her own car and tied his hands and covered his mouth. Then she got into his car and drove it a couple blocks away, where it couldn't be seen.

Juliet walked back to the warehouse, adrenaline still pooling through her entire body. Hopefully, the threat to Evan had passed, because she didn't think she could possibly be any help to him at this moment even if he needed it. She clenched her jaw in an attempt to stop her teeth from chattering. Mark Bolick was the closest she'd come to any sort of physical altercation—hell, almost any physical contact—with a stranger since her attack.

Juliet crouched down, focusing on her breathing and getting in as much oxygen as possible. Eventually, her hands stopped shaking and her heart rate settled into a less frantic pace. She made a call to Omega, reporting the location of Bolick's car and that he could be found in the trunk. Someone from headquarters would handle it and make sure Bolick was kept out of the picture while Evan was undercover with Cady.

Feeling a little better, she stood up. Her job here was finished, right? Mark Bolick no longer posed a threat to Evan's mission, so she was free to return to the safety of the Omega offices. Juliet began walking toward her car, but then stopped abruptly.

She couldn't just leave. Yes, Bolick was out of the picture, but she couldn't just go, not knowing if Evan was okay. Why couldn't he be reached? Why couldn't they track his phone? Juliet knew she would never be able to forgive herself if he was in trouble and she had left him to run back to safety.

Observe. That's all she had to do. She wouldn't need to make her presence known. She wouldn't interfere. She'd just make sure nobody was about to kill Evan or anything like that.

And if he *was* in trouble? Then she'd call for backup. Juliet took out her phone. As a matter of fact, she'd call Omega right now, let them know her status and get Baltimore PD on standby if necessary. Done. She could do this.

Keeping her breath slow and even, Juliet turned and began walking back toward the warehouse, deciding to go to a rear door she knew each of these buildings contained. She rubbed her damp palms on the thighs of her jeans as she silently made her way along the wall, her weapon still tucked in the waistband under her lightweight sweater.

She just prayed she wouldn't have to use it. And if she did, that she wouldn't freeze up. Sweat broke out on her forehead just thinking about it.

Juliet opened the door to the warehouse as silently as possible. She could hear some people talking, but couldn't make out the words. She eased inside.

She wasn't prepared for the hand that grabbed her shoulder from behind. She stopped. Everything stopped.

Her movements, her thoughts, her breathing, even her heartbeat—it all stopped. Neither fight nor flight was an option. She had forgotten how to do both.

She felt the cold muzzle of a weapon against the back of her neck and realized it didn't matter, she couldn't do either, anyway. So much for just observing.

"What are you doing here?" the man said from behind her.

Juliet fought to get a grip on her terror. "N-nothing," she stammered. "I got lost."

He used his free hand to push her, face forward, against the door she'd just closed. She sucked in a breath, gasping for air, her skin clammy. Squeezed her eyes shut and struggled to withhold a whimper as the man began running his hand down her back.

Juliet felt bile rise in her throat at his touch. She might vomit right here. Her shudders returned full force.

Blessedly, the hand stopped when it reached the Glock tucked in her jeans.

"What's this?" he barked close to her ear. She cringed, unable to answer even if she had a good plan for what to say. Which she very definitely didn't.

"Thomas, what's going on back there?" a voice from the center of the warehouse called out.

"I found an intruder, Mr. Cady. A woman coming in through the back door."

Juliet tried to calm her breathing enough to listen for Evan's voice, but couldn't manage it. She was spending all her energy attempting to control her panic.

Her captor grabbed her arm and began dragging her toward the middle of the warehouse. Juliet didn't resist much, especially when they rounded a stack of boxes and she could see what was going on with Cady and his men.

She expected to find weapons trained at her, but found them pointed in the opposite direction.

At Evan.

Juliet had to give him credit; he kept his wits about him even with her showing up so unexpectedly. She couldn't figure out what to say, just stared at Evan as the man holding her arm steered her closer to the group.

Evan sighed dramatically and rolled his eyes.

"Damn it, Lisa, I thought we agreed you were going to stay out of sight at the pier. What the hell are you doing here?"

Chapter Seven

Evan knew he was taking a huge risk engaging Juliet as Lisa Sinclair, but didn't see any other choice. Cady didn't trust Bob Sinclair, thinking it suspicious that he was here without his "wife." Well, she was here now.

Why Juliet was, Evan had no idea. She should be behind a desk at Omega, where she felt safe. What the hell was going on?

Juliet seemed only a moment away from complete panic, if her expression was anything to go by. She pulled as far as she could from the man holding her arm. Evan knew she didn't like anyone touching her, and was sure that went double for some thug she didn't know.

"Cady, have your guy let her go. My wife doesn't like to be manhandled."

Cady nodded at the man and he released her. She floundered for just a second, not seeming to know what to do, but then rushed over to Evan. He put his arm around her— loosely, so she wouldn't feel trapped—and slid her behind him. Keeping himself between her and the guns still pointed his way.

Vince Cady chuckled. "Looks like you haven't quite been honest with me, Bob. You made me think your lovely wife had left you for good. Yet here she is."

"Yeah, well, she wasn't supposed to be."

"And why is that?"

Juliet still didn't seem to be capable of any sort of speech, so Evan just kept talking, well aware of all the weapons trained on them. "She was supposed to stay at the car, back at the pier. Away from all this, and people throwing her around." Evan gestured toward the guy who had brought her into the warehouse.

"She was armed, Mr. Cady. I didn't know why she was here," the guy chirped, holding Juliet's Glock out as proof.

"Lisa is always armed," Evan interjected quickly. He didn't want to take a chance on Cady linking the words *armed* and *law enforcement* together. "She had an…accident a while ago and feels better carrying a gun with her." Evan could feel Juliet stiffen behind him, but couldn't do anything to make her more comfortable. He shrugged and smiled at Cady. "I personally find an armed woman very sexy."

Cady looked at Evan and Juliet for a long moment, then gave the motion—finally—for his men to lower their weapons. Evan felt a little better, but knew they were still far from safe.

"Yes, that was another rumor I heard about your wife. That someone had tried to kill her," Cady declared.

Evan gave a curt nod. "We don't like to talk about it. But Lisa and I decided she would stay out of the business side of things after that incident."

"And yet here she is at our meeting." Cady's eyebrow was raised.

"Not by my choice." Now that the guns were no longer pointed at them, Evan drew Juliet from behind him and wrapped his arm around her. He could feel fine trembles racking her body. "She must have gotten a little scared and followed us when you decided to switch the location. Is that right, honey?"

Evan looked down at Juliet and squeezed her closer, trying to get a reaction from her. She nodded blankly. Not great, but enough.

He pulled her even nearer to his side. "Look, Mr. Cady, ever since Lisa got attacked she's been a little skittish. She doesn't like being touched by people she doesn't know, and she doesn't like being surrounded by a roomful of men with weapons. That's why we've been keeping a low profile for the past few months."

Evan hated using Juliet's attack as a tactic to get ahead in this situation, but didn't see any way around it.

Cady broke into a smile. "Trying to keep your woman safe. No wonder you were acting so suspiciously! I can totally respect that. I am a family man myself. I have a wife who means a great deal to me, as yours obviously does to you."

For the first time, Cady's men seemed to relax, as if they finally believed their boss was okay with the situation. Evan smiled also. "Exactly."

"Thomas, give Mrs. Sinclair back her gun. She obviously doesn't feel safe without it."

"But, Mr. Cady, are you sure you want her to have a weapon?"

"These people aren't our enemy, Thomas." Cady gestured to Juliet. "Would you feel better about this situation if you had your gun back?"

Juliet nodded.

"But please don't shoot poor Thomas. He was just doing his job."

She nodded again. When her captor walked over and handed Juliet the Glock, she kept it in her hand, down at her side. Evan could tell she felt much better having it in her possession, although the lack of color in her face still worried him.

It was a nice gesture on Cady's part to give Juliet the security blanket she so obviously needed, although Evan was
sure the man's motives were not altruistic. He was trying to
form some sort of bond between them. But Evan was also
aware that there were at least four men in the room who
could kill both him and Juliet immediately if she began
to raise her weapon in a threatening manner. Having the
gun in her hand provided a slim facade of control at best.

"I'm sorry for what happened to you, Mrs. Sinclair."
Cady bowed his head slightly. "I would never condone that
sort of behavior from any employees of mine."

"All right, Cady, let's cut the chitchat. You have some
surface-to-air missiles to sell. I have a buyer, possibly multiple buyers, who are interested."

"Good, good. I also have other items, much more important items, to be auctioned off. Including something
acquired only recently."

"More important than SAMs?" Evan raised an eyebrow.
"I find that hard to believe."

"How about access to override codes that would allow
someone to turn US military drones onto any target they
so desire. Attacks untraceable back to them."

Evan swallowed the expletive he so desperately wanted
to let loose. Instead he gave an impressed whistle through
his teeth. "You have drone override codes available for
sale?"

Cady had the gall to casually flick a piece of lint off
his shirt. "I do, in fact."

"Wow!" Evan feigned excitement. "That's some next
level stuff. Where did you get them?"

"I'm sure your buyers would not actually care, correct?
They would only want to be sure that the codes work."

Evan could feel Juliet stiffen beside him. How the hell

did Cady have drone override codes in his possession? Things had just gone from bad to critical.

Evan sure as hell cared where and how Cady had gotten the codes, but Bob Sinclair wouldn't press. Evan had to let it go. "That's true, and it's also pretty impressive, Mr. Cady. I was worried that since DS-13 seemed to be out of business, there would be a gap in merchandise available for sale. But it seems that's not the case at all. As long as everything works, I'm sure my buyers will be interested, no matter where the codes came from."

"I'm glad to hear that. I plan to have an auction on Monday. A few choice buyers, you included. I will be in touch with more details."

Monday. That was only three days away.

Cady walked over and held out his hand. Evan reluctantly unwrapped his arm from around Juliet to shake it. She still didn't seem too steady on her feet and he knew he needed to get her out of here as soon as possible. He willed her to stay strong.

"Like I said, I am a family man," Cady told Evan. "One of the reasons I contacted you in the first place is because the two of you work together as a couple. Call me a romantic, but I find that love makes people more trustworthy."

Cady turned to Juliet. "I know you don't enjoy the business any longer, but I hope that you will see coming to my home as more than business. I can promise your safety."

Evan didn't like where this was heading. "Mr. Cady—"

The man stepped back from them. "In any case, my invitation to the auction at my house is for you as a pair. If your lovely wife decides she cannot make it, there is no reason for you to come, either, Mr. Sinclair. My wife will be expecting a couple, not a single man. I am not interested in letting her down on this matter."

"I just think it would be better—"

"Both or neither, Mr. Sinclair." Cady seemed uninterested in any argument, so Evan just shut his mouth.

The drug lord turned and began walking toward his men. "I assume, since your wife had to arrive in some sort of vehicle, you won't need my men to escort you back to the pier."

Evan looked down at Juliet, who nodded again. "Yes, we've got our own ride, thanks."

"Then I'll be in touch and look forward to seeing you both again soon." Cady and his men walked out the door.

EVAN WATCHED THEM LEAVE, then tucked Juliet more firmly to his side. "Hang in there, baby," he whispered.

"Evan, I can't…" Her voice was barely more than a whisper.

"Don't think about anything right now. Let's just get out to your car. Where is it?"

"In the back alley, on the northeast side of the building." Her words had an uneven cadence.

Evan led her out through the door she'd come in. They made it to her car.

If possible Juliet looked even more pale out in the sunlight. Evan leaned her up against the vehicle "Where are the keys, Jules? Under the mat?"

She nodded.

"Okay. Let's get you in the car and back home. All right?"

"Evan, I'm going to be s—" Juliet didn't even get all the words out before she bent over and was violently ill all over the pavement.

Evan offered his support by touching her back, but she waved him away. Even after she lost the contents of her stomach she continued to dry heave.

Evan knew there was nothing he could do. Her system

was in shock and just needed to run its course. He winced as she once again heaved. It was painful to watch, and he was just glad she had been able to keep herself under control for so long.

Eventually Juliet pulled herself to an upright position, although she kept her arms wrapped tightly around her stomach. "I think I'm okay now." Her voice was cracked and hoarse.

Evan helped her into the car, thankful that her face had some color in it now and the shaking seemed to have stopped.

"Juliet, what the hell are you doing here?" he finally asked, as they pulled away from the warehouse area and headed back toward DC.

She sat with her eyes closed, leaning back against the headrest. "Mark Bolick, one of the guys you arrested from DS-13 last month with Sawyer, has ties to Cady and was about to blow your cover."

Evan cursed under his breath. Things had already been going pretty poorly before Juliet arrived. If Bolick had stumbled in and accused him of being a cop, that would've been it for Evan.

"You saved my life," he told Juliet.

She gave a bark of mirthless laughter. "Not on purpose. If there had been anyone else around I could've called, I would have, believe me."

"Well, you did it and that's what counts. Plus, Cady was pretty antsy about why Lisa Sinclair wasn't with me. You showing up when you did probably saved my life again, or at the very least the whole case."

Juliet still had her eyes closed. "Like I said, I didn't do that on purpose, either. Then I almost blew the whole thing."

"But you didn't."

She shrugged and Evan knew better than to argue with her. She refused to acknowledge her own success because of her physical reaction afterward.

"You did good, Jules. It was a dicey situation. Cady was ready to call the whole thing off, or maybe even get rid of me completely, because you weren't there."

"I thought you had a plan for what you were going to say."

Evan took the exit for the interstate leading to Washington. "I had a bunch of possibilities, based on how the situation was going. But Cady started up about you almost right away. I was still reeling from the change of locations and my phone sinking to the bottom of the harbor."

"No wonder we couldn't contact you. I tried to let you know about Bolick, then sent Baltimore PD to the pier."

"Evidently, Cady's even more security-conscious than we thought. And definitely pro-family. He was not interested in talking to me at all if you weren't in the picture. Every excuse I had—that we had broken up, that you just weren't interested in the business anymore—wasn't going to fly, I could tell."

Out of the corner of his eye, Evan could see tension fill Juliet's body and her breathing become more rapid, although she was still leaning against the headrest.

"What? Are you okay? Are you going to be sick again?"

"Evan, Cady's not going to deal with you if I'm not involved."

He reached over and took her hand, shocked when she didn't jerk away instantly. He had touched Juliet more in the past hour than he had in the whole past year.

"It'll be all right, Jules. I can make it work without you."

Now Juliet opened her pretty green eyes to look at him, her breathing becoming even more pronounced. "How, Evan? You heard Cady. He was *adamant* about the two of us being together or you not bothering to come to the auction at all. And he has drone override codes."

Juliet was right. Despite his assurances, Evan couldn't see how he was going to make it into the auction without her. If he had known what a hangup Cady would have for Juliet's attendance with him, Evan would've gotten another agent—someone who could pass for Juliet—and gone in with her. Sure, that plan had its own problems, but it was better than where they were now: having an open invitation to infiltrate a huge crime lord's organization, but not being able to move on it.

Evan cursed silently. He couldn't force Juliet to go back undercover; after what he'd seen today, he knew the price would be too high.

And honestly, despite the confidence he had in her overall, and the firm belief she could again become the great agent she had once been, he wasn't sure she could do it right now. Not that she was willing, anyway.

Evan glanced over at Juliet, watching her trying to get herself under control. She didn't look like a law enforcement agent right now. She looked like a woman who was frightened. She still had her Glock clutched in her small fist.

He would just have to find another way to get into the auction with Vince Cady. But hell if he had a single damned idea of how he would do so.

He felt Juliet slip her hand out of his as she turned her head to the window. Silence permeated the car. Evan didn't know what he could possibly say to make this better, so he didn't even try.

They drove all the way back to DC—Evan would have to send someone else to get his car at the pier—and pulled into the Omega parking garage without Juliet saying another word. At one point Evan had wondered if she'd fallen asleep. But at least her breathing was even and she had color in her face. All signs of her earlier panic attack seemed to be gone.

Maybe that was why he was so shocked when she turned to him as he parked her car.

"I'll go back under, Evan. It's our only hope."

Chapter Eight

"We sat in this very room yesterday and had this exact conversation. You weren't ready then. You can't possibly be ready now."

Sawyer spoke to Juliet, but wasn't looking at her; he was glaring at Evan. The conversation had been going on for the past twenty minutes. It was the first time in memory that Juliet could recall wishing that a bomber still threatened Washington, DC.

At least then her brothers wouldn't be here trying to convince her of something she already knew: this was a bad idea.

"Sawyer, it's the only option." Juliet didn't raise her voice.

"Hell no, it's not the only option. And even if it was, we'd figure out something else."

Silence flooded the room. That was the problem—there really weren't any other options. Not ones that could solve the problem in the amount of time they had. None of the four people in the room, Juliet, Evan, Sawyer or Cameron, had much that could be offered by way of an alternate plan.

Juliet spoke calmly. "It was bad enough when Cady had the surface-to-air missiles. But now he has the drone override codes. If anyone has an alternate plan I'm willing to listen to it. If not…"

More silence. Which was broken by the phone ringing on the conference room table.

"Why did a call get routed in here?" Evan asked.

"Because it's Dylan. I gave him a heads-up and told him to call." Sawyer looked at Juliet, eyebrow raised.

She could feel her nostrils flare; she couldn't believe they had brought their oldest brother into this. This was her decision, not theirs. She slammed her palm over the handset before Cameron could pick it up. "You know what you two are? Tattletales."

Cameron brushed her hand away and pressed the button for the speakerphone. "Hey, Dylan."

Dylan had been an Omega agent for a long time before getting out a few years ago to start his own charter airplane business in the western part of Virginia. He wasn't one to beat around the bush. "What's going on, Jules?"

There were few people in the world Juliet had more respect for than her oldest brother. He, more than anyone else knew the price of undercover work. "It looks like I need to go back under, Dylan. As Lisa Sinclair."

Dylan knew what had happened eighteen months before. Juliet didn't need to explain it to him. "Do you want to do it?" he asked.

"I think saying I *want* to do it would be a gross overstatement. But I don't think there's any way around it. Vince Cady has somehow acquired drone override codes, Dyl."

Juliet could hear him whistle through his teeth. He knew the ramifications of having these codes in the wrong hands.

"Evan, are you there?" Dylan finally asked.

"Yeah, man, I'm here."

"What happened today? How did Juliet even get drawn into this?"

Evan explained about Bolick, playing up the part about

Juliet knocking him unconscious and locking him in his own trunk. Then he told about Cady's proclivity for hiring people who had family, or at least loved ones, and how the criminal wasn't interested in Evan coming in as a single man working alone.

"Sounds like Juliet was caught unawares in this situation," Dylan stated plainly. "You felt like she handled everything all right?"

Juliet wasn't offended by her brother's question to Evan. He could give a much more accurate description of what happened.

Evan looked at her. "She held it together. Everything was dicey for a while, but she didn't blow our cover. Although I can definitely attest she wasn't having a good time."

He conveniently left out the part about her throwing up all over the place as soon as they got out of the warehouse. That wouldn't reassure anyone.

"Evan, it's your life on the line, too, if you go under together. Are you sure this is what you want?" Dylan asked.

"Look, Dylan, I'll be honest. If we had a bunch of other choices, I would weigh them all before throwing Juliet back into this. But we don't, so there's not much point in talking hypotheticals."

Dylan's days as an Omega team leader were clearly evident in his voice as he said, "But do you believe the objective is obtainable if you and Juliet resume cover?"

"Honestly, I don't know." Evan shook his head. "But without her, at this point, we have a zero percent chance for success."

Dylan's sigh was tired.

Juliet had been glaring at her brothers as the two other men spoke. Sawyer and Cameron shouldn't have called Dylan; he had been through enough. He didn't need to be dragged back into this. But her younger brothers were impervious to her irritation, convinced that her resuming her undercover role was the wrong thing for her to do, and willing to go to any lengths to stop it.

"Can you guys clear out for a couple of minutes? I want to talk to Juliet alone," Dylan said after a few moments of silence.

Juliet picked up the handset as the three men filed out, her brothers grumbling under their breath. "Yeah, Dylan, they're gone."

"Listen, sis, here's the deal. You and Evan were a tight team once. He has always held to the opinion that you would one day resume duties as an active agent again. I know him, and he believes you can do this."

"It didn't sound that way a minute ago."

"It's not an easy case, Juliet, and you don't have much time to prepare. Plus you're still dealing with trauma and haven't been out there for over a year. Evan is just giving his honest opinion."

"Yeah, I know." And honestly, nobody knew even the half of what was going on with her. If they did, they sure wouldn't trust Juliet with their life.

"If it was anybody else but Evan you'd be going with, I'd tell you to refuse, no matter what. But he has always been…"

She waited for Dylan to finish his thought. "Always been what?"

"Nothing. Never mind. You should just know that he has your back. You can always trust that about Evan. He would die before he let anyone hurt you again."

"I don't know if I can do this, Dylan." The words came out as little more than a whisper. "What if I get both Evan and myself killed?"

"Jules, listen, you have good instincts. Follow those and trust them. And stay as close to him as you can."

Juliet's heart gave a little thump. The thought of being close to Evan was both thrilling and terrifying at the same time.

"But hey," Dylan continued, "I'm the first one on your side if you don't want to do this. I know Cady has the codes and I know it's bad. But it can be somebody else's job to get in there, some other way, and pull this off."

But Juliet knew that in the time it would take to come up with and implement a new plan, the codes would be sold and ultimately lives would be lost. And it would be her fault.

She took a deep breath. "No, I can do it, Dylan."

"I never doubted it for a second, sis."

They said their goodbyes and Juliet hung up. So this was it. She was going back undercover. Juliet walked toward the door. There was no point delaying; she needed all the time she could get before they were to meet with Cady in just a few days.

The guys weren't in the hallway, so she began walking to her office. There were a few things she needed to take care of before throwing herself into the Lisa Sinclair role.

Juliet was totally unprepared for the hands that grabbed her from behind as she walked. For the second time that day, her heart dropped into her stomach. For a moment she froze, terrified.

But then, unlike this morning, without a second thought she sprang into action. She rammed her elbow into the solar plexus behind her, and heard a whoosh of air release at her ear. The hands gripping her momentarily loosened, and she grabbed one of her attacker's arms and pulled it over her shoulder. Then she dropped her weight, widened her stance and flipped the person over her back. He was a large male, but weight didn't matter in this maneuver, just momentum.

Juliet was coming down with a punch to finish her attack when she realized she was looking into the face of her brother Cameron. Her dazed brother. She barely stopped her fist from connecting with his face.

"Cameron, what the hell are you doing?" Evan yelled.

Juliet stepped back and attempted to relax her arms at her sides, though it was difficult with the adrenaline rushing through her. Her fists were still clenched, ready to take on her attacker. Who happened to be her stupid brother.

"I was trying to prove a point," he finally said from where he lay on the floor, after getting his breath back.

Other people were coming out into the hallway to see what the commotion was about. But evidently a Branson brother lying on the floor wasn't much cause for concern, because most headed back the way they'd come without much real interest.

Sawyer reached down to help his brother up. "And what point was that?"

"That Juliet isn't ready. She can't stand to be touched. She's unpredictable."

Juliet could still feel tension coursing through her body. Fight or flight instincts, although neither were needed now.

Evan just shook his head. "I think all you successfully proved, you moron, is that your sister can kick your ass."

Cameron dusted off his clothes. "What is she going to do, flip everyone who touches her at Vince Cady's house?" He clenched his jaw, his exasperation clear.

"Well, then they'll learn pretty darn quickly not to touch her if they don't want to end up staring at the ceiling, wondering what the hell happened," Evan retorted.

"She's not ready, Evan," Cameron all but growled. "You're forcing her into something she doesn't want to do."

"I'm not forcing her into anything, Cam." Evan's rigid posture spoke volumes. "The situation sucks, I'm the first to admit it. But people are going to die if we don't get the drone codes out of Cady's hands, or whoever he plans to sell them to."

Juliet had had enough of this. All of it. "Why are you guys talking about me like I'm not even here?"

Cameron began to answer, but she cut him off. "You zip it. You lost your right to speak when you were lying on the floor. You're lucky I didn't break your nose."

Sawyer snickered. Juliet turned and pointed at him. "You be quiet, too. Just because you weren't stupid enough to try something so asinine doesn't mean you're off the hook."

Evan wisely made no sound at all.

"I know this situation isn't optimal. I know I'm not a good candidate for undercover work. Believe me, I've been thinking about that every day for the past eighteen months."

Both Cameron and Sawyer began to speak, but she held out her hand to stop them. "However, we don't have any other options that won't end up costing other people their lives. So I'm going to do it." She glanced at Evan. "And hopefully not get both of us killed in the process."

Evan nodded with a half smile, still smart enough to keep quiet.

"You two—" she waved at her brothers "—need to either get behind me on this or completely out of the way. No more trying to point out my shortcomings. I need your support."

With that, Juliet turned and walked down the hallway toward her office. She knew she didn't have to say anything more. Her brothers were hardheaded and often pretty stupid—Cameron's little stunt was plenty of proof of that—but she knew they loved her. And now that they understood she was serious about this, she knew they would stop their antics and help her and Evan in any way they could.

Juliet just hoped it would be enough.

Chapter Nine

Evan watched Juliet walk down the hall.

"All right. I guess this is really happening," Cameron muttered. "I didn't expect her to drop me like that."

"Yeah, she's in top shape. I saw her sparring yesterday. If anything, she's even more quick and strong than when she was an active agent," Evan said. It was damn impressive.

"But she's not consistent," Sawyer told him. "Yeah, she took Cameron down, but was just as likely to freeze up and do nothing."

"She'll get her rhythm back. She just needs more time to get used to being an agent again."

Sawyer slapped him on the back. "Well, unfortunately, that's the one thing you don't have—time."

Evan nodded. "Then I better not waste any more of it talking to you guys."

Sawyer stopped him. "Evan, you know we only said all that because we want to protect Juliet. I don't know if she'd survive another—" Sawyer lowered his voice "—incident. Like what happened before."

"Nothing like that's going to happen. I'll make sure of it." That was the one thing Evan knew he could promise.

"If she's made up her mind, then we want to help any

way we can," Cameron added. "We can clear our schedule, work with you for the next couple of days if you want."

Evan shook his head. He knew what needed to be worked on first and foremost with Juliet, and her brothers couldn't help. "Thanks, guys. I'll let you know if we need anything. Besides, she's pretty pissed at you two right now. I think you better steer clear."

"Yeah, the demonstration maybe wasn't such a great idea," Cameron mumbled.

"I could've told you that if you'd asked me beforehand, dumbass," Evan declared. "It's amazing you ever got your gorgeous fiancée to agree to marry someone as stupid as you."

"That's the truth," Sawyer said in agreement. "I never would've done something so dumb."

Evan didn't have much mercy for Sawyer, either, even though they'd been best friends since elementary school. "Yeah, I recall you saying some pretty stupid things to your own fiancée a few months ago, so you can't talk much either."

The Branson brothers began walking down the corridor, grumbling at each other about who was the most stupid when it came to women. Evan turned in the direction of Juliet's office. One thing was definitely true: they didn't have much time. They needed a crash course in working together, and it had to begin immediately.

Because if Lisa Sinclair jerked away every time her loving husband touched her—or flipped him over her shoulder—everyone in Cady's operation was going to get suspicious real fast.

She had to learn to let "Bob" touch her, to be around her. To kiss her.

Seeing that she had withdrawn from even the slightest

physical contact with anyone over the past year and a half, undoing it in a little over two days wasn't going to be easy.

Plus, Evan wanted to do some surveillance on Cady's house, at least the outer grounds, before they went in on Wednesday. The more they knew about the location, the better it would be.

Theoretically.

Evan tapped on Juliet's office door. "I come in peace."

She looked up from where she sat at her desk. "I know my brothers are your best friends, but they are really idiots sometimes."

"No argument here." Evan sat down in a nearby chair. "But if it helps, they're on board now. Anything you need or want for this op, just ask them and they'll get it to you."

Juliet nodded. "I know they're worried about me. I don't blame them."

"You're going to do fine." Looking at her now, so comfortable in her office, her color just slightly heightened from the fight with her brother, Evan believed his own words.

"I noticed when you were telling Dylan what happened that you left out the part where I hurled my guts all over the pavement. That's not exactly the most confidence-inspiring action."

Evan shrugged. "We've all lost it a time or two. Throwing up isn't the worst way someone's dealt with the stress of an op. Plus, you didn't do it while we were surrounded by Cady and his men. That's what counts."

"But what if I had, Evan?" Juliet's posture was hunched, her voice strained. "What if I had lost it right there in the middle of everything?"

"Then we would've dealt with it. Like anything that doesn't go your way while you're undercover. We would've blamed the guy who grabbed you, or the Avian flu, or told them you were pregnant. But we would've come up with something."

Juliet didn't look convinced.

"We can't prepare for every possibility in the field. That's why not everyone is cut out for working undercover. You have to think on your feet and be ready for anything."

"Yeah, well, I don't know that I'm able to do that anymore. I could barely think at all at the warehouse this morning."

"We'll stick together as much as possible, have each other's backs. And always, if you don't know what to say, the best bet is to say as little as possible."

Juliet's grin was wry. "That shouldn't be a problem for me."

"Are you nearly done here? I don't think we can afford to waste any time. We're going to need every bit of the days we have before meeting Cady."

She nodded. "Yeah. Burgamy all but jumped for joy when I told him I was going back undercover as Lisa Sinclair. Then got this very smug look on his face, like he knew it would happen all along. He had Chantelle clear everything off my plate for the next couple of weeks."

"Poor Chantelle. I don't know how she can bear being that close to Burgamy all the time."

Juliet began gathering up papers, straightening her desk. "I won't waste any more time around here, so you and I can get to work prepping for the op. And I won't be offended, Evan, if you feel we need to start back at the very beginning. As if I'm fresh out of the academy." But he could tell she found the thought distasteful.

"Even if you were straight out of the FBI Academy, you've still got good instincts, Jules. You're just going to need to learn not to panic. You've got the skills, we just have to hone them. It'll all come back."

Evan walked over to her desk and helped her collect and stack the files that had to do with Vince Cady. Juliet's discomfort grew as he got closer to her. Normally he would've backed off, given her the space she requested with her nonverbal communication. But not now.

Physical distance between the two of them was over. Their lives would depend on it.

Evan never actually touched her, but definitely came near enough to invade her personal space. Juliet didn't say anything, but shifted away, avoiding eye contact and rocking slightly.

That sort of behavior was more likely to get them killed while undercover than anything else. She couldn't cringe every time he was near.

"Jules." Evan kept his tone soft, even. "Lisa Sinclair wouldn't shy away from Bob. He's her husband. They love each other."

She nodded jerkily and stopped sliding farther away. But she was obviously still uncomfortable. Evan moved nearer.

"It's just me, Jules," he said softly into her ear. "I've been this close to you a hundred times before."

JULIET KNEW WHAT Evan said was true. They had been this close countless times before. She had known him since they were teenagers. He'd been running around with her brothers for almost as long as she could remember.

Evan was never going to hurt her.

Juliet tried to relax into that knowledge. The presence of such a large man—she came only up to his chin—so close beside her was still unsettling, but this was Evan. It was okay. Juliet took a deep breath and let the fear ease out of her system.

This is Evan. She repeated it in her head like a mantra.

They finished stacking the files. Evan helped her put them into her bag.

"So what's the plan?" Juliet asked him.

"When was the last time you fired your weapon?"

"I've kept current. Been at the range at least weekly."

"Good, because we don't have time to mess with that. We've got more important things to do, like go grocery shopping."

Of all the things Juliet could think of that needed to be done before their next meeting with Cady—memorization of her undercover role, brushing up on hand-to-hand combat, going over details about Cady and his known associates, coming up with a solid overall *plan*—none involved walking leisurely through a grocery store.

But that's where she found herself forty-five minutes later. Strolling through the local grocery store, pushing a cart, Evan right next to her helping her pick out produce.

As if they were on their fifth date and about to make a romantic meal together.

And the crazy thing was, for the first time in as long as Juliet could remember, the thought of a romantic meal didn't make her want to be sick to her stomach.

Evan didn't talk to her about the case or Vince Cady. He just talked about normal stuff, as if they were getting to know each other.

"Fresh strawberry pie is my favorite. Although apple pie with ice cream…I don't know that anything in the world is much better than that. How about you?"

Juliet stared at him as he handed her a pint of strawberries to put in their cart. His thumb grazed her hand as he did it. Juliet could swear she could feel where his thumb had touched her skin even after he moved away. "How about me, what?"

"What's your favorite kind of pie?" Evan took a small step closer and smiled at her.

That smile—the one that brought out the dimple in his chin—did something to Juliet's insides. Something she hadn't felt in a long time. Something she hadn't been sure she'd ever feel again.

The faintest stirrings of desire.

She immediately took a step back. "I don't know. I guess key lime pie is my favorite."

Yeah, Evan wanted her to be comfortable with him, but he didn't want her actually *wanting* him, she was sure. Plus, she totally couldn't think about feelings right now. Just surviving the next few days.

But she couldn't stop looking at the dimple in his chin.

Juliet tried to keep everything professional, yet friendly between them as they walked around the store. It was hard, given the way Evan constantly touched her, just briefly, or smiled, or said something funny to make her laugh.

Eventually they gathered all the food Evan deemed necessary for whatever meal he had planned, then paid and went out to his car. He had insisted she leave hers at Omega.

"Your house?" he asked her. "It's closest."

Juliet froze in the middle of putting a bag of groceries in the back of his Jeep. Evan couldn't see her house, not the state it was in right now. "No, let's go to your town house. That'll be better. Mine's a mess."

And she wasn't just talking about a mess, although it was a mess. She was talking about something else.

He didn't seem to have any argument with that, and Juliet relaxed. Evan just wouldn't understand what she'd done in her house. *Juliet* didn't even understand it.

Evan's town house wasn't too far from her place, just

a couple miles. They both lived north of DC, in College Park, a popular area for young professionals.

She had been to Evan's home a few years ago, but never just the two of them together. They pulled into his designated parking spot.

His home was different than Juliet remembered. Previously it had been more of a bachelor pad, with mismatched furniture, no color on the walls. She'd made fun of Evan and her brothers, about their poor taste in decorating, and the fact that some boxes remained unpacked in the middle of their living rooms. She had called all their places the bachelor death pads. They'd argued that they worked too much to be at home very often, anyway.

Now Evan's house couldn't be any more different. The walls were a deep teal, causing the white trim and molding to stand out brightly. The old couch and folding chairs in his living room had been replaced by a lovely overstuffed sofa and matching armchair, both of which fairly begged you to sit down, get comfortable and watch a movie with a loved one.

The room appealed to all Juliet's senses. She walked inside, looking around, amazed. "This is gorgeous. When did you do all this?"

Evan seemed uncomfortable, although Juliet had no idea why. "A little over a year ago. I thought it was finally time to grow up and stop looking like I was about to move out any second. I hired a decorator to help pick things out, although I did most of the work myself."

"Well, it's unbelievable." She spun away from him to look at the couch. "I couldn't have picked out a better color myself. And this sofa? I just want to sink into it and stay there forever."

Juliet knew she was gushing, but couldn't help it. She

loved everything about this room. Smiling widely, she turned back to Evan.

Only to find him looking at her with something akin to agony in his eyes.

"Evan? What's wrong?" She rushed to his side. "Are you okay?"

"Fine. Let's get this stuff into the kitchen." He blinked and his easy smile slid back into place. Juliet wondered if she had imagined the whole thing.

The kitchen was just as tastefully decorated as the living room. Evan now had matching appliances and granite countertops. An island rested in the middle of the space, two stools slid neatly underneath.

"Wow, whoever your decorator was, I want to kiss him or her."

"Her. Kimberly's pretty brilliant."

Juliet could hear the admiration Evan had for this woman. Had they been lovers? All of a sudden Juliet wasn't as enthralled with the colors and textures as she had been a moment ago.

Were they still lovers now? Juliet had avoided any personal conversations with Evan for a long time. She realized she had no idea what was going on in his life. For all she knew he could be seriously involved with someone. The thought that she was standing here, leaning against some other woman's kitchen island, did not sit well with her.

Juliet knew she had no claim on Evan, no say about his intimacy with other women. Because what could she do? It wasn't as if she could get involved with him, even if he wasn't dating someone. Men tended not to like it when their woman shied away from them every time they were touched.

So what did it matter if Evan had a gorgeous interior decorating girlfriend? If the woman didn't care if Evan went undercover as someone else's husband, then it was none of Juliet's business.

"Does, uh…Kimberly mind you going undercover for long periods?"

Evan looked up from where he was putting the fruits and vegetables into the refrigerator. "We're not dating. As a matter of fact, I think you might be more her type than I am."

Juliet just nodded, ignoring the fact that she suddenly loved everything about the town house again.

"Oh. Well, she did a great job in decorating. I love it here. Definitely not a bachelor death pad any longer."

Evan stopped and looked at her for a long moment.

"What?" Juliet finally asked.

"Nothing," he said. "Get over here and let's cook dinner."

Chapter Ten

All through the evening, as they cooked, ate and washed dishes, Evan tried to touch Juliet as much as he could. He stayed as close to her as possible, invading her space, even bumping her leg with his under the kitchen island as they ate dinner together.

She often shied away or flinched, and while something in Evan's soul shattered each time he saw those little reflexive reactions, he never brought it up. Talking about them wouldn't do any good.

It was time to change Juliet's basic muscle memory. Words weren't going to get her any more comfortable with being around him. Only being around him would do that.

Not that it was any hardship for Evan, being this close to Juliet. If he'd had his way he would've been this close to Juliet long before now. And would still be long after the case closed.

Yeah, this was forced intimacy rushed along for the sake of working undercover together. But Evan didn't mind at all. As a matter of fact, the closeness, the flirtation, just having her around felt totally right to him.

And her scent. Something about the smell of her hair—not fancy, just clean and fresh—made Evan want to keep her with him for about the next fifty years.

When she had commented on the decor and furniture

changes he'd made in his house, Evan had come to an
abrupt realization. All of it had been for her. Not consciously. He'd never once thought *oh, Juliet will like this*
while he'd worked with Kimberly, picking out colors and
furniture a year ago.

But now, having Juliet here, seeing how much she genuinely liked what he'd done with the place, he realized it
had all been for her. He had wanted her to have a place
where she felt comfortable. Where she felt safe.

His subconscious hadn't had any grander plans than
that. He hadn't been thinking she might move in and live
here. He'd just wanted it to be a place where she could visit,
and not think of it as a bachelor death pad.

He hadn't been sure when she might ever come here.
He'd just wanted to have it ready whenever she finally did.

Now they were sitting side by side on the couch in his
newly decorated living room, looking over files from the
case. Juliet reached for another folder, then kicked one
shoe off and tucked her foot beneath her when she sat
back down. That caused her to slide a little closer to him.
But she didn't move away, almost didn't seem to notice
the proximity.

Evan smiled to himself. Maybe there was hope for this
plan, after all.

"I've been studying Cady and everything we know
about him for the past two days," she said. "He's a slippery bastard—has his fingers into everything. But honestly, I'm not sure his son, Christopher, isn't going to be
more of a problem."

"Christopher? I don't know much about him. He's in
his early twenties, right?"

"Yes, and is just starting to become an important part
of his father's business."

"Why now?"

"We're not exactly sure. Intel suggests that he's been back in Vince's organization for only the last year."

"Where was he before that?" Evan asked.

Juliet reached forward and threw the very thin file Omega had on Christopher Cady onto the table. When she sat back, she moved farther away from Evan, leaning on the arm of the couch. "No one knows. We can't get any official word or record. But evidently, he hasn't been living in his parents' house since he was seventeen."

"But he's involved with his dad now?"

"Yes, for sure. Although he wasn't at the warehouse today."

"Hmm." Evan reached over and gently clasped the foot Juliet had tucked under her, drawing it onto his lap. He didn't want to give her a chance to begin withdrawing.

She looked at him sharply, then down at her foot, but didn't move away. "Word is that Christopher was in Europe. Cady has family over there. But nobody knows why he was living there instead of here."

Her eyelids began to close almost automatically when Evan started rubbing her foot through her thin sock. He found a knot of tension in the arch and applied pressure there with his thumb. She let out a soft little moan.

"What are you doing?" Juliet asked. But Evan noticed she didn't pull her foot away.

"Just trying to get some of the tension out of your system, so you can think clearly. It's been a pretty stressful day for you."

"But—"

"No buts, Jules. Just relax. And hand me your other foot while you're at it."

Evan just kept rubbing her instep as Juliet thought it through. He could almost see the emotions play out on her face: pleasure, confusion, even consternation. But no real fear. Eventually, the pleasure won out. She kicked off her other shoe and stretched that foot out, too, then leaned back into the arm of the couch as he worked his magic. Her eyes drifted shut.

"It's okay to go to sleep. Like I said, you've had a hard day."

"No, I'm not going to sleep. But I'll just rest here for a little while," Juliet murmured.

Evan loved how she burrowed back into the cushions just a little. He kept firmly rubbing her feet and ankles, easing tension out as best he could.

Slowly, her legs became heavier in his hands as she let go of more and more of her control. Despite her protests she was falling asleep. Good, she needed it. It was late; they'd both had an exhausting day. Plus they had even more to do over the next forty-eight hours, including scoping out as much as they could of the Cady residence before going there for the auction.

Evan debated about whether to carry Juliet upstairs to his bed, but decided against it. She'd probably wake up when he tried to move her, and demand to go home. He didn't want to let her out of his sight, or touch, for as many hours as possible. He wanted her subconscious to become used to him being around.

And hell, he could admit it, at least to himself, that he wanted everything about Juliet to become used to him being there, not just her subconscious.

Evan gently shifted her feet off his lap. He got up and turned off the lights, except for the hallway one, which he left on so Juliet wouldn't feel disoriented if she woke in the middle of the night. He walked back over to the couch and looked down at her sleeping form. No fear or worry seemed to surround her now. She had rolled onto her side and tucked one arm under her head.

Evan removed his shoes, then eased himself into the space between her and the back cushions of the couch. She stirred but didn't wake up.

Evan longed to pull her against him, but knew she might feel restrained if she woke up with arms around her. But he had to put his arm somewhere, so rested it on her hip. Juliet relaxed back against him and Evan fell asleep thinking he'd rather be on this cramped couch with her than alone on the largest, most comfortable bed.

JULIET WOKE UP with a start, unsure where she was. Not in her own home, that much she knew with certainty. Her back wasn't against the corner wall where she always slept in her house. Was she in her office?

Juliet wasn't in a panic. Odd. She couldn't remember the last time she'd woken up and wasn't in at least a little panic.

It didn't take long to remember where she was. Evan's house. In his wonderfully decorated living room, on his cozy couch.

And, based on the arm flung over her hip, Evan lay on the cozy couch with her.

Juliet waited in the dark for the fear to come. In the nest she had made for herself at home, the fear always came, stealing away any chance of falling back to sleep. Four or five hours of sleep had become the norm, although often she was able to take a nap on the sofa in her office.

But the fear wasn't coming now. Juliet relaxed slightly against Evan's sleeping form.

From where she lay, she could just see the window at the front of his town house. The sun was beginning to creep up. With a sense of shock, Juliet realized she had slept the entire night, not waking up once.

No nightmares. No screaming. No fighting nonexistent monsters in the darkness.

She shifted so she was lying on her back and could see Evan a little better in the dim light. He looked so relaxed and peaceful in his sleep. His brown hair fell slightly over his forehead. The growth on his cheeks was hours past a five o'clock shadow.

That tiny dimple was still there on his chin.

Juliet was amazed at how good it felt to just lie here. How right it felt. She wanted to stay here forever.

Beautiful hazel eyes slowly blinked open and looked at her. The smile that followed caused her heart to skip a beat.

"Hi," Evan murmured, his voice deep with sleep.

Juliet just stared at him for a long moment. Evan had been a source of strength for so long, a good friend, but always something more than that. And here she was, lying in his arms, fear nowhere to be found.

She was so very tired of being afraid.

Juliet closed the small distance between their bodies and kissed him. She didn't let herself think about it, just let herself feel.

Then Evan kissed her back and all she could do was feel. He teased her lips apart and drew her closer, rolling onto his back so she was half lying on top of him. She felt one of his hands on her waist, the other cupping her neck to keep her close.

Juliet remembered their kiss in front of the lighthouse, how intense it had been. But she didn't remember this heat, this electricity, running through her. She just wanted to get closer to Evan, and stay here forever.

But after a long moment he eased back, then sat up, bringing her with him.

"Wow," he murmured. He kept an arm around her and smiled at her tenderly.

"Yeah, wow," Juliet echoed. But she didn't want to talk about how good the kiss was, she just wanted to kiss some more. She started to reach for him again, but stopped at his words.

"That sort of thing ought to definitely convince Vince Cady and his group that we're happily married."

Her arm froze in midair, then dropped back to her side.

This was all just undercover practice for Evan, of course. Duh.

That hadn't been a real kiss for him, and especially hadn't been real emotion. It had just been practice for the roles they were playing. The heat had obviously been only one-sided.

"Yep." Juliet popped the *p*, trying to sound casual. She slid away from him on the couch. "We're definitely getting closer to being ready."

He pulled her back. "You're doing great, Jules." She could feel him kiss the side of her head. "It's all going to work."

Juliet thought of the drone override codes Cady planned to sell, and the damage those could do. Yeah, Evan was right to keep his focus on the job at hand. She needed to do the same.

And she needed to remember that nothing Evan did, despite how good it might make her feel, was real in any way. He wasn't attracted to her; this was the job.

Juliet's phone buzzed from the coffee table. She picked it up, cringing as she saw the screen. Lisa Sinclair had received another email.

Sweetheart, I'm so worried about you. You should be mine, no one else's. We'll be together soon.

Chapter Eleven

Evan watched as Juliet all but threw her phone across the table. She jumped off the couch as if it had burned her and walked over to the window.

"Everything okay? What happened?"

"Nothing. It's fine. Nothing."

She was looking out the window, rubbing a fist against her stomach as if something inside hurt. And she wasn't just glancing out, she seemed to be looking for something or someone in particular.

Evan reached over and grabbed her phone to see if it held clues, but there was nothing on the screen.

He joined her at the window. The reflection showed her pinched expression. "It's obviously not nothing, Juliet. Are you looking for someone?" He peered out the window himself, but there was no one to be seen in the early dawn. The streets were empty.

Evan touched Juliet's shoulders, wanting to let her know that she wasn't alone in whatever was upsetting her, but she jerked away.

Damn it, were they back to square one?

He reached out again to rub her arm, but she shrugged him off and walked back to the couch.

"What's going on, Juliet? Seriously."

She shook her head. "Nothing. I don't want to talk about it."

His jaw clenched. "That's the problem, isn't it? You never want to talk about it. Never want to talk about anything, to let any of us in."

Juliet didn't respond, just walked over to the gym bag she'd brought from the office. "I'm not ready to talk about stuff yet." Her voice was soft as she rifled through the bag. She pulled out running shorts and a top, not looking at him. "I don't know if I'm ready for any of this, Evan."

He rubbed a weary hand across his forehead. He didn't want to push, didn't want to lose all the progress that they'd made over the past few hours. And that kiss a few minutes ago—Evan couldn't even allow himself to think about that right now. He'd have to process it later.

"Okay, let's go for a run. Together. No talking necessary," he told her.

He thought she might refuse, but then she nodded. "Okay."

They were out the door just a few minutes later, headed toward a local park. Juliet had no problem keeping up with the pace Evan set, even given her shorter stride, further testament of what good shape she'd kept herself in. Her brain might not quite be ready for her to resume an active agent position, but the same couldn't be said for her body.

They jogged around and through the park without talking, Juliet obviously not interested in sharing what was on her mind. Evan wished he could tell her that no matter how fast or how far she ran, the demons she tried to leave behind would still be there when she stopped. You couldn't outrun your demons.

You had to face them. Maybe it was time to help her do that.

They reached a large fountain in the middle of the park

and Evan stopped, rather abruptly. Juliet looked over at him in concern. "Are you okay?"

"Yes," he told her between breaths. They were both sweating and breathing hard. They had kept up a strong pace for at least five or six miles. "I want you to close your eyes."

"Why?"

"Just do it, okay, Jules? For me."

Juliet shook her head, but closed her eyes as he asked.

Evan looked around the park, now much more active, since it wasn't so early.

"Okay, without looking, I want you to tell me what's going on around here."

"What?" Juliet's tone was uncertain, her eyebrows squished together over her closed eyes.

"What's happening in this park right now? If you had to describe it to someone, what would you say?"

Juliet shook her head, obviously thinking he had lost it, but took a deep breath through her nose and blew it out of her mouth.

"A mother with two toddlers at the southwest corner, heading toward the playground. Another woman with a stroller coming in from the other direction. Male Caucasian runner, age thirty-five to forty-five, dark hair, six foot one, 170 pounds, running counterclockwise on the inner loop. Blonde female speed walking with German shepherd on inner loop, probably five foot three, 150 pounds. African-American couple, early twenties, strolling together five hundred yards from the fountain. Drinking coffee from nearby coffeehouse—"

"That's fine." Evan chuckled. "You can open your eyes. I think you proved my point."

"And what the heck was that?" Juliet asked as she

opened her eyes and looked around, obviously checking to see what she had missed.

Which was nothing.

"Your brain saw and processed everything, Jules. Even though you were running at a hard pace and there was no reason to keep track of what was going on, your brain still did it automatically."

"So?"

"So? Your body still works like an agent and so does your mind. Your situational awareness is off the charts. Only your fears are holding you back." Evan prayed he wasn't pushing her further away from him. "I'm not saying you should just get over what happened. I'm just saying I think you can move forward."

Juliet looked around the park again, then stared at him for a long time. At first he thought she was going to argue, but she didn't. She looked down at the phone she held in her hand, then back up at him, her expression resolved.

"Okay, Evan, you want the truth about my fears? We're not far from my house. Let's go there."

EVAN WASN'T SURE what her house had to do with her fears, but jogged the mile or so to her place, slowing down and walking the last few blocks with her. He hadn't been here since the attack, although he had hung out here all the time with her brothers before that.

Juliet hadn't wanted to go to any of their bachelor death pads, so she'd had them over to her place when they wanted to eat or hang out or watch a movie. Her space was smaller, but it was always clean and inviting, and most importantly, usually had real food.

As Juliet let Evan in, using a key she had kept in her running belt, shock reverberated through him. Even from just inside the door, he couldn't believe this was the same place. He blinked rapidly as if the scene before him might change to what it was supposed to be—a light, airy, friendly house.

Not the hovel that stood before him.

The chic wooden blinds that used to cover the windows had been replaced by heavy curtains that obviously hadn't been opened in months. Barely any illumination from the sun made it through, casting the entire place in an eerie light. Every flat surface was piled with papers and files and *stuff*, not to mention layers of dust. There was nowhere to sit even if you wanted to.

Obviously, Juliet hadn't done any entertaining in her house recently. It looked as if she hadn't even been here herself. Had she moved somewhere else and left her furniture behind?

But when Evan turned and looked into the kitchen, which was located across the small foyer from her living room, he realized that wasn't the case. The kitchen was in slightly better shape. No food was left out, and dishes were washed and sitting on the drying rack, but there were newspapers and books stacked on the small table. Obviously, she did use this kitchen, but evidently ate while standing at the counter.

Evan scrambled to understand what he was seeing. Juliet said nothing and closed the door they'd just walked through. And then began locking the most locks Evan had ever seen at a single entrance.

There were at least a half dozen that bolted her door into the wall. He watched with an aching chest as she rapidly clicked each lock into place—a testament of how often she did it.

Yes, Juliet did live here, in this house, in its current state. But you couldn't call it her home. You couldn't have called this *anybody's* home.

Juliet still didn't speak, just walked into the kitchen and grabbed a water bottle for each of them, then headed down the hall into one of the two bedrooms. Not hers, but the room she'd made into her home office.

This room was obviously used often. Her desk, complete with lamp and computer, was like her office at Omega: meticulous and clean, the exact opposite state of her living room. No dust, no piles of junk. At the other end was a small couch, a pillow and blanket thrown over it.

Juliet pointed to the couch. "I sleep there every once in a while."

Evan supposed that sleeping some nights on a couch might not be unusual for a person who had been through what she had. Heaven knew, he had his own nightmares about that day. He imagined Juliet's were much worse, since she had lived through it.

"Nobody can blame you for having bad nights, Jules. Sleeping on the couch every once in a while happens to everyone."

She studied him for a moment, then crossed into her master bedroom, motioning for him to follow. There were heavy drapes over the window in here, also, allowing in very little light. Her queen-size bed, with its beautiful four posters—Evan remembered how delighted Juliet had been when she'd found it at a secondhand store about five years ago—obviously hadn't been slept in for months, maybe longer. Like the kitchen table and furniture in the living room, it was covered with stuff: jackets, boxes, papers.

But Evan was totally unprepared when Juliet pulled open the door to her walk-in closet and pointed down at the floor—to a makeshift bed of a couple blankets and a pillow. Next to it lay a rifle—a .308 Winchester, it looked like—and a Glock G42, similar to the handgun Juliet used as an agent.

"That's where I sleep—*attempt* to sleep—almost all the time. I haven't slept in a bed since the attack."

She turned and walked out of the closet and her bedroom. Evan remained, staring at the pitiful pallet that spoke volumes about Juliet's solitude and fear.

He'd had no idea. None of them had known Juliet was struggling to such a degree. All of them knew she spent a lot of time at work and hadn't been home much. Looking around now, Evan could see why. No one would want to spend much time here. And obviously, a lot of the time she spent here was in fear.

Evan's heart broke just thinking about it. But anger wasn't far behind.

He followed her into the kitchen, where she leaned against the sink.

"So, obviously, I'm not fit for duty. You know I've been talking to therapists for months, all different types, but never seem to mention this." Juliet laughed nervously and gestured with her hand. "This is barely a step up from that reality show about hoarding. Criminals probably wish I would become an agent again, because obviously, I'm damaged beyond—"

Evan pulled her into his arms. He didn't care if the movement might startle her or make her tense. He just wanted her to know she wasn't alone. Not anymore.

By God, never again would she have to go through any of this alone. If she wasn't getting better, then Evan, not to mention her brothers, would help her. In any way she needed, whatever way she needed.

"Jules, why didn't you tell us?" Evan whispered against her hair, glad that she didn't try to pull away. "We all knew you didn't like to be touched, but none of us knew you were struggling so much here at home." Evan couldn't wrap his head around it.

"I didn't know what to say."

"None of us expect you to just get over what happened, but hasn't it gotten any better at all? This place…" Evan glanced into the living room. "It's like you're waiting for another attack."

"That's what I feel like whenever I'm here. Like I'm not safe." Juliet removed herself from his arms and pointed at the locks. "Although it would seem impossible with all that."

"Jules, why are you still so afraid? The man who attacked and raped you is dead. His accomplice is in federal prison. Neither of them can hurt you anymore."

"Somebody is still out there, Evan."

Evan ran a weary hand over his forehead and eyes. This was so much worse than he'd thought. If Juliet was still this scared after eighteen months, and thought someone was after her, then the psychological scarring must be much deeper. She was definitely not ready to go back undercover. He would need to cancel the mission and find another way to get the drone codes from Cady.

Because honestly, Evan was worried for Juliet's very sanity.

How had he not seen this? How had they all been so blind to what Juliet was really going through? She should have been getting better, not worse. And now, thinking someone was after her when it was impossible…

Evan walked toward where she stood in the middle of the room, moving slowly, as if she were a wild animal he didn't want to spook. "Juliet, there's nobody who can hurt you anymore. There hasn't been since the arrest. You don't need to be afraid of that."

She looked torn between wanting to accept his embrace and argue the point further, but then froze when her phone chirped. The same sound it had made this morning.

Evan watched all the color leak from Juliet's face as she stared at the device.

"That's the reason I know someone is still out there, still after me. He's been sending me—well, Lisa Sinclair—messages for nearly a year."

Chapter Twelve

Evan pulled Juliet to his side—she had her fist clutched against her stomach again—and grabbed the phone. It was a link to an email she'd received as Lisa Sinclair, and that had been forwarded to her phone.

Are you thinking about me as much as I'm thinking about you? It's so hard for us to be apart, isn't it? Soon, sweetheart.

There was no signature line or name. Nothing to give away the identity of the sender.

The questions flew through Evan's mind almost faster than he could ask them. "Juliet, what the hell is this? How long has it been happening? Why didn't you tell anybody about it?"

Juliet shrugged. "I was trying to handle it myself. I don't know who it's from—and believe me, I've tried every resource Omega has to figure that out. It's someone with advanced hacking and cloaking skills sending those messages."

"How many have there been?"

"Dozens. Escalating in the past few months. Here, I'll show you." She led him back to the room that contained her computer.

Juliet opened the file with the emails and got up from the chair so Evan could sit there. Rage pooled in his stomach as he read.

It's hard to be alone, isn't it? Soon we'll be together, sweetheart.

I'd never let anything so horrible happen to you. Don't worry sweetheart, I know you'll want me.

I'm much better for you than that no-good husband of yours, sweetheart. We'll get rid of him so we can be together.

The only tears I'd ever make you cry are ones of pleasure, sweetheart.

Don't worry, sweetheart. When we're together you'll never think of your past again.

Soon, sweetheart, soon. Be patient. I'm coming for you.

Thirty or so more, all like that. All with the same sick use of the word *sweetheart*, and many with intimate, graphic descriptions of Juliet's rape a year and a half ago. The blood pounded in Evan's ears, his desire to put a fist through the closest wall almost overwhelming.

He closed his eyes, tried to focus on the task at hand.

"They're all addressed to Lisa Sinclair, with no link to you or anything with Omega?" He spun the chair around to face Juliet.

She sat on the couch, clutching the pillow to her chest. "No. I don't think it's someone who knew Lisa Sinclair was just my undercover persona. It's someone who thinks she's real. That I'm really her."

Evan leaned back in the chair. "Have you had any indication of anyone following you? Is it possible that your association with Omega has been compromised?"

"No, I've never seen anyone. And believe me, I've

looked. I don't think it's someone who knows me as Juliet Branson, but…"

"But it's someone who has details he shouldn't have about your attack," Evan finished.

Juliet nodded.

She had never made the extent of her attack public knowledge at Omega. All details had been struck from her file. Most people knew she had been hurt—she'd been in the hospital too long for that to go unnoticed—but none of them would have the sick details present in these emails.

"It has to be someone who was there." Juliet's voice was barely more than a whisper.

The Avilo brothers had taken her in the middle of the night, while she was sleeping. Knocked her unconscious, then dragged her out to the nearby boat shed. Evan and Juliet had been undercover as Bob and Lisa, staying at a local weapons dealer's mansion, for buys that were occurring all weekend. There had been multiple third parties around, including the buyers who had become so upset at Bob and Lisa's success.

Evan had been playing poker with the men, trying to wring any information he could from them, and Juliet had been back in their locked room alone.

A single lock hadn't kept out her attackers, which probably explained her need for a half dozen on her door now.

When Evan had gotten back to their room and found it empty, he had immediately begun looking for her. Juliet would not have left it in the middle of the night without giving him any notification, unless it was under duress.

It was under the worst possible duress.

Finding her haunted Evan's dreams even now. She'd been mostly naked and tied to a post, with a broken leg, cracked ribs from brutal kicks, covered in bruises and blood. Moaning, barely coherent.

Both her eyes had been swollen shut from punches, and she hadn't known it was Evan when he'd first approached her. She had tried to scream, but it had come out a broken croak, barely audible.

Evan had reassured her the best he could, untied her and wrapped her in his shirt, screaming for an ambulance. At that moment, he couldn't have cared less that they were undercover. He'd just wanted Juliet to get the medical attention she needed. Although no one had figured out they were undercover, anyway.

Juliet had been too traumatized to talk then, but two days later, when he found out the extent of what had happened, and who was responsible—Robert and Marco Avilo—Evan had made sure they had gone down. One was dead, the other in prison.

But had he missed someone?

"Was a third person there that night, Juliet?" Evan asked in the gentlest tone he could muster. He knew she didn't like talking about it.

"No. I've gone over it in my head, believe me. The Avilo brothers were only the two people involved. One who held me down and the other—" Juliet put the pillow aside and stood up.

"The messages started almost a year ago. Honestly, at first I didn't know what to think. Maybe that it was some twisted joke from someone inside Omega. And then…" Juliet was pacing now.

"And then what?" Evan finally asked.

"Remember when I took those personal days about ten months ago?"

He nodded. They'd all been relieved that she was going to spend a few days down in Florida with some girlfriends at the beach. It had seemed a step in the direction of healing.

"Well, actually, I went down to the federal penitentiary in Louisiana to talk to the warden."

Evan instantly put together what she saying. "You went to see if Robert Avilo, the surviving brother, was the one sending you the emails."

Juliet stopped her pacing. "Robert Avilo wasn't the one who actually raped me, but he was there. He has the knowledge of the sick stuff in those emails. I had to know if it was him, Evan."

Evan didn't blame her. "What did you find out?"

"That it couldn't have been him. That he had no access to any computers, nor had he sent or received any correspondence since he'd been in prison. Evidently, his brother Marco was the only family he had."

"Robert didn't strike me as someone who could've hacked an IP address, anyway. Marco always seemed to be the brains of their little ring. Robert took orders from Marco."

Evan could see Juliet grinding her teeth from where he sat. She sank back down on the couch. "That was my thought, too." She shook her head. "I know you told me Marco had been killed while resisting arrest, and I wanted that to be true with every fiber of my being."

"But?" Evan could hear the *but* as clear as day.

"But I had to be sure."

He was afraid he knew where she was going with this. His shoulders slumped. "What did you do, Juliet?"

"I got a court order and had the body exhumed. I checked it for DNA."

"And?"

"And it was Marco Avilo. You were right. He had died of a bullet wound taken after he resisted arrest and shot at some officers."

Juliet shrugged. "So that left me back at ground zero.

Marco was dead and Robert had no access to any computer or any visitors. I just thought if I ignored the emails long enough, whoever was sending them would give up. I never responded. But it's gotten so much worse in the last three months. There have been so many more emails." She looked around as if seeing the shambles her house was in for the first time. "I should've said something."

Evan couldn't stand to hear the smallness of Juliet's voice. She shouldn't have tried to go through this alone, but she had nothing to be ashamed of.

He went to sit next to her on the couch, then picked her up and settled her on his lap, his arms around her. She drew in a startled breath, but didn't pull away.

"Yes, you should've said something." Evan put his lips against her temple. "But because this threat is real and anyone in this situation would need support, not because you're weak."

"I didn't want to bother anyone. You all had your own cases, your own problems. I didn't want to be a burden."

Evan didn't know whether to shake her or never let her out of his arms again. "Nothing about you could ever be a burden to me, Jules."

"I was afraid I was losing my mind." Juliet actually cuddled in closer to him. "Look at this place, Evan. It's not healthy. I knew that, but I couldn't seem to do anything about it."

"Well, you don't have to try to go through any of this alone anymore. That's the first step." He rubbed small circles on her back. "And we need to get some more people working on this email issue. Omega takes stalking seriously, regardless of the circumstances."

Juliet nodded. "I know. But once we tell Sawyer, Cam and Dylan, they're going to go crazy with the overprotectiveness. They're bad enough as it is."

Reluctantly, Evan shifted her from his lap. "Yeah, I should call them right now. We can let them know about this while we start working on a different plan for the case with Cady."

"Why do we need a different plan for Cady?"

"Juliet," Evan said softly, gently. "I was wrong to force you to go back undercover. You don't have to do it. We'll find another way."

She shot off the couch, turned and glared at him. "You didn't *force* me to go back under, Evan. I agreed to do it because it was the right thing, and because if those drone codes get out there, a lot of people are going to die."

Evan looked around at the shambles of her house. "Jules—"

"Okay, I'll admit I've been having problems. Here, alone at night, my demons come out and obviously I haven't been terribly successful at battling them. But that doesn't change the situation with Cady. Bob and Lisa Sinclair *as a couple* is the only good option for getting the codes out before they're sold to someone else on the black market."

What Juliet said was true, but the thought of doing any further damage to her psyche tore at Evan. He wanted to protect her more than anything else.

Juliet was looking at him with something akin to pleading in her eyes. "Evan, is what you said in the park today true? Do you really feel like I have it in me to be a successful agent, to get the job done at Cady's?"

Was he making her beg to do something she didn't even really want to do?

"Juliet, wait—"

"Because I don't want to get either of us hurt or killed. And I'm scared. But I'm more scared of the drones being used on innocent people. I couldn't live with myself if I had a chance to stop it, but was too much of a coward."

Evan couldn't take any more. He rose and went to her. He gripped her biceps gently, running his thumbs along the smooth skin of her arms. "Yes, I believe all those things I said. Nothing has changed that—even though you're now the one with the bachelor death pad."

Evan kissed her softly, briefly. But he knew this wasn't the time for anything more, so he pulled away. "You can do anything you set your mind to. I've never doubted that for a moment."

"I'm afraid I'll screw up."

"I'm afraid I'll screw up, too. But we won't. We'll just work together and do what we do best," Evan said with a wink. "Catch some bad guys and save the world."

Chapter Thirteen

Something released inside Juliet. A weight lifted off her shoulders now that the truth about the sweetheart emails, as they decided to call them, was out in the open. They took her computer to Omega to be examined. She explained to Evan that she'd tried using Omega resources before, but agreed the sheer volume of emails she'd received over the past few weeks warranted a second look. Maybe there'd be some clue about who was sending them.

Evan also helped Juliet make a dent in cleaning up her house. It wasn't actually dirty—she hadn't left food out or anything that had attracted any sort of bugs, and none of it was garbage. Instead, the clutter consisted mostly of old reports, files, books, maps, mail.

Almost as if her subconscious had attempted to build a fortress of paper around her.

When Evan opened the drapes covering her windows, Juliet watched, blinking rapidly as her eyes attempted to adjust. It had been months since this much light had been let into this house. Letting light in being a fitting metaphor.

They didn't spend all day in the house, knowing there was too much other pressing business from the case. Juliet packed a bag so she could stay at Evan's place for a few days. It would be better, just in case they were ever followed, if they seemed to live in the same house.

Juliet knew that tomorrow they would need to move into full agent mode, including infiltrating and scoping out Cady's house as much as possible tomorrow night. Any information they had before going in on Wednesday would only help them. Plus it would give Juliet a chance to reacclimate herself with clandestine incursion tactics.

Surprisingly, she felt equal parts ready and scared to death.

Dinner was nice, just the two of them at Evan's town house. But afterward, while discussing the case and the details of Vince Cady's residence, Juliet heard the dreaded chirp from her phone, the sound she had assigned to signify the receipt of another sweetheart email.

She didn't realize how relaxed she'd become in Evan's presence until the tension flooded back through her.

This was the third email she'd received that day. The frequency of the messages was definitely escalating, particularly today.

"You okay?" he asked, reaching for her hand.

"I won't lie, I don't like getting these. And three in one day?" She chewed at her bottom lip, but then forced herself to stop. "But I'm glad you know, Evan." She grasped his outstretched hand. Even through the fear she could feel little sparks of attraction where their palms touched. She wondered if it was the same for him.

"I'm glad you don't have to go through this alone anymore. Nobody should have to." Evan squeezed her hand.

"I just hope receiving these emails won't interfere with the case. I don't want to just ignore them in case the perp slips up and says something useful that'll help us catch him."

Evan nodded. "How about if we look at them together from now on when you get one. Keep everything in perspective and on an even keel."

"That would be great." Juliet kissed him on the cheek. "Thank you, Evan. I know today hasn't been easy on you, either."

"We'll just take it as it comes. But no more hiding stuff."

"Deal." She smiled, and for the first time in a long while, it wasn't forced.

Evan stood. "I'm going to go shower and get ready for bed. I left a towel and stuff out for you in the guest bathroom."

"Okay, thanks."

He turned as he was heading out of the living room. "And Jules, I was thinking…" He seemed uncharacteristically at a loss for words. "At your house you showed me the couch and the pallet in the closet where you said you've slept since the attack. That you haven't been back in a bed?"

Juliet sighed inwardly. It must have seemed ludicrous to him, her blankets on the closet floor. "Do you think I'm crazy?"

"Not at all." His smile was gentle. "You did what you had to do to get by. Nobody would think that's crazy. But once we get to Vince Cady's house, you can't sleep on the floor."

She hadn't really thought of that. "Right, yeah."

"And we'll probably be under surveillance, so I wanted to address that now. You can't be all tense and nervous getting into bed with me there."

"Right, yeah." Juliet felt like a parrot.

"So, it would probably be a good idea for both of us to sleep together in my bed tonight. So you're more used to being in a bed…"

"And being with *you* in a bed."

Evan grinned. "I promise to stay on my side, if that's any consolation."

The thing was, Juliet wasn't sure if it was or not. And she wondered what Evan would do if she told him that.

She needed to remember that this intimacy, the heat she could feel between them, was just because of his undercover skills, not because of any real attraction. At least on his part.

But she'd like to see some more of his "undercover" skills.

The thought popped into her head before she could stop it. Shocked, Juliet brought both hands up to cover her mouth, just in case the words came shooting out. And she giggled.

She didn't know who was more surprised by the sound, Evan or her.

"What's going on in that head of yours?" he asked, still grinning.

"Nothing." Juliet tried to pull herself together. "Got it. Bed, together, for the case. No problem. I'm going to take a shower, too. Um, in the guest shower, I mean. I'll see you in a few minutes."

She was still snickering as she fled the scene of the crime.

Undercover.

SHAKING HIS HEAD, Evan watched Juliet all but run down the hallway. What the heck had just happened? He had no idea.

But if it made her smile and giggle like that, he'd take it no matter what it was.

Since the information about the sweetheart emails had come to light, Juliet had been more relaxed, freer, than Evan could remember seeing her since the attack. And she didn't cringe from his touch. At least not as much. And sometimes even initiated a touch herself.

Evan found it difficult to believe how happy it made him

when Juliet touched him of her own accord. Even something as simple as a brush of her hand on his arm meant more to him than entire embraces from other women.

He was feeling better about this operation than he had since Juliet showed up at the warehouse yesterday morning. He'd lost faith for a little while when he'd seen the state of her house, but now, understanding the reason, he could even understand that.

And she had just giggled and run out of the room.

And they were about to sleep together in his bed.

The thought of it thrilled Evan in ways he never would have thought. And it wasn't about sex. Obviously, Juliet wasn't agreeing to have sex with him, so he could just push that thought right out of his mind. Which, surprisingly, didn't upset him one bit.

Just the thought of being in bed next to her was more than enough. Able to help her if she needed him, or just knowing she was sleeping peacefully even if he didn't.

In the dark, lying with her after their respective showers, he could feel Juliet's discomfort. At first she fidgeted, tossed and turned. Obviously, being back in a bed reminded her of the attack. He wasn't sure what he could do, if anything, to help.

"I'll be okay. I just need to get used to it." She answered his thoughts before he could even voice them.

"I'm never going to let something like that happen again," Evan told her softly, reaching out to touch her back.

Juliet slid a little closer. He wrapped an arm around her, pulling her all the way over to his chest.

"Right now just try to get some sleep," he murmured.

It was as if her body needed a haven, a place where her mind felt safe, and Juliet was almost instantly asleep.

Long after he could hear her even breathing, Evan stayed awake, appreciating having Juliet in his arms. What

he'd said to her was true. He would die before he let anything like the attack happen to her again. While they were
undercover he didn't plan to let her out of his sight. But
for now he just held her gently while she slept, and eventually fell asleep himself.

Evan awoke a few hours later to a knocking on his
door. The sun was already up, but Juliet was still asleep.
He glanced over at the clock: 6:30 a.m. Later than he had
been sleeping, for sure, but still too early for someone to
be knocking.

Evan reached for the Glock on his bedside table, easing away from Juliet's sleeping form. His phone buzzed
with a message.

At your door. Hurry up, sleeping beauty.

Sawyer. Evan was tempted to ignore Juliet's brother's
message, but knew he'd just start knocking louder. Evan
slid out of the bed, slipped on a T-shirt with his pajama
pants and went to open the door.

Sawyer and Cameron. Great. But at least they had
doughnuts.

"Why the hell are you two here at this ungodly hour
in the morning?"

Cameron dropped the doughnut box on the table. Sawyer, quite familiar with Evan's house, began making coffee.

"We had an idea. Wanted to run it by you first before
talking to Juliet," Sawyer told him.

"Do I need coffee before hearing this grand plan?" Evan
wondered if he should mention that Juliet was asleep upstairs.

"It's not a grand plan so much as a safety precaution
for Juliet," Cameron said. "We were talking to one of the
geeks in the tech department…"

"Excuse you, I happen to sleep with the head geek from the tech department every night," Sawyer said, pouring himself a cup of coffee from the pot before it was even finished brewing.

"Okay, so you guys were talking to Megan, and she told you what?" Evan asked. Megan was Sawyer's genius fiancée, who had recently come to work for Omega.

"Tech has developed a short-range tracker/emergency response initiator that is virtually undetectable, even with a scanner, or someone monitoring frequencies," Cameron replied, pushing Sawyer out of the way so he could get his own coffee.

"And you want Juliet to have it."

"Yes." Both men said it at the same time.

"An added safety measure for everybody. Plus, it would probably make her feel better about the entire operation," Cameron stated.

Evan nodded. Even though he had no plans to let Juliet out of his sight the entire time they were on Cady's property, a backup safety measure was never a bad idea.

"She's going to do fine. Although she's been getting a string of emails from some sick secret-admirer-type bastard. So this distress mechanism Megan designed might help Juliet more than you even thought."

"What the hell emails are you talking about?" Sawyer demanded. Both his and Cameron's posture stiffened.

"They're not actually coming to Juliet, they're addressed to Lisa Sinclair. Creepy stuff that mentions specific details about her attack last year. I'll show you." Evan got out Juliet's laptop and showed her brothers what she'd been dealing with for nearly a year.

Sawyer dropped into a chair. "Why didn't she tell us about all this?"

Evan shook his head. "She said she didn't want to put

a burden on anyone. That we had 'real' cases we were working on."

Sawyer's expletive was ugly. "That's the most asinine thing I've ever heard. This stalker thing is obviously escalating. Look at how many more there have been in the last three months. And that ratio quadrupled in the last couple of days."

"I know." Evan gave a long exhalation. "I don't like it. As soon as we get the drone codes situation under control with Cady, I'm going to make this top of my priority list."

Cameron had been leaning against the counter, silent since Evan had shown them the emails. He spoke up softly now. "She shouldn't have had to go through this alone. Not after what she's been through. I'm going over to her house right now to talk to her."

Evan put out an arm to stop him. "Cam, that won't work."

"I'm her brother. She'll let me in. I just want her to know she's not alone in this."

Evan sighed. "She's not at her house."

"Where the hell is she?" Sawyer asked. "Is she back at Omega again? She spends too much time there."

"No," Evan said, and cleared his throat. "She's upstairs. Asleep. In my bed."

Evan watched as the two men he had been friends with for over fifteen years looked at him as though he was an adversary. Sawyer stood next to Cameron, both glaring at Evan.

"What do you mean, she's up there in your bed?" They studied his clothes. Obviously, Evan had also been sleeping when they had gotten there a half hour ago. It didn't take them longer than the average three-year-old to put the details together.

"What the hell are you doing, Evan?" Sawyer's words were quiet, making them all the more menacing.

"Did she want to go to bed with you or did you push it?" Cameron's voice wasn't as quiet.

Evan's whole body tensed. "You two are my best friends in the world, but you better watch what you say right now. I would never put Juliet in a situation like you're suggesting."

Sawyer's breath flew out in a huff, and he relaxed against the counter. "Damn it, we know that, Evan. It's just, first the undercover work, then those emails, and now you tell us she's sleeping with you."

"It's too much, too soon," Cameron agreed.

"She wasn't *sleeping* sleeping with me. You both know she and I can't go under at Vince Cady's house with her cringing every time I touch her. So we've been spending as much time as possible together in the last thirty-six hours."

Evan thought mentioning her house and the shape it had been in probably wouldn't help the situation overall. Her brothers would feel the same way she had at first. As if there was no way she could handle the case.

"She can handle the case," Evan said, as much to himself as to Sawyer and Cameron. "I believe that."

"You be careful not to let things get out of hand, Evan. Don't take it too far."

Evan reminded himself that these were Juliet's brothers. Brothers who loved her very much, which was why they were being so overprotective. But they knew him, knew how long Evan had carried a torch for their sister. They just didn't like that anyone would care that much about her.

"You know how I feel." Evan snapped his mouth shut and reached for the coffee, to give himself a moment to formulate his words.

"How you feel about what?" Juliet's voice chimed in from the kitchen doorway.

Evan stopped, frozen. How much had she heard?

"Hey, little sis. We were just talking about some tracking and emergency equipment the tech department has come up with," Cameron said.

Thank God. Evan really didn't want to get into his feelings for Juliet, with two of her brothers sitting in his kitchen, while he was wearing his pajama pants. Juliet, thankfully, had changed out of the T-shirt and boxers she had slept in, and put on yoga pants and a sweatshirt before coming downstairs.

Sawyer hugged his sister. "Yeah, Megan came up with something we'd like you to wear while undercover. It's a tracking and distress device. Only good short-range, but completely undetectable. Perfect for while you're at Cady's house."

"We were dropping by to see what Evan thought of it. Didn't expect to find you here this early in the morning." Cameron's eyebrow rose.

Juliet flushed just a little bit, but she was used to dealing with her brothers. "It's not what you think."

"So Evan assures us."

Evan poured Juliet a cup of coffee and handed it to her. How he wished it *was* what it looked like. Nothing would make him happier.

Chapter Fourteen

Getting rid of her brothers took a couple hours. Juliet loved them, she really did, but they were ridiculously overprotective. When her oldest brother was around it was even worse, although Dylan was usually the most reasonable. He understood, by experience, that sometimes no matter how traumatic the event, you just wanted to be left alone.

Juliet definitely didn't want to talk with her brothers about being in bed with Evan. No matter how innocent it had been.

And definitely didn't want to talk about how good it had been to lie there with him.

She had avoided sleeping in a bed all these months because of her fears. But being in one with Evan, she'd found her fears hadn't really crossed her mind. She'd been too busy thinking about him. About how close he was and how good he smelled.

And how she was nervous about being in the bed with him, but it was a *good* nervousness, not a bad kind.

And how she wanted to kiss him again. And more.

She knew Evan had lain in bed last night, so close, and watched her. But it was because he was worried about her, not because there was any real interest on his part.

This was all just part of a critical case for him. Undercover work. She needed to remember that.

But Juliet was definitely beginning to wish it was more.

She looked over at him, dressed all in black now, as she was, ready to go do the reconnaissance work at Cady's house. There were others who could handle it, providing details about the outside of Cady's house and his security. But both Juliet and Evan felt it important to do it themselves.

She looked forward to it, actually.

They weren't really going onto the grounds, just nearby, to see what they could see. Covered by darkness, they would be counting guards, getting a lay of the land, so to speak. Juliet suspected this entire escapade was for her benefit, and she didn't mind.

"You ready?" Evan asked.

"Yep."

"Okay, we'll need to park a couple of miles away. We're not sure how far out Cady's guards patrol. We don't want to take any chances."

They drove one of Omega's cars rather than Evan's Jeep, since it would be less recognizable.

"Have you got the tracker Megan and her tech people made?"

Juliet reached down and grabbed the locket hanging around her neck. "It fit in here perfectly, even behind the picture. It's crazy how thin that thing is."

"Yeah, well, Megan's mind is pretty amazing."

Juliet didn't bring up how she had once accused Megan of working for the very enemy Megan now worked so hard to defeat. She knew how in love Sawyer and Megan were; Juliet had never been happier to be wrong.

"Let's just hope we don't have to use it tonight," she said, looking out the window as they drove into Anne Arundel County.

"Such a huge criminal sitting right under the navy's

nose. Hard to believe, isn't it?" Evan parked the car. The Naval Academy was only a few miles away.

"Cady has a lot of gall being right out here in the open," Juliet said as she got out of the car.

"He's very selective about whom he deals with. That's why we've never been able to get close to him. I'm still amazed he approached Bob Sinclair in the first place."

Juliet asked, "Are you worried? Do you think Cady is suspicious?"

"He hasn't survived this long without being so. But I don't think he's any more suspicious of us than he is of anyone else."

Juliet wasn't sure if that made her feel better or worse. "Let's hope it stays that way and that I don't do anything to freak him out."

Evan squeezed her hand. "You won't."

They left the car and walked through the shadows until they reached the top of a very small hill just outside the gated property line of Vince Cady's estate. From here they had a pretty clear, although not complete, view of the house and grounds. But there shouldn't be any danger of them being caught.

They both stood silently, using night vision goggles to study the premises for a long while. Juliet counted two sets of three roaming guards passing by every eight minutes.

"Do you see the ones on the roof?"

She moved her focus upward. "Roger that. Looks like two sets of two."

"Yeah. That's a pretty well covered place. Cady definitely isn't taking chances."

"If we have to get out of there in a hurry, it's going to be nearly impossible."

"I know." Evan's voice reflected all the solemnity Juliet

felt. It was going to be more important than ever that she keep it together and do her job.

"Let's get the amplifier planted."

Juliet followed Evan down the hill, closer to the wall that surrounded the property. They needed to get the device as near as they could without it touching the structure, which probably had some sort of sensor.

"Why does it need to be so close?" Juliet asked quietly.

"It helps amplify the signal of your tracker, but it also contains a small explosive. Not enough to do any real damage, but enough to cause a distraction if we need it."

"That makes me feel a little better." Sometimes being just a couple seconds ahead of everyone else was enough when you were undercover.

They weren't expecting a guard on this side of the wall, so far away from the others, but evidently Cady even had someone patrolling the exterior. Juliet's gaze flew to Evan's as they heard him coming toward them.

The guard was alone and talking on his radio, so evidently he wasn't aware they were there. But that wouldn't stop him from bringing this whole operation crashing down on them if he caught them.

He'd be directly on them in just a second.

Juliet felt a moment of panic as Evan grabbed her by the waist, spun her around and pushed her to the ground. Knowing he was trying to get them under the cover of a fallen tree, she slid back as far as she could, and he scooted with her. She didn't let the fear overwhelm her. It was Evan this close to her; it was okay.

He didn't have time to turn around before the guard came by, which left Juliet and Evan in a lover-like embrace. She quickly pulled her dark sleeves over her hands and wrapped her arms around Evan's neck, trying to cover as much of his exposed skin as possible.

Both of them were silent as the guard passed by only feet from where they hid. He began walking away, then stopped.

Juliet's heart hammered in her chest. Had he seen them? Could he have possibly seen the amplifier?

Evan's arm moved just the slightest bit, and she realized he was removing his weapon from his shoulder holster. There was no way Juliet could get to hers, the way they were wound together, bodies pressed up against each other from chest to toe. And Evan was facing the wrong direction to shoot.

His hand skimmed up to where her arms were wrapped around his neck. Silently, he pushed his Glock into her hand.

If the guard became a dire threat, Juliet was going to have to be the one to take him out.

There was no doubt the man was armed. Like the other patrols they had seen, he carried a modified HK-33 submachine gun. The guard might have orders to shoot on sight. Hopefully, it wouldn't come to that, but Juliet had to be ready.

Evan trusted her to be.

Why was the guard still stopped? Did he see something? Sense something was off?

Juliet relaxed minutely against Evan when the man lit a cigarette in the darkness. He didn't know about them at all; he was just trying to get away with having a smoke on the boss's dime.

Evan and Juliet waited as the guard took drag after drag on his cigarette. Although Juliet didn't relax, she knew there was no way he would be casually smoking if he suspected there was anyone hiding nearby.

Evan obviously knew it, too. Because Juliet could feel his fingers begin to trace up and down her back. All of a sudden she was very aware of all the places their bodies were touching.

All the places.

Evan ran his hand down her spine and splayed it over her hip, pulling her the slightest bit closer. His hot breath rushed across her neck.

The guard finished his cigarette and reported in on his radio that all was clear and he was headed to the south end of the property.

Juliet and Evan didn't move from where they lay, although she relaxed the arm that held the Glock. Evan's hand remained on her hip, his hard body pressed up against hers.

She couldn't hold back a little sigh when she felt the breath against her neck turn into little kisses there.

Evan rolled onto his back, but didn't release her, so she rolled over on top of him. Neither spoke as he threaded his hands into her hair and pulled her lips down to his.

There was no hesitation, no faking, no fear. Only heat. Evan kissed her as though he couldn't get enough of her. A knot of need twisted inside her.

They broke apart from the kiss, breathing heavily. This was neither the time nor the place to give in to what they were feeling. Evan pulled her in for one more brief kiss, then got up from the ground and helped her up, too.

With a minimum of words they set up the amplifier/ detonator close to the wall and began the trek back to the car. They saw no sign of the guard.

Juliet handed Evan's weapon back to him. "I'm glad I didn't need to use this."

"Yeah, it would've been weird kissing you with a dead body lying right next to us."

Juliet rolled her eyes at Evan's black humor. "Not to

mention the two dozen guards that would've been chasing us once they heard my weapon fire."

They reached the car and Evan turned to her, cupping her cheek. "You did good, Jules. You kept your head, didn't panic, didn't fight me when we had to roll under that log."

"Well, I was pretty scared."

"It's all right to feel scared. It's what you *do* when you're scared that's important. You handled it like a trained agent. Nobody can ask for more."

Juliet didn't say much on the way back to DC. There was too much she was thinking about. Evan was right; she had handled the situation with the guard well. She hadn't panicked, not even when Evan had grabbed her and all but threw her down.

Because her mind was used to Evan. Not him throwing her to the ground, but him being around. His presence. His touch. Even his smell.

Evan had been gentling her over the past two days as if she were some sort of wild mare. Accustoming her to his touch, getting her mind to accept his presence as normal.

And although Juliet didn't like to compare herself to an animal, damned if it hadn't worked. After a split second of fear, she hadn't even worried about Evan's proximity; had only focused on the real danger: discovery by the guard.

The scene kept playing through her mind as they returned the borrowed car to Omega Headquarters and headed back to Evan's town house. For the first time Juliet felt assured about her abilities as an agent as they went undercover at Cady's mansion tomorrow. She might not be completely up to speed, but she would be able to get the job done. They would be able to recover the drone codes before anyone was killed.

She and Evan walked through his front door. He took off his jacket and hung it over one of the kitchen bar stools.

How had Juliet never really noticed how ripped Evan was? His black T-shirt didn't do much to hide the muscles of his biceps, pecs or abs. Thank God.

Evan turned to the fridge for a couple water bottles. He took a big sip out of one, leaning back against the counter.

"You want?" He held up a bottle, his dimple showing with this smile.

Looking at him, Juliet realized she did indeed want.

Evan. Right now. Tonight.

She knew he wanted her, too. That much had become evident while hiding under the log. This wasn't just an undercover op for Evan. *She* wasn't just an undercover op for him.

This time she didn't plan to take no for an answer. She had let the attack steal too many months of her life. She didn't plan to let it have even one more day. She wanted Evan and she knew he wanted her.

What was that saying? Leap and the net will appear.

Juliet leaped.

She slid her own jacket off and walked over to him. "Yeah, I want." She took the water bottle out of his hand and put it on the counter.

She pressed herself flush against him and reached up to wrap her arms around his neck. His hands instantly moved to her hips. She pulled his lips down to hers.

Yes. Finally. That was what she had been craving. His warm lips against hers. Evan tried to keep it soft and light, but Juliet had no interest in that. She pulled him hard against her and stood up on her tiptoes so she could get even closer.

"Juliet," Evan murmured against her mouth. "I'm not sure we should—"

She became even more aggressive in her kiss. "Not sure we should what?" Juliet finally asked.

Evan broke away just for a moment so he could look her in the eyes. "I just want to make sure this is what you really want."

"I'm pretty sure I want this more than I want to continue breathing."

With that, Evan scooped her up by the waist and spun, placing her on the kitchen counter. He grabbed her hips and slid her forward so they were as close as possible. And kissed her again, stealing her breath.

Yes, this was how Juliet wanted to feel, had thought she would never feel again. Evan's lips brushed over the underside of her jaw and down her neck. She couldn't stop the soft moan.

"I've waited a long time for this," Evan murmured against her throat.

"It's been a long time for me, too." Juliet found she could say it without bad memories coming up to swamp her.

Evan pulled back a little so they were looking eye to eye. "I've wanted you for years, Juliet. But it was never the right time."

She grabbed him by the collar and pulled him closer. "Well, it's the right time now. For both of us." Then she reached down and pulled Evan's shirt over his chest and head, letting it fall to the ground. Heat coursed through her. Everywhere their bodies touched was on fire.

Evan didn't say anything, just swung her up in his arms and carried her to his bed.

Chapter Fifteen

Evan lay in bed, watching Juliet curled up next to him, sound asleep. His mind was blown by their lovemaking a few hours before. Better, hotter, just plain more awesome than he would've ever expected.

He had tried to keep himself on a tight leash. If Juliet had any moments of panic, he wanted to be able to stop and help her through it.

But evidently the only panic she'd experienced had been about him not getting their clothes off fast enough. A couple steps up the stairs, while he was carrying her, she had been running her hands all over his chest and kissing his neck. He'd stopped right there, lowered her, backed her up against the wall and kissed her thoroughly. She'd pulled her own shirt off, and he'd made quick work of her bra, so they could be skin to skin.

Nothing had ever felt so right in his entire life.

"If we don't cut it out, we're never going to make it to the bed," he'd said.

The most beautiful smile he'd ever seen had lit up Juliet's face. "I don't want to make it to the bed. I want to make love right here, on the stairs."

Evan had been more than happy to oblige. In fact, he'd almost ripped their clothes off in an effort to oblige.

They had finally made it to the bed, afterward, with a

stop by the shower first. Now Juliet was sleeping and he needed to do the same. Tomorrow they'd be heading to Vince Cady's mansion.

Juliet's phone chirped on the nightstand by her side of the bed. That chirp—the one that signified Lisa Sinclair had received another sweetheart email. Evan tried to reach over and grab the phone before it woke Juliet, but he felt the tension flood through her. She'd already heard it.

"Just leave it," he told her as she reached for the phone.

"I can't." She was wide-awake. "Not knowing what it says makes me just as crazy as knowing."

Evan doubted that, but knew he couldn't stop her.

Sweetheart, we'll be together soon. Don't worry about your husband, I have special plans for him. He doesn't deserve you.

Evan hated the way fear crept back into Juliet's green eyes. She didn't openly panic, but the stress and tension had obviously returned.

"Jules, it's going to be fine."

"But now it looks like he's targeting *you*, Evan. And the last thing we need while we're undercover with Cady is some freak trying to track us down for some alone time with me."

"Well, we know the two are unrelated, so for now let's put the emails on the back burner. Once we finish with Cady, then we can concentrate on tracking down whoever is sending them."

Juliet looked uncomfortable, but nodded. "Okay. I'll turn off my phone notifications for that email account. I'll still get them, and so will the tech peeps at Omega, but we'll only see them when I choose to open them."

She set the phone down and Evan pulled her against

him. "That will be better. You'll be able to concentrate on the case, rather than worrying about the emails."

"You're right," Juliet whispered. "It's just, they freak me out. Throw my mind to crazy places. Sometimes it's hard to come back from that."

Evan kissed her on the forehead. "I know, baby. But you don't have to battle this alone anymore. I'm going to be here to help you every step of the way. Not to mention all three of your dumbass brothers."

Juliet smiled at that, as he had hoped, then pushed him back against the pillows and swung her leg so she straddled his hips.

"You know, we have to be at Cady's house in just a few short hours. We better get some sleep," she told him, but her wicked grin said something much different.

"Later," he growled, pulling her mouth down to his. "There'll be time for sleep later."

JULIET'S SOBS WOKE EVAN. For a moment of sleep-induced confusion, he forgot where he was and thought he was having another nightmare, with Juliet's agony in his head. But he quickly realized the sobs were coming from Juliet herself, asleep in his bed, dressed only in one of his T-shirts.

Her fitful thrashing and quiet sobs broke Evan's heart. He had hoped her nightmare days were behind her, but he also knew recovery was never a straightforward line. Steps backward were also part of the process. All he could do was keep his word and show Juliet she wasn't alone any longer.

Because she damn sure would never sleep on a closet floor again.

"Juliet." Evan kept his voice even and didn't touch her, not wanting to cause her further duress. "It's Evan, baby. Can you wake up? You're safe. It's okay."

He spoke the calming words over and over, and began gently and very loosely stroking her arm. Nothing that would seem like a grasp.

At first Juliet became more fitful, but then began to relax, almost as if his words were sinking in. He hoped that was true. He would've given his own life to have saved her from the brutality that now haunted her dreams with such poignancy.

"Evan?" Juliet's eyes fluttered open.

Thank God. "Yes, baby. I'm right here. It's okay. You were having a nightmare."

"I'm sorry. I didn't mean to wake you. Us sleeping together was probably a bad idea."

Evan wasn't sure if she meant the actual act of sleeping or their lovemaking earlier. Either way, she was wrong.

"No, it was the best idea either of us have ever had."

Juliet shrugged. "I'm not a great sleeper."

"You have nightmares. So do I. The important thing is you don't have to wake up alone anymore. You don't have to fight these demons by yourself."

She nodded, but Evan could tell she was still upset by what had happened. He wasn't quite certain what upset her more, the nightmare or him being there to witness it. She got up and headed to the shower. Evan let her go. She needed space.

And if she stuck around his bed, he was afraid he might start talking to her about *always* being there when she awoke, and holding her through any nightmares. It was too soon to be discussing that, and it might scare her off even more.

Evan could be patient. He'd been patient for years, even before the attack. He could be again.

And besides, now was not the time to worry about the future. They both needed to be concentrating on today, and Cady and retrieval of the codes. Everything else would have to wait.

A few hours later they were on their way to the estate near Annapolis. They had stopped by Omega so Megan could fine-tune the tracker and mayday device Juliet wore.

"Okay, remember the acoustic homing signal echoes off the magnetic ray with the tracker, and vertical trajectory also comes into play if the device is utilized as part of a denotation stratagem, so that needs to be taken into consideration. But because of the alloy elements, it's virtually imperceptible to discovery," Megan, one of the leading computer scientists in the country, had told them. "Any questions?"

Juliet and Evan had just looked at each other, neither really having any idea what the younger woman had just said. Fortunately, Sawyer was there to interpret, putting his arm around Megan, obvious love in his eyes.

"What giant brain here is trying to say is that Vince Cady and his men are not going to find the device on you, but it is definitely short-range," he'd explained.

"Sawyer, that's exactly what I said to them!" Megan blinked at them through her glasses, obviously believing it.

"I know, honey," he'd responded in a stage whisper. "They're just slow. Don't worry."

The little bit of humor had been just what they needed. Juliet had turned to Evan, shaking her head, her eyes twinkling. She was ready.

They were ready.

As they pulled up to a guardhouse at Cady's property an hour later in Evan's Jeep, Juliet slipped her hand into his. He gave it a reassuring squeeze.

"Bob and Lisa Sinclair, here by Mr. Cady's invitation," Evan told the guard.

The man looked it up on a small computerized tablet, then nodded and gave them instructions on where to go.

There were a number of cars already parked near the house, all high-end automobiles. Neither the number nor the caliber of the vehicles was surprising. Cady did not deal with lowlifes. His dealings were not something small-time criminals could afford.

Especially when it came to the drone override codes. Anybody interested in buying them would definitely be a big-time player. Someone Omega would need to start keeping tabs on, if they weren't already.

Like Evan, Juliet was taking stock of the different vehicles. Some of these people would be associates they'd worked with before. Others would be new. All could be potentially deadly.

Evan pulled the Bob Sinclair cloak around him—a friendly guy, good with people, not quite the sharpest tool in the shed, but smart enough. He enjoyed creature comforts and good food, but also had an adventurous side, thus the Jeep as his chosen vehicle.

Evan could tell that Juliet was fully into her role as Lisa Sinclair. Lisa was smart—not a stretch for Juliet—but also liked to pamper herself, and cared more about her appearance than Juliet ever did. She wore expensive jewelry: a diamond bracelet, two almost gaudy rings on her hands, and of course, the locket around her neck.

Lisa's clothes were a far cry from what Juliet normally wore; her tailored pants and blouse, coupled with high heels, were quite different from Juliet's more casual jeans and sweaters. But Evan was sure Lisa Sinclair's outfit helped Juliet dig more into character.

She appeared confident, professional and no-nonsense. Evan loved Juliet's casual style, but had to admit she could pull off Lisa's look as if she was born to it. It was a turn-on, for sure.

Evan parked the Jeep, then hopped out to come around and open the passenger door. He helped Juliet down from her seat and kept his hand at the small of her back as they walked toward the main door of the house.

"You look great," he whispered.

One eyebrow arched. "Of course I do," she responded, smiling. She was already Lisa Sinclair. "These shoes are Manolo Blahnik. Any girl would look fabulous."

Evan pulled her close and kissed the top of her head, partly because he knew they were being watched and the action would be in character.

But partly because he just couldn't help himself.

A member of Cady's staff opened the door as the two of them approached the steps.

"Welcome, Mr. and Ms. Sinclair," the woman said. "Mr. Cady is expecting you. We will have you join the other guests in just a moment, but first please follow our security team."

Juliet and Evan were led to a smallish room off the foyer. One man used a wand to scan Evan, while another did the same to Juliet. Evan could see her tension at the man's proximity. She glanced at Evan and he gave her a reassuring nod. She flinched when the guard touched her shoulder and asked her to turn around.

Evan had a moment of slight panic when the wand beeped as it passed over Juliet's locket. Megan had said it was undetectable as a short-range device. Had she been wrong? Was the very thing that was supposed to assure Juliet's safety going to get them both killed?

"Would you mind removing that locket, please, ma'am?" the guard asked politely, but his tone brooked no refusal.

Juliet took a step back and removed the jewelry. Evan

hoped it was as undetectable as Megan and Sawyer claimed it was.

Juliet cringed and couldn't seem to find anything to say, so Evan stepped in for her. "That was her mother's, so be careful with it." Juliet grasped his hand, nodding.

The guard opened the locket, and after much studying, and even removing the picture that was in it, put everything back and returned it to Juliet.

"Sorry," he said. "Any piece of jewelry this size must be inspected."

"Fine, just give it to me," Juliet told him in an acerbic tone. The guard handed it to her and she returned it to her neck. "Are we free to go or are we going to be subjected to more humiliation?"

"You're free to go. Sorry for the trouble."

"I would think so."

It was easy to see why Lisa Sinclair had a reputation as being a bitch. Because she was one. Juliet, once she'd found her tongue, seemed to remember Lisa well.

The woman who had met them at the front door led Evan and Juliet into a large room with multiple windows. People were milling around, talking. Waitstaff were walking around with trays of food and drink.

With his hand resting on her waist, Evan felt Juliet's tension growing, but none of it showed in her expression. A smooth, alert-but-somewhat-bored look remained planted on her face. It was damn near perfect.

"There you are!" Vince Cady came at them from across the room. "I wondered if you were going to make it at all, after our last…encounter."

Evan shook the older man's hand. "Lisa convinced me this wasn't something we'd want to miss out on."

"Well, the lovely Mrs. Sinclair has good taste." Cady gestured to Juliet's outfit. "As always." When he bent forward to kiss her cheek, she stiffened slightly, but didn't withdraw. Cady didn't seem to notice her discomfort.

"Thank you for having us in your home, Mr. Cady," she said, her tone a nice mixture of friendly and cold. "We much prefer this to an empty warehouse or other dirty building with weapons pointed at us."

Cady's laughter was booming. "Yes, this is much more comfortable for everyone. And it's only going to get better, you'll see."

More comfortable than an entire staff providing for their every whim? Evan found that hard to believe.

"But let me introduce you to my family. This is my wife, Maria, and our son, Christopher."

Maria Cady had hard, small eyes. Her smile seemed forced, although she politely murmured, "Pleased to meet you," as she shook Evan's hand.

Definitely not the friendly type, or at all personable or charming like her husband.

Evan turned to Vince's son, only to find the younger man staring at Juliet with unadulterated lust. Juliet didn't see it, because she was shaking hands with Maria. Evan wrapped his arm tightly around Juliet's waist and pulled her up against him.

Christopher Cady turned to Evan, his face smoothing out into a blank mask, friendly even. Had Evan imagined what he'd just seen in the younger man's face?

With a smile, Christopher offered his hand to shake. "Pleasure," he said.

"Same," Evan lied. He'd definitely be keeping an eye on Christopher.

"Maria, Christopher and I must go say hello to some other guests," Vince told them. "We have over twenty coming in all. The drone codes have brought out interest from quite a few buyers."

Cady was so excited Evan was surprised he didn't rub his hands together in glee. The man obviously loved being in a position of power.

"I'm not surprised," Juliet told him. "Your reputation for having quality items and not wasting buyers' time is well known, Mr. Cady."

"Please, both of you call me Vince. We should be informal, don't you think?"

"Absolutely." Evan and Juliet spoke at the same time, then looked at each other and grinned.

"Such a lovely couple." Maria smiled at them, but the smile didn't reach her eyes.

"Please enjoy yourselves," Vince said. "Eat. Drink. We'll provide further instructions once everyone has arrived."

Vince took his scary family and began wandering toward other guests.

"So far, so good," Juliet whispered to Evan. "What do we do now?"

"Like the man said, let's eat and drink. Mingle."

"Get as much information as possible."

"Exactly." Evan winked down at her. They began working their way toward a table that held different hors d'oeuvres: the scallops wrapped in bacon looked particularly delicious. "Who should be our first targets?"

Juliet placed some food on a plate as she looked around casually. Then Evan saw all the color drain from her face. The plate in her hand fell from lifeless fingers and crashed onto the hardwood floor, shattering.

Evan rushed immediately to her side. "What's wrong?"

"That man over by the door." Juliet couldn't seem to tear her eyes away. "He's Heath Morel, close friend of the Avilo brothers, who attacked me. He could be the one sending me the emails."

Chapter Sixteen

Nausea roiled in Juliet's stomach. What was Heath Morel doing here? Although he hadn't been there the night the Avilo brothers had attacked her, everyone knew he and the Avilos not only worked together, but were close friends.

Suddenly, the sweetheart emails made sense to Juliet. Before he died, Marco Avilo could've provided details about the attack to Morel, or Robert could have, before he'd gone to prison.

Evan led her to one side of the room as concerned staff members began cleaning up the mess she had made when she'd dropped her plate. All talking had stopped at Juliet's social faux pas, but now was slowly resuming its previous volume. Eyes that had been glued to her and Evan were now starting to look away, having found nothing of interest to hold their stares.

Except for those of Cady and his son. Juliet glanced their way again and found them still gazing at her. At first she thought it was because of their duty as hosts— was Juliet okay? Had something happened to her to make her disrupt the party? But then she saw Cady look over at Heath Morel, a small smile on his face.

Juliet turned her back to them, so she was facing Evan. Had Cady planned this? Had he invited Morel, to get some sort of rise out of her?

"Hey," Evan said and bent down so they were eye to eye. "Are you okay?"

She nodded tightly, unable to say anything right at this second.

"We knew there would be people from our past here," he continued. "You're still okay. We can do this."

Juliet took a couple long breaths. Evan was right; Heath Morel was here, but nothing had changed. She could still do this. The emails didn't have anything to do with the drone override codes.

"You're right," she whispered. "I'm okay. I can do this."

Evan drew her in for a hug. "Good girl. No more throwing plates, okay?"

"Got it." Juliet turned so she was standing beside him and facing everyone in the room again. "I think Cady might have invited Heath Morel on purpose, just to see my reaction. He was looking at Morel with a weird smile a minute ago."

"Wouldn't surprise me at all. That's the kind of sick stuff Cady is known for. Even more reason not to let it get to you."

"And if Morel is the one sending me the emails? It has to be him."

Evan pulled her closer and kissed the side of her forehead. "Then we're one step closer to catching him, aren't we?"

Evan was exactly right. That was how Juliet needed to look at it. She didn't need to hide from Morel; she could use this time to draw him out.

"Thank you." The words were inadequate to describe how grateful Juliet felt toward Evan. He was helping her remember how to stand and fight, rather than run and hide. She couldn't have done it by herself.

"For what?"

"For being here. For knowing what to say. For just being you."

Evan winked at her. "No problem."

The two of them began making their way around the room, talking to different people. Most of it was just chit-chat. No one wanted to give up very much information. After all, they were competitors vying for the same prize. But Juliet made mental notes of every person there, absorbing as much detail as possible to report later. She knew Evan was doing the same.

They avoided Morel, and Juliet noticed he seemed to be avoiding them also. He didn't have anything to do with her attack—he'd been in a different part of the country at the time—but that didn't mean he hadn't known about the plan. And it made complete sense that he was the one sending her the emails.

Juliet wasn't sure if she wanted to confront the bastard or just stay away from him altogether. But putting a face to the emails somehow made her feel better. Confronting the demon she did know rather than fighting the ones she made up in her head.

And speaking of demons, Juliet always felt as if someone was watching her. It didn't seem to be Morel. He was studiously trying *not* to look at her, as far as she could tell. Juliet never could pinpoint who it might be, but she seemed to always feel eyes on her. Maybe her imagination was running away with her. It wouldn't be the first time.

And maybe it was that she was in a room full of criminals and everyone was eyeing everybody else, while trying not to make it obvious.

Vince Cady certainly seemed to enjoy playing lord of the manor, talking to everyone, holding court. Everyone was doing what they could to get in his favor, in case that would help when the bidding began.

Juliet knew the auction probably wouldn't be until to-night, possibly tomorrow morning. Until then they had to play nice. Evan certainly seemed to have no problem with that. Bob Sinclair was charming with everyone. Of course, that wasn't a stretch for Evan; almost everyone liked him. But his Bob Sinclair persona hid his fierce intelligence. People tended to underestimate him, and he used it to his advantage.

Lisa Sinclair was more silent and snooty. Juliet didn't mind not talking. It gave her a chance to study people. And not have them touch her. Although she was doing better in general, she still did not like people casually touching her. She slid a little closer to Evan.

After an appropriate time to mingle, Cady held up his hand to get everyone's attention from where he stood in the doorway. "Thank you all for coming. I know we have important business to attend to. And we will soon, I promise.

"I would like to give you a tour of my house, and show you where you will be staying," he continued. He looked at his son, who was grinning slightly and nodding. "But Christopher had a much better idea, and perfect for security reasons."

Cady waited until he had everyone's undivided attention. "I will have my staff get all of your belongings. We will be going to my yacht for the next few days and conducting all business there."

Silence reigned for a few moments before murmuring broke out. Juliet looked up at Evan, concerned. He slipped an arm around her waist and drew her closer, putting his lips against her hair as if kissing her.

"It's a test. Don't show any emotion."

The words were so soft, Juliet almost couldn't hear them. She schooled her expression into a blank mask. Lisa

Sinclair would not care if they were going on a yacht. She would just want to get to business.

Christopher joined his father and held up a small metal box. He didn't explain what it was, but Juliet knew.

The transmitter/detonator she and Evan had planted yesterday. She felt Evan's arm tighten around her waist.

"Here on land there can be security compromises, but on the yacht we can assure everyone's comfort, safety and privacy."

Both Christopher and Vince were looking around the room carefully. They couldn't know for sure it was some-one here who had planted the device, and even if they did, it wasn't an item that particularly screamed police.

Lawmen didn't tend to plant detonation devices. Of course, Omega Sector wasn't your everyday law enforcement.

"Anyone not interested in joining us on the yacht may leave now. Your association with the Cady family will be finished for good," Vince proclaimed.

That certainly upped the stakes for everyone. Silence fell over the room once more.

"Well, we're in! Just point us to the boat and we're ready. It'll be like a second honeymoon, won't it, honey?" Evan broke the silence with his enthusiastic response, mov-ing toward the doorway where Cady stood, bringing Juliet along with him.

She just plastered a smile on her face, although it was the last thing she felt like doing.

Moving to a yacht changed everything. All their plans, the information they'd gleaned from their surveillance work about Cady's security forces, all wasted. The trans-mitting device her brothers had given her would be worth-less out in the Chesapeake Bay with no amplifier.

They'd be going in blind, with no way to contact Omega for support. They'd be totally on their own.

And Evan, instead of trying to figure a way of gracefully bowing out, had just enthusiastically agreed to be the first ones on the ship.

Things had just gone from iffy to downright impossible.

EVAN DIDN'T LIKE the yacht idea, but there wasn't any way around it, so he decided to at least make it look as if he embraced the concept.

Cady was smart. This abrupt change put everyone on edge and changed all the game plans. Including Juliet and Evan's. On the yacht Cady would have all the advantages.

They'd found the transmitter where Evan and Juliet had left it, but hadn't identified it as law enforcement equipment. It could just as easily belong to someone who had more nefarious purposes in mind.

Juliet hadn't reacted to the transmitter's appearance, thank goodness. Vince and Christopher had both been watching everyone, looking for a reaction. Evan knew Juliet couldn't be happy about this change of plans. The safety net, feeble as it was, had just been yanked right out from under them.

But there was no time to talk about it, no time to get a new game plan together. They just had to go with it and watch each other's backs.

"When do we head out?" Evan asked Cady. Hopefully, keeping up the bravado would remove all suspicion from them.

"If you will just provide your luggage to my staff, we have cars ready to take you all to the ship."

Evan nodded and led the way out of the room, arm wrapped around Juliet's waist. Others followed, while a few stayed behind to press for further details from Cady, or maybe even to bow out altogether. Good. Anyone leaving now would be one less problem for him and Juliet to deal with, while also strengthening their cover.

Evan walked with her out to the Jeep. Her pinched expression tugged at his heart, but he couldn't stop to reassure her. Too many ears around.

He got their luggage out of the trunk. Immediately, one of Cady's staff members appeared to assist. Evan freely handed them over, but knew the contents would be thoroughly searched before he and Juliet saw them again.

It was all part of Cady's plan, and it was a good one. He would now control what went onto the vessel, including weapons. This would eliminate anybody planning to double-cross him. Also, once they were out in the Chesapeake Bay, cell phone reception might be sketchy, and most certainly monitored by Cady's people.

Calling in the cavalry wasn't going to be an option.

They needed to get a message about the change in situation to Omega now, but Evan couldn't figure out how to do it without being obvious. Any call they made would be heard; texts would be monitored.

"I'm going to text Aunt Mildred and let her know that we may need her to watch the dogs a couple extra days. I don't want to take a chance on being out at sea and not being able to get a message to her. You know how she would worry," Juliet said to him, already getting out her phone.

Evan could've kissed her. As usual, Juliet was one step ahead of everybody with the plan-making. Thank goodness for the Branson family and all their crazy codes with each other.

"She'll like that we're going on a boat. You know she just went on a cruise last fall." Juliet spoke as she typed. "I need to mention to her how to turn the satellite television on, too. Just in case she wants to watch while she's there, you know, since the transmitter isn't working anymore."

It looked as if Juliet would be able to get the important info out to her brothers. They would be on a ship, Omega needed to use the satellite to locate them, and the transmitter was no longer an option.

This was a perfect example of what made Juliet such a great agent. She thought out of the box and acted quickly.

She slipped her phone back into her purse. "Okay, sent. I hope it makes it through."

"Everything will be okay, either way." Evan took her hand and she slid closer to him.

Three black limousines pulled up to take the guests to the yacht. Evan helped Juliet into the closest one.

There was no going back now.

Chapter Seventeen

The yacht was everything Evan would expect of a criminal of Vince Cady's caliber. Large, able to easily sleep the twenty guests he had invited, plus the staff and security Cady had on board.

The limos had taken them to a private boatyard near Annapolis Harbor. Everyone had been shown on board and soon they were on their way into the Chesapeake Bay, with champagne served as they sailed away.

As if they were going on some sort of pleasure cruise rather than an auction of items that could potentially cost the lives of thousands of people.

Evan had to admit he was impressed by the ship's luxury. He and Juliet had been shown to their plush stateroom. A bed filled the space, surrounded by tasteful mahogany woodwork and trim. Under any other circumstance, he would be delighted to be here with Juliet.

But the fact that the room was most definitely bugged, that all their belongings had been searched and they were in the middle of a dangerous situation with little or no backup tended to kill the romance.

Evan still hadn't been able to talk to Juliet about this new change in situation. He was sure that was part of Cady's plan: keeping everyone on edge and giving them very little privacy.

"Hey, baby, we're on a cruise. Just like we always wanted to be." Evan walked over, hooked an arm around Juliet's waist and began kissing her neck, working his way up to her ear. Her shivers delighted him, but this embrace was business.

"Room is bugged. Audio, maybe visual," he whispered.

She tensed, but then nodded and kissed him. "Well, this wasn't exactly what I had in mind. I was thinking more along the lines of the Bahamas," she said out loud.

"If we secure this deal with Cady, I promise to take you there. The commission on the drone override codes will be outrageous."

"Yeah, yeah, yeah. I've heard all that before, Bob."

"Aw, don't say that, baby." He pulled her in for another hug. "Let's take a shower together so we can get ready for tonight."

Juliet nodded. "I definitely feel like I need one, especially with some of the people Cady invited. Go turn the water on."

The bathroom was just as opulent as the bedroom. Evan switched on the shower, knowing it would be their only chance to talk privately.

Not that he minded getting in a shower with Juliet for any reason.

He undressed and entered the stall, a large walk-in one with granite tiles and a clear glass door. Evan turned the water to hot to make the glass steam. He wasn't sure if the surveillance was just audio or had a visual component, and he wanted to protect their privacy as much as he could.

Evan tried to stay focused on the case, but found it difficult when Juliet opened the shower door a few minutes later.

"Wow, this is nice. We should get something like this at home," she said, loudly enough to be overheard.

"I know. Get in here."

Evan wrapped his arms around her and brought her flush up against his body. He couldn't control his reaction to her, but forced himself to concentrate on the business at hand. This might be the only time they could talk freely with one another.

"Surveillance in the room, without a doubt. Cady wouldn't bring us all out here otherwise," Evan whispered in her ear, at a level that couldn't possibly be overheard with the water falling all around them.

Juliet nodded, but he felt her stiffen. She didn't like the thought of someone watching her naked. Neither did he. "Sorry."

"Our plan is still the same, right?" she asked. "We make sure we have the highest bid when the codes become available."

"Yes."

"What about Heath Morel?"

Morel complicated things, especially since Juliet was right—it seemed most likely that he was behind the emails to her.

"We can't let him distract us."

The water rushed down over both of them for long moments. "This is all hard enough for me. I'm not sure I can do it with him around. Just seeing him, knowing he has those sick details…"

Evan skimmed his fingers up and down her spine. "I know, but you'll have to, baby. You have to just push it aside."

He could feel her sigh against him. He didn't blame her. The whole Cady case was difficult enough without Morel thrown into the mix.

"We'll get him, Jules. I promise. Within twenty-four hours of being back on shore, we'll make sure Morel gets picked up for questioning. We'll put an end to all those emails. But it will have to wait until after. Can you do that?"

Juliet nodded her head against his chest. They stood in silence for another moment, water pouring around them. Then Evan felt her hands slide up his arms to his shoulders and link behind his neck. "I don't want to talk about Heath Morel anymore."

Her body brushed up against him. Evan's body responded in kind.

"Do you think there's any chance of cameras being inside this shower?" Juliet asked, planting kisses along his chest.

"No, not with all the steam. They wouldn't be able to see anything."

"Good," she murmured, and pulled his lips down to hers.

AFTER THEIR SHOWER, Juliet and Evan got dressed and walked around the yacht. They strolled as if they were just enjoying being out on the Chesapeake Bay, but they really wanted to glean as much intel as possible.

As far as Juliet could tell, the ship had five levels. The bottom one seemed to be staff quarters, the galley and the engine and maintenance areas. She and Evan hadn't been able to get down there at all. They'd been met by an armed guard at every entrance they'd strolled by.

The other floors held guest rooms, a large dining area, multiple decks to sit out on and enjoy the views, even a swimming pool. There was also a lounge with couches and seats. Juliet concluded that's where the auction would probably be held.

All and all, their walk gave them lots to see and admire, but very little info in terms of strategy.

Now they were back in their room, dressing for dinner. Juliet tried not to let the thought of cameras spying on them from somewhere in the room bother her, but it did. She changed clothes as quickly as she could.

Her dress wasn't formal or particularly fancy, but Juliet knew she looked good in it. The quintessential little black dress, but in a rich plum color instead, the perfect foil for her blond hair. The dress fell to just above her knees and had a slightly naughty V neckline. Nude-colored, high-heeled sandals completed the outfit.

"Wow." Evan was slowly looking her up and down. "I'm not sure we're going to make it out of this room."

Juliet smiled. "Too much?"

He shook his head slowly. "No. Definitely no. Just enough."

Juliet loved the hungry look in Evan's eyes. She never thought she'd let someone close enough to see that look again.

Evan himself looked dashing in his jeans and black T-shirt, coupled with a stylish beige sports coat. He offered his arm. "Shall we go to dinner?"

Juliet hooked her arm through his. It was almost as if they were on a date, except for the being on board a ship miles from land, with over a dozen known criminals.

The plan while they were at dinner was for Evan to corner Morel and make some barely veiled threats about the emails. After all, Bob was Lisa's husband. He wouldn't like for her to be receiving emails of that type from anyone.

She'd already received three more since her arrival at Cady's house this morning. The emails were escalating in number, in tone, in desperation. Juliet had turned off notifications for when she received an email, but she was still able to check them manually, which she'd done just before dinner.

She and Evan had gone over them together. And while they no longer caused that sick feeling of dread to course through her, she still hated reading them. Especially hated the word *sweetheart*.

Hopefully, Bob's talk with Morel would eliminate the email problem altogether, or at least while they were working this case.

Dinner went smoothly, with Vince Cady announcing that the auction for the different items, including the drone codes, would take place the next afternoon. After dinner, they were herded, gently and tastefully, of course, by the staff into the large sitting room. It opened out to the water and people milled around with their drinks and desserts.

Juliet spoke with Maria Cady for a while, mostly just polite chitchat. The woman seemed very tight-lipped. Juliet wondered how much she knew about her husband's business. Did she know what was really going on here? Did she deliberately turn a blind eye? Ultimately, it wouldn't really matter.

Juliet noticed Evan talking to Morel across the room. Part of her wanted to go over and stand by Evan while he let Morel have it, but the bigger part of her wanted to stay away from the man completely. Just looking at him brought up memories of the Avilo brothers, making her stomach turn.

Juliet gave a polite excuse to Maria and went to stand outside near the railing. It was peaceful out here, darker and cooler, with no need to talk or even listen to other voices. Juliet breathed in the fresh night air and her stomach settled. She could handle this.

The sound of a match being lit just a few feet away startled her. She turned and saw Christopher Cady's face as he brought the flame up to his slim cigar. He took a couple steps toward her.

Juliet started to back up, but forced herself to stop.

Don't panic. You're fine.

"Enjoying the peace and quiet out here?" Christopher asked.

He's just a man talking to a woman. Making conversation. Don't panic.

But tension suffused her body. "Yeah, it's a nice night and it got a little stuffy inside. So I decided to come out so I could be alone." Juliet hoped he would get the hint.

But no. Instead, Christopher took a step closer. "It's beautiful out here, isn't it? I love boats. They can take you to lots of private places, romantic places."

Juliet just stared at the man. Lisa Sinclair was *married*, for heaven's sake. Was Christopher hitting on her? She took another step farther away. Unfortunately, this led her into a little more darkness.

Even more unfortunately, Christopher took another step toward her. Juliet looked over to the main room where everyone was talking and mulling around. No one, not even Evan, was looking this way or paying her and Christopher the slightest bit of attention.

"I think I'm going to go back inside," Juliet said. She didn't want to be rude to Vince Cady's son, but didn't want to stay out here alone with him, either. He gave her the creeps, and the sweet smell of his thin cigar soured her stomach. "Bob will wonder where I am if I stay away too long."

Christopher leaned forward and grabbed her arm where it rested on the railing. "Bob is a fool to allow you to be out here alone at all. No one should leave a woman as beautiful as you unattended."

Juliet's panic spiked at the feel of Christopher's hand on her. But she forced herself to ease away rather than yank. "I have to go."

"I would like you to stay and talk to me. I can tell you more about the boat. There's lots of interesting facts about it you don't know. Of course, some are better shown."

Juliet turned away. "No, thanks."

But Christopher wasn't interested in taking no for an answer. He grabbed her arm again, just above the elbow. Juliet cringed, her flesh crawling. She forced herself to take a cleansing breath in through her nose and out through her mouth. "I'm really not interested. Please just leave me alone."

Christopher's darkly handsome face took on a cruel look. "I'm Vince Cady's son. If you want any sort of chance at winning the auction tomorrow it would be in your best interest to be nice to me."

What he said was probably true, but Juliet didn't care. She couldn't stay there with him even a minute longer without retching all over the place. She twisted out of his hold. "I have to go."

This time Christopher grabbed her shoulder in a painful grip. Juliet's reflexes took over. She turned slightly into the stronger man's grasp, then rammed her elbow into his solar plexus. She heard the breath whoosh out of him, but didn't stop. Instead, she grabbed his arm with both hands, pulled him closer and, with a yank and shift of her body weight, flipped him over her back.

Before Juliet even realized what she was doing, Christopher Cady lay gasping on the yacht's wooden deck, staring up at the sky.

Chapter Eighteen

It happened faster than she thought possible. Juliet still held Christopher's wrist, now in a grip that would allow her to break bones if he tried anything else. Reflexes still in full-alert mode, she looked around for any potential threats.

But all she saw was Evan rushing toward them. And a dozen concerned faces behind him. And the Cady security team.

"Hey, what's going on here? Lisa, is everything all right?" Evan asked her.

She immediately let go of Christopher's hand. Awareness of the situation crept into her brain. Oh no, what had she done? Probably just cost them the case, maybe worse.

Evan stepped around Christopher and stood right in front of Juliet, offering them a little bit of privacy from the prying eyes with his body. "You okay, honey?"

He trailed a finger down her cheek, but didn't try to embrace her. Juliet appreciated the distance. "He grabbed me and instincts just took over. I'm so sorry." She stared down at her feet.

Evan tipped her chin up with one finger. "It'll be fine. He shouldn't have grabbed you." Evan took his sports coat off and wrapped it around her shoulders. Juliet didn't even realize she had been trembling. She snuggled into the warmth.

Evan turned around to face Christopher, who was now sitting up on the floor. Security guards were rushing to assist him.

"I'm taking my wife back to our cabin. As I'm sure you now realize, she doesn't like people to grab her. I trust nothing like this will happen again."

Christopher didn't say anything, just glared at them. Evan returned to where Juliet had propped herself against the railing, put his arm around her and led her away.

The magnitude of what she'd done hit Juliet. She brought her fist up to her mouth. "Oh no, Evan, I've ruined everything." She couldn't help it; tears welled in her eyes. "What's going to happen?"

He stopped and pulled her into his arms. They were far enough away now that no one could see or hear them. "Hey, we'll deal with it."

"But I assaulted Cady's son! I may have just blown everything."

"He wasn't hurt, you just knocked the wind out of him. It's late. Let's head back to the room and let everything die down."

Juliet nodded. She couldn't think of any way to undo the damage she'd done.

"My brothers were afraid something like this would happen. They were right."

"They were right about what? That you would be able to handle yourself if some guy started forcing his attention on you? Christopher Cady won't make that mistake again."

"I guess not," Juliet whispered, but she didn't feel any better. What if, after everything they'd done to get here, she and Evan got booted off the ship because she hadn't been able to keep her cool?

"You just need to get some rest, Lisa. Everything will

feel better in the morning," Evan said a little too loudly as he opened the door to their cabin.

Juliet took the hint. It wasn't safe for them to talk anymore, at least not about blowing the case. But even Lisa Sinclair would be worried about the ramifications of assaulting Cady's only son.

"I'm worried what Vince is going to do when he finds out."

Evan nodded and gave her a little squeeze. "We'll deal with that as it comes."

EVAN COULD TELL Juliet didn't get much sleep. Her tossing around had little to do with the patch of rougher waters the boat had hit and everything to do with her apprehension over what had happened with Christopher Cady.

Evan should never have left her alone. His talk with Heath Morel, trying to get the other man to agree not to send any more emails to Lisa, had been pretty fruitless, anyway. Morel had played his cards very close to his chest, refusing to admit to any knowledge whatsoever about the emails. And Evan hadn't wanted to make a big scene that would get them noticed, so force was out of the question.

Which was about the time he had looked up and seen Christopher Cady flying through the air over Juliet's shoulder. Evan's immediate concern had been for her safety. Had Cady assaulted her? Tried to harm her in some way?

But once Evan made it over there and realized Juliet wasn't harmed—and neither was Cady—he'd also been concerned for the case. Although he'd tried to assure her otherwise, Juliet was right to be worried about how Vince would respond to her aggression against his son.

But it was already morning, so evidently Cady wasn't planning to kill them. He would've done that last night, although even for Cady that was a bit extreme. But Evan wouldn't be surprised if they were put off the ship altogether, or at the very least not allowed to participate in the auctions.

Which would put the drone codes out in the open. They couldn't allow that to happen.

But hell if Evan had any sort of plan B.

A sharp knock at their cabin door startled Evan and had Juliet sitting up in the bed, clutching the sheet to her chest. Evan looked around for anything he could use as a weapon, but there wasn't much. He pulled his jeans on and answered the door.

"Yes?" He opened the door the smallest crack possible.

It was one of Cady's security force. "Mr. Cady would like to extend an invitation for you to join him for breakfast in his private dining area in one hour. I'll return then to escort you."

The man didn't wait for an answer; just turned to leave. Evan closed the door and found Juliet up and already starting to get dressed.

"Breakfast with Cady. Is that bad or good?"

Evan honestly didn't know. "We'll just have to see and go from there."

True to his word, the guard was back to escort them an hour later. Evan and Juliet hadn't said much to each other during that time. There wasn't much that could be discussed when they knew their conversation would be overheard.

Her expression was tight and she kept biting at her lip as they walked toward Cady's dining room. Evan wished he could reassure her, but had no idea how.

"Good morning, Bob, Lisa," Vince said to them as they were shown into the room. He sat at a small table that held settings for four. "Please sit down."

Coffee and juice were already on the table, but no food

had arrived. Evan held out a seat for Juliet, then took the one next to her.

Juliet glanced quickly at him, then turned her attention to Vince. "Mr. Cady, please allow me to apologize for what happened with your son last night. I am afraid I still have some…residual issues from some…occurrences in my past."

Vince didn't respond, just added some cream to his coffee.

"Mr. Cady," Juliet continued, "I hope you will take into consideration that it was only me who assaulted your son. Bob had nothing to do with it. He wasn't even with me at the time."

Evan stared at her. What the heck was she doing?

"I don't blame you if you want me to leave. But I hope you will not penalize Bob, or the people we work for, because of my actions. Please allow Bob to remain for the auction today."

Cady turned his head and looked at her while stirring his coffee. "You assaulted my son."

Damn it. Evan knew he should've stepped in before now. *Assaulted* was such an ugly word. "Mr. Cady, my wife—"

"I'm just trying to tell you that it was me. It had nothing to do with Bob." Juliet cut him off.

Cady leaned back in his chair and took a sip of his coffee. "No offense, Mrs. Sinclair, but you don't look like you would be big or strong enough to assault anyone. Much less someone as large as Christopher."

Juliet started to speak again, but Cady held out his hand to silence her. "Furthermore, I know Christopher well, and I have no doubt that if you flipped him over your shoulder, then he did something to deserve it."

For the first time since last evening Evan could relax slightly. Cady wasn't mad. He was impressed with Juliet.

"I just don't like to be touched, once I've told somebody not to."

Cady took another sip of his coffee, laughing. "That's right. No means no. Well, you've certainly helped Christopher learn that lesson. One I'd hoped he'd learned, but evidently had not."

Two waiters brought out trays of food, setting plates before each of them. "My wife was going to join us, but she's not feeling well because of the rough waters." Cady was referring to the empty chair. "Please go ahead and eat."

Evan was a few bites into his delicious meal of eggs, bacon and fruit when Christopher Cady walked in. When he saw Evan and Juliet his expression turned from bored to irritated to smug.

"You wanted to see me, Father?"

Evan saw Juliet's fork hesitate halfway up to her mouth. Did Cady expect her to apologize to Christopher? She would do it to save the case, but Evan wasn't sure he could stomach it. He reached over and grasped her free hand.

"Mr. Cady—"

Cady held out a palm to silence Evan.

"Christopher, I was just speaking to Bob and Lisa about what happened last night."

The younger Cady could barely tear his gaze away from Juliet to answer. "A misunderstanding, Father. I'm sure Lisa did not mean any harm by what happened."

"I'm sure you're right. You, on the other hand, I cannot speak so confidently about."

Now Vince had Christopher's attention. A growing awareness of his father's feelings about the situation dawned over his dark features. And he wasn't happy about it.

"Father—"

"Christopher, I want you to apologize to Mrs. Sinclair for your behavior last night." Vince cut him off without even waiting to hear the rest of the excuse.

At first Evan thought Christopher would refuse, defying his father. But then he turned stiffly to Juliet. "Please accept my apology. It was never my intention to hurt or frighten you in any way."

Juliet nodded, but didn't say anything. There wasn't anything she really could say. Christopher returned her nod and turned to leave, but Vince stopped him.

"I want you to apologize to Mr. Sinclair, too. After all, it was his wife you traumatized."

Evan caught Juliet's concerned gaze. She knew, as he did, that this was going too far. Evan didn't understand all the dynamics between father and son, but obviously there was some sort of power struggle going on.

Evan had not expected—or wanted—an apology from Christopher. Neither had Juliet. The best both of them had hoped for was just not having to abandon the case because of what had happened. Evan wasn't sure what buttons Vince wanted to push with Christopher, but wished it didn't involve him and Juliet.

"Mr. Cady. That's not necessary. Truly." Evan tried to defuse the situation.

"Oh, I think it is," Cady replied, while casually eating his breakfast. Obviously, putting his son in this humiliating situation didn't bother him at all. The opposite, in fact.

Christopher stared at his father for a long moment, then finally turned to Evan. "Then my apologies to you also, Mr. Sinclair."

The words were calm, but his gaze murderous. Evan wasn't sure if Christopher directed the sentiment toward him or toward his father, but knew he'd just made an enemy.

But this wasn't Evan's first enemy. It wouldn't be his last.

Vince evidently decided his son's lessons in humility were over, because he didn't stop him as he turned again to leave.

"There, glad we got that settled," the drug lord said as he took another bite of his eggs Benedict.

"Well, thank you for understanding, Mr. Cady," Juliet said to him. Evan noticed she wasn't really eating, just pushing her food around on the plate. He didn't blame her. He'd lost the taste for his.

"Vince, please, Lisa. Call me Vince."

"Vince." Juliet smiled at the older man, but the smile didn't reach her eyes. Her instincts were right. Vince Cady wasn't to be trusted.

Cady lifted his water glass. "Here's to a fruitful business partnership for years to come."

Juliet and Evan both lifted their glasses. Evan gave his own silent toast: *Here's to the day we take you and your entire enterprise down, you bastard.*

The clinking of glasses was sweet to his ears.

Chapter Nineteen

The auction late that afternoon wasn't very different from other ones for art or antiques. It certainly wasn't like the cattle auctions Evan had been to a few times as a child, with a guy up front speaking very rapidly and with a Southern accent. This was much more subdued.

Some people were here bidding on items for themselves that they would either keep or sell later. Others were representatives of a specific buyer. They were authorized to bid up to a certain amount and no more. Bidding was tricky; definitely an art form.

Acquiring the drone override codes would be difficult. Although not everyone would be bidding on them, there were at least three parties who were here specifically to do so, Evan knew. Omega had given him and Juliet an unlimited ceiling for bidding for the codes. After all, Omega would recoup the money when Cady was arrested and his accounts frozen in the next few months, after Evan had a chance to glean as much information as possible about the drug lord's associates and suppliers.

Keeping the codes from reaching the streets was critical, but just as important was figuring out how and from whom Cady had gotten them in the first place. That's why Omega hadn't just taken the drone codes by force. They needed Cady's connection inside the military. Undercover work was the only way to figure out who that was. If Evan and Juliet didn't win the codes in the auction, then Omega would have to move much more drastically. Figuring out Cady's supplier would no longer be an option. It was better if Evan and Juliet could just buy the codes. Their cover would remain intact to use as long as possible.

Never burn a cover if you didn't have to.

But bidding was a skill. Going in with an extremely high bid would do nothing but throw suspicion on Evan and Juliet. They would need to use all their cunning in the bidding process. Win, but make sure it looked close.

Evan was ready to get this all over with. There were just too many unknowns on the yacht. Things he couldn't control. The situation with Vince that morning was just plain weird. Christopher had seemed ready to kill them at any moment. And Heath Morel being here had Juliet in a frenzy.

Potential for disaster abounded. And although Juliet thus far had held up pretty well, better than most people would have under the circumstances, Evan wanted to get her off this ship and back in a situation where they had more control. Maybe not the upper hand, but at least *a* hand. Right now it felt as if he was trying to do everything with both hands tied behind his back.

Not to mention the storm had really picked up and was rocking the yacht, even with its powerful stabilizers, all over the place. Almost everyone had a slightly green tinge.

Evan looked around for various items as the auction continued, some art of questionable origins, and weapons, both legal and illegal. These weren't what Evan and Juliet were here for, although every once in a while they would bid on something just to shake things up a bit.

Another piece of artwork came up for auction. Juliet sipped at the champagne a waiter, struggling to keep glasses upright on his tray, had provided. "I'm going to bid on that," she murmured.

Evan turned to study it more closely. "Why? Do you know something about it I don't?" She had learned a lot in the past year as an analyst, Evan knew. She had deep knowledge of many more cases than just the ones Evan worked on. Perhaps this piece of art held some importance.

"I know it's hideous."

He looked over to find her smiling at him. "And that's why you want to buy it?"

"Yeah, you could hang it in your bathroom."

Evan grasped her hand and linked their fingers together. He gazed at the painting more closely. It really was ugly.

"Um, yeah. Maybe we should pass on that. Save us the paperwork and explanations later."

"Oh, all right. I'm disappointed."

Evan smiled to see Juliet relaxed enough to make a joke. Keeping a firm grip on reality was important when undercover. Despite the mishap with Christopher last night, she seemed to have rebounded quite well.

"You're doing great." Evan leaned over and kissed her temple, whispering the words in her ear. "Hang on just a few more hours and we'll be done here. You're amazing."

Juliet smiled at him crookedly. He knew she didn't believe him. He wished he could make her realize how amazing she really was.

The bid for the drone codes came up, drawing Evan's attention away from Juliet. This was it.

The bidding started slowly. Everyone's attention focused on this big-ticket item regardless of whether they were bidding or not. Evan could see Vince Cady watching the proceedings closely.

A pair of Ukrainian buyers were their biggest competition, according to the rumors Evan had heard over the past day. They were buying for themselves, leaving clear ideas of their intent. To do as much damage as possible to their enemies, which included the United States.

Right now the Ukrainians were being bid up by a young man with a Caribbean accent Evan had met briefly. He knew this was just a Hail Mary for the younger man. He had no real shot at winning.

Juliet was in charge of bidding for them. She sat, looking almost bored, as the action continued, not putting in a bid at all.

"Planning to jump in at some point?" Doing nothing made Evan nervous.

"I have a plan. Just simmer down." Juliet winked at him.

Evan sat back in his chair. He didn't exactly relax, but one thing he had learned was that when Juliet had a plan, it was almost always a good one. He kept telling her to trust herself. Now was his chance to show her that he trusted her, too.

Juliet did nothing as the Ukrainians continued to bid, forcing Caribbean Accent out of the running. Evan thought surely she would jump in then, but it was Heath Morel who bid instead.

Juliet tensed, but didn't say or do anything. She and everybody else watched as the bidding went back and forth like a Ping-Pong match between the Ukrainians and Morel. Evan wanted to prod her to get in there, but forced himself not to.

Juliet could handle this.

The bidding slowed down and began growing in increments of five thousand dollars rather than the twenty thousand just moments before. Juliet made her play. She raised her hand to get the auctioneer's attention and made a bid one hundred thousand dollars above the current price.

A collective gasp echoed through the sitting area. Cady

grinned, all but rubbing his hands together. Morel turned to glare at Juliet, and Evan slipped an arm around her shoulders for support.

The bidding was now too high for Morel. He stormed out of the room. The Ukrainians bid again, five thousand higher than Juliet's huge bump. She countered with fifty thousand dollars more.

No gasps this time, just silence. Juliet had obviously proved herself as the person to be beat in this auction. Evan turned to watch the Ukrainians argue with each other in short, quiet barks. One obviously wanted to keep bidding. The other recognized the truth: Juliet was going to win.

She'd handled it perfectly. Throwing around the exact amount of money to stop the bidding cold. Letting the others know she was serious, but not seeming wasteful. As she'd told him, she'd had a plan. And it had worked.

The Ukrainians finally shook their heads at the auctioneer. He asked for any other offers, waited a few moments, then closed the bidding. Juliet now owned the drone override codes.

Evan's relief was palpable. Their biggest obstacle had just been overcome. Cady walked up to congratulate them, Christopher by his side.

"Well bid, my dear," Vince said, holding out his hand to Juliet. She gave it to him, but instead of shaking it, he brought it to his lips.

Evan could see Juliet didn't like the feel of Cady's lips on her skin, but she held it together.

"Thank you, Vince. Sometimes it just takes a woman's touch."

"And a very deft one it was. Although it seems like you've made some other people quite unhappy."

Evan noticed that Christopher had inched closer to Juliet. Evan wasn't sure whether it had been done on purpose or not, but he still didn't want the younger man anywhere near her. Evan slipped an arm around her and pulled her against him, farther from Christopher.

"Some people are sore losers," he told Vince.

"I'd like to know some more about the people you buy for," Vince said, while leading them toward the dining area. Now that the bidding was complete, dinner would be served. Although it looked as if neither Morel nor the Ukrainians had much of an appetite. They were nowhere to be found.

"We buy for different people at different times," Evan told Vince.

"But none of our clients like us to talk about them." Juliet smiled charmingly at the Cadys.

"And that is why you are so good at what you do." Vince returned Juliet's smile, but his was much more calculating. This had probably been a test to see if the Sinclairs kept their heads, and their mouths shut, even when feeling a little cocky, having just come off a win.

"It's a shame you've been out of the game for so many months," Christopher said.

Juliet wrapped her arm more tightly around Evan as the boat rocked again, and looked up at him. "Bob and I just needed some time to ourselves."

"And why was that?" Christopher asked.

Evan didn't know why the man was pushing this point, but was determined not to give him anything to use against them. "Everybody needs a break sometimes. Plus, can you blame me for wanting to spend more time with someone this beautiful?" He bent down and kissed Juliet's cheek.

Vince chuckled. Christopher seemed less amused. "Yes, if I had someone so lovely I would never let her out of my sight," he responded stiffly. "Excuse me."

Christopher walked toward some of the other guests.

"Ignore my son. Maria spoiled him as a child and he has not had such good luck with the ladies," Vince told them. "He lived in Europe until recent months, near his mother's family. He's had a difficult time adjusting to American culture."

Evan winked at Vince. "Not everyone can be as charming and witty as you and I, Vince. Know what I mean?"

Juliet rolled her eyes. Vince chuckled ruefully. "Well, he is my son. Someday all of this gets handed down to him, so I'm trying to teach him as much as possible." He looked toward where Christopher had stormed off. "But often it's difficult."

Evan slapped Vince on the back. As both Bob Sinclair and Evan Karcz, he was thrilled that they'd won the auction, and wasn't afraid to show it. "Ah, kids today. What are you going to do? Let's get a drink."

They enjoyed dinner, sitting again at Vince's table. Evan told stories of growing up in Virginia and the trouble he'd gotten into as a kid. Almost all the stories were true, just with names changed or certain facts left out. That was always the best bet when working undercover. Keep your stories as close to the truth as possible. The fewer lies to remember the better.

His lightness caused Vince to open up a little, which was what Evan had hoped. Although the older man didn't say anything they would directly use against him when the eventual arrest and prosecution occurred, they were one step closer to entering Cady's inner circle. It wouldn't happen today, maybe not anytime soon, but eventually Evan would be the one to bring this bastard down.

And a friendly dinner with lots of laughs didn't make Evan forget that. Vince Cady was a criminal. Had killed, at the very least indirectly, through his sales. But probably directly, as well.

"Shall we head back to my cabin? I can present you with the drone override codes, which I'm sure you'll want to authenticate. Then you can transfer the money."

Chapter Twenty

Evan met Juliet's eyes as she glanced at him sharply. This would be the opportunity for them to get a message to Omega—coordinates letting headquarters know exactly where they were, in case emergency extraction became necessary, although it didn't look as if it would. He and Juliet had done pretty damn well on their own. But they hadn't checked in for over twenty-four hours. Evan knew Juliet's brothers were worried.

"Sure, Vince, let's do it." Juliet smiled and put her napkin down next to her plate.

Evan stood and helped her with her chair. She took his arm and they followed Vince out of the dining area, stumbling slightly at the rough seas.

Angry eyes drilled into their backs as they left the room. Could be the Ukrainians, could be Heath Morel, could be Christopher. The list of people angry with them grew by the hour.

Vince's cabin was much larger and more elaborate than theirs. The sleeping space was tucked away from sight and a sitting area with beautiful views and a private deck took up over half the room. Two guards stood just outside the door. No one got in or out without them noticing.

Cady motioned for them to sit in the chairs, left for just

a moment, then returned with a briefcase in hand. "Here you are, as promised. The drone override codes."

Cady undid the clasps, revealing a computer attached to the outer casing. It was obviously military grade or something damn close. He typed in a few passwords and the specs of a drone appeared on the screen, as well as a number underneath.

"I assume whoever you're buying for already has access to the Department of Defense mainframe. Without that, these codes won't be of much use. I can, of course, provide that for your client, but it would be a separate charge and would take a little more time."

Juliet took the briefcase from Cady, smiling ruefully. "It's not our first time playing in the big leagues, Vince. We'll take care of the DOD mainframe for our client." She made a tsking noise.

The drug lord chuckled, obviously charmed by her. "Just checking, Lisa. I never miss out on an opportunity to make money."

"I don't blame you. Sometime you'll have to tell me how a businessman like you can get access to the DOD mainframe."

"It's always who you know, my dear. Always who you know."

A knock on the door interrupted them. Christopher walked in.

"Ah, son, I'm glad you're here. We're just about to finish the transaction. Mrs. Sinclair is validating the codes."

Christopher nodded and remained standing just inside the door.

"Is it okay for me to call our client? I'm assuming you've lifted the signal that's been blocking cell phones since we left port?"

"An important security measure," Vince told them. "But, yes, you are free to make your call now."

Juliet brought out her cell phone and dialed a number. She knew every word she said would be overheard both by Vince right now and probably someone else on his security force monitoring all cell phone traffic coming into or leaving the yacht.

"Do you mind putting your call on speaker, Mrs. Sinclair?"

Juliet didn't even hesitate. "Sure." She pressed a button and set the phone on the table in front of her.

Although Cady was all smiles, and even the sullen Christopher looked neutral, Evan knew this was yet another test. One wrong word from Juliet or anyone on the other end and everything they'd worked for would be blown to bits.

As soon as someone answered, Juliet began speaking. "This is Lisa Sinclair calling on an unsecure line for Mr. X."

There was a moment of silence. "Yes, please hold."

Christopher Cady's lips pressed into a white slash. Obviously, he had hoped to get a least a name out of the conversation. Juliet noticed his annoyed look. "Sorry, we have security measures of our own."

Vince still appeared relaxed as they waited for "Mr. X" to pick up. Evan prayed it was someone from Omega intimately detailed with the case. He imagined the scramble going on at Omega headquarters as they attempted to determine the best person to talk to Juliet.

As the silence dragged out, Christopher spoke. "It sounds like Mr. X doesn't have time for you."

"Mr. X is an important man. If it is taking him a while to get to the phone, I'm sure he has his reasons."

Such as tracking this call, Evan knew. Omega would have started running the trace as soon as the call came in.

"Perhaps we need to just give the drone codes to the next highest bidder, Father. Since the Sinclairs can't seem to get in touch with their buyers."

Juliet tried her charm on the younger Cady also. "Christopher, I assure you, Mr. X will be on the line momentarily. We've been out of touch for a couple of days, so he wasn't expecting my call just now. Give it a few more moments."

Christopher didn't look convinced, but didn't say anything further.

Finally a voice came on the line. "Lisa. You've been out of touch for some time now. I was beginning to get a little frantic."

It was Juliet's brother Cameron.

"My apologies, Mr. X. There was a change in plans, although I must admit I ended up on a lovely yacht. As a matter of fact, I'm sitting right here with the yacht's owner."

Evan knew Cameron would take the hint.

"I see. And with Bob, too, I hope. Or have you thrown him overboard?"

"No, I'm still here, Mr. X. Enjoying my time with my lovely wife," Evan responded.

"And were you able to secure the items we discussed, in the midst of what seems like a mini-vacation?"

"Yes, sir," Juliet said. "Even came in under budget. I have the first of the codes to be authenticated. Once that is done—and I'm sure there won't be any problem—the money can be transferred. Is Dr. Fuller nearby, sir?"

Why did she want Sawyer's fiancée to be there?

"I'm sure she's around here."

"You'll need her to access the code. She's the one able to do what needs to be done, in terms of authentication. She'll know what to do with the code. I'll be sending it to you, and the account number to route the money, right after our conversation."

"Well, good job, as always, Lisa. And you, too, Bob. When can I expect to see you again?"

"Soon, sir. We've enjoyed the boat. Water is turning a bit choppy, but nothing too rough."

"Do I need to send a lifeboat to rescue you?" Cameron asked.

Evan and Juliet both laughed lightly, but they knew what Cameron was really asking. Were they in trouble? They weren't. But getting these codes into safekeeping would definitely be a good idea.

"Well, if you happen to have a lifeboat nearby, that would be great. Otherwise I guess Lisa and I will just suffer through the gourmet food and fine company a couple more days," Evan interjected.

Cameron pretended to laugh, too. "I'll see what I can do. But it looks like you're being well taken care of."

"We're just glad to have the codes for you, sir. Getting them to you is the most important thing." Juliet was on the same page as Evan. If they could get those codes off the ship tonight, that would be the best thing for everyone.

"I'll have Dr. Fuller authenticate, then we'll transfer the money. Tell your seller to expect it within the hour."

"Thanks, sir. Transferring the data now. See you soon."

Juliet disconnected the call. "I'll just email this code and your account number in an encrypted file. Like Mr. X said, it shouldn't take long."

She sat down with her phone and began sending the information.

"Lisa's pretty amazing, isn't she?" Evan told the other men. Vince smiled, but Christopher just glared at him.

Vince was right, his son definitely did not have much going for him when it came to the ladies. That was okay;

soon he'd be rotting away in prison with his father. His lack of game wouldn't matter then.

"Okay, finished." Juliet turned to Evan and nodded. He wasn't sure exactly what she'd just sent to Cameron, and wished he could get her out of this room so they could discuss it. But he didn't want to leave without the rest of the codes.

"Great." He held out a hand to her as she stood. The ship was beginning to take on more movement now from the waves outside. Juliet was looking a little green from the rocking. Evan knew his own coloring probably wasn't much better. They walked over to the balcony so they could get some air. Ominous clouds hung low in the sky. The sun was going down, although finding it was nearly impossible given the cloud cover. It wasn't raining yet, but would be soon.

"You doing okay?" Evan asked her. Vince and Christopher could hear them, so there was no opportunity to talk about important stuff yet.

"I'll be better after we get the confirmation we need."

It didn't take long, thank goodness. The Cadys were already antsy enough, especially Christopher. Juliet received the text.

"Okay, your money is in your account. You can check it," she announced.

Christopher sat at the laptop at the table. A few moments later he confirmed it. "It's there, Father. Everything looks good." He stood back up.

Evan took Juliet's arm. "Okay then." He grabbed the briefcase with the codes. "We're going back to the upper floors, where maybe this rocking isn't so bad. It's been a pleasure doing business, Vince."

He turned with Juliet to leave, and for a moment thought

Christopher was going to stop them, but the younger man just looked at her before stepping aside.

Juliet clung to Evan's arm as they walked down the hallway.

"I sent our coordinates to Cameron. Megan should be able to decipher them amid the numbers, especially if she knows she's looking for something," Juliet told him.

That's why she had asked if Dr. Fuller was around. Juliet had wanted to make sure someone would recognize the coordinates. Sawyer's fiancée would be sure to spot them.

"Good. Hopefully, they'll come tonight, so we can at least offload the codes. We should get those into safe hands as soon as possible." They couldn't take a chance on them being intercepted during an electronic submission. The codes needed to be handed off person to person.

Evan grabbed a railing to help with balance. This storm was turning nasty. Rain and nightfall made getting around even more difficult.

"Let's just head back to the room. There's no point staying out here," he muttered.

Juliet nodded. "Okay. We have until 3:00 a.m. before whoever Omega is sending will be here. They'll be at the back of the ship."

"How do you know that?"

She held up her cell phone. "Message from Cameron or Megan or whoever from Omega ended up sending it. It says 'Code received and verified. Money deposited in given account. Further contact can be made through Mr. Stern, extension 0300.'"

Evan smiled. "Stern of the boat, zero three hundred hours. Very clever."

"I know." Juliet grinned at him. "I'd forgotten how much I like this part. The thinking on my feet, figuring out ways around barriers."

Evan brushed a strand of her now very wet hair behind her ear. "You've definitely got a natural talent. I hope you'll think about that for cases in the future."

She shrugged. "Maybe. I know I'm doing better. I'll think about it, that's all I can promise."

"Sounds reasonable to me. Now let's get back to our cabin. I think a hot shower would be in order to warm us up after all this rain."

"Absolutely." Juliet grabbed his arm. "And we definitely should take one together. I'd hate to be wasteful."

Evan loved the heat building in Juliet's eyes, but also the smile he saw in them. He picked up speed, leading them to their cabin. "Yes, let's go do our part in saving the planet."

Chapter Twenty-One

Juliet awoke to find someone's hand over her mouth. Terror flooded her. Her eyes instantly flew open, but she couldn't make out much in the dark room. One thing she knew for sure, Evan wasn't in the bed next to her.

She immediately began fighting, grasping her assailant's wrist and attempting to pull him closer so she could hit him. But she couldn't get a good angle to strike, so began to claw at his face. Juliet heard a foul curse as her fingernails found skin.

It was so similar to her attack by the Avilo brothers. Juliet still couldn't see who was in the room. Was it Heath Morel?

No matter who it was, she wasn't going to allow it to happen again.

Juliet struggled against the hand that held her head pinned to the mattress. She attempted to pull her legs around to gain a better position.

And where was Evan? He'd been in bed with her when they'd gone to sleep a few hours ago. He wouldn't have left without telling her.

Juliet scratched at the face again. The hand was removed for just a moment, but before she could make any sound, a fist crashed into her cheek. Blood filled her mouth.

Juliet fought to hold on to consciousness while the world

spun and weaved. From across the room she heard a muffled ruckus, but couldn't see what was going on. Was it
Evan?

A crash and then silence. Had Evan been hurt? Juliet
renewed her efforts against her attacker. She rolled quickly
off the side of the bed, landing on her feet. She was able to
get off two sharp kicks to the attacker's midriff, but then
the boat lurched and she lost her balance. Her opponent
took advantage and Juliet received another blow to the jaw.

This time she couldn't hang on to consciousness. She
moaned as blackness closed in around her.

When she awoke she was being tied to a chair. They
weren't in the cabin any longer; it looked as if they were
in the ship's galley. Evan was tied to another chair, unconscious, still in his sweatpants and shirt, his head bleeding
from a nasty gash near his temple.

And it wasn't Heath Morel who had done this. It was
the Ukrainians. One was tying Juliet, the other keeping
watch at the galley door.

"Vince Cady isn't going to stand for this, you know. His
men will be here any second to break up this little party."
Juliet tried to make the words as clear as possible, but it
was difficult with her swelling jaw.

"I don't think Mr. Cady is going to know about this
at all. At least not until it is too late." The man's accent
was thick.

"Our room was bugged. Cady's men are probably on
their way right now."

"You mean bugged with these?" He held out two trans-
mitting devices in his hand. "I'm sure Mr. Cady's security team will figure out there is a problem, but will most
likely blame it on the storm."

Juliet was afraid they were right.

"We want the drone codes," the man said.

"Look, maybe we can talk about a sale. But Bob and I spent our buyer's money to get the codes. We can't just give them to you. Our reputation would be shot." Juliet knew she needed to stall. To come up with a plan.

"More than just your reputation will be shot if you do not provide us with the codes. Or maybe not shot." The man pulled out a knife, but instead of using it on Juliet, he walked over to Evan's unconscious form. "Let's see if we can get your husband to wake up."

He began poking his knife into Evan's shoulder. Not deep, but enough to cause the wounds to bleed through his shirt. Evan moaned and began to awaken.

"Look, fine, stop, okay?" Juliet struggled against the zip ties that held her to the chair, but there was no give. She saw Evan's eyes open, glazed over in pain. The Ukrainian poked the knife into his shoulder again, twisting it. Evan's lips clamped together and he sucked air through his nose.

"Stop! Okay? Just stop," Juliet pleaded. She couldn't stand to see Evan in that much pain, but she knew she couldn't give the codes to the Ukrainians. "You need the briefcase Cady gave us."

Juliet didn't tell him that they'd already downloaded all the drone codes off the computer that was inside the briefcase and wiped the computer clean. She and Evan had put the codes on a hard drive in preparation to handing it off to Omega at 3:00 a.m. It now rested inside Juliet's pillowcase.

What time was it now? Maybe she wouldn't have to rely on Cady's security team to get their act together. Maybe the Omega agents would soon be on board. When Juliet and Evan didn't meet them at the rear of the ship, the agents would come looking for them, right? That's what Juliet's brothers would do. Although she knew Omega wouldn't be sending Sawyer or Cameron. The wounds they'd sustained recently would prevent them from scaling the side of the yacht.

Juliet glanced at the clock on the galley stove. Only a couple minutes after two. Damn it, it was too early for the Omega team. The Ukrainians would have Evan chopped up into pieces by three.

"This briefcase?" the man asked. He had it on one of the kitchen counters.

Damn. They already had it here. This was going to play out quickly, not giving them the time Juliet had hoped for. She looked over at Evan. More blood oozed from his shirt at the shoulder.

Think.

Juliet watched as one of the Ukrainians opened the briefcase and booted the small computer. She knew it wouldn't take him long to figure out there was nothing on it.

Think!

She racked her brain. Yelling wouldn't help. They were in the galley, distant from the rest of the ship. Plus the storm was too loud for anyone to hear much. She was going to have to find a way of getting them out of this on her own. The first thing she needed them to do was untie her from this chair. Until then, she was useless.

The man turned from the computer to glare at her, his lips pulled back, teeth bared. "It does not boot up. There is no information on here."

"Damn it." Juliet did her best indignant impression. "Cady must have double-crossed me."

The Ukrainian stared at her in silence for a moment, then in one fluid motion took the two steps to her and backhanded her across the face.

Juliet's head jerked all the way to the side and blood flew from her mouth, spraying onto the floor. She could feel her eye already beginning to swell shut from the ring the man wore.

"I will waste no more time with you!" In his anger, the accent became thicker.

The man grabbed his knife from the table and walked over to Evan. He took the wicked blade and jammed it into the front of Evan's already injured shoulder, this time much deeper.

Evan couldn't control the groan that escaped him. Juliet watched as all color drained from his face and sweat began dripping down his brow.

The Ukrainian turned back to her. "Again?" he asked. "Your husband is much tougher than I gave him credit for. I think he can take it."

"Lisa, no…" Evan could hardly get the words out.

The Ukrainian pulled his knife out, causing Evan to give an agonizing gasp, and raised his arm again.

"No!" Juliet screamed.

"Then you will tell me where the codes are."

"Yes," Juliet sobbed the word. "They're in our cabin."

"Tell me where."

She knew if she told him, she and Evan would both be dead. Not to mention a known enemy of the United States would possess drone codes that could cost the lives of thousands of innocent people.

"I have to show you. It's a hidden safe and has biometric coding. Only Bob or I can open it." The lies flew out of Juliet's mouth, but at least it would get her out of this damn chair.

"Fine." The Ukrainian came and cut her loose. He turned to his partner and spoke in their native tongue. The other man nodded, grinning evilly.

"I just told my partner that if we are not back with the codes in fifteen minutes, he is to kill your husband. By gutting him from top to bottom with his knife. Slowly." Both men laughed. Juliet's stomach turned. She nodded.

The Ukrainian kept her close by his side as they left, knife poking into her ribs. He made sure she could feel the blade.

Juliet had no idea what she was going to do. The chances of her being able to take down this hulking beast in fewer than fifteen minutes, and then defeat his partner, were remote. Both were armed and probably waiting for her to try something like that.

They walked down the empty hallway in silence. Her captor led her to a service elevator at the rear of the ship. None of the guests would be out at this time of night, especially not in the middle of a storm.

The elevator was empty, as expected, but Juliet could see some water pooling on the floor in one of the back corners. A wet person had been in this elevator recently. As inconspicuously as she could manage, she touched the wet wall and then brought her fingertips to her lips.

Salty.

Juliet had grown up in Virginia and vacationed at the Chesapeake Bay her whole life. And her mother, a high school science teacher, had always used every opportunity to teach her children—even during vacations.

The Bay was a unique water source, an estuary. It started with fresh water north of Baltimore, but by the time it got south of Annapolis—where they were now— the water was brackish, becoming more and more salty.

In this storm, anybody could've made a watery mess in the elevator. But only someone who had just come out of the Bay would've made a *salt*water mess.

Omega agents were on this ship.

For the first time since she'd come on board, Juliet had a sense of hope. She needed to be ready, and prayed that

Omega had sent a good agent. She wished Sawyer and Cameron weren't injured and that Dylan wasn't retired. Her brothers were the best the agency had to offer. But of course, right now Juliet would take even a rookie straight out of Quantico.

The Ukrainian didn't notice anything suspicious. As the elevator doors opened, he grabbed Juliet's arm again and pressed the knife against her ribs. They walked this way down to Juliet's room. She didn't have a key and just reached for the doorknob.

"Glad you guys had the good sense to leave the door unlocked," she said, just a hair too loudly. Wherever the Omega agent was, she wanted to make herself as noticeable as possible, without making the Ukrainian aware of that, of course.

Her captor shoved her into the room. "Why do you waste time? Perhaps you want to be a widow and allow my partner to viciously kill your husband? Maybe I'll just sit here and let the minutes count down."

"No." Juliet shook her head. "No, please."

"Then where is this hidden safe you mentioned?"

"I lied. There is no hidden safe."

The Ukrainian stepped toward her, his nostrils flaring, his skin mottled. "Then I hope you enjoy pain, and that your husband does, as well. You will suffer mightily before you die."

"No, I have the codes. They're right here, look." Juliet walked over to her pillow and retrieved the drive from the case. She tossed it to the Ukrainian. He inspected it, then looked back at her.

"Good, now you do not need to suffer. But unfortunately, you still need to die."

Chapter Twenty-Two

The Ukrainian came barreling toward Juliet, knife extended. She grabbed the pillow off the bed—it wouldn't help much, but at least it was something—and shifted her weight sideways as the large, beefy man came at her. She used the pillow to help push the Ukrainian to the side, using his own momentum against him. He stumbled, but didn't fall all the way to the floor.

Juliet knew this would be her only chance for escape. She ran toward the door, but the Ukrainian was too quick. He grabbed her ankle and yanked, pulling her down. She tried to kick him off, but he was stronger. He reached over to grab his knife and Juliet knew this was the end.

She opened her mouth to scream, not knowing if it would be heard in this storm, but she had to try. The sound hadn't even left her mouth when the door slammed open and a figure dressed from head to toe in black neoprene flew through the air, tackling the Ukrainian. Juliet backed away, out of reach of the knife.

She couldn't see his face, but knew the Omega agent was here.

The Ukrainian was determined to kill this new arrival. The agent, on the other hand, at first used nonlethal blows, but when it became obvious they weren't going to work, the man's stance altered.

Juliet could see the change, recognize the training. The Ukrainian didn't know it yet, but he was a dead man. And this Omega agent? He definitely wasn't a rookie.

It was over in a matter of moments. The Ukrainian came at his attacker, knife aimed at his heart. The agent twisted and stepped out of the way, flipping his foot out and tripping him. Then he straightened quickly and knocked the other man forward with his elbow. The Ukrainian couldn't recover his balance.

He fell to the floor, landing with his own knife in his chest, dead just seconds later.

The agent whipped his hood off and ran to Juliet. Shock pooled through her.

"Dylan?"

What was her oldest brother doing here? He wasn't even an active agent anymore, for heaven's sake. Not that you could tell that from the fight that had just occurred.

Dylan put his face next to Juliet's and spoke almost silently. "Is this room under surveillance?"

She shook her head. "Not in here. It's been dismantled."

He pulled her into a hug. "Jules, are you all right? Where's Evan? You've got a load of bruises on your face. Are you hurt?"

"What are you doing here, Dylan?"

He gently framed her face with his hands. "Juliet, are you hurt?" he repeated.

"No, I'm fine. I'm fine. Just some bruises. But I have to get back to Evan. That guy's partner—" she pointed to the body lying on the ground "—has instructions to kill Evan if we're not back in about five minutes."

"I'll help you with the other guy."

"Dylan, why are *you* here?"

"When Cam and Sawyer told me about the yacht and all the changes yesterday, I flew in to headquarters to see if there was anything I could do. When we got your message, both Sawyer and Cam wanted to be the ones who came here, but neither were up to the physical aspect of getting on board."

"Didn't Omega have anyone else to send?"

"Of course they did, but we weren't sure what condition you would be in. Everyone thought it would be best if a family member met you, in case there was…trauma."

Juliet quickly hugged him. "I'm fine, Dylan. Trauma-free. Although I was probably about to get myself killed by that guy. Thank you, by the way. You may not be an Omega agent anymore, but nobody would've known it from what I just saw."

He bent and kissed her on the forehead. "You look great, little sis, um, except for the massive bruising and swelling."

Juliet rolled the eye that wasn't swollen shut. "Thanks."

"No, I mean you seem together. Prepared. In charge. You look better than I've seen you look in eighteen months."

"I'm doing better, Dylan. I really am. Evan was right, I just needed something to force me to get back in the game."

"Karcz being right, now there's a first." Dylan winked at her. "Let's go get him."

She opened the door, but when she heard voices down the hall, immediately closed it again. "People are out there, Dylan."

She handed him the hard drive with the codes. "Here, you take this, find your other Omega guy and move out. I'll get Cady and his security people to help me with the other Ukrainian and Evan."

"Are you sure? I hate to send you to Cady for anything."

"No, it will be fine. Vince will be furious that the Ukrainians tried this right under his nose. I'll tell him I killed this guy. It will work."

"Okay. Be safe, sis. See you soon." Dylan kissed her forehead, then pulled his neoprene mask back over his face. Juliet opened the door and headed toward the voices she heard, while her brother made his way in the other direction. Halfway down the hall, she turned to check Dylan's progress, but he was nowhere to be seen.

Omega had lost a brilliant agent the day they had lost Dylan Branson. But Juliet knew he had his reasons for quitting.

Knowing he was clear, she started screaming her head off.

"Help! I need help!" Forcing hysteria wasn't difficult.

Juliet was sure she looked a sight—bruised, bleeding, screaming, in her T-shirt and torn yoga pants. It didn't take long for everyone to find her. Security, guests, even Vince and Christopher Cady were soon in the hallway, despite the late hour.

Juliet grabbed the biggest guy in the corridor, pretty sure he had to be part of the security team, and started dragging him toward the galley.

The fifteen minutes was almost up and she was afraid the other Ukrainian might already be torturing Evan with his knife, even if he hadn't killed him.

"The Ukrainians are trying to kill us. One has my husband in the galley." Juliet tried to make the words as clear as possible, but her mouth felt like mush from the punches she'd taken. The security guy had drawn his weapon, so evidently he understood the gist of what she was saying. Another security person was attempting crowd control, trying to get everyone to return to their assigned cabins.

Juliet left them behind, running down the hall toward the elevator. The ride down the three levels seemed to go on forever. She didn't waste time talking to the guard. The moment the door slipped open just enough for her to fit, she was through. The guard was right on her heels.

Juliet barreled through the galley door, instantly taking stock of the situation. Evan was alive, but the Ukrainian stood in front of him, knife raised. Juliet didn't hesitate, didn't take even a moment to consider her own safety, just threw herself at the thug before he could figure out what was going on and harm Evan.

She took him to the ground, where they landed side by side, legs entangled. Juliet steeled herself against the pain of the collision, but found it difficult to see straight. The big man was quick to shake off the effects of the fall, and before she knew it, his knife was raised and coming toward her.

Evan yelled her name and she prepared to block the knife.

Until a shot was fired and the Ukrainian fell backward, a bullet hole in his forehead.

Juliet pulled her legs out from under the dead man's and looked over at the galley door. She expected to see the guard with a raised weapon, but instead it was Christopher Cady who had shot the Ukrainian. The gun was still in his hand, his arm still raised.

Juliet didn't care who had killed the other man. She was just glad to be alive and that Evan was, too.

She got up and stumbled over to him.

"Damn it, woman, are you all right? What the hell were you doing, tackling him like that?" Evan looked like hell. Half his shirt was bright red with blood from his shoulder.

"Are you okay?" She wasn't sure if she should apply pressure to the wounds, or if that would just cause him more pain without really helping him. "Somebody cut him loose."

One of the guards immediately sliced the plastic ties

that bound him to the chair. Evan wrapped his arms around Juliet, pulling her into his lap. "Where's the other psycho?" he whispered in her ear.

"Dead. In our room. Long story."

"And the codes?"

"Safe in the place they need to be. In good hands. Even longer story."

Evan raised his eyebrow at that, but said nothing. Juliet was sure that, like her, he was just glad something had gone right in this whole brouhaha.

Vince Cady made his way over, followed by his son. The older man looked aghast. "Lisa, Bob, I cannot believe this has happened while you were under my protection. My men are already investigating. It looks like the Ukrainians went to great lengths to circumvent our security measures."

Juliet noticed Cady didn't mention having the rooms bugged, only "security measures."

"Yeah, well, the other member of that merry little gang is dead in our cabin. Thanks to the storm, he tripped and fell on his own knife."

"Yes, he has already been found. And I am quite proud of Christopher, that he did not hesitate to do what needed to be done."

Juliet looked over at the dead Ukrainian. She was glad Christopher hadn't hesitated, either, or it might've been her lying there. "Thank you," she offered. Christopher still gave her the creeps, but in this case she owed him her thanks. She smiled and held out her hand.

He took it, but instead of shaking it, brought it to his lips. Juliet barely contained her shudder. She withdrew her hand as politely as possible.

Evan's arms tightened around her.

"Bob needs medical attention. Those psychos stabbed him in the shoulder," Juliet stated.

Vince nodded. "We have a medical professional on staff. I will have someone escort you both. You have injuries, too, Lisa." The older man grimaced as he glanced at her face. She must look pretty bad.

Vince and Christopher both left to confer with the security team, anger clear in both men's stance and tone. Vince Cady might be a criminal, but his sense of honor had been contravened, his own sanctuary violated.

Heads would roll that something like this could happen without the security team's awareness.

Juliet looked over to the doorway and found Heath Morel standing there, staring at her, malice evident in his expression. He turned and left before she could respond. Not that she'd know what to say or do.

"Are you okay?" Evan whispered, now that they were relatively alone. He obviously hadn't seen Morel, and Juliet didn't mention him. "How did you take down that Ukrainian? What the hell happened?"

"Dylan happened," Juliet murmured back.

"*Dylan*? Here on the ship? Now?"

"Well, hopefully not anymore. I gave him the drive. Omega sent him, since they didn't know what shape I'd be in. Didn't want to send a stranger."

"Then that poor Ukrainian bastard didn't have a chance."

Juliet sighed and shook her head. "My thoughts exactly."

"Are you sure you're okay, baby?" Evan stroked her bruised face, grimacing.

"Surprisingly, yes." Juliet shrugged. "Battered face notwithstanding. You were right. I can handle more than I give myself credit for."

"See? You should listen to me more often."

Juliet brushed Evan's hair away from his forehead with

gentle fingers. "You're worried about me? You're the one who got stabbed."

He kissed her gently on her bruised, swollen lips. "It's only a flesh wound. But if my arm falls off be sure to pick it up for me, okay?"

Juliet could see sweat still beading on Evan's forehead. She knew he must be in pain. But that he would worry about her and make jokes to help her feel more comfortable even now…

God, how she loved him.

Her eyes flew back to his and she drew in a startled breath. Where had the thought of love come from? After her rape, she had figured that love wouldn't be in the cards for her, that she would never again be comfortable enough with a man to be close.

But here she was, sitting on the lap of the man she trusted most in the world, as comfortable as she could ever dream of being. They were both wounded, exhausted and surrounded by criminals, but Juliet felt safe.

So maybe love wasn't such a crazy idea, after all.

"What? What is that look? You look like you've just had a breakthrough in quantum physics or something." Evan smiled, shaking his head.

"Yeah, something like that." This wasn't the place for declarations of love. But she did lean in and kiss him tenderly. "You're a pretty good husband, Mr. Sinclair."

Evan's smile got even brighter. "Well, you're a pretty good wife, Mrs. Sinclair."

They probably would've stayed there awhile, just holding on to each other, if the staff member hadn't come to lead them to the medical attention they needed.

Chapter Twenty-Three

Evan watched the distant port of Annapolis come into view. It would take only an hour or two now before they docked and were able to disembark. He was ready to get off this yacht.

He glanced at Juliet, who sat in an overstuffed love seat enjoying the late afternoon sunshine. Her eyes were closed and her battered face turned up toward the sun, which had chased away all traces of the storm. The sight of her wounded face brought back many unpleasant memories for Evan, but Juliet seemed to be doing fine.

More than fine, if her slight smile gave any hint.

Truly, she had handled the entire situation with the Ukrainians like a champ. She may have been out of the game for the past eighteen months, but no one would have known that last night. Evan could still feel the terror that had washed over him when that bastard had taken her out of the galley to go get the codes.

Not knowing what the Ukrainian was doing to Juliet—whether he would kill her as soon as he had what he wanted—had been much worse than the pain in Evan's shoulder. And then to see her come flying back through the galley like some professional wrestler, tackling a guy twice her size? Yeah, she'd saved Evan's life, but she'd also taken ten years off it as he'd watched, helpless, as the second Ukrainian raised that knife at her.

So thank God for Christopher Cady and his good aim. *That* was a sentence Evan never thought he'd say.

Vince Cady, although thrilled with his son's actions, was truly appalled at what had happened. He'd moved Evan and Juliet into a huge cabin for the little of the night that was left and had apologized profusely. Multiple times.

In the end, Evan had no doubt this incident would strengthen their relationship with the miscreant. It was always good when a criminal owed you a favor. Vince was less likely to be suspicious of them in the future when he remembered what they had gone through under his watch.

Cady would eventually be arrested for his crimes, but first he would inadvertently provide Omega all sorts of intel about his criminal network. Evan would see to that.

But most of all, everything had become crystal clear to Evan last night. He was not going to live without Juliet any longer. Life was too short, too fragile. And he'd loved her too damn long to be without her anymore. Whatever it took to convince her of that, he would do it. He'd made the mistake of giving her space for too long.

He wouldn't be making it again.

"You doing okay over there?" Juliet asked him from her chair. "How's the shoulder?"

The yacht's medic had stitched him up and given him a tetanus shot and some painkillers. It didn't seem as though any permanent damage had been done, especially since Evan had full range of motion. But the doctor had suggested he get himself completely checked out once they reached shore. None of Juliet's bruises and swelling would have any permanent effects, either, he predicted.

Evan turned and leaned against the railing so he was facing her. "Not too bad. How about you?"

"I'm just glad that ridiculous storm is over. This is much more what I think of when I envision myself on a yacht."

Yeah, they'd made it through all sorts of storms last night.

Evan went to sit next to her on the love seat. He didn't see anybody within earshot, but just in case, he pulled her close.

"How about, when we get off the boat, you come and stay with me at my town house?"

Juliet opened her one good eye. "You mean, for the op?" Her voice was barely more than a whisper. "In case they're following us?"

He shrugged, then brought his face near hers. "Yeah, that. But mostly because I want you there, Jules." He kissed her gently. "Now. When this case is over. Forever."

Juliet sighed. "I'm still pretty messed up, you know."

"We're all messed up in this business. We'll just take each day as it comes. Together." He wanted to tell her he loved her, but was afraid it was too soon, that it might scare her off. If she agreed to come stay with him, hopefully live with him, that would be enough for right now.

Evan held her close as the ship headed to Annapolis. He enjoyed just being there with Juliet. Omega safely held the drone codes. And because of their injuries, nobody was bothering them.

He felt Juliet stiffen as she leaned back in his good arm. His gaze followed hers and he realized the problem. Heath Morel. That bastard was still throwing malicious glances their way every chance he got.

Evan and Juliet hadn't checked for the past twenty-four hours to see if she had received any more sweetheart emails. But regardless, Evan had had enough of that nonsense. As soon as they were back on dry land, he was going to make sure Cameron or Sawyer picked up Morel.

The man needed to be questioned about the emails so they could get to the bottom of this. So Juliet could move on with her life. They probably couldn't actually arrest and prosecute Morel, as the emails weren't threatening in nature. But they could see him charged with other crimes.

"We'll get him, don't worry," Evan vowed. "He may not spend any time in jail for those emails, but I'll have your brothers breathing down his neck. He'll keep his distance."

"I just want to move forward. To stop having to worry about those emails and the past in general."

Evan kissed her temple. "I know, hon. And you will. We'll handle it for you. Let's just concentrate on the future."

Juliet smiled and turned her face back up toward the sun. "That's no problem at all."

A FEW HOURS later Juliet and Evan were finally off the yacht and on their way back to Omega to debrief. At the first pay phone they saw, just in case their cell phones had been bugged by Cady, Evan stopped to call Cameron and Sawyer. He wanted Heath Morel picked up as soon as possible, before the man went underground and they couldn't find him.

As Juliet had said, it was time to start concentrating on the future. The sooner they took care of Morel, the sooner that would happen.

He and Juliet both were looking forward to not having to worry about what they said or if someone was watching or listening. And he knew they both wanted to wash the filth of the past few days off them.

After they had gotten off the ship and returned to Cady's house via limousine, Cady had apologized again, Christopher right by his side, as they were leaving. "I hope this incident won't jeopardize our business dealings in the future," Vince had told them.

"It's not like you planned this," Evan had responded.

"Although next time, we trust your security team will be more on the ball." Lisa's snooty tone came through loud and clear.

"Oh, believe me, they will," Vince promised.

"And thanks again, Christopher, for your quick trigger finger." Evan shook hands with him, noting that his gaze remained riveted on Juliet.

"Yes, thank you, Christopher," she had murmured, when he'd let go of Evan's hand to shake hers.

"Au revoir," Christopher had replied.

French? Evan barely refrained from rolling his eyes. He had ushered Juliet to the Jeep immediately.

They both just wanted to go home and crash. Evan especially, since Juliet had agreed to stay at his house, but they both needed to debrief, so here they were.

They barely made it out of the parking garage and into the building before Juliet was engulfed in hugs by her brothers. All three were still there, even though Dylan didn't technically work there any longer. The eyes of each shone, locked on Juliet.

Relief and pride were evident in their every motion, every statement.

Juliet smiled at Evan from the circle of brotherly limbs and torsos. Her chin was high, her voice animated as she told some of the story of what had happened on the yacht.

Good. She deserved to be confident and satisfied in what she had accomplished. Because it was a lot, on both a professional and personal level.

After greetings, they were ushered to the Omega physician, who reevaluated their wounds. Although Evan's shoulder hurt like hell, the doc agreed with the ship's medical professional. It didn't look as if there had been any permanent damage, given Evan's range of motion. The doctor gave him a round of antibiotics and pain medication, warning him not to take the latter until he was near a bed he didn't need to get out of for at least eighteen hours.

Juliet's wounds, now a myriad of purples, greens and blues all over her face, were also superficial. Painful, but not serious.

Their boss, Dennis Burgamy, with his overworked assistant Chantelle by his side as always, found Evan and Juliet. He congratulated them on a job well done, obviously thrilled that Omega would be able to take credit for recovery of the drone codes.

Yeah, Burgamy always had his eye on the truly important stuff. Like accolades.

But at least he told them to go home and get some rest. Debriefings could take place tomorrow, since nothing involved with the case was pressing.

Evan was thrilled at the thought of sleeping with Juliet at his side. Someplace where he didn't have to watch what he said because other people were listening. Where he could actually call her *Juliet*. Although he didn't think either of them were up to anything too physical, he still just wanted to be with her. Holding her. That was more than enough to make him happy.

Of course, he didn't necessarily want to explain any of this to her brothers just yet, even if they were his best friends.

Evan grabbed Juliet's hand and pulled her around a corner, out of earshot of everyone else. "You're still coming back to my place, right?" He kissed her briefly, gently on the lips.

Juliet nodded. "I need a ride, since you drove me here.

And my brothers are going to have a field day with this, you know."

Evan rolled his eyes. "Oh, believe me, I know. I was hoping maybe not to get into all that with them tonight. I'd like to be fully functional and able to defend myself before telling them that I'm having my wicked way with their sister."

Juliet leaned in a little closer. "Your wicked way with me? I think I like the sound of that."

"Then let's get to my house." He kissed her again; he couldn't help it. It was all he could do not to back her up against this wall and kiss her until both of them couldn't see straight. Brothers be damned. Evan would take his chances.

And what was that nonsense he'd been thinking, about just holding her tonight? Not the way both of them were feeling right now.

At least Juliet still had the sense to remember that a lot of their colleagues, not to mention their boss, were just right around the corner. She pushed Evan back. "Okay, we'll just need to stop by my house and grab a few things. Then I'm all yours."

At those words, he leaned in again, but she stopped him with a hand on his chest, a playful smile on her face.

Not a moment too soon. Sawyer stuck his head around the corner. His eyes narrowed at their close proximity, but he didn't say anything about it. "Hey, Evan, Baltimore PD just nabbed Heath Morel. They're not sure what to hold him on. Cam and I were going to go question him. You want to come observe in case you can help?"

Evan sighed. All he wanted to do was go home with Juliet this very second. But the sooner they dealt with Morel and got those sweetheart emails stopped, the sooner she would be able to move on with her future.

Their future.

"Yeah, I want to come," Evan told him. "We can't let Morel see me, of course. But I can feed you info from the other side of the glass."

"Okay, we're headed out."

Evan nodded. "I'll be right there."

Sawyer left and Evan turned back to Juliet, smiling ruefully. "I guess we'll have to put those other thoughts on hold for a few hours. Here are my keys, to the Jeep and my house. I'll see you in a little while, okay?" He tucked a strand of Juliet's blond hair behind her ear, then kissed her again.

"I'll be waiting," she murmured against his lips.

Chapter Twenty-Four

A couple hours later, after Evan and her brothers had left
to question Morel and Juliet had finished a little of the paperwork at Omega, she pulled up to her house in Evan's
Jeep. She just sat in the vehicle looking at her home, dark
and empty, for a minute. How she had hated coming here
for the past eighteen months. Hated knowing she was alone
and weak and a coward.

Hated knowing she'd be trying to sleep in that damn
closet, like a child afraid of the monsters under the bed.

But now, after the past week, her perspective had
changed. She had found her footing in the case and realized how much she truly enjoyed undercover work. She'd
kept her wits about her and successfully completed a dangerous mission, possibly saving thousands of lives in the
process.

Just as importantly, she'd found out she could still respond passionately to a man. At least when that man was
Evan, whom she had known—somewhere in the depths
of her subconscious—was in love with her. Had been in
love with her for a long time.

Just as she had been with him.

They had been floating toward each other for years and
things probably would've happened a lot quicker if it hadn't
been for the attack. But Juliet didn't begrudge that any-

more. The past was the past and she wasn't going to let it control her. She and Evan were stronger together because of what had happened. And they would remain strong.

She got out of the Jeep and made her way inside her house. For the first time in eighteen months, she didn't bolt all the multiple locks on her door when it closed behind her. She didn't have to live in fear any longer.

Juliet looked around. She liked the thought of leaving this house for good. It held too many bad memories she didn't want to battle anymore. Even if she wasn't moving in with Evan she would've been looking for a new place. Moving forward.

She didn't rush through her house. She knew Evan would be hours with Heath Morel. That was another part of her past she wanted to have done with. She was glad they'd arrested him. Her brothers would take care of this for her. For once their excessive overprotectiveness would come in handy. She didn't expect to have much future trouble from Morel.

Juliet got a suitcase out and packed clothes and toiletries. Her house was still a disaster, even with the work she and Evan had done a few days ago. But she'd deal with that later.

She grabbed a soda from her fridge and decided to catch up on a little office work on her computer. She smiled. Once Evan got home, who knew when she'd be interested in checking emails again? She'd have better things to do.

She checked her own personal stuff first. Not much there. Then she decided to go ahead and check Lisa Sinclair's emails. She knew there would be new ones. Undoubtedly Morel had sent her some since she'd turned off the email indicator chirps on her phone.

And there were. Juliet was aghast to see fifty-seven new messages in the past two days.

Oh my God. Morel was obviously more sick than they had thought. Being around Juliet and seeing her on the yacht must have made him downright crazy.

Fifty-seven messages.

At one time she would have read them all. Pored over each one, here alone, fighting and losing the battle to not let fear overwhelm her.

But she wasn't going to do that. Not tonight. She'd wait until tomorrow, or the day after, when Evan, or even the entire Omega staff, was with her. Waiting didn't make her weak or a coward. It meant she was growing, learning. Facing her fears in a better, more effective, way.

She would just go on over to Evan's house. She didn't need to stay here anymore. But as she scrolled up to close the email account, she noticed the date and time of the latest sweetheart email that had been sent.

Today. Five minutes ago.

What the hell? This one Juliet opened.

Just you and me together at last, sweetheart. We've had to wait a long time, haven't we? You're so beautiful.

She sat staring at the screen. If Heath Morel was in custody, there was no way he could've sent that email.

And then she smelled it, a sickly sweet odor coming from her hallway. One she recognized from just a few days before. The smell of a cigar.

Oh no, they'd made a horrible mistake. Juliet turned slowly in her chair and faced the doorway.

There stood Christopher Cady. "Hello, my sweetheart."

EVAN WATCHED FROM the other side of the two-way mirror as Cameron and Sawyer questioned Morel. Dylan watched with him, since he wasn't actually law enforcement.

For nearly forty-five minutes Cameron and Sawyer had been at it, at first drilling Morel about his criminal activities, although very specifically not mentioning Vince Cady, and then moving on to the emails sent to Lisa Sinclair. Morel had looked a little uncomfortable when they'd mentioned his shady activities, although he hadn't said anything that incriminated himself. But his stare was completely blank when they mentioned the emails.

"I know I've been out of the game for a few years," Dylan said to Evan as they both watched the action in the interrogation room. "But if I had to guess, I would say that Morel has no idea what they're talking about with the emails."

"But I've read them all, Dylan. They contain details that no one could know if they hadn't been there or been communicating with Robert Avilo. And Avilo hasn't been communicating with anyone. It has to be Morel."

Through the glass, Cameron continued questioning the man, but Sawyer was looking at a text he'd just received. Confusion suffused his face and he glanced over at the two-way mirror. When he walked over to Cameron and showed him the text, his brother got the same befuddled look, then gestured with his head for Sawyer to go to the observation room.

"What's going on?" Evan demanded as soon as he arrived.

"I just got a text from Megan. She's still at the Omega computer lab. She said another email came in for Lisa Sinclair fifteen minutes ago."

"Is it on a scheduled timer or something?" Dylan asked.

"No. It was actually sent then. No timer. Megan is sure."

Nobody dismissed Sawyer's fiancée. She was smarter than all three of them put together.

But if she was right, that meant Heath Morel wasn't their perp. Damn it, Evan had really wanted this to be over with.

He rubbed his eyes. "Okay, I guess it's not him, then. Tell Cam to ask a few more random questions to throw Morel off any scent and—"

Evan froze as his and every other phone in the room began buzzing. They all grabbed for them. Another text from Megan at the Omega office.

Juliet had just activated the emergency transmitter in her locket. She was in trouble.

Evan was running out the door before he even finished reading the message. Dylan and Sawyer were right behind him. Cameron would have to stay with Morel.

They made it to the car, Evan letting Dylan drive because of his shoulder. Sawyer was already on the phone with Megan. He put her on speaker.

"Honey, what's going on?"

"Juliet pushed the panic button on the locket." They could all hear Megan clicking away at the keyboard while speaking to them. Multitasking wasn't a problem for her.

"Are you sure it wasn't an accident or something? A mistake?"

"No, setting it off accidentally is nearly impossible. And I've already tried to call and text her. No response."

"Is the tracker working, Megan?" Evan asked.

"Yes, Evan. She's at her house. She hasn't moved any significant distance since the transmitter was turned on."

Evan tried not to panic. There was more than one reason Juliet could have hit the emergency button without it actually being a life-threatening situation. She'd gotten smacked around by the Ukrainians pretty hard. Maybe she was just having problems from that.

Evan could recognize the holes in his own theory, but

he clung to it. He couldn't stand the thought of her being hurt again.

As if Dylan could read Evan's thoughts, he pushed down on the gas and the car shot forward.

Juliet wouldn't have activated the device if it wasn't truly an emergency. Everybody in the car knew that.

"Oh crap," Megan said. Evan had forgotten they still had her on speakerphone.

"What?" All three men responded in unison.

"Hold. Processing." Megan was a scientist to her core.

If she was telling them to wait, she had a good reason to do so, but those moments were some of the longest in Evan's life.

"Oh crap," she repeated.

Evan closed his eyes and forced himself not to scream at her.

"We've been digging more deeply into Robert Avilo, since he knew the most about Juliet's rape. Details that were in the emails."

"Yeah?" Evan replied. "Juliet talked to the warden at his prison and he said Avilo hadn't had any contact— written, phone calls, visitors, anything—since he'd been in jail. Evidently Robert's brother Marco was his only friend, and Marco's dead."

Good thing, too, because Evan was pretty sure he would've killed him for what he'd done to Juliet if the man wasn't already in the ground.

"No, that looks correct. Robert Avilo hasn't had any outside contact with anyone, as far as we can tell," Megan confirmed.

"But…" Evan prodded.

"But Avilo's cellmate sends out letters all the time. Some-times two or three a week. All going to the same person and place. His cousin, a resident of a mental hospital–country club type place in Croatia."

"Croatia? Like Europe Croatia?" Evan asked. And what the hell did this have to do with Juliet?

"It's a place where rich parents send their bad teenagers and young adults when they've gotten into trouble, and they want to keep them out of prison or out of sight. Non-extradition. Of course, that's interesting, because Croatia has traditionally been a democratic-supporting country at least in terms of socioeconomic—"

"Honey," Sawyer said. "Focus."

"I'm sorry," Megan replied. "Anyway, Robert Avilo's roommate writes to his cousin there all the time. We were able to get a scan of one of the letters, and although it doesn't mention any names, it definitely includes some details about a rape."

Evan could feel cold pooling in his chest. "Who is the cousin, Megan?"

"It's not the cousin that's a big deal. It's the cousin's BFF at the hospital, who was just released back to his family about six months ago."

"Who?"

"Christopher Cady. Vince's son. According to records I hacked, Cady sent him there five years ago at the ripe old age of seventeen, after a fourth woman claimed Christopher attacked her. The Cady family couldn't buy her off, like they had the others, so needed him out of the country quick."

"Juliet said the emails have been coming for about a year," Evan stated. "Would Christopher have had access to email at this hospital place?"

"Without a doubt. It's not a prison, it's more of a retreat. And when Cady got home six months ago? That's when the pickup in emails really started."

So many things made sense. How the emails became more excitable a few days ago, after Cady met Juliet for the first time. And the looks Evan had seen on Christopher's face while on the yacht.

Obsession.

A man obsessed with Juliet had her in his clutches. The cold in Evan's chest spread further.

"Wait, she's on the move now, actually headed toward you." Megan provided them coordinates. "Do you want me to send in local PD?"

"No," Evan told her. "Police might cause Christopher to do something desperate. But have them on standby." Evan didn't want to risk Juliet's life.

"Hurry," Megan said. "If she gets out of range, we'll lose her. That transmitter is limited. I'll keep giving you coordinates. Right now, she's still headed north."

"Drive faster," Evan whispered to Dylan. He prayed they would get to her in time.

Chapter Twenty-Five

Christopher Cady was certifiably insane. Juliet wasn't sure how she hadn't seen it before. Now she wished when she'd flipped him on the yacht that he'd fallen overboard.

Because he was crazy. He really was.

He had found her by tracking her phone, Christopher had told her. They were in his car back at Annapolis Harbor. Juliet had driven, with Christopher pointing his gun at her and stroking her hair the entire way.

The gun didn't freak her out nearly as much as the hair-stroking did. Every touch caused her to cringe, flinch, her flesh crawling.

She had to keep it together, keep her wits about her, and pray like never before that the emergency transmitter in her necklace was working.

Evan would get to her. He had to.

She couldn't believe they were back at Annapolis Harbor. From where they were parked, Juliet could see the unique three-pronged flagpole in the middle of Susan Campbell Park. It was late; the harbor was empty. Juliet had tried to buy more time by driving as slowly as possible, but she could go only so slow without Christopher realizing she was stalling.

"I know you don't love me now, sweetheart." Christopher twisted a strand of her hair between his fingers as they sat in the parked car. "But you will. I have another boat, one that doesn't require a staff. It will be just you and me."

He got out of the car, keeping his gun pointed at her the entire time as he walked around to her door. He opened it and pulled her out.

"Christopher, what about Bob? I'm married. I can't just leave him and run off with you."

"Don't worry. I'm going to get you situated in the boat, then come back and finish your husband for good."

"What?"

"He doesn't deserve to live, sweetheart. He didn't protect you when you needed it most. Not eighteen months ago and not yesterday."

"Christopher—" Juliet wanted to break through to her captor, but there didn't seem to be much chance.

"It was *me* who protected you yesterday, not him. Because we are meant to be together, you and I."

Juliet wasn't prepared for Christopher's kiss. Something snapped in her. She bit down on his lip and then pushed him away with all her strength.

But he was ready for that. She found herself being spun around and flung against the car, Christopher using his weight to hold her there while he yanked her arms behind her back and bound her wrists together with a zip tie. Juliet tried to breathe through the panic.

"I should be angry, but I'm not. You're not ready yet, but you will be soon." He tightened the tie. "This will just help me keep you on the boat until I can take care of Bob. I have to admit I was hoping he would be with you at your house, so I could get rid of him before even talking to you."

Thank God they'd arrested Heath Morel and Evan had gone with her brothers to question him. Otherwise, Evan would probably be dead now.

Christopher grabbed Juliet by the arm and started marching her toward the pier. She knew she couldn't allow him to get her on that boat. If she did it would cost both her and Evan their lives.

"Stay quiet. If you yell and someone comes to investigate, I'll be forced to kill them. You don't want that on your conscience, do you?"

No, she didn't, but she didn't want to get on that vessel with this lunatic, either. The docks were pretty quiet at this time of night and Juliet didn't see anyone she could yell to, anyway.

They were nearing the boat slips now, Christopher angling her toward one of the last ones, where a large sailboat floated serenely in the water. Under other circumstances Juliet would have loved to climb aboard, but now she just wanted to get away. She kept testing the zip tie, hoping to find a way out of it, but to no avail.

She would have to try to fight Christopher with her arms restrained. Because she sure as hell wasn't getting on the boat of her own accord.

Juliet tensed, about to make a move by throwing herself back at Christopher, when a voice called out from the darkness. "I'm not going to let you just take my wife, Christopher."

Evan. Thank God.

Christopher immediately turned toward him, using Juliet as a shield. The two men pointed their weapons at each other.

"You don't deserve her. You don't take care of her. Don't protect her. She deserves to be with me." Christopher spat the words.

"Well…" Evan took a step forward, weapon still raised. "Why don't we go sit down and talk about this, the three of us? If Lisa wants to leave me to be with you, I'm man enough to accept that."

"No!" Christopher's near hysteria echoed now. "You would try to trick her."

He took another few steps backward, dragging Juliet with him until they were on the gangplank that led to the boat.

"Just put the gun down, Christopher, before someone gets hurt." Evan tried to talk reason into the younger man, but he was far beyond that at this point.

"You're the only one who's going to get hurt!" he growled.

Juliet realized he was no longer waving his gun so wildly. He was taking aim at Evan, ready to shoot.

"No!" She screamed, throwing her weight into her captor, but he had already gotten off a shot.

Christopher crumpled onto her. He had been shot from a different angle, not by Evan. He seemed to be badly wounded, but wasn't dead. His eyes fastened on hers as they hit the railing of the gangplank together.

"It's over, Christopher. Bob's never going to let you leave here with me. Just let me go," she told the younger man.

Christopher looked over toward Evan, then back at her. He ran his fingers, now bloody, down her cheek. "We're destined to be together, sweetheart. Even if it's in death."

Before Juliet could figure out what he meant to do, he threw all his weight forward over the railing, dragging her with him. She could hear Evan yelling for her as she fell with a splash into Annapolis Harbor.

The freezing water stole Juliet's breath. Darkness and cold surrounded her, making orientation impossible. She fought to free herself from Christopher's grip, but with her arms tied behind her back, there was little she could do. He didn't fight, just wrapped his arms around her as they sank deeper and deeper. She finally hit the bottom of the harbor, landing face-first, with him on top of her.

Juliet's lungs screamed for air. She bucked and twisted, to no avail, and was giving up hope when she felt Christopher's body finally—*finally*—shift away. In the dark water she couldn't tell what had happened. Had he lost consciousness? Died? Had someone pulled him off?

Juliet pushed off against the bottom as hard as she could, then kept kicking, but it wasn't enough. With her hands restrained behind her back and the weight of her waterlogged clothes and shoes, she couldn't get to the surface. She fought as hard as she could, but couldn't reach the precious air. Juliet wasn't even sure if she was heading in the right direction any longer. Blackness surrounded her.

She wouldn't give up. She kept kicking, but the need for oxygen overrode everything. Instinct took over and she opened her mouth to breathe, but all she took in was water.

She stopped fighting as the blackness consumed her.

EVAN DIVED UNDER the water of the harbor again, as did Dylan and Sawyer. All of them screaming for Juliet.

It had been only moments since Christopher Cady had pulled her into the dark bay. But they were running out of time. *Juliet* was running out of time. Evan had found Cady in the depths, but hadn't been able to find her. Evan didn't even bother dragging Christopher up, just pushed him aside and kept searching for Juliet.

He couldn't lose her. Not now, when they'd really just found each other.

But the black water seemed to swallow everything whole.

Evan wouldn't give up. No matter what, he would keep searching for Juliet. He dived again, but in the opposite direction from where they'd been searching. He stretched his arms out as far as they would reach, hoping to feel her, since there was no way he'd be able to see her. He swam around until the need for air once again forced him upward.

And that's when he felt something hit against his ankle. He immediately spun around in the water.

Juliet!

But she wasn't swimming. Oh God, she wasn't moving at all.

Evan grabbed her lifeless form and began dragging them both toward the surface. As he broke through, drawing in much-needed air, he realized Juliet wasn't breathing.

"Sawyer, Dylan! I've got her!" They had to get her to shore so they could start CPR. It wasn't too late. She hadn't been in there that long.

It couldn't be too late.

Evan dragged Juliet over to the pier, where her brothers had made their way out of the water. He handed her still form up to them.

Somebody cut the zip tie off her hands so she could lie flat on the pier. Both her brothers immediately began CPR, one giving breaths, one doing chest compressions, as Evan climbed up beside them.

In the pale light of the poorly lit pier, Juliet's skin had a horrible bluish tinge to it. He didn't know if it was from cold or lack of oxygen. Her lifelessness was the scariest thing Evan had ever seen.

He knelt beside her. "Come on, baby. Don't you give up. Not now, not when we've just found each other." Evan didn't care if her brothers heard.

"Jules, I love you. I always have. Fight, baby. Fight for us." Evan couldn't stop the tears that were streaming down his cheeks. "I love you. I can't live without you," he whispered.

Juliet's whole body seemed to convulse, causing her brothers to stop the CPR and pull back. They turned her to the side as she vomited half the harbor. Finally, she rolled onto her back of her own accord. Although she shivered, her skin had lost much of its blue tinge. Dylan and Sawyer slid her over and began wrapping their dry jackets, which they'd left on the dock before diving into the water to save Juliet, around her for warmth.

Juliet had eyes only for Evan. "Hey." Her voice was raspy, strained from the vomiting.

Evan smiled and pushed a strand of hair out of her face. "Hey, gorgeous."

Sawyer slapped him on the back. "Congrats, man. First time I've seen a declaration of undying love cause a woman to puke her guts out. Impressive."

Evan smiled, but didn't take his eyes from Juliet.

"You want to tell me exactly what's going on with you two?" Sawyer asked.

"We'll give you guys a minute." Dylan cut Sawyer off. "Go call this in. Get Jules a real blanket." He grabbed his younger brother and start pulling him away, despite Sawyer's indignant responses.

All Evan wanted to do was look at Juliet. To touch her. To know she was alive.

"I heard you, you know," she croaked. "So did my brothers. No going back now, because I love you, too. You're stuck with me."

Relief flooded Evan, chasing away every last bit of panic. Juliet loved him the way he loved her.

"I wouldn't have it any other way." He took her hand in his. "You're still wearing Lisa Sinclair's wedding band, you know."

"Yeah, I didn't have a chance to take it off."

"How about if we get a set that's yours and mine, rather than Lisa and Bob's?"

Juliet smiled even though she was shivering. "You've got yourself a deal. Although I'm going to make you propose again, properly this time, once you get me a ring."

She started to sit up, so Evan helped her. "That would be my pleasure." He wrapped his arms around her and pulled her close.

"But we'll still get to be Lisa and Bob in the future, right? I want to take Vince Cady down," Juliet told him from against his chest. A worried note came into her voice. "Do you think we've ruined everything with the case? Christopher's dead, right?"

"Don't worry. You and I won't even be placed at the scene by the time the report gets back to Vince Cady. Bob and Lisa will have their chance to make sure Cady goes down."

"Good. I'm ready, not so scared anymore."

Evan kissed her forehead. "There will be times when we're both scared, but we'll face it together. You and I make a pretty good team."

"Both on cases and off." She pulled his arms more securely around her.

Neither of them had any doubts about it.

* * * * *

Janie Crouch's OMEGA SECTOR *miniseries comes to a gripping conclusion next month with Dylan's story. Look for* LEVERAGE!

"Tristan?" she whispered. "You're real."

It wasn't a question. Not exactly. Because he was real. She knew it. The water dripping off his hair and clothes was wet on her skin. The face she was touching was sickly white, yes, but it was warm and fleshy and, most important, it was not fading before her eyes. She grabbed a handful of hair and squeezed it. Her hand came away soaking wet. She looked at it and laughed, but the laugh turned into a sob.

His brown eyes turned darker. "I'm real," he said, his mouth stretching into a wry smile as a dampness glistened in his eyes.

She sobbed again and put her hand over her mouth, hoping to stop them before they stole what little oxygen she had left in her lungs.

"It's okay, San. It's okay."

"Okay? Is it?" she snapped, still stunned by the vision before her. "Where did you come from? We. Buried. You."

SECURITY BREACH

BY
MALLORY KANE

MILLS & BOON

Published in Great Britain 2015
by Mills & Boon, an imprint of Harlequin (UK) Limited,
Eton House, 18-24 Paradise Road, Richmond, Surrey, TW9 1SR

© 2015 Rickey R. Mallory

ISBN: 978-0-263-25308-5

46-0615

Mallory Kane has two great reasons for loving to write. Her mother, a librarian, taught her to love and respect books. Her father could hold listeners spellbound for hours with his stories. His oral histories are chronicled in numerous places, including the Library of Congress Veterans History Project. He was always her biggest fan. To learn more about Mallory, visit her online at www.mallorykane.com.

This one is for the readers. Thank you for liking my books. Thanks for the letters and emails and Facebook posts. For your insights, your compliments and your critiques. I love you all.

Chapter One

Murray Cho had always worked hard, as a boy in Vietnam after his parents were killed and in America after he immigrated. But the so-called land of opportunity was not accurately named, at least not for a poor immigrant from Vietnam. Eventually, he managed to buy a shrimp boat in a small town in South Louisiana on Bayou Bonne Chance and make enough of a living to take a wife and have a son.

But when Patrick was five, Murray's wife ran off, leaving him to rear his son alone. He and Patrick had made it just fine until two months ago, when gun smugglers hid their booty in Murray's shrimp warehouse and hurt his reputation. So Murray moved himself, Patrick and his shrimp boat to a dock near Gulfport.

For a couple of weeks, Murray had thought the move was a good one, until an ominous voice on his phone had shattered his peaceful fisherman's existence. The voice threatened harm to his son, Patrick, if he didn't follow their directions with no questions.

It wasn't difficult to figure out why the men had chosen him. He was at once familiar and suspicious to the people of Bonne Chance. Brandishing a gun at and threatening the smugglers who'd used the old seafood warehouse he'd bought as a depository for the automatic handguns they were smuggling into the United States had not helped his reputation in the town.

Stealing a laptop from Tristan DuChaud's home had been a piece of cake, once Patrick had shown him how to disarm a security system. He didn't want to know how his son knew that. All he wanted to do was leave the laptop computer where he'd been instructed and go back to his simple life. With any luck that was the last he'd hear from the men.

Murray reattached the rope he'd just mended to the rear of the boat, and then headed across the dock and through the gate, locking it behind him. The RV that he and Patrick lived in was across the parking lot. It was tiny but it served. He slept in the bedroom and the boy slept on the couch.

Murray opened the door quietly, frowning to find it unlocked. Patrick always promised to lock the door before he went to sleep, but he was barely eighteen. He had trouble remembering to close the door, much less lock it.

The interior of the RV was dark and quiet. It was after ten o'clock on a school night. His son should be home studying or in bed. Irritated and a little worried, Murray dialed Patrick's number. No answer. Then before the display went off, the phone rang.

"Patrick, where are you?" he snapped.

"Murray Cho?" a familiar voice said. It was the same man who'd sent him into Tristan's house for the laptop.

Murray's heart pounded. "Where's Patrick? If you've done something to him—"

"Listen to me," the voice said. "We've got your son. He's alive—for now."

"What? For now? What's going on? I want to speak to him."

"I said *listen*! You did a good job of getting the laptop. Now we've got another job for you. DuChaud's wife is back in the DuChaud house, by herself. My boss is wondering why she didn't stay with her mother-in-law. What do you know about Tristan DuChaud?"

The dread that had squeezed his chest the first time the man had called him seized him again. "DuChaud?" Murray stammered. "He's dead."

"Is he?" the voice on the phone asked. "How do you know?"

"Th-there was a funeral," Murray stammered. "Please. Let me talk to Patrick."

"We'll make you a deal. You get us proof that Du-Chaud is alive and we won't kill your son."

Murray's heart seized in terror at the man's words. "No! Please! I'll do anything, but don't hurt my son."

The man sighed. "Come on, Cho. You think begging me is going to do any good? I've got orders from my boss to get this information or my ass is on the line. I picked you because you're known around that area and nobody would think it unusual if you were seen around the dock or the DuChaud house."

"I—I don't understand," Murray stammered.

"Look, we're not bad people. We don't want to hurt you or your kid, but if we don't get this job done it's going to hurt us—permanently. That's another reason I picked you. Because you have a kid, you're motivated. So get me some proof. If he's alive, my boss wants to see proof. If he's dead—" The man gave a little snort. "That'll be harder to prove."

"Who's your boss?"

"Nope. Now, Cho, you should know I can't tell you that. Just do what you're told and don't ask questions."

Murray shook his head numbly. He had no choice. His son's life was on the line.

"We'll take care of your son as long as we can. You need to concentrate on what I'm saying."

Murray did his best to remember what the man had said the boss wanted. "Y-your boss wants proof Tristan DuChaud is alive? But he's dead. They buried his body. I can't prove he's alive."

"You're not helping yourself or your boy by arguing. We're going to check with you every day and find out what you're doing. This better not take long, Cho. And if you even think about going to the authorities, your son will suffer, and I do mean suffer." The phone went dead. The caller had hung up.

Murray stared at the phone's screen until it went black while the man's voice echoed in his ears. *You get us proof...and we won't kill your son.*

He had to do something. Had to rescue Patrick. But how? How could he prove that a dead man was alive?

IT WAS AT DUSK, the end of the day, when she missed Tristan the most. A thousand years ago, someone in Britain had known enough about loneliness to name this time of day the gloaming. A little later, it was called eventide. These days, most people said twilight or dusk. Pretty words, but depressing, according to Sandy DuChaud.

Sandy preferred the sunrise. The beginning of the day. Each rising sun was a new promise, a bright beginning that called to her. She'd loved to roust Tristan out of bed, thrust a hot mug of coffee into his hand and make him watch the sunrise with her. And he in turn had delighted in making her take a walk with him at sunset. With Tristan at her side, she'd begun to get over her innate sadness at the fading of the sun's light.

But Tristan was gone now, and even the sunrise didn't cheer her.

"Do you know what today is, bean?" Sandy asked her unborn baby as she rubbed the sore spot on her baby bump where he liked to kick. "No? Little bean, you need to keep up. It's been two months since your daddy died—" Her voice gave out and her breath caught in a sob.

"Come on," she said. "We need to unpack." Yesterday afternoon, she'd walked into their house on the outskirts of Bonne Chance, Louisiana, for the first time since the day after her husband's funeral. It had been so quiet, so empty, so lonely.

At first, she had been overwhelmed with grief and sadness that Tristan wasn't there and would never be there again. But as she'd stood looking out the French doors past the patio and the driveway to the graceful, drooping trees, vines and Spanish moss of Bayou Bonne Chance, she'd felt a serenity inside her like nothing she'd ever felt before.

The faint sound of the surf and the mellow ring of the wind chimes on the patio washed over her, adding to her peace and calm.

This was why she'd come back to Bonne Chance and their home and all the memories, good and bad. She could hear Tristan's laughter in the organic, spiritual sounds of nature. It called to her as the sun always had.

Forgetting about unpacking, she slid open the French doors and walked outside. The air in June seldom got cool in South Louisiana. Oh, sometimes a storm would send a chilly breeze in from the Gulf. But anyone who lived in the Deep South knew that chilly and cool were not the same thing.

Cool was pleasant—afternoons on the front porch with the ceiling fan rotating, watermelon or iced tea and desultory conversation about nothing more important than how well the fish were biting. Chilly, on the other hand, was a damp breeze that cut through any material, even wool, and made fingers and toes stiff and cold.

"We seem to be all about word choices today, bean," she said. Lifting her head, she let the evening breeze blow her hair back from her face. When she opened her eyes, there was still a faint pink glow in the western sky.

"Okay. Yes. The sunset is kind of pretty," she admitted reluctantly. "I'll give you that. But it will be completely dark in less than fifteen minutes. I'd planned to walk over to the dock and back this afternoon, but I let the time get away from me. It's too close to dark now."

She'd walked over there late the day before. She still wasn't sure why. Maybe hoping to feel Tristan's presence there, where he'd spent so much time. That dock had been his second favorite place all through his childhood. Boudreau's cabin had been his first.

Tristan had always liked swimming in the Gulf this time of the day. He'd pointed out to her that as the sun went down, everything calmed. The breezes that normally seemed to carry sound died, the birds and animals quieted, and the waters of the Gulf became calm and slick as glass. He'd said it was as if the whole world hushed in respect for vespers.

Sandy recalled the dark form she'd seen in the water, diving and swimming out beyond the shallows at the dock. She'd been looking into the setting sun and so all she could see was a sinuous silhouette sliding between the waves. She'd thought it was a dolphin.

But now, thinking back, she could convince herself it looked human.

The sky was getting darker every second. As Sandy turned back toward the house, a faint whispering stopped her. It sounded like voices.

She went still, listening. Disturbed by her sudden anxiety, the baby kicked. Sandy patted her belly reassuringly.

Within a few seconds, the sounds became repetitive and she realized her ears had played tricks on her. The susurrus noise wasn't voices. It was leaves and twigs rustling as something or someone moved through the tangled jungle of the swamp. Something or someone large.

But who—or what? And was it as close as it sounded?

She shivered. There were a lot of wild animals in the swamp, some very large, like alligators or bears. But she'd lived here all her life. It wasn't the prospect of meeting a wild animal that made her tremble.

It was the memory of the dark form swimming gracefully in the Gulf. Had it been a person? Who would be swimming at dusk and then walking through the swamp, the way Tristan once had?

No. She had to stop imagining that each breeze that lifted the curtains or each murmur of waves licking the shore could be Tristan—or his ghost.

There had been nothing ghostly about whatever was moving through the tangle of trees and vines just now. Those sounds were real.

There was no reason she could think of for anyone to be on DuChaud property, not at this time of day— or any time of day, actually. The DuChaud's home was eight miles from the town of Bonne Chance. Everybody knew where the beautiful hand-built house was, but the road from town turned from asphalt to shells and gravel about two miles away and ended at the DuChaud's patio. It was not a road that invited casual drivers.

A different noise broke the silence of the early darkness, again faint, but recognizable. The sound of snapping twigs and crunching leaves.

Whatever or whoever was out there was on the move and didn't care who heard him. Sandy inched her way backward, away from the trees and toward her house, both hands cradling her tummy protectively. She ran through the French doors as if the hounds of hell were nipping at her heels, locked them and set the alarm.

Only then did she breathe a sigh of relief. "Sorry, bean," she muttered. "I know it's silly, but I think I scared myself."

All at once, her eyes began stinging. Blinking furiously, she tried to make the tears disappear, but they still welled and slipped down her cheeks.

"Damn it, I don't want to be afraid in my house. But like it or not, you and I are here alone. We have to be careful. Besides, that's our dock—your daddy's dock," she said, her voice tightening with grief.

"Oh, Tristan," she whispered. "I need you so much. I'm doing my best to live without you. Why are you still. Right. Here?" She slapped her forehead with two stiff fingers.

"Right here in the very front of my brain. Why aren't you fading, like a perfect memory should—" Her voice cracked and a couple of sobs escaped her throat. She pressed her lips together, hoping to hold in any more sobs. She didn't want to cry. The more upset she got, the more restless the little bean.

In all the years she'd been married to Tristan, in all the years she'd known him before that—essentially their whole lives—she'd never been afraid of anything. But the sound of footsteps had spooked her.

"Don't worry, bean. I'm not turning into a scaredy-cat. I came back here for the peace and quiet, and no alligator or poacher—or whatever that was—is going to scare me away." Her brave words made her feel better, and as she relaxed, she realized how tired she was.

Yawning, she checked the alarm system and armed the doors and windows, then headed toward the master bedroom.

As she passed the closed door to her office, which they'd converted into a nursery, she realized she hadn't even thought about checking her email. Too distracted by memories, she supposed.

When she turned on the light, the desktop was empty. Her laptop wasn't there, where it always sat. Automatically, she glanced around as if it might have gotten set aside by someone during the time she'd been in Baton Rouge with her mother-in-law.

But by whom? And when? A chill ran down her spine at the thought of someone coming into her house.

No, she told herself. *Don't start panicking. Think rationally about who of all the people who must have had access to the house could have done it.* Obviously Maddy Tierney or Zach Winter, but Maddy would have told her, right? So…people from the crime scene unit? But all the evidence of Maddy's kidnapping by the captain of the *Pleiades Seagull* was in the master bedroom. Why would they need to take her laptop computer?

But if not them? Then she had a thought that sent her heart hammering. What if it had been Tristan? What if he was out there, hiding, and needed something from the laptop.

"Stop it!" she cried. "You can't go there every time something odd happens or you hear a strange sound. He's dead and nothing is going to bring him back to life!" Blinking, she forced away all her silly romantic thoughts of Tristan out there somewhere, alive and hurt.

Forget all the evidence about how he had died. Forget everything except one fact. He'd gone overboard into the dark, dangerous water and had never come out. That, if nothing else, told her he was really dead. If he were still alive, he would move heaven and earth to get to her. Tristan would die before he'd allow her to believe he was dead.

With a quick shake of her head, she forced away thoughts of Tristan and concentrated on the missing laptop.

Before she jumped to any conclusions, she should check with Maddy and Zach. They may have had to confiscate it so the hard drive and memory cards could be reviewed.

Maybe Homeland Security or the NSA had needed it for evidence. That made sense, except for the fact that there was nothing on her laptop that could possibly be interesting to anyone other than herself.

She checked her watch. It was just after ten. That was eleven Eastern time. She hesitated for a second, then pulled out her phone. Maddy had told her to call anytime if she needed anything.

When her friend answered, she blurted out, "Maddy, did you or Zach take my laptop?"

"What? Sandy? Are you all right?"

"I'm fine. Did either of you take my computer, or see someone else take it?"

"It's not there?"

"No. It always sits on my desk in the nursery. Always. And it's not there."

"No, we didn't. We searched it. Remember, you gave us the password. We went through all the saved files, looking for anything that might have been related to Tristan's death or the smuggling, but it was there when I left." Maddy paused for a beat. "Have you seen any other signs that someone has been in your house?"

Sandy's tummy did a flip, which woke up the baby. He wriggled and kicked. "I don't think so. The nursery is the only room I hadn't been in. You're sure it was here when you guys left?"

"I am," Maddy said. "Did you check with the crime scene unit or the sheriff?"

"No," Sandy said. "I called you first."

"Well, you need to call them. If they took it you should have gotten a receipt, but people forget things."

"So it disappeared after you left." She paused, thinking. "Wait. Come to think of it, the alarm wasn't set when I came in yesterday. It didn't beep."

"So whoever took the laptop disarmed the alarm. Do a lot of people know the code?"

Sandy shook her head. "Just me and Tristan."

"Maybe the crime scene team didn't know how to arm it and didn't realize you weren't there."

"So someone's been in the house," Sandy murmured.

"Listen to me, Sandy. It could be nothing, but just to be on the safe side, maybe you should go into town and stay at the hotel, or go back to Baton Rouge."

"No," Sandy said. "This was probably some kid."

"Hold on a minute."

She heard Maddy talking to Zach, then suddenly the phone went silent. Maddy must have put it on mute. It didn't matter, because Sandy knew what they were saying. They were discussing whether there was still any danger to Sandy or anyone else in Bonne Chance.

"Maddy—" Sandy muttered. "Come on. Hurry up."

Finally Maddy unmuted her phone. "Sandy, if anything happens, call us, okay? We're not on the case anymore, but it hasn't been closed. So either Homeland Security or the NSA might reactivate it."

That quickly, the confidence that Sandy had in knowing that Homeland Security and the NSA had finished with Bonne Chance, the smugglers and Tristan's death drained away. "Why would they do that?"

Maddy hesitated—not for long, but it was long enough for Sandy to notice. "Maddy? You told me all the smugglers were arrested and the captain was killed by Boudreau. I thought that was the end of it."

"There are some things that we're not allowed to talk about. There are some things we're not even allowed to know."

"But you do know, don't you? I *knew* you and Zach weren't telling me everything. There's more to Tristan's death than you told me, isn't there?"

"Sandy, don't."

"Maddy, I swear I will come over there and wring your neck if you don't tell me what you know."

"Hang on a minute."

"No! Wait—" But Maddy was gone. Sandy waited impatiently. After about twenty seconds, she came back on the line.

"Sandy, listen carefully, because I can only say this

once. It's possible—just possible—that your husband's death was not an accident."

Sandy sat down. It was a good thing there was a chair right there. "What? So Zach was right? What happened? Is there some new evidence?"

"Listen to me. We spent a week in your house while we searched for answers to what happened to Tristan and all we could come up with was that his death was suspicious." Maddy took a breath. "So now Homeland Security is ramping up listening devices as well as working with the Coast Guard to do more spot inspections of the oil rigs. They're obviously worried that there may be another group out there that's planning something. Bonne Chance is probably one of the least populated and least noticed places on the Gulf Coast. It doesn't even have streetlights except on Main Street."

"I know. Out here, we can barely see lights from the town on clear nights, or if there's a fire we can see flames and smoke."

"Well, the darkness and isolation makes it desirable for smugglers."

"Maddy, you have to tell me why Zach—"

"Sandy!" Maddy snapped. "What did I just tell you?"

"A lot of vague stuff that you won't explain. Fine. I'll let you know if anything happens. That is if I'm able to." Sandy was being sarcastic, but Maddy had just laid a new and awful truth on her and refused to explain it.

Her husband may have been murdered.

"Sandy, call the sheriff and get him to take fingerprints off the desk. That's the easiest way to figure out who did it."

"If their prints are on file. But they probably aren't."

"Call the sheriff, Sandy," Maddy said.

"Maddy, this might not make any sense to you, but I don't want anyone in my house. I just got home. All I want to do is be here with the baby. We have a lot of things to sort out, him and me. There's no real reason to get fingerprints, is there?"

"Sandy, I mean it. I'm supposed to be in training this whole week, but I'll take a break and call you if I have to."

"All right. I'll call. Now can we talk about something else?"

"Sure. How are you feeling? Is the baby doing well?"

"Yes. We're both doing fine."

"Did that little thing ever fall off?"

"Little thing?" Sandy said. "Oh, right. That's what the doctor said about the sonogram. Not that I know of. It's still there."

"So did he actually say it's a boy?"

"No. Apparently physicians don't like to actually commit, but he sounded pretty sure. You know," she said with a sad smile, "Tristan said we were having a boy. He really believed it."

"Aw, honey."

"I know. Don't worry. I'm fine." Sandy forced a laugh.

"Have you thought of a name yet?"

"No. Not yet."

"So you're back there in Bonne Chance. Are you and the baby going to stay there?"

"I plan to," she said. "But I might go back over to Baton Rouge when I'm closer to the delivery date. It might be easier, having Tristan's mother to help me."

She barely listened as Maddy went on and on about what a great idea it was to go back to Baton Rouge. When she had a chance, she broke in and said goodbye, that she was going to sleep. Maddy warned her again what would happen if she didn't call the sheriff, then they hung up.

"Okay, bean. How about you? Do you think I should call the sheriff about the computer? Yeah. Me neither. Although I think I'll go see Boudreau tomorrow. Let him know I'm back. He might have seen someone sneaking around the house."

She smiled as she rubbed the side of her tummy. "Although, if Boudreau saw somebody he didn't know going into Tristan's house when I wasn't there, he'd probably shoot them."

Chapter Two

Tristan woke up feeling relaxed. The early-morning sun shone across his bed, warming his legs. He took in a deep breath, scented with gardenias. *Sandy.* She'd glowed the last time he'd seen her, just as a pregnant woman should.

As he smiled sleepily and turned toward her, searing pain tore through his calf, igniting painful memories.

He wasn't in his bed with his wife beside him. He was on a cot in his old Cajun friend Boudreau's cabin, where he'd been since Boudreau saved his life.

A memory of dark water and bright shark's teeth hit his brain. His muscles tensed and the hot pain in his calf, where muscle had been ripped away by thick, sharp teeth, seized him again.

Clenching his jaw and groaning quietly, he consciously relaxed his leg. He'd learned the hard way that if he could avoid tightening the tendons and whatever muscles were left on that side, it didn't hurt quite so bad.

The pain finally faded, but it was no relief. All he felt was a gaping emptiness inside. He was supposed to be dead. Was dead, as far as his hometown, Bonne Chance, Louisiana, and his family knew.

He couldn't have notified his family if he'd wanted to. According to Boudreau, he'd spent nearly two weeks unconscious, then when he finally woke up, he was too weak to stand and walk.

Since then, he'd forced himself to walk every day, pushing through the awful pain. He couldn't imagine how his mangled leg would ever work right, but if determination had anything to do with it, he would be successful.

Every morning, he sent up a prayer of thanks to God for letting him live. He'd been granted quite a few miracles in the past two months, and that one was the greatest.

He needed another miracle, though. He needed to walk across the dock from Boudreau's cabin to his family home. The miracle he envisioned was that once he got to the house, Sandy would be there waiting for him, beautiful and happy because he was alive.

He'd run to her without limping or falling and take her in his arms, feeling the swell of her tummy between them. She would take his hand and place it in just the right spot to feel their baby kick.

But Sandy wasn't there. She was in Baton Rouge with his mother, thank God.

Thank God for several reasons. First, while seeing her might be his fondest dream, that wasn't his primary motivation to recover as fast as he could. He had to find and bring to justice the man who'd ordered him killed.

And to do that, he needed to retrieve a vital piece of evidence—at least, he hoped it would be vital. But he had to get his hands on it and it was in the house.

As much as he longed for Sandy, he prayed she wouldn't come back to Bonne Chance. Not until he'd tracked down the person who had tried to kill him and wanted him dead.

While he'd been daydreaming about Sandy and their

baby, the sun had risen above the window casing. From the floor, he picked up the bumpy cypress walking stick Boudreau had whittled for him,

He took a deep, fortifying breath, then slowly sat up and swung his feet off the bed to the floor. Putting on his shoes was a painful chore, but not as painful as standing.

He used the stick to lever himself upright. As he balanced, putting weight on his right leg, he grimaced in anticipation.

And there it was. The pain. He cringed and tightened his grip on the walking stick. Outside, the morning sun shone through leaves and sent dappled shadows dancing across the ground.

Tristan lifted his face and let the energizing sun's heat soak through him, trying to keep his mind clear and open, trying to be glad he was alive.

But as hard as he tried to stay in the warm, bright present, the nightmare of his struggle with death clutched at him. He couldn't shake the memory of plunging into the dark, churning water off the oil rig.

He relived each terrifying moment, as dark, chill salt water seeped in through his mouth and nose and the shock of cold on his skin paralyzed his muscles.

He'd felt but hadn't reacted to the bumps and nibbles and flesh-ripping bites of the sharks that circled him until he'd opened his eyes and saw blood everywhere. His blood. It had swirled and wafted past him like ink dripped in water, darker than the brownish water of the Gulf.

Tristan gagged and coughed reflexively, and greedily sucked in fresh air until the horrible memories began to fade. He was beginning to appreciate the small things in life, like breathing. A wry smile touched his lips for a second as he limped over to a rough-hewn bench Boudreau had built under a pecan tree.

He didn't sit, because then he'd have to stand up again. Instead, he propped the walking stick against the bench and watched the morning come alive. Birds circled the yard, stopping to peck for seeds and nuts and insects.

Boudreau had a goat tethered to a tree with a generous amount of line so it could wander almost uninhibited. A vague memory of cool milk sliding down his throat took away the remembered burn of salt water.

As the quiet of dawn turned into the hustle and bustle of daytime in the bayou, Tristan made a decision. There was no more time for rest and recuperation. He had to solve the mystery of his near murder, and there was no better time than now. He would walk a mile today, all the way down to the dock and back. He was ready to walk that far. He had to be.

When Boudreau appeared, carrying a bucketful of water from a hidden artesian spring, Tristan told him his plan.

"What for you thinking about going down there?" Boudreau shook a finger at him. "You ain't got the stamina yet, you. You want somewhere to go? Strip the sheets off that cot and take them down to the spring and wash them. Use that Ivory soap. It don't hurt the water too much." He stalked past Tristan into the house and within a moment came back out, carrying the bucket, now empty.

"Haul up a bucketful of water when you're done washing. See how that goes, then we'll talk about how far you think you can walk."

"Boudreau," Tristan said. "You saved my life. If you hadn't been out fishing that morning and stopped the bleeding in my leg, I wouldn't be alive now. I owe you too much and respect you too much to argue with you, but I can't lie in bed any longer. I've got to strengthen this leg as much as I can, although I know it's never going to be as good as it was." He sighed. "There's enough I won't be able to do. I don't want it to wither down to complete uselessness."

"Wither? Son, ain't no use making up stories about what ain't happened yet. The future gonna happen, yeah, but its story ain't been writ yet. You start pushing yourself too much, you'll undo the good you've done and, before you know it, you'll accidently throw yourself into that future of your own making. See?"

"So what should I picture, rather than the truth that without most of the muscle in my calf, I'll never do better than a slow and painful limp for the rest of my life?" he asked bitterly.

Boudreau studied him for a moment. "How 'bout you picture that pretty little wife of yours back home and mourning for you. See if that's a better motivation."

"What? Sandy's back? Here?" Shocked, he glanced in the direction of the house. Then one of the many things Boudreau had told him during the past few weeks came into his mind.

He recalled his friend telling him that Murray Cho had gotten into the house without setting off the alarm and had come out a few moments later with what looked like Sandy's laptop computer.

Tristan had been surprised—he'd never imagined Murray Cho as a thief.

"She can't be back," he cried. "Murray could come back. He thinks she's gone, and if she surprises him—"

"There you go again, making a surefire mountain out

of a piece of ground where there might be a molehill one day. Slow down, son. Let things happen as they will. Just be ready when they do." Boudreau assessed him. "Meanwhile, how come you think she's not safe? You left her alone when you worked on the rigs."

He thought of Sandy, waiting for him week after week, never having a full-time husband, and he never having a full-time wife. Now she was less than a mile away.

He wanted to run to her and grab her up and kiss her until they both were panting with desire. He wanted to see how much her tiny baby bump had grown. And he wanted to put his hands on it and feel the child they had created, the child he already thought of as his son.

But he was afraid. Not only did he not want to show his face, he didn't want to chance her telling someone— her best friend, or his.

"I had no choice. Besides, I didn't know they were going to kill me. If they find out I'm alive, what's to stop them from doing it right this time?"

"Who's them? That captain's dead. Everybody's gone from the oil rig now."

"Come on, Boudreau. The captain was never the man in charge. The boss is still out there. He's some big muckety-muck in the company that owned the oil rig, Lee Drilling. And that man knows I can potentially identify him."

"Yeah?" Boudreau said. "Who is he?"

"I said *potentially*. I don't know who he is. The first time I heard the captain talking about a plan to smuggle illegal weapons into the US and give them out to kids on the streets, it was a complete accident. I realized I was listening to terrorists, and that was only one side of the conversation. I put together a program to capture and save every conversation that took place on that satellite phone."

"And that captain never said a name?"

"I don't know. I never had a chance to listen to all the recordings. Too afraid I'd get caught. I stored them on a flash drive, hoping I could get it to Homeland Security. They can use voice recognition technology to identify the man, and that will implicate him in the smuggling operation.

"Something went wrong with my program and the captain caught me fooling with his satellite phone. He kicked me out of his office and never said anything, but I know that's why they tried to have me killed."

"So where's that flash drive? You for sure didn't have nothing on you when I fished you out of the Gulf."

"That's just it. I hid it in the house the last time I was home. My plan was to get it to Homeland Security on my next week off. But I never got that week off. Now I don't know if Murray found it when he got the laptop."

"That's why you don't want Sandy back here."

Tristan nodded grimly. "I'd like to get Homeland Security to put a guard on her, but to do that, I'd have to let them know I'm alive. And as soon as they hear from me, they'll pull me in to DC for debriefing. Oh, they'd honor my request to guard her, but I can't be sure she's safe if I'm not the one protecting her. I mean look at how many good soldiers who have the protection of the government have been killed. How many innocent civilians."

"I get you wanting to protect her yourself, but, son, you ain't capable right now."

Tristan pinched the bridge of his nose. "So what are you saying? That my only choice is to notify Homeland Security? I'd be signing her death warrant. Somebody as high up as the captain's boss would know as soon as I surfaced. He'd have plenty of time to kidnap her before Homeland Security could react. She might end up being tortured for information she doesn't even have. And I wouldn't be here to rescue her."

SANDY FELT AS THOUGH she hadn't slept at all and therefore the little bean had been restless, too. She hadn't been able to shut her brain off. Every time she'd go to sleep, her dreams had been filled with images of Tristan sinking into the cold, dark water as hungry sharks circled around him. It was like a slideshow that wouldn't stop. *Click—murdered. Click—murdered. Click—murdered.*

Then she would wake up with her heart racing and tears wetting her cheeks and pillow.

Finally, around seven o'clock, she got up and bathed and dressed and headed into the kitchen. For a second, she stared at the coffeepot in longing. But she'd sworn off coffee for the pregnancy, not wanting to have a baby who was hooked on caffeine.

She yawned. "You have no idea how much I would enjoy a cup of coffee this morning. And there might be some decaf in the freezer. But my tummy has let me know in no uncertain terms that it likes grape juice and only grape juice." She patted her belly. "So grape juice it is, right?"

As she sat at the kitchen table and drank the juice, she looked at her phone, recalling Maddy's warning from the night before. She wanted to blow off the Homeland Security agent who had become her friend, but she knew Maddy would bug her until she called the sheriff. If she refused, Maddy would call him herself.

"No choice but to do it," she muttered as she got up

and went into the nursery. It was the only place in or out of the house where she could get a reliable cell signal. She dialed the sheriff's office.

"Baylor," she said when Sheriff Baylor Nehigh answered. "It's Sandy."

"Well, hello. I didn't know you were back in town," he said. "How're you doing? How's the baby?"

"Fine. We're fine," she said. "The baby's fine. Baylor—"

"Now how far along are you? I'm trying to remember."

Sandy closed her eyes and prayed for patience. If she couldn't get her question in, Baylor would be off on Tristan's death and she'd have to listen to his theories for at least twenty minutes before she could get another word in edgewise.

"Five and a half months, Baylor. I think someone got into the house while I was gone. My laptop computer is gone."

"Now, what? You say a computer is missing? Well, now, we can't be responsible for that. You'd have to talk to the crime scene unit, although my guess is that oil rig captain took it when he broke in to kidnap Agent Tierney," he said. "If it was him you'll never get any money for it."

"Baylor! That's not why I'm calling. The laptop went missing while I was gone. I thought if you or the crime lab had it then I don't need to worry that someone got into my house while I was away."

"I'll be glad to check on that for you, but do understand, my budget is too small to replace your laptop."

"I'm not asking you to. I'll buy a new one." She paused. "You don't want to take fingerprints or anything, do you?"

"I can send my deputy out there when he gets back.

It'll probably be after dark. He's gone to Houma to deliver some paperwork. I need a courier, but like I said—my budget won't handle it."

"No, no," Sandy said, feeling relieved. She didn't want anyone coming into her house right now. She'd come back to be alone with her baby and try to come to peace with Tristan's death. "I'm sure you're right about how it happened."

"Anything else I can do for you, Sandy?"

"No, Baylor. Thanks."

Sandy hung up while he was telling her to take care of herself. She rinsed her glass, then headed out to walk to Boudreau's cabin. She took a deep breath of clean morning air and yawned again. "I'm sorry about last night, bean. I couldn't get what Maddy said out of my head."

She wondered if talking to her unborn baby about things that upset her was bad for him. She hoped not, because talking to Tristan's child soothed her, and according to the latest baby books, it was good to let the baby become used to the mother's voice.

"Did you know your daddy was an undercover agent? Wait. What am I thinking? You were there when Zach told me. Naturally I had to hear it from his oldest friend, because Tristan apparently thought I didn't need to know that little tidbit." She heard the bitterness in her voice. She didn't want to sound like that when she talked about Tristan. Certainly not to her baby.

With an effort, she made her voice light and soft, the way she talked when she told him a fairy tale or quoted a poem. "He was a real-life spy, I guess. He worked for Homeland Security, catching bad guys. Until one day, one of the bad guys killed him."

She stopped talking because she had to. She was

breathing hard, mostly from trying not to cry, and she'd arrived at the dock. It was a beautiful morning. The sun glared and glistened off the water. "I should have gotten up earlier and watched the sunrise," she said wistfully. "Although without Tristan…" Her voice trailed off and she smiled sadly at the memories of sunrises and making love and being happy.

"Okay," she said briskly. "Let's go. I want to talk to Boudreau."

As she turned toward the path to Boudreau's cabin, she noticed slide marks in the mud. Stepping closer to the wooden pier, she studied the markings. Someone had pulled a boat up there since the last rain. She shook her head. It was probably Boudreau. He used the dock all the time.

"I've got to be careful," she murmured. "I'm seeing terrorists and bad guys everywhere."

The sun was already yellow and hot when she stepped out of the tangle of vines and branches into Boudreau's front yard. Boudreau was sitting on an old, rough-hewn bench, mending a tear in a fishing net.

"Well, now, you are moving much faster this—" he said, looking up. "What the hell you doing here?" he snapped, glaring at her.

"Boudreau, it's Sandy. Tristan's wife." He'd known her for years, and the last time she'd been here was on that awful night, when she'd come to tell him Tristan was missing and feared dead. But when he talked nonsense, like just now, she wasn't sure he remembered her.

Boudreau stood, dropping the fishing net and stalking toward her, the darning needle in one hand and his knife in the other. "I ask you a question. What you doing

here? You go on now. Get out of here." He stopped, pointing the tip of the knife back the way she'd come. "Go!"

"But I need to talk to you. I want to close the dock—"

"Get out of here, Mrs. DuChaud. Get!" Boudreau
shooed her as if he were shooing a chicken, with a sweep-
ing motion of his hands. "Get!" he yelled again.

Sandy stared at him in openmouthed disbelief. This
wasn't confusion. It was hostility. Did he think Tristan's
death was her fault?

"Boudreau, please, listen to me. This is important."

He eyed her suspiciously. "I come down to your house
one day soon. We talk then. Now you get out of here and
back to your house *tout de suite* or I'll sic my dog on you,
I guarantee."

She didn't know a lot about Boudreau except what
Tristan had told her and he'd never mentioned the man
being violent. But he had shot that oil rig captain in cold
blood, so maybe the best thing to do was to leave.

"Please, come talk to me," she called out over her
shoulder as she turned and headed back down the path
she'd walked up to his shack.

"You just get gone and stay gone," she heard him say.

By the time she got to the dock she was breathing hard
again, so she stopped for a few moments. She stood on the
dock and looked out over the dark, greenish-gray waters
of the Gulf of Mexico. And there, diving and surfacing
as the sun glared off the water with such intensity it was
difficult to see anything but the splashes and waves, was
the creature that she'd seen the day before yesterday, frol-
icking in the water. She squinted and shaded her eyes,
wishing she'd brought her sunglasses with her.

Nothing helped her see any better, though. The sun
was higher now and the glare was too bright. And all at

once, it seemed that whatever the creature was, it had sensed that she was watching, because the splashing stopped. Sandy blinked and put both hands up to deflect the sun, but the water was glassy and smooth and the sun reflected off it like a mirror.

Whatever—or whoever—had been playing in the water just beyond the shallows was gone now.

"I'm going to have to get up early one morning, bean, and get out here so I can catch whoever or whatever that is. Maybe it's a mermaid." She smiled and rubbed the side of her belly. "Or a merman."

Back at the house, she made herself some breakfast. By the time she'd finished eating, she'd convinced herself that Boudreau had shooed her away for her own protection. Maybe he knew there was a fox or a bobcat or an alligator running around that might do her harm. And he had promised to come see her. She knew from Tristan that if Boudreau said he would do something, he would.

"I guess we've got to wait for him, bean. He could have been nicer, though. He didn't have to yell like that. Kind of hurt my feelings." She drank the last of her juice and rinsed her glass and plate and set them on the drain board.

A glance at the clock told her it was just now eleven o'clock. "I still need to talk to him, though. He may have a better idea of how to keep people away from the dock," she told the baby. "He may already be guarding it. Maybe that *was* him I heard last night, checking to be sure no one was using the dock."

She yawned again. She'd been tired before she went to Boudreau's. "We've got to take a nap, bean. I'm about to fall asleep standing up. Then we've got to drive into Houma and get some groceries and buy me a new, smaller computer. A notebook. That'll be our big, exciting adventure for the day." As she said the words, a faint echo of a chill ran down her spine. "I hope," she added.

Chapter Three

It was almost dark when Sandy got back from shopping in Houma, which was twenty-five miles north of Bonne Chance, and if she'd been tired before, she was about to collapse from exhaustion now. She had stopped and bought a chocolate milk shake on the way. It was melted now, but she could put some ice in it and rejuvenate it a bit. Even melted, it sounded better than any of the food she'd bought at the grocery store. She was too tired to cook anything. Swallowing the melted shake would probably take the last of her strength.

She parked on the driveway just beyond the patio and grabbed her groceries and the new computer box in one hand and her house keys in the other. She was almost all the way across the patio to the door when she saw the footprints.

She nearly dropped the groceries. Automatically, she glanced around, but there was nothing to see. She stepped around the muddy tracks and tried the French doors. They were still locked.

She looked at the threshold, but there was no mud there. Relieved, she went inside and locked the doors behind her. Then she stood there and studied the muddy prints through the glass panes.

It was hard to tell how big or small the shoes were because the prints were smeared and the concrete was wet from an earlier rain. It looked as though they had no tread, though. So either the shoes were worn-out or they were soled in smooth leather.

Boudreau wore old, cracked leather boots. Maybe he'd walked over here while she was gone.

Of course, she thought with a sigh of relief. It was Boudreau who'd made the prints. It made her feel better that he'd come. Tristan had always told her that when he was away, Boudreau would watch over her.

She glanced at the clock on her phone. Eight o'clock. She stretched and yawned. "What do you think, bean? Too early to go to bed?"

She walked to the alarm box and set the door and window alarms, grabbed a glass of water and her milk shake, which she'd cooled with a couple of ice cubes, then headed into the master bedroom.

She'd already climbed into bed before she realized she'd left the curtains open. She didn't want to get up, but she certainly didn't want to sleep with the curtains like that, not after what had happened the last time she was here, when Murray Cho's son had spied on her.

She closed the curtains and climbed back under the covers. She picked up a book she'd begun at her mother-in-law's house, but it didn't take long for her to recall why she hadn't finished it before. She tossed it onto the floor and pulled an old fashion magazine from the shelf of the nightstand. It took practically zero concentration to glance through the ads and the fashion spreads.

She was nodding off over an ad for Bulgari earrings when the bean decided he was restless. "Ow!" she said. "Wow, bean. That was a good one."

She rubbed the place where he'd planted his tiny foot, not that it helped much. It was like scratching your thumb because your nose itched. The place that hurt was on the inside, so rubbing the outside, while it seemed like a good idea, didn't help much.

"Settle down. You're going to make me go to the bathroom again. Please don't kick my bladder." She grunted. "And there you go. That was my bladder. I'm so glad you mind well."

She stepped into the bathroom and saw that the curtains in there were open, too. She closed them, used the bathroom, then looked at herself in the mirror as she washed her hands. Her eyes were wide and dark.

"Come on, Sandy," she muttered. She looked like a pitiful heroine in a horror movie, although there was no reason to feel afraid in this house.

"This house is very safe," she said to the baby. "It's your daddy's house. It was his daddy's and his grand-daddy's house. He promised me he would always keep me safe here. Me and you now." She felt tears starting up in her eyes and dashed them away angrily.

"This is Murray Cho's fault," she said. "It was his son, Patrick, who'd peeked in the window on the day of your daddy's funeral." She'd been terrified to see two men looking in her window, gaping into her private life.

"*Our* private life. I'm not sure I'll ever be the same." She sighed. "Not even when you get here," she said softly, patting her tummy where she thought his little back was. "It's their fault I'm scared."

She turned out the light and lay down, but there was no way she was going to fall asleep. It was just like the night before. Every time she closed her eyes, horrific visions haunted her. With a sigh, she sat up and turned on the lamp.

Opening the bedside table drawer, she picked up the prescription bottle and considered the label. *Take one or two for sleep.* She could take one. One would be safe. Extra safe, since the doctor had prescribed two.

She swallowed the pill with water. "Okay, let's try again," she whispered, then lay down on her side and cradled her pudgy tummy.

"Good night, little bean," she said as she felt something wet trickle down the side of her face to the pillow. "Why am I crying?" she grumbled out loud. She rarely cried and seldom ever needed help sleeping. But tonight, there was something bothering her and it wasn't the memory of two men peeking in her window.

She'd insisted on coming back here, had declared to Tristan's mother that she had to come back to the house where she and Tristan had lived together. She'd told her it was the only way she could heal. She'd meant it then, but now she wasn't so sure she'd made the best decision. An impossible thought had occurred to her while she'd been on the phone with Maddy. A ridiculous thought. A thought that couldn't possibly ever be true. But, whether it made sense or not, she couldn't get it out of her head.

What if it wasn't the Chos who had spawned this fear and dread that was keeping her from sleeping? What if it was the figure she'd seen at the window later on the night of Tristan's funeral? The figure that had to be a dream. Or was he? What if he'd been the one who'd taken her laptop computer?

Was it Tristan—or his ghost—that she was really afraid of?

She remembered him standing there just inside the

bedroom window, dripping wet, his face pale and haggard. Blood had dribbled down the side of his head, mixing with the water. Sandy shuddered. She never wanted to see that apparition again as long as she lived. She did not believe in voodoo. She did not believe in ghosts or demons or goblins—not on this earth. But she knew she couldn't live here if Tristan was going to keep showing up, even if he was just a figment of her grief-stricken imagination.

She knew he was only in her imagination, because if he were alive, he would never hurt her by pretending he was dead.

If Tristan were alive, he'd be here with her and their unborn baby.

TRISTAN UNLOCKED THE French doors of his home with the spare key that had been hidden in a fake flowerpot bottom for as long as he could remember. He shook himself, trying to get rid of the rainwater dripping off him.

Boudreau was right again. He'd been sure Tristan wasn't strong enough yet. Now, with his leg throbbing with pain and his head fuzzy with fatigue, Tristan had to agree. But he'd had no other choice.

Boudreau had told him about Sandy showing up at his cabin that morning while Tristan was swimming. But Tristan already knew she'd been out walking.

He'd gotten a glimpse of her at the dock from the water. She'd been shading her eyes and craning her neck, so the odds were that she couldn't see him because of the sun's glare. The fact that she hadn't shouted at him or marched back up to Boudreau's asking about him had been reassuring.

According to Boudreau she'd been agitated and nervous, as if she was afraid of something. And she'd seemed desperate to talk to him. But Boudreau, knowing that Tristan would soon be coming up the same path that Sandy would be walking down, had put her off and sent her home, hopefully in time to prevent them from running into each other.

Tristan made his way across the kitchen floor to the alarm control box behind the hall door, worrying about the squeaking of his sneakers. He disabled the alarm with two seconds to spare. He was way too slow.

He shook his head in disgust. He'd brought his walking stick with him, but he'd abandoned it by the French doors. He didn't want to use it inside the house and take a chance on dropping it or banging it into something.

He hobbled down the hall to the nursery, where he'd hidden the flash drive in plain sight. He'd thought at the time that he'd chosen an excellent hiding place. He had no idea how well it had worked, although he figured if anyone had found it, Boudreau would know.

So unless Sandy had noticed it, the device was probably still exactly where he'd put it. He'd grab it and go, and Sandy would no longer have anything that anyone wanted.

Of course, he'd have to figure out a way to assure the mysterious head of the terrorist group that had tried to smuggle guns, using his dock, that Sandy had no idea that he had been working undercover, nor was there anything in the house that could incriminate him.

But he would work that out later. Right now he just needed to get the drive and get out of the house without Sandy hearing him.

As he started to open the nursery door, he heard a

sound from behind him. He stopped dead still and listened.

Nothing. What had he heard, exactly? He reached for the knob and heard the same sound again. It was soft and low-pitched, and his heart wrenched when he realized what it was.

That was Sandy. He was sure of it. She was talking. It was almost two o'clock in the morning. She should be sound asleep. She was a lark, an early riser. She'd never stayed up past midnight or gotten up later than seven or seven-thirty. Although she *was* pregnant now, and he remembered his mom telling her that she'd be going to the bathroom almost constantly by the time the baby was born.

That was probably it. She'd gotten up to go to the bathroom. On the other hand, maybe she was talking or moaning in her sleep.

He waited, listening. He was in no hurry. Once she settled down he could sneak out without her ever knowing he'd been there.

He stood there on his left foot, flexing the right, trying to stretch and exercise the muscles that were left beneath the ugly scar where Boudreau had stitched up the gaping wound. Point then flex. Point then flex.

After a few moments without a sound, he turned the knob again. He was just about to push the door open and slip into the nursery when he heard a familiar sound that twisted his aching heart even more. The sound of Sandy's bare feet on the hardwood floor. Then the knob on the master bedroom door turned. Within the couple of seconds while he wondered if he had time to push the door open, slip through and ease it shut, the master bedroom door opened and his wife stepped through it into the hall.

In the dim glow of a night-light from the kitchen, he saw that she had on pajama pants and a little sleeveless pajama top that stretched over an obvious baby bump. She'd hardly been showing at all the last time he'd seen her.

He stared at her smooth, rounded belly barely covered by her pajama top. He wanted to touch it, to kiss it, to feel the movements of the tiny little child growing inside. He had missed her so much, and here she was, close enough that he could reach out and take her into his arms, and he couldn't.

If she knew he was alive, she would be furious—more than furious—that he'd let her believe he was dead. She wouldn't understand the danger. She'd spent her entire life in the belief that just because he was with her, she was safe.

That was the one thing about her that had always awed him.

Sandy had always believed in him.

He just prayed that she loved him enough to forgive him for this unforgivable hurt he'd caused her.

She yawned and pushed her fingers through her hair, leaving it sticking out in tangled waves all over her head. He smiled. He knew her, knew her every move, her every little gesture. She was three-quarters asleep, padding on autopilot to the kitchen in her bare feet. Her habit of getting a drink of water without ever completely waking up might save him if he stood perfectly still. Often, people only noticed things that moved.

He concentrated on keeping his bad leg still. If he tensed it too much, the muscles jerked involuntarily. "It's okay," she whispered.

Shock flashed through his body like lightning and instantly the muscles in his right leg cramped. He clenched his jaw. Was she talking to him? He couldn't move. Didn't dare.

"Ow. Watch it, bean. I know I woke you up. Just need some ice for my water and maybe a couple of crackers. Kinda nauseated," she murmured, rubbing the side of her belly. "Then we'll get back in bed."

She wasn't talking to him. She was talking to her baby. To *their* baby. Tristan's eyes stung. It hurt his heart to know how much he had missed. He'd been gone too much, working on the oil rig for two weeks or more at a time, and he'd missed most of the pregnancy. And now... now she thought he was dead.

He held his breath as she took her first step up the hall. There was no way she could pass by without seeing him. He debated whether he should speak to her or wait and let her notice him on her own. Which would be less traumatic?

Sandy jerked as the baby's foot knocked the haze of sleep right out of her head. "Oh, why do you have to kick, bean," Sandy said, rubbing her belly. "One day your foot's going to kick right through—"

She gasped and stopped cold. What was that? Her heart suddenly vied with the baby's foot to see which could burst through her skin first. She pressed her fist to her chest.

Dear God help her. There was someone there. In the dark. Right in front of her. Her first instinct was to turn and run, but she couldn't move. Her arms and legs were numb with fear.

"Who are you? Wh-what do you want?" she asked, trying to force a cold sternness into her voice, but hearing it quaver.

The dark shadow didn't move. She took a step backward as the nausea that had woken her hit her again. She felt hot and cold and terrified.

"Get out," she said hoarsely, then filled her lungs and shrieked, "Get out! Get out now!" She ran out of breath too fast. Her heart was drumming against her chest wall now. *Boom-boom run! Boom-boom run! Boom-boom!*

"Sandy," a voice that could not possibly be speaking said.

She recoiled, her back slamming against the wall. Her throat closed up. Her lungs burned with the need for oxygen. Another scream built behind her throat, but when she opened her mouth all that escaped was a quiet squeak.

She pressed her hands flat against the wall behind her, as if she could make it move, and dug her heels into the hardwood floor, trying to get away from the thing that was hovering in front of her. "Oh, please," she whispered desperately. "Come on, Sandy, wake up. *Stupid dream.*"

"San, you're not asleep," the voice said gently. "Don't be afraid."

She tried one more time to get air past her strictured throat into her lungs, but she couldn't. Her fingers curled at her constricted throat, then stars danced before her eyes and the next thing she knew, she was crumpled on the floor and the wet, haggard ghost from her nightmare was crouching above her, dripping water on her and calling her name.

"I'm asleep," she muttered. "In bed, asleep."

"You're not asleep," a familiar voice said softly.

"No, no, not again," she whispered, shaking her head back and forth. Then she felt a wet hand on her cheek and she squealed and propelled herself backward as fast and hard as she could, but she was already up against the wall.

"No!" she cried. "No, no. Get away."

"Sandy, listen to me. I'm sorry. I'm so sorry. I didn't mean to scare you."

She felt his hand and the soft whisper of his breath against her cheek. Water dripped down his pale, drawn face, just as it had in her dream.

She understood now that on the night of his funeral what she'd seen had been a dream. He'd hovered by the same window where Patrick Cho had peeped in on her. But unlike Patrick, Tristan had been insubstantial, a shimmering awful specter that had dissolved into nothing as she'd watched.

Tonight he was not dissolving. She touched his face. "Tristan?" she whispered. "You're real." It wasn't a question.

The water dripping off his hair and clothes was wet on her skin. The face she was touching was sickly white, yes, but it was warm and fleshy and, most important, it was not fading before her eyes. She grabbed a handful of his hair and squeezed it. Her hand came away soaking wet. She looked at it and laughed, but the laugh turned into a sob.

His brown eyes turned darker. "I'm real," he said, his mouth stretching into a wry smile as a dampness glistened in his eyes.

She sobbed again and put her hand over her mouth, hoping to stop the hiccuping sobs before they stole what little oxygen she had left in her lungs.

"It's okay, San. It's okay."

"How—" She reached out to touch him, hesitated,

then gingerly touched his shoulder. It was firm, strong, alive. Oh, dear God.

She met his gaze and found him watching her intently. He didn't try to pull her close or hug her, and she was fine with that.

He was here, and his hair was dripping with real water and his face was damp. But there was a part of her that was afraid to trust her own eyes and ears and fingers. She looked at her hand, then back at him.

"San? It's okay," he said again. "It's me."

The voice. The eyes. "It is you," she said. "How? Shouldn't you be dead?"

"Almost was," he muttered. "How're you doing? How's—"

"But where?" she broke in. "Where have you been? Where did you go? It's been two months!"

"Boudreau found me. He's been taking care of me."

"Boudreau? You mean you've been right over there all this time?" She dug her heels into the hardwood floor to push away from him.

"We. Buried. You. We had a funeral. We cried. We mourned you. I thought I was going to die because I would never see you again. And you were *less than a mile* away the whole time?" She pushed at his chest and he almost toppled over. He caught himself with a hand to the floor just in time.

"Sandy, it's okay."

"Okay?" She laughed hollowly. "You think so? I wake up in the middle of the night and find my dead husband sneaking into my home and looking cornered when I run into him. What the hell are you doing here?"

Suddenly, the floodgates opened in her mind. Thoughts and questions whirled around in her head so fast that she could barely speak. As soon as she started to demand one answer, another question pushed its way to the forefront, insisting on being asked. A still shot of memory flashed across her inner vision.

The casket at the open door of the DuChaud vault as Father Duffy deliberately turned her away from the sight and asked her a distracting question.

She stared at him in horror, her mouth turning dry with trepidation. "Who was in there?" She pressed a hand to her lips. "Who's in the vault? Who's…buried in—" she giggled a bit hysterically "—in Tristan's tomb?" She hiccuped.

Tristan stared at her for a brief moment. "My…tomb?" he echoed, as if the fact that a casket was placed in the DuChaud family tomb had never occurred to him. "I don't know," he said, his eyes burning like dark fire.

Then he sat back, put his hands on the floor and maneuvered his left foot under him. She could barely see his face, which was in profile to her, but his jaw tensed and he bared his teeth as he used just his left foot and his hands to push himself to his feet.

She watched and realized why he'd almost toppled over when she'd pushed him.

"Oh, my God," she whispered.

He finally got himself upright. He stood with his head bowed, his breaths sawing loudly in his throat. He flattened a palm against the wall to steady himself. In the dark, his pale face floated above his dark clothes like a disembodied head.

"What happened to you?" She was still sitting with her back to the wall. She pushed herself to her feet, murmuring to her little bean encouragingly as she stood.

"It's okay, bean. You're fine. I'm fine." She looked

up, realizing that her fear and panic had drained away and the only thing left inside her was anger, rising to the surface like a bubble in a lake.

"Tristan? Talk to me," she said through gritted teeth.

He glanced at her sidelong. "Sorry, San. It's a long story." He huffed. It could have been a chuckle, except that his expression didn't change. "A very long story," he mumbled.

The bubble burst and fury washed over her like a red tide. This was Tristan, standing in front of her. He was real. And he'd been alive. All this time, he'd been alive. "A long story? That's your answer?"

She realized that the anger felt good. It didn't weigh on her like grief and sorrow. It invigorated her. She clenched her fingers into fists. Her husband was alive and she was pissed off.

He glanced at her for an instant, then looked away. "I didn't mean to wake you up. I should have been in and out of here in, like, two minutes."

"In and out?" she echoed.

He spread his hands. "I don't know where to start. It's—"

"A long story. Yeah. I got that," she said. "Not a problem, *sweetheart*. I've got all night."

Chapter Four

Ten minutes later, Sandy sat at the kitchen table, clutching a rapidly cooling mug of decaf coffee that her husband, who was supposed to be dead, had made for her.

It was a cliché, but she really did feel as though she'd walked into a play where everyone knew their lines except her. In fact, she was reminded of a movie about a man whose entire life was a TV show, and he was the only one who thought it was his real life. She almost glanced around to see if she could spot hidden cameras.

Across from her, Tristan sat, staring into his mug. She studied him as long as she could, which was only a few seconds, then looked away. If she looked at him for longer, it did awful, painful things to her insides.

But his tortured expression wasn't the worst thing. Nor was the fact that he looked so tired and sick she couldn't believe he was upright. It wasn't even that she could feel his pain. No. The worst thing was that her heart and head and gut throbbed with anger at him.

"You said if I hadn't gotten up you'd have been in and out in a few minutes."

Tristan glanced up. "I did?"

"You know you did. What were you doing here? Obviously you didn't come to tell me that you are still alive and doing fine."

He looked down. "I had to get something," he muttered.

"What? Tris, look at me."

"I said I had to get something. San—"

"Don't San me. When exactly did you think you'd let me know that you didn't *die*?"

"Look, I'm sorry, but there are other things to consider here."

"Other things? *Other things?* You mean than letting your wife know you're alive? Or coming home to your unborn child? If I had any sense I'd kill you myself, right now."

His gaze flickered downward to her tummy and an expression of longing and sadness crossed his face. Sandy almost reached out to him, but then he looked away and muttered something she couldn't understand.

"Would you speak up? What did you just say?"

He waved a hand. "Nothing." He went back to staring into his mug.

"I think I hate you," she said, her voice as flat and cold as an iceberg. It made her shiver. She squeezed the mug more tightly, until her fingers ached.

Tristan nodded sagely. "Trust me, San, I know." He lifted his mug to his lips, then frowned and set it down. "I kinda hate me, too."

"Well, you should." Sandy stood. She couldn't look at the changing expressions on his face. If she did she'd start feeling sorry for him and that would lead to feeling other things and she was not about to get sucked back into the evocative vortex of loving Tristan. She couldn't. Not now, when he'd proven that, even after a lifetime of love, he wasn't the trustworthy protector she'd always depended on.

She picked up his mug and took it to the sink along with hers. With her back to him, she blinked and looked up, trying to force the tears to flow backward, back to where they came from. But as usual, they were determined to fall. She rinsed the mugs and then splashed cold water onto her face.

Picking up a dish towel, she turned around and leaned back against the counter. Water she'd splashed onto the countertop seeped into her pajamas, wetting her lower back and sending a chill through her.

"So, wh-where have you been?" she stammered. It was the first question she wanted to ask and the last answer she wanted to hear.

She was dying to know, but she knew when he told her it was going to break her heart.

At the same time, a sickening dread told her she didn't have to wait to find out. She already knew what he was going to say. All this time, while she mourned him and ached for him and lay in her lonely bed, he was less than a mile away, at Boudreau's.

She waited for him to tell her that, but he didn't answer. He stood and limped over to stare out the French doors.

Sandy tried not to compare him with the man she'd last seen three months ago when he'd left for his monthlong work shift on the *Pleiades Seagull*. That man had been irritating, grouchy and depressed, but he'd been healthy and handsome and sun-browned despite the sunscreen she tucked into his duffel bag every time he headed back out to the oil rig. His hair had been streaked with golden-blond highlights put there by the sun, his shoulders had been broad and he, for all his faults, had been the man she knew and loved better than anyone in the world. The man she'd always known she could trust.

This person, although he sported Tristan's blazing dark brown eyes, straight nose and wide mouth, was not him. When that thought hit her, she sobbed. It was a small hiccup that barely made a sound, but Tristan's head turned toward her.

She put a hand over her mouth. That stiff, strong back, the lines of pain that scored his face from his nose to his chin, told a story of horror that she had not been a part of nor could ever understand. And that horror, those two long months of suffering, had changed him. His dark eyes were wide and too bright above sunken cheeks and pinched nostrils. His hair was too long, mousy brown and lifeless.

His back was ramrod straight, with a desperate dignity she'd never seen in him before. He'd lost at least fifteen pounds, maybe more, from a frame that had always been lean.

Her gaze traveled down his straight back and she pressed her hand hard against her lips and teeth, swallowing another sob. The pants he wore were too big, held up by a belt that had been tightened to the very last hole. The material was cotton and soaking wet, so it clung revealingly to his thighs and calves. She could see exactly what had happened to his right leg. Beneath the material, the right calf was no more than half the size of his left.

She remembered what Zach had told her about the strip of calf muscle that had been recovered from the water and identified as coming from Tristan's body. Just one of the several things that had convinced the authorities that Tristan could not have survived.

Sudden nausea, hot and sour and insistent, swept over her. She barely had time to turn to the sink before she threw up. It took forever for her stomach to stop heaving and spasming.

When she was done and had rinsed her mouth with a handful of water, she reached for the dish towel. With a shuddering moan, she dried her face and held the towel against it until she was certain that the spasms were dying down and she wouldn't gag anymore.

When she turned around and lowered the towel, Tristan was facing her. His face wasn't just ghostly—it had turned a sickly shade of green.

"Are you okay?" he asked.

She nodded.

His gaze dropped to her swollen belly. "You still have morning sickness?"

She shook her head.

"But—" he gestured vaguely.

"That? Oh, I don't know. Maybe a combination of no dinner, finding an intruder in my house and seeing my dead husband."

"How's—" His hand reached out, but stopped in mid-air. He stared at her baby bump, looking slightly bewildered.

"The baby?" she said, irritation rising and pushing the nausea away. "The baby is fine."

"San? I didn't mean for this to happen. I wasn't— I couldn't—" He stopped. Moving awkwardly, he stepped close to her. He lifted a hand and brushed her hair away from her forehead.

His hand was surprisingly warm, given his drenched state. Her head inclined naturally toward it. "Oh, Tris, I missed you so," she whispered.

He bent his head and pressed his forehead against hers. "I'm so sorry," he said, then pulled back. "Is it okay if I touch you?"

"You want to feel the baby?" she asked. "He kicks all the time these days."

Tristan gingerly laid his palm against her swollen tummy. Again, she was surprised at how warm it was.

He stood there, his hand caressing her belly, for a long time. "I can't believe it's been two months," he murmured.

Immediately, her anger swelled again. She pushed his hand away. "Two months in which I mourned you and thought I'd have to live the rest of my life without you. And if you'd had your way, I'd still think you were dead. I can't believe you came here and expected to leave without waking me."

She drew a shaky breath. "I don't understand why you didn't want to see me. To tell me you were alive. My husband would have crawled here if he couldn't walk, to let me see him and know that I had not lost the love of my life. My husband would not have made me grieve and mourn and hurt for two months."

"San, listen to me," Tristan said. "I was unconscious—"

"That is no excuse. What about Boudreau? Why didn't he come and tell me? A true friend of my husband would have let me know." She sucked in a harsh breath.

"Don't blame Boudreau."

"So, that is where you've been all this time? Right across the dock at Boudreau's cabin, less than a mile away? Oh, get out! Get out of here!" she cried, knowing as the words left her mouth that she didn't mean them.

Tristan stepped backward, away from her. He stared

at her for a moment, then nodded to himself as if he'd made a decision or come to a realization.

He smiled, but that wasn't aimed at her, either. It was the subtlest, saddest smile she'd ever seen. It made her want to cry, to go to him and take him in her arms and promise him that everything was going to be fine, even though she knew it wasn't.

Just about the time she'd decided he was too sick and wounded and in too much pain to be sent out to make his way back to Boudreau's, he turned and twisted the knob on the French doors and opened them.

"Tristan?" she said hoarsely. "Where are you going?"

He turned to look at her. "Back to Boudreau's," he said.

"Fine. Go. Stay there."

Awkwardly, he bent over and picked up a carved walking stick that she hadn't noticed on the floor beside the doors.

Once he had the stick and was leaning on it, he raised his gaze to her. "You said he."

"What?"

"You said *he* kicks all the time. The baby's a boy?"

His face was suddenly so filled with hope and longing that she thought her heart would shatter. "That's what the doctor said."

"A boy," he repeated, his voice tight. He turned back toward the door.

"You're still going?" she asked, surprised.

He didn't answer. He just stepped through the French doors and headed toward the overgrown path.

HE'D WALKED OUT. Now if he could just keep going. He hadn't wanted to leave. What he'd wanted to do was hold his wife, breathe in the sweet, familiar scent of her hair and touch her petal-soft skin.

He wanted her to wrap her arms around him and welcome him back. But even more than that, he'd wanted to lay his palms on her tummy and feel their baby—their son.

But she'd been so angry and hurt. He could not, would not, force himself back into her life.

He walked slowly and awkwardly across the patio and onto the slippery wet grass in the yard, hoping he could make it out of her sight before he collapsed from pain and fatigue.

There was no way he could make it over to Boudreau's cabin.

He heard Sandy's voice behind him.

"Could you come back in here, please?" she asked harshly. "You can't get up that hill tonight. Not with your leg in that condition. And even if you could, it's pitch-dark out there. You're liable to slip and end up drowning in gumbo mud. I don't want to be responsible for you *really* dying this time."

"You're not responsible for me," he yelled. "So don't worry about it."

"Not re—" She laughed bitterly. "What about those vows? Did they mean nothing? Of course I'm responsible for you. You're my husband. I—"

Tristan knew what she'd been about to say. *I love you.* But she hadn't been able to force out the words. That disturbed him. She'd never been shy about saying it. She'd sung it in the middle of church one Sunday when they were around ten years old. She'd written it on the chalk-boards in their classes several times every school year.

And she'd had it printed on a huge banner that hung suspended over the pulpit on the day of their wedding.

So it was ominous that she couldn't bring herself to say it on the night that her dead husband reappeared, alive and well—or almost well.

"Okay, then," she said, apparently taking his silence for agreement. "Get in here and let's get you settled in. Maybe you'd be comfortable in the guest room," Sandy said. "That way—"

"Wait a minute. I didn't say I'd stay." He couldn't spend the night anywhere close to her. Just a few whiffs of her hair had nearly driven him crazy.

His calf muscle cramped and the leg nearly gave way, a not-so-gentle reminder that no matter what he wanted, how much he longed to be close to her, no matter what seeing her did to him, the simple truth was that in his current condition, even if he wanted to make love with her, even if she invited him to, he couldn't. He was still weak, and his leg couldn't take the workout involved.

He shook his head and opened his mouth to tell her that he was fine and that walking through the overgrown paths that led to Boudreau's house wasn't a problem, but at that instant it began to rain hard. He grimaced.

"Well, you can't go now," she said ungraciously. "The ground will be even more slippery."

"I've got to get back. I need—" He stopped himself. He'd almost told her he needed the concoction that Boudreau had brewed up. It was a mixture of natural herbs and substances. According to Boudreau it had a natural painkiller, natural immune-system boosters and something to help him sleep. Without realizing on a conscious level that he'd moved, he found himself walking back across the patio and through the French doors.

Sandy handed him a towel. He took it while continuing to protest.

"Boudreau needs me," he said and saw in her face that she didn't believe him for a second.

"Boudreau needs *you*," she stated wryly. "He needs you? Come on, Tris, don't give me that. *I'm looking at you*." Sighing, she spread her hands in a supplicating gesture. "There was a time I believed every word you said. And it wasn't that long ago."

Tris saw her eyes begin to shine more brightly.

"Sandy, don't complicate this. I haven't been on my feet but a few days. There was no big conspiracy to keep me hidden. Certainly not from you. I came here as soon as I could walk this far."

She stared at him, shaking her head. "Right. You already told me you came here to get something. You probably thought I was still in Baton Rouge."

He shook his head. "No. I told you. It's very simple. Boudreau told me you were back."

"Damn it, Tristan, you're doing what you've always done. You're simplifying the situation beyond belief. You're acting like we're nine years old and you're trying to convince me that my dad won't hit me if I just go on and tell him it was me who dented the car with a baseball, if he's not drinking. Trouble is he was never not drinking. So you were wrong about that and you're wrong about his. You let me think you were dead. This can't be solved with a little strip bandage or a kiss from Mommy or a great, big *I'm sorry, pumpkin* from Daddy Dearest."

"Really, San? You think I'm oversimplifying anything? Look at me. Look. At. Me." He reached for her arm.

She recoiled, her eyes wide.

"You really believe that I think a little bandage will solve anything? You know me better than that. Or at least I thought you did. But you were never happy that I went to work on an oil rig, were you? You thought you were going to get a veterinarian and all you got was a blue-collar worker."

"I did hate you working offshore. And it was bad enough when you were just working there. When you started working for Homeland Security and were not only gone all the time, but distracted and worried when you were here, I hated it more."

He was surprised and she saw it in his face.

"That's right. I figured out what you were really doing on that rig. I don't understand why you couldn't tell me, but I can respect that you had to keep it secret. But letting me believe that you died? That was low." She studied him and her big blue eyes filled with tears. "Great, now I'm crying."

Tristan almost smiled. It didn't matter what was going on—wedding, funeral or silly movie, Sandy cried.

"I see that. I'm a little surprised, though. This isn't exactly a Hallmark commercial." He winced internally when he heard the sarcastic tone in his voice.

Her jaw tensed and she glared at him. "No. It's real life and it's not going away. We still need to talk about it."

"Talk about it?" His tone grated. "You mean like this? This isn't talking. You want to talk? Let's talk about this—you going back to Baton Rouge and staying with my mom. You'll be safe there."

"Safe? From what?"

"Did you miss the part where somebody tried to kill me? Or here's an idea. You and Mom should go somewhere, then. Somewhere nobody can trace you. Maybe go to DC and stay with Zach until I can clear all this up." He liked that idea. His old friend from childhood who'd become an NSA undercover agent would know how to keep them safe.

But Sandy's instant anger told him that he'd made another mistake. He could almost see smoke coming out of her ears.

She put one hand on her little baby bump and raised the other, her index finger pointing at him. "You're crazy if you think I am going to go away somewhere and leave you with Boudreau to take care of you."

"He's done okay so far," Tristan interjected.

"What? Look at you. You can barely walk. You're at least fifteen pounds—maybe more—underweight. Just where is the good job he did?"

"Right here." Tristan jabbed a thumb into his chest. "Right here. If it hadn't been for him I would be dead now."

Her eyes widened for an instant. "Oh, please, Tris. He's crazy and he's Cajun. That in itself is a lethal combination. What did he do? Give you a potion, then touch your forehead and say, 'Stand up and walk, I guarantee'?" Her tone was bitter as she mocked Boudreau.

She had the potion right, but what Boudreau had said was *You get your own self up and go swim. Or your legs gonna be withered and you be crawling around like a cripple the rest of your life, you.*

"What he did that saved me was not waste time trying to get me to a doctor or a hospital." Tristan cut a hand through the air. "Never mind. You're not going to believe a word I say right now, are you?"

"No, I'm not. You lied to me and that means you're

a lying liar. So no. I'll be assuming from now on that if your mouth is open, you're telling me a lie."

Tristan wiped his face with an unsteady hand.

"And look at you," she said. "If you don't get some real care, real medications and real cleansing and bandaging of those wounds, you could die of…of sepsis or infection." Her voice cracked as she continued to fight tears. "Why can't *you* go to DC? Why can't you tell Zach everything and let him protect you?"

Tristan shook his head. "Have you not heard a word I've said? I. Am. Not. The. Only. One. In. Danger. Should I repeat that, so you're clear?"

"Oh, I'm clear," she snapped. "I'm starting to see a lot of things clearly that I never saw before."

"Sandy—" Tristan started.

Sandy held up her hand. "Okay, then. We can both go, together. I'll drive."

But he was already shaking his head. "That doesn't work. If we do that, they'll get Boudreau."

"Then we can take him with us."

"Right. Take Boudreau. Besides, don't you think they know who Zach is by now? Just listen to me. Boudreau and I are going to work something out."

Sandy growled. "Ooooh, you've just got an answer for everything, don't you?" She clenched her fists. *"Everything."*

He couldn't help but stare at her. She was furious and he was so frustrated he could almost be tempted to wring her pretty neck, but when she got mad her eyes sparkled like sapphires, her cheeks turned a nice shade of pink and her hands wrapped protectively around her stomach. His heart felt as though it would burst with love for her and the baby.

"What are you staring at?" she snapped. "Could you try to help me come up with something? There has to be an answer."

Then suddenly, for no apparent reason, all the discussion and planning and rejecting of plans that he and Boudreau had been doing coalesced and he had it. He looked at her thoughtfully. "There is an answer," he said.

"Well, then, tell me. Why have you been beating around the bush—" She frowned at him. "Wait a minute. What are you talking about?"

But he didn't have to answer. She was already putting it together.

"Oh, no," Sandy said, shaking her head. "No, no, no! You are *not* setting yourself up as bait. They'll kill you."

"San, this is not a discussion and it's not up for a vote. It's the only way I can stop them."

"I said no!"

But Tristan didn't hear the word *no*. It was drowned out by a deafening explosion.

Chapter Five

Sandy shrieked involuntarily, but she couldn't hear herself. The explosion was too loud. It took her a fraction of a second to realize that the thunderous crash had actually been thunder. She remembered a quick, bright flash of light right before the noise.

Now, at least for the moment, the sky was dark and the explosion of thunder was fading to a deep rumble. In the suddenly dark kitchen, Sandy felt disoriented.

She lost her balance and fell against Tristan, who almost toppled. He caught himself against the facing of the French doors as she scrambled to get her feet under her and push away from him. But his arms slid around her and tightened and everything changed.

He held her tightly against him and all the things about him that she'd missed were right there, molded to her body, just as they should be. His strong arms, his warm broad chest and his chin, under which her head fit perfectly.

She slid her arms around his waist, trying not to think about how fragile he felt, with ribs sticking out on his sides and back. All she wanted to do was bury herself in him and drink in his familiar scent, and the hard-planed muscles under his smooth skin.

She turned her head and pressed her lips against his collarbone. "Tris," she whispered, "I missed you. I missed this so much."

He took a sharp breath. "Sandy, I—" He let go of her and stared through the glass panes of the doors. Just at that instant, lightning flashed again.

"Get down," he growled.

"What? What is it?" she asked.

"Keep your head down and go into the living room!" His hand raised, pointing, silhouetted by a flash of lightning.

She bent over and crept away from the French doors and into the living room. "What did you see?" she whispered.

"Shh," he said, cutting the air with his flattened hand.

Sandy waited, both irritated at his orders and grateful that he was there. Whatever he'd spotted in the flashes of lightning, she was glad she didn't have to face it on her own.

It was about five minutes before he came into the living room, massaging his forehead with his fingertips.

"Well?" she said. "What was out there?"

"Nothing. A trick of the lightning."

"Liar! Lying liar!" Sandy pulled herself upright by grabbing the door frame. "You expect me to believe that you acted like that over some waving branches? You used to play outside in thunderstorms."

He shrugged. "I'm just telling you what I saw. Something looked a little odd, but I never saw it again."

"Tristan, stop it, please. You're acting—I don't know—different. I know you saw something, or somebody, out there. Why can't you tell me like you always have, and we'll deal with it together."

"I'm not different. It's the situation. Someone tried to kill me. That same person wants to smuggle automatic handguns into the US. I'm the only one who even has a chance of identifying him. But, Sandy, I promise you. Nothing has changed. I'm still the same person I always was."

"N-nothing has changed?" she sputtered, as her tears changed to a bitter laughter. "You…can't be…serious!" she gasped, laughing. "Maybe you think you haven't changed, Tristan, but everything, *everything*, around you has. You may still live in the same world as before you fell overboard, but I don't. Did I tell you the rest of it? Did I tell you that they told me they'd found parts of your body that the…sharks didn't eat?"

She could barely repeat the words the ME had told her.

Tristan stood without moving, his face averted. She kept going. "I had to pick out a casket and talk to Father Duffy about a service. I had to choose flowers for the top of the casket." She stopped to take a deep breath.

"Do you understand what I'm saying? Do you get that *you were dead*? I had nothing to hold on to. No hope. *Nothing!*" She was almost out of control and she knew it. She had to calm down, for the baby's sake. He was wriggling and kicking, upset because she was upset.

"Sandy, I never meant—"

She held up her hands. "No!" she snapped. "I can't do this anymore. Just leave," she said brokenly. "Leave!"

"I'm not leaving. I don't know what I saw, but I'm not taking any chances."

"I knew it," she said flatly. "I knew you saw more than a branch. At this point, I feel more capable of facing whoever is out there than you. And you're upsetting the baby." She pressed her hand against the side of her belly where the bean's little foot was.

"Do whatever you want to. I don't care as long as I don't have to…look at you." She turned on her heel and stalked down the hall to her bedroom with as much dignity as she could muster.

THE BEDROOM DOOR SLAMMED. Tristan spat a curse in Cajun French and slammed the heel of his palm into the door facing. He cursed again when his hand throbbed with pain. "Ow. *Fils de putain—*" He clamped his jaw, shook his hand and tried to get his anger under control.

In one way, he understood why Sandy was so angry at him. When his dad died right before his high school graduation, he'd been furious and terrified. As much as he'd hated his father's job, he had loved his father. But with him gone, Tristan had known that the future he'd hoped to have as a veterinarian was impossible. He'd had to drop out of school and take a job on the oil rigs, just like his old man.

His family was there, too, with all the churning emotions Sandy had described. The only difference was that his dad hadn't shown up later.

She'd had to experience the trauma and grief of finding out he was dead, and then the equally traumatic experience of finding out he was alive. Of course she'd be angry, at least at first.

He was angry, too.

There had been a time, not too long ago, when he'd have sworn that he and Sandy had never and would never have a serious fight. They'd known each other practically all their lives and had learned long ago that they were perfectly suited for each other.

But then he'd started keeping secrets. He'd never told her about his job with Homeland Security. He'd lied to her and he'd pretended he was dead.

Lightning was still flashing in the sky, fainter than before. Tristan took a step closer to the door and looked out. There wasn't as much rain and he wasn't hearing thunder anywhere. The storm was over.

Of course, he knew as well as Sandy that it would be days before their electricity came back on. Meanwhile, at least they had candles and a camping stove. They were in the laundry room, just off the kitchen.

Before he could start in that direction, he saw something move outside. He froze. It was a larger shadow among the smaller, darker ones out beyond the patio. The shadow was noticeable because it was moving, not just quivering as the raindrops hit the leaves or swaying in the shifting wind.

His muscles tensed, but he remained perfectly still, his eyes straining as he stared at the shadow, waiting for it to move again.

He stole a glance into the living room, where his dad had kept a pair of guns hanging above the fireplace. One was a double-barreled shotgun and the other was some kind of rifle.

Tristan didn't like guns. Never had, not even when he was a kid and almost all of his friends wanted to play cops and killers.

He stared at the two weapons now, trying to decide which one he could carry more easily. The rifle was less bulky than the shotgun. He took it down and loaded it.

When he stood, the rifle's weight played havoc with the careful balance he'd just begun to learn that allowed him to favor his right leg. But he couldn't go out there without a weapon. He had no idea who was lurking in the shadow of the swamp, but he'd seen enough of a silhouette to know for a fact it was human, a two-legged rather than a four-legged predator.

Tristan set the alarm and carefully unlocked the French doors, making as little noise as possible. He chambered a round in the rifle and slipped out onto the patio. It was fortunate that the electricity was off. Otherwise the motion-detector lights on the patio and garage would come on, spotlighting him. When he reached the far corner of the garage, he stopped. His leg was aching badly and he was sweating in the rain-soaked air.

He stood with his back straight and solid against the exterior of the garage, as close as he could get to the corner without being seen. Then, carefully, keeping his gun at his side, he angled his head around and took a look at the area where he'd seen the shadow moving.

And there he was. Tristan took a quick mental picture of what he saw, then pulled back, flattening himself against the wall of the garage again. Staying alert to any sound, he ran the picture his brain had made. What all had he seen?

First, the shadow was not as tall as he'd initially thought. Could it be a kid, sneaking around, looking for alligators to poach?

He shook his head. No. The way the man stood upright, not crouched, the way he moved his upper body and the shape and size of his torso and head, told Tristan he was a full-grown man.

But what innocent reason would a man have to sneak around out here? The answer was, none. He had to be someone connected with the man who'd ordered Tristan's murder. But that man thought Tristan was dead. A horrible notion hit him.

As far as anyone knew, he *was* dead. So there was only one explanation for why the intruder was sneaking around. He was spying on Sandy.

Tristan glanced up at the sky, where clouds still hung low. He wished the moon would come out, but any light that illuminated the lurker's face would also illuminate his, so if the clouds parted, he needed to be ready for anything. He decided to take another look. When he angled his head around the corner of the building, his fears were realized.

The man held binoculars to his eyes. Even in the dark the vague shape of the man holding the binoculars and the direction he was looking were unmistakable. He was looking at the house. He was spying on Sandy.

The surprise morphed into anger, undercut by a gnawing fear. Who was he? Who had sent him?

Tristan picked up the rifle and took a deep breath. He had a lot to concentrate on. He had to aim the rifle, keep his balance, maintain his cool and keep an eagle eye on the other man.

He knew he was at a disadvantage, because he was to the man's left, so he'd have to step out into the open before he could even aim the rifle.

But when he peeked one more time, the lurker had lowered the binoculars and bent down. He was sneaking away.

After the man crawled for about a third of the way around the edge of the yard, he stood and ran toward the road. Tristan sneaked around the garage, hugging the wall, trying for one last glimpse of him.

He had reached the road now and was sprinting. In

the sky, the thunderclouds had begun to break up and a bit of pale moonlight shone through.

Tristan squinted. Even from this far away, as the man quickly ran toward the road, he looked familiar. He looked like Murray Cho.

"YOU HAVEN'T KEPT UP your end of the bargain," the voice said through the phone Murray held.

"But…I've done everything I can," Murray stammered. "It's not that easy. Have you ever tried to stalk someone?" The instant he heard himself say those words, he regretted them.

What the hell was he doing asking a question like that to someone who was ruthless enough to kidnap an innocent boy to coerce his father into spying on another innocent person?

The man could have stalked dozens of people and killed them for all Murray knew. His gruff, guttural voice certainly *sounded* cold and hard enough to be a killer's.

"Are you *kidding* me?" the man said with a harsh laugh. "You listen to me, Murray. My boss wants this information and he wants it fast! What's the big holdup?"

"I can't go around there in the daytime and it's hard to see anything at night. It's a new moon right now and—"

"I'm warning you, you little whiner—"

"Hold on," Murray said with much more bravado than he felt. "I'll not do anything until I find out if my son is alive—" He stopped because his voice broke. He cleared his throat. "Alive and well. I want to talk to him."

"You're skating on thin ice. There's only so much my boss will put up with and he's already had more than one problem this year. He's extremely nervous."

"I want to see my son. Kill me, but I won't do anything until I know he's alive."

"You can't see him until my boss sees what you've got," the man said harshly. "But I can let you hear his voice. Will that do?"

"Yes. Yes. Please."

Murray heard the other man cursing. Then he heard him calling loudly. "Get that punk in here." Pause. "You don't need to know why." More cursing. "Over here. Sit," he ordered.

Holding his breath, Murray listened for every sound. The man was obviously talking to his son. His heart squeezed in his chest until he thought it would burst from the pressure.

Then he heard his son's voice and a half sob caught in his throat. "Patrick!" he cried. "Patrick, are you all right?"

"Dad? What's going on? I don't get it—"

"All right, that's enough. Hey, you guys. Get him out of here."

"Dad! I think we're at—" Patrick's voice was cut off by an unmistakable sound. It was the sound of a fist hitting flesh.

"No!" Murray shouted. "Don't you touch my boy!"

"He's okay," the man said. "He just needs to learn to do what he's told and not try to be a smart-ass."

"He will. I promise he will."

"Listen to me. I don't need promises. I need action. Now, I'm going to give you a number to call and we'd better hear from you in forty-eight hours with the proof the boss needs, or neither you nor your son will see another sunset. Got it?"

Murray ached to tell the man what he wanted to know.

All he had to do was report that he'd seen a man with Mrs. DuChaud in her home through the binoculars, and he could get his son back safe and sound. He hoped.

But just as he opened his mouth he realized he'd be giving away everything with no promise of return. He couldn't prove to the kidnappers that the man with Mrs. DuChaud was Tristan DuChaud. He needed that proof as leverage.

"Yes. Got it," Murray said. With any luck he had the perfect way to ensure his son's safety. To get the proof he needed, he'd have to risk getting a lot closer to the house, and going in the daytime. That was not a problem. He'd do anything he had to in order to get a photo of Tristan DuChaud, because that was the only thing he could do to save his boy's life.

Chapter Six

The first thing Sandy noticed when she woke up the next morning was the smell of coffee. For a fleeting instant the dark aroma took her back to the days just after she'd found out she was pregnant, when Tristan was so excited about the baby. Knowing how much she loved coffee, he'd gone on a safari through South Louisiana looking for the absolute best decaf coffee in the state.

But on the heels of that poignant memory came harsh reality. This wasn't those early days. This was now.

Tristan was back from the dead and he'd spent the night in their house. She'd known he had because after she'd stormed out of the kitchen and down the hall to the master bedroom, she'd listened for the French doors to slam. They didn't.

She'd lain there for a few seconds, wondering if he'd left quietly. Then she heard the familiar, comforting beep of the alarm being armed. She'd gone right to sleep.

Sitting up and taking another whiff of the aroma of coffee sifting into the room, Sandy realized it had been five and a half months—her entire pregnancy so far—since she'd wanted a cup of coffee.

She turned on the lamp, but nothing happened. She'd forgotten the electricity was out. How had Tristan made coffee?

And what was the other aroma? Bacon? It must have been in the freezer. Maddy had put all the food that made Sandy nauseous into the freezer, and bacon had been a big culprit.

Right now, however, both the coffee and the bacon smelled heavenly. Sandy didn't care how Tristan had made them. She just hoped her nausea didn't come back as soon as she walked into the kitchen and got the full effects of the smells.

She jumped up, took a quick shower and dressed in a white skirt and pink top. The skirt had to go on top of her baby bump, so it came to just below her knees instead of just above her ankles, where it was supposed to be. But it looked fresh and new and maybe it would be a portent for the morning with Tristan.

When she stepped through the door into the kitchen, she understood how Tristan had cooked. He'd used the gas stove they kept in the laundry room for these circumstances. He'd used one burner to fry the bacon and had boiled water in a pan to make boiled coffee, sometimes known as hobo coffee.

He was at the kitchen table, sipping at a mug and playing with his food.

"What are you doing here?" she asked grumpily.

"Didn't you say you didn't care what I did, as long as you didn't have to look at me? I slept on the couch. I'll sleep outside tonight if you want me to."

"I *don't* want you to. I don't need you to protect me. You know how I know?" she asked. "I know because you left me alone for over two months. If you were so sure I needed protection, why didn't you come home? It's not like it was a long trip."

Tristan grimaced. "I couldn't."

She knew that. Of course he couldn't have, because he was in bed, at the very best too weak to stand, at worst, in a coma. She knew she'd have to ask Boudreau what had gone on during those weeks, because Tristan would never tell her.

"You went to a lot of trouble to find the gas stove and make breakfast. Why aren't you eating?"

He looked up at her and smiled, a tired smile that made her heart start to break. "I made it for you," he said. "You've lost weight and, at risk of sounding clichéd, you're eating for two."

"I've been nauseated at even the *thought* of bacon for months," she said, suppressing a smile. "And didn't you remember that all I could drink was grape juice?"

Tristan looked blank for a second, then his face turned a bright pink. He ducked his head. "Sorry," he said as he pushed his chair back from the table. "I'd forgotten that. I'll make you some toast."

"No." She put her hand on his arm. "Don't get up. The bacon and the coffee both smell good. I want to try them."

He looked down at her hand on his arm and, embarrassed, she pulled it away and sat down. She poured herself some coffee from the pot at her right hand, added a little sugar and stirred it. "Decaf?" she asked.

"Sure," he said, picking up a piece of bacon, then putting it down. He picked it up a second time and pressed it against the plate to break it. The bottom half shattered. "Bacon might be a little crisp," he said, sticking the half that was still intact into his mouth.

Sandy chuckled. "We never came to a compromise

about bacon, did we?" She picked up a piece and took a bite. "It *is* crispy," she said, making a face.

"That's what I just said."

She glanced up. He sounded irritated. "What's wrong?" she asked.

He shook his head and sighed.

"Don't sigh at me. What's wrong with you?"

He grabbed the wooden arms of the chair and shoved himself up out of the seat. "That's not the question," he barked. "The question is what's wrong with you? With *us*?" He pointed back and forth between them.

She watched him warily. She'd never seen him angry, not at her, and it sent a heart-thumping burst of adrenaline through her. An instant later, the baby stirred restlessly and she rubbed the side of her belly. "Are you saying—"

His gaze went to her hand and the look on his face made her heart hurt. "I'm saying I don't understand your attitude. I thought you'd at least be happy to see me."

Sandy gave him a shocked look. "Happy? I suppose you mean because you were so thrilled to see me and you came all this way. In case you don't remember, when I saw you, you were trying to sneak in and out of here without me catching you. Name one thing—just one—about it that should make me *happy*?"

He leveled his gaze on her in a game of visual chicken. "Maybe the fact that I wasn't dead?" he said softly.

She couldn't hold his gaze. Of course he was right. She *had* been stunned and thrilled that he was alive, after she'd recovered from the initial shock. Then she'd woken up thinking she was having another hallucination. There had been no room inside her for happiness.

"When I first saw you—" She held up a hand. "No. I'm not going to go into all that again. Tristan, you know how I feel. If you can't accept that I have a right to be angry, then…well, I don't know what else I can tell you."

He didn't like her answer. There was no mistaking that. A muscle in his lean jaw ticked and at his temple, a vein stood out in sharp relief. "Oh, great," he said, his voice heavy with irony. "That explains everything."

She opened her mouth to spit out a sharp retort, but he kept talking.

"I'm headed over to Boudreau's," he said through gritted teeth, "but first I'm going to take a look around the area where I saw Murray last night. Now that the sun's up, I might be able to find a clue as to what he was doing here this time."

"Whoa! What?" Sandy gasped. "You saw Murray? Are you talking about Murray Cho?"

Tristan muttered a curse under his breath. He obviously had not meant to say that out loud. He opened his mouth, then closed it, then opened it again.

"Damn it, Tristan. Stop trying to not tell me anything. I need to know what's going on so I can take care of myself."

"Fine. Yes, it was Murray Cho. He was sneaking around in the weeds on the other side of the garage."

"Murray? But he's in Gulfport. He moved."

"All I can say is I saw him and recognized him. I can't tell you why he was here. That's why I'm going to check," he said with exaggerated patience.

She crossed her arms, a little creeped out. "I saw Murray's son peeking in the master bedroom window on the day of your funeral. Murray was behind him."

"What were they doing?"

Sandy shook her head. "I assumed Patrick had wandered around the house and was peeking in to see what he could see. Murray followed him to stop him." She paused. "How are you so sure this was Murray?"

"I saw his face when the moon came out for a few seconds."

"What do you think he was doing here?" she said. "Do you know he was involved in bringing down the smugglers?"

Tristan nodded. "Yeah. Boudreau told me he showed up at the seafood warehouse threatening to take them all down."

"Did Boudreau tell you he shot first? Boudreau killed the oil rig captain without blinking an eye." She sent him a sidelong glance. "Maddy told me Boudreau said, 'This is for Tristan,' or something like that."

Tristan's brows shot up. "No. He never mentioned that, but I suppose he wouldn't." He was quiet for a moment.

"There's something else about Murray, isn't there? You said 'this time.'"

He looked down at his hands and back up at her. "Did I?"

She set her jaw and stared at him. "Don't be coy. You said, 'What he was doing here this time.'"

"Have you got your laptop?" he asked.

"No. As a matter of fact, somebody stole it from the nursery. It was gone when I got back here." The look on his face unnerved her. "Why?"

"Boudreau was checking on the house a couple of weeks ago and he saw Murray coming out the French doors with what looked like your laptop."

"And he's sure it was Murray. A hundred percent sure?"

"What is it with you and Murray?"

"Nothing," Sandy said. "I felt bad that he thought he

had to leave Bonne Chance after the incident with the smugglers at his seafood warehouse. He always seemed so nice and quiet. But this makes the third time he's been sneaking around. What do you think he's looking for?"

"He's watching you."

That surprised her. "Me? Why? Are you sure?"

"Oh, I'm sure."

Sandy stared at him. His tone had been almost amused. "I don't get it. How can you be?"

"Because you were here in the kitchen and he was directly across the yard, in that patch of weeds, with binoculars."

Sandy looked in the direction Tristan pointed. It had been frightening to see Patrick Cho and his father standing at her bedroom window on the day of Tristan's funeral. But as she pictured Murray lurking out there in the dark and watching her through binoculars, she felt sick.

She turned back to Tristan, but he was gone. She hadn't heard him open the door. She stepped out onto the patio and looked in the direction of the dock, but he'd already disappeared into the heavy canopy of branches, weeds and vines that hid the path from casual view. He'd gone back to Boudreau's cabin.

She went inside, her fury at him rising with every breath she took. How dare he act so supercilious? He wasn't the only person who'd been hurt. She'd nearly died of grief and unbearable loss when she found out he was dead. The only thing that had kept her alive during those first hours and days was the knowledge that if she took her life, she'd be taking another innocent life with her.

She hadn't been able to even think about doing that to her baby. Instead, she'd vowed to make sure her child lacked for nothing and knew everything she could possibly tell him...or her...about his father.

"I swear, little bean, sometimes I don't know why I bother. What's the matter with him? Staying away for my safety. What a jerk. If everyone thinks he's dead, how could he possibly draw the bad guys to me?" She stopped. "Unless— Oh, dear God."

She sat down and cradled her tummy in her hands. "That's what's bothering Tristan—your daddy," she said. "Murray Cho is working for...for whoever tried to kill him. He must have been sent by them to watch me, to see if I acted strangely. He must be trying to find out if Tristan is really dead. Because if Tristan is alive, he could ruin them—maybe even put them in prison.

"What if Murray saw him, bean?"

BY LATE AFTERNOON, Sandy was climbing the walls. She'd tried to distract herself by taking inventory of their stock of food and planning what to cook, but that only kept her occupied for about a half hour.

So she decided to practice her crochet. She'd taken a class and now she was knitting the bean a pair of booties, but they were looking a little more like gloves than booties. Her stitches stuck out here and there.

Finally, she tossed the crocheting aside and stood and looked out the French doors toward the path to the dock, but nothing was stirring. Maybe Tristan had decided he needed some peace and quiet, so he was planning to stay at Boudreau's.

It had been around five hours or so since he'd left. Under normal circumstances he occasionally spent all afternoon and sometimes all evening with his Cajun friend, talking and fishing or just drinking beer.

But these weren't normal circumstances and Sandy wanted to talk to her husband.

She flung the French doors open and stepped out onto the patio. "You're not going to leave me here all day and night by myself, Tristan DuChaud. Not now that I know you're alive, you lying liar." She patted the side of her belly where the bean was beginning to kick.

"Hey, bean, it's okay. Don't worry. I'm not really *that* mad at your daddy. It's just that he's the stubbornest, most arrogant man in three counties." The baby kicked her again.

"Okay, okay," she whispered. "I'm through being mad. We're going to go over to Boudreau's place and find your daddy. And when we do, I'm playing the alone-and-scared card. Because if there's one thing you need to remember, it's that your daddy might be stubborn, but your mama is downright obstinate." She chuckled. "With us for parents, you're going to be a piece of work, aren't you?"

She walked briskly across the yard to the overgrown path. Before she stepped into the tangle of weeds and vines, she glanced toward the place where Tristan had said that Murray Cho had been hiding and watching her. *Through binoculars.* She drew her shoulders up as a frisson of aversion slithered down her spine.

She stood still for a moment and closed her eyes. Did she feel someone's eyes on her? She didn't think so. But would she, even if there were someone watching her? She had no idea.

Just as she put out a hand to brush away hanging vines so she could step onto the path, she heard something—footsteps—coming her way. Maybe it was Tristan. Her heart fluttered a little bit.

But what if it was Murray? Suddenly frightened, she turned to run back across the yard, but the person who'd been trampling down the path ran slap into her, grunting at the impact.

"Tristan!" she cried as he stumbled against her, trying not to lose his footing on the slippery leaves and sticky vines on the ground. She heard a muffled thump as his walking stick hit the ground.

"Sandy! What are you doing out here? Where do you think you're going?"

"To find you. You've been gone for hours," she complained.

"Well, you told me to leave, and in no uncertain terms, either."

"I did not," she shot back, but then she remembered. She'd said, *Leave. Just leave.*

"I didn't mean for you to stay gone. I was afraid you weren't coming back. It hurt so much I wanted to die when I found out you were dead. Staying away, letting me think you were dead, just might be the worst thing any man has ever done to his wife."

He shook his head. "I think that's a bit of an exaggeration," he said in that reasonable, mockingly patient tone that always made her furious. And right now was no different.

"Oh!" she shrieked, doubling her hands into fists. "I swear you make me so mad, I could—I could—"

"What, Sandy?" Tristan asked, stepping toward her, his pale face drawn, his eyes dark and deep as brown bottle glass in the sun. He was in her face and she couldn't look away.

"That's just it. I don't know. What I'd like to do is reach into your heart and pull out the man I married. Because you're not him. You think you haven't changed? Well, you're wrong. You've changed, a lot."

Tristan's jaw tensed.

"And I'm not talking about just since you went overboard. No. It's been going on for a long time now. A year, at least." She stopped, calculating in her head. "Oh, my God, that's it, isn't it? You became a Homeland Security agent a year ago." She stopped, but he didn't say anything. "Isn't it?" she cried.

Tristan's face hadn't changed, but his dark brown eyes seemed to get even darker. "Yes," he said.

She didn't want to look at him. She'd told him the truth. He was not the person she'd known all her life, not the person she'd married. She turned away. "I don't know who you are anymore."

She felt his gaze burning into her back, but he didn't say a word.

"I think Murray is working for the man who tried to have you killed," she said.

For a couple of seconds, Tristan stayed quiet. Finally he said, "I do, too."

"You do?" She stared at him. "What are you going to do? We've got to stop him!"

"That's what Boudreau and I have been talking about."

"Tell me something. If you're so worried about me, why are we still here? Why haven't we gone somewhere else—somewhere safe, where I can have my baby without having to worry that his father is going to be dead before he's born?" She took a deep breath.

"And while you're explaining things, what are we supposed to do without you? What is your child supposed to do?" Anger flared inside her and constricted her throat.

She struggled to take a full breath. "I'll promise you

this, Tristan Francois DuChaud," she continued, walking up to him and jabbing her forefinger into the middle of his chest. "I will protect this baby with all my power. I'll risk *anything*," she said. "My life—even yours—for this baby's life."

Tristan grabbed her by the upper arms and pulled her so close that his face was a mere fraction of an inch from hers.

"You don't think I would do the same thing?" he said through clenched teeth. After all this time—after a lifetime together—are you telling me you don't know that? You don't know that I would die for you or for our baby? But I don't intend for it to come to that. Boudreau and I are working on a plan to keep you and the baby safe until we can figure out who is behind all this and how to get to him."

"Stop it," Sandy cried. She'd never had the full effect of Tristan's blazing eyes boring into hers in anger. "Let go. You're scaring me."

He let go instantly—so fast that Sandy had to catch herself to keep from losing her balance. The anger drained from his face. "Sorry. I didn't mean to do that."

"That's just it, Tristan. You didn't mean to scare me. You didn't mean to make me think you were dead. You didn't *mean to do* a lot of things. But you have. And I know it's because of that stupid job. Why would you do that? Why on earth would you become an undercover agent? That's not you."

He looked at her for a moment, then turned toward the house. "Go inside and go to bed. You need some sleep. I'll lock up the house and put the alarm on."

"No. I want an answer."

But she didn't get one. Tristan started walking in his

awkward way toward the house. She had no choice but to follow him or stand outside alone. Inside, he set the alarm and asked her if she wanted coffee.

She shook her head.

"Yeah, me neither," he said. He walked down the hall into the master bedroom.

Sandy didn't know what to say, so she followed him. Finally, he spoke.

"I never wanted to work on the oil rigs," he said. "I saw my dad turn hard and distant. He was out there more than he was home. I hated that and I swore I would never do that to my—" He stopped.

"To your family," Sandy supplied, hearing the bitter note in her voice.

"But I had no choice."

"Are you blaming me?"

He shook his head. "No, of course not. I'm not blaming anyone. Dad died and I had to forget about veterinary school and get a job. The oil rigs have always paid the best.

"It happened. Nobody's fault. But when Homeland Security contacted me and told me they wanted an agent on the *Pleiades Seagull* who was a local and would never be suspected of being undercover for the government, it sounded like a way of making the job meaningful. I wouldn't just be one man on one of the thousands of oil rigs in the Gulf of Mexico—I'd be doing something for my country." He shrugged.

Sandy's heart wrenched, listening to his dreams. She took a step toward him, reached out and put her hand on his shoulder. "I guess I never realized how much it meant to you to be able to contribute to the safety and security of the country."

His back stiffened. "I'll sleep on the sofa in the living room," he said flatly. "That way I can see and hear anyone who might be sneaking around the house. We'll have the alarm, but I'd like to get a look at whoever it is that's hanging around. If I do see someone, I might set off the alarm myself just to be able to get to him and beat the crap out of him."

She scowled at him. "Don't even try," she said with more than a dash of sarcasm. "You couldn't beat the crap out of a stuffed toy bear in the condition you're in."

Chapter Seven

As soon as the words were out of her mouth, Sandy was sorry. Tristan's face went still and his mouth flattened.

"You've always underestimated me, San. I'm not sure why."

"I'm not underestimating you. I'm looking at you. You're injured. You don't have your strength back. Of course you can't fight until you're healed. But you're not by nature a fighter, anyhow. You're a romantic. A peacekeeper." She held up a hand when Tristan started to speak.

"I know. I know you can take care of yourself—and me. I've never doubted that. But you've never been the type to go looking for trouble."

He shook his head. "That's not what I'm doing. I'm talking about protecting my house. Protecting you and the baby. But there you go, underestimating me again." He looked down then back up at her. "I'll see you in the morning."

"Tristan?" she called out just as he was about to close the door behind him.

He looked at her. "Yeah?"

"Don't go."

"I thought you were so mad at me you could do something drastic."

"I am— I was."

"So what were you thinking of?" he asked, his mood lightening. His mouth turned up in a mischievous smile. "This?" And he drew her to him and kissed her.

Sandy was completely caught off guard. She wouldn't have been surprised if he'd shaken her or pushed her out of the way and strode out of the house. But kiss her? That, she'd never suspected.

All those thoughts flitted through her head in a split second. Practically no time. Yet time enough for him to begin to nibble at her lips and flick them with his tongue in a tentative invitation for her to open her mouth.

She had no problem complying with that request. Nothing about this part of their life together had changed at all. She was still in love with her husband, still turned on by the faintest pressure of his lips on hers, the quickest, lightest nibble on the flesh of her lips and tongue and every breathtaking inch that his hands caressed as they moved from her back around to the sides of her breasts.

She moaned and opened her mouth, using her tongue the way he was using his, to thrust and explore and ease her way closer and closer. She felt faint with desire, a sensation she'd known—*known*—she would never feel again, because the man she'd loved ever since they were children was dead. And if it hadn't been for his child who was growing within her, her heart would have died, too.

From long before they'd experimented with something more than kissing or innocent hand holding or hugging, she'd been insatiably drawn to him. She'd wanted him touching her, molding his body to hers, loving her, all the time. They'd both been seventeen, too young and yet plenty old enough.

Still, once they'd done *it*, there was no turning back. They had loved each other all their lives. And that love had always been multifaceted. It embodied every kind of love in existence: sexual, sensual, platonic, innocent and jaded all at once. They were not perfect people, by any means, but they were perfect together.

As the fuel of desire flowed through Sandy, her longing for the man she had and would always love and whom she'd thought she'd lost forever grew until she was on the verge of bursting into climactic flame just from his mouth on hers and his hands caressing her.

"This is probably not a good idea," he murmured against her lips.

"You started it," she teased, but she felt the change in him. He was withdrawing. She didn't know what his problem was, but she wasn't about to give up so easily.

She had always wanted him, but at this moment, her desire for him was a burning urge like nothing she'd ever felt before. He'd been dead and now he was alive, his skin vibrant and hot, his body coursing with life. She slid her arms around his waist and kept kissing him.

For an instant he yielded. He deepened his kiss, sending electric pulses through her, each one bringing her closer and closer to the brink of climax. She pressed her body against his.

"No," he said. He stiffened and pulled away.

Sandy moaned. "Don't stop now," she whispered.

"San," he said, putting his hands on her upper arms and holding her at arm's length. He met her gaze, then he looked away. "I'm not sure I can...do this," he muttered.

She looked up at him with a small smile. "I'm sure

you can," she said, sliding her fingers across the front of his pants.

He stepped away from her and turned his back. "That's not what I'm talking about."

"Then what?" she asked.

He said something, too softly for her to understand.

She went to him and tried to wrap her arms around him from behind, but he pulled away and turned, his face dark with anger.

"Damn it, Sandy, I can barely walk. My damn leg will never hold up to—" He gestured vaguely.

Sandy gave a short laugh. "You don't have to. I can definitely handle that workload myself. I'll be on top and—"

"I said no!" he snapped, looking cornered.

Sandy held up her hands, palms out. She took a step backward. "Fine. Sorry," she said. Her whole body ached with the pain of thwarted desire as well as hurt at his rejection.

He shot her a glare, then said, "Okay, well, I'm going to lie down on the couch."

She closed her eyes and then opened them again. "I'd feel a lot better if you'd stay in my—our—room," she said. "If you want, you can sleep on the daybed."

Tristan looked at the small bed then back at her. "Nope. I'm not sleeping on some child-sized bed in my own bedroom in my own house. You can forget that. If you want me to stay in this room—our room—it will be in my bed with my wife."

At his words, the flame inside her that he'd so successfully damped just a few seconds ago reignited.

It was a flame that had been banked for a long time. Too long. It had been a long time since she'd been in the same bed with her husband. Before he'd fallen or been pushed overboard, he'd been on the rig for a month. The last time he'd come home she'd been dealing with a severe bout of morning sickness. Amazed, she realized it had been over four months since they had made love.

"Good night," Tristan said, heading out the door again. "Get some sleep."

"Wait!" she cried.

He stopped and stood in the doorway, rubbing his temple with his fingers.

She looked at him. He was a miracle by anyone's account. He'd been declared dead. He'd had funeral rites spoken over a casket that supposedly contained his remains. Now he had returned. And she needed him as close to her as was humanly possible. "All right," she said.

"All right what?" he asked, earning a glare from her. "Just so we're clear."

"Please sleep in here with me, in the bed," she said. "I need you with me."

He nodded slowly, his dark eyes shimmering like gems in the low light.

IT WAS A long time before Tristan came to bed. Sandy didn't know exactly what time he'd slipped beneath the covers, but when she awoke at 2:00 a.m., her heart pounding and her breath puffing in shallow gasps, he was there.

He'd put his hand on her arm and bent his head to her ear. "Go back to sleep, *cher.* I'm here now."

"Tristan?" she whispered, turning over and snuggling into his arms. "I heard something."

She felt him stiffen slightly and couldn't tell if it was because she'd turned a casual gesture of comfort into an embrace or because of what she'd said.

"I know," he said. "It's probably the wind."

"Probably? You think it might be something to worry about?" She snuggled closer.

His breath caught. "San, be careful."

"Oh, Tristan, did I hurt you? I'm sorry," she said.

"No, but you're going to wake us up if you don't stop talking."

She pressed her nose into the side of his neck. He smelled the same as he always had. Warm, clean, masculine. She'd never quite figured out what the combination of scents was. Something like soap and shaving cream and maybe a little toothpaste, mingled with a masculine undertone that was uniquely his. To her, he smelled like the man she'd sworn to live the rest of her life with.

"Are you sure you want me to be careful?" she whispered into his ear.

He shivered and she felt goose bumps raise on the sensitive skin beneath his ear. She blew on it, hoping to keep the goose bumps there for as long as possible.

"Is that careful enough?" she whispered. She shouldn't be trying to seduce him. She knew that. For one thing, she was still angry with him for not letting her know that he was alive for two whole months. Granted, he'd spent most of one of those months either unconscious or asleep, recuperating on any day of those two months. But Boudreau could have walked over and saved her hours and days of horrible grief and sadness. He could have told her that Tristan was alive.

But even more than anger, she was feeling a deep, exquisitely painful yearning for him. He was her husband and it had been way too long since they'd made love.

"What are you doing?" he asked, his voice breathy and deep.

"I'm doing what I thought you wanted me to do," she said, thinking she was treading on dangerous ground. If he chose to get annoyed with her for bringing that up, she'd lose her chance to make love with her husband.

Tristan rose up on his elbow and looked down at her. "And what's that, *cher*?" he whispered.

She smiled up at him, knowing from the tone of his voice and the soft look in his dark eyes that he'd made his decision. He was ready to be her husband, her living, breathing, virile husband.

"Welcoming you home," she breathed, barely even making a sound. But she knew he heard it and understood it. He pulled her into his arms and kissed her with as much intensity, as much desire, as much love as he ever had.

Sandy melted into his embrace and took his kiss, fully, returning it the same way. When he touched and caressed her, when he kissed her, she felt like an ethereal, exquisite fairy, floating in a beautiful world that belonged to just the two of them, her and Tristan. Three, now that the little bean was with them.

Tristan slid a hand down over her rounded belly. "Hi, bean," he whispered. Then he bent his head and kissed the taut skin. "Hey, my little boy. My son. How're you doing in there?"

Sandy felt his hand travel down the slope of the baby bump and farther, to caress her intimately. When his fingers touched her, a painfully thrilling spasm shot through her with the speed and sense of an electric shock. She cried out.

Immediately, he tried to pull his hand away, but she held it there with hers. "Don't stop, please. It's been so long."

"I know," he gasped. "I didn't mean to leave you alone so long." He bent to lick and nibble on her distended nipples as his arousal hardened against her thigh.

Sandy arched her back, the twin sensations of his mouth on her nipples and his fingers inside her driving her to a second climax, stronger than the first. While she was still receiving little aftershocks of that second climax, Tristan suckled on a nipple.

"Tris, just so you know, I'm getting some—"

He jerked backward so quickly that, even though she was in the middle of explaining what he might encounter, it shocked Sandy.

"What? Did you hear something?" she asked, but she was pretty sure he wasn't fixated on anything that had happened outside.

He was wiping his mouth and staring at her breast. "Was that—" he asked, looking pale.

She nodded and smiled. "Milk. Just a little bit. I've been noticing little droplets every so often."

"I'm not sure I want to know that," he muttered.

She was still shaky from her climaxes, so when she reached out for him, her hand trembled. "It's fine, Tris. It's perfectly natural. In fact, some couples do this. It stimulates the production of the milk and makes it easier for—"

"Okay," he snapped, swiping a hand through the air. "Could you just stop?" He pulled away from her and got up. "I'm going to sleep on the couch, like I said I would in the first place," he said more calmly. "I need some sleep and I'm sure you do, too."

He stood, steadying himself against the bedpost as he retrieved his jeans from a chair. As he headed out the door, she saw his silhouette in briefs and a T-shirt. His right lower leg appeared to be nothing but skin and bone.

He closed the door behind him and Sandy flopped down on the bed, staring at the ceiling. She needed a few seconds to recover from the two—had it just been two?—climaxes.

The feeling of Tristan touching her, caressing her, dipping into her, was so sharp and sweetly painful that she wanted to capture as much of it as she could before the last of the tiny aftershocks faded.

She also wanted to get up and follow Tristan and force him with kisses and touches to finish what he'd started. It was late, though, and he'd been shocked and repulsed when he'd tasted the milk from her breast. He hadn't been ready for that.

A deep pain arrowed through her entire body. Maybe he would never be ready for it, or for her, again, after the horror he'd been through. She couldn't imagine the pain and fear he'd suffered, certain he would die, or if he lived that he would be scarred and, worse, never have full use of his leg again.

For the first time it occurred to her that she may have had it easier than he had. It was beyond awful to find out the love of your life was dead, but was it worse than experiencing death? Especially a violent death? Was it worse than watching a vicious creature rip away a part of your body? Was it worse than needing air and sucking in seawater instead?

Tears slipped down her cheeks and wet her face and her pillow as she allowed herself to think about what it had been like for him. Dear God, how she loved him. And how she had let him down.

WHEN SHE WOKE just after eight o'clock, Tristan was in bed with her. She was lying on her side and his body was spooning hers. His half-hard arousal was pressed against her and his deep, even breaths tickled her ear. But what sent a poignant ache through her was that his hand was resting protectively on her tummy. She wanted to turn and lay her hands over his, wanted to show him the heart-filling thrill of feeling his baby kick and squirm inside her. She longed to lie there in his arms and tell him how the doctor had joked about that little thing he saw on the sonogram that made him sure the baby was a boy.

She listened to Tristan's soft, even breaths and felt the supple firmness of his arm embracing her. He was sleeping soundly. From the shadows beneath his eyes, she knew it had been a long time since he'd slept well, so she didn't want to disturb him.

She dozed for another hour before her own restlessness forced her to slide quietly out of bed, doing her best not to wake him.

As she poured a glass of juice, she glanced at the calendar. It was still on April. She took it off the wall and turned it to June. She'd spent almost two months in a grief-stricken haze, staying with her mother-in-law. Then last week she'd decided to come home. She'd gotten here Sunday. Her finger slid across the calendar page. And today was Friday.

Her mind reeled, thinking about all that had happened in just five days.

She hung the calendar back up and made a pot of hobo coffee on the gas stove, then wiped stray grounds off the counter.

Five days and she'd gone from widow back to wife—abandoned wife.

Throughout their entire lives, through good times and bad, she'd always believed she could count on Tristan's love to overcome any and all obstacles. His love had always been so steady, always there as a foundation that their relationship rested on, no matter what.

But now he'd done the one thing that just might crumble their marriage. From the time they were nine years old, he'd been by her side.

Then, within a heartbeat, he was gone.

The hilarious irony was that he hadn't died after all—he'd abandoned her. He'd left her alone and carrying his child. She folded the dishrag and laid it on the edge of the sink, then she rubbed her baby bump.

"I don't know if we can survive this, little bean." She blinked away tears and took a deep breath, ordering herself not to cry. "We'll try, I know. For your sake. And more than anything, I want to protect you. Because if your daddy could let me think he was dead, how can I risk that he might do something similar to you?"

The idea of her little boy looking for their father and finding him gone ate a hole the size of a shark bite into Sandy's heart. She could not—she *would not*—allow that to happen to her child. Not even if she had to give up love.

At that instant something large and heavy crashed into the French doors, sending Sandy stumbling backward in an instinctive fight-or-flight response.

The doors hadn't broken as she'd instantly thought, but all she could see was a bizarrely flattened face and hands pressed against the door. She half screamed. Her chest contracted and her scalp burned with fear. She took another step backward and another, until her back hit the refrigerator.

"Tris—" she started, but her voice fell flat. There wasn't enough air from her paralyzed lungs to make a sound. She struggled just to breathe. Her arms and legs were limp.

Forcing herself to reach for one of the knives in the block on the counter, she tried to wrap her fingers around its handle, but they weren't working right, which was probably just as well. What she thought she would do with the knife if she could grab it, she had no idea.

She sucked in air again, this time managing to get a full breath. "Tristan," she cried, dismayed at her tentative, breathy tone.

She was still staring at the misshapen face when suddenly it jerked backward and she could make out features. She almost fainted in surprise and fear. It was Murray Cho.

"No!" she cried. "Tristan!" She felt behind her as she sidled toward the edge of the refrigerator so she could make a beeline for the hall.

To her surprise, Murray didn't move. He didn't try to break down the doors or run. He appeared to be paralyzed, or frozen with fear himself. His dark, almond-shaped eyes pleaded with her, for what, she didn't know.

He looked as scared, if not more, than she felt. Then within a heartbeat, he flew backward as if pulled by a bungee cord and his expression changed to surprise, then pure terror.

Before she could wonder what had happened, she saw something behind him move. Her brain was still having trouble reconciling what she saw with reality, because the reality was that Murray looked as if he were being jerked around by a puppet master.

She kept inching toward the door.

"Tristan!" she yelled, and this time her voice worked. She was just about to duck around the door facing into the hall and shove it closed when she caught a glimpse of another face, this one dark and familiar. It was Boudreau. His dark gaze met hers.

"Tris-tan!" she shrieked.

He burst into the kitchen as Boudreau reached for the door handle.

"San? Are you all right?" he cried, stopping cold when he saw Boudreau.

"Hold it!" Tristan called out and backtracked into the hall to turn off the alarm. Then he opened the French doors. "Boudreau," Tristan greeted the older man.

"Tristan," Boudreau replied.

"What have you got here?" Tristan said as if he were looking at a gift bag in Boudreau's hand, rather than a man at the end of his gun barrel.

"Me, I'm thinking I caught me a poacher, yeah," Boudreau said. "Found him wandering around here early this morning. I spent some time talking to him, but he don't want to talk to me. So me, I brought him to you."

Sandy gasped and looked at Murray. She'd always thought he was a nice, quiet man, even after the incident at her bedroom window.

But Boudreau had seen him leaving her house with her laptop, and Tristan had seen him spying on them with binoculars.

Right now, he looked terrified. She frowned, trying to reconcile the pleasant fisherman with a man who was essentially stalking her.

Boudreau described exactly how he'd gotten the drop on Murray. "Was he armed?" Tristan asked.

"*Oui*, in a manner of speaking," Boudreau said. He pulled a smartphone and a small pair of binoculars out of his pocket. "Not dangerous weapons, unless they get into the wrong hands."

"What's going on here, Murray? I saw you the other night, sneaking around the side of my garage with those binoculars. I know you took my wife's laptop."

"Mr. DuChaud, please," Murray Cho said. "Can I talk to you? I try to explain to Mr. Boudreau, but he won't listen."

Sandy noticed that Murray's English was deteriorating. Could fear do that? Because he was obviously afraid. He was sweating profusely and looked as if he were being led to the hangman's noose. His eyes were sunken, as were his cheeks.

"Please, Mr. DuChaud," he begged.

"Tristan?" Sandy called, wanting to tell him to not be too hard on him. But Tristan waved a hand at her dismissively.

That made her angry. She walked closer to the doors, her arms crossed, intent on hearing every scrap of conversation. Tristan glanced toward her, frowning, but she ignored him.

"Where was he?" he asked Boudreau.

"Right back there," Boudreau said, pointing to the other side of the garage. "He looked like he was waiting to sneak up to the house and grab some pictures."

"Murray," Sandy said quickly. "What's going on? Why were you spying on us?"

Murray turned his gaze to her, hope flaring like a tiny candle flame in a storm.

"Sandy," Tristan said warningly.

"He's terrified," she shot back at him. "Can't you see that?"

"He oughtta be. I got my double-barrel pointed right at his heart," Boudreau responded.

"You don't think this is more than just fear of being caught?" She stepped closer. "Murray? I know the day of the funeral you were just trying to stop Patrick from looking in my window. I understand that. Your son is what—barely eighteen? But you're afraid of more than that, aren't you? What is it, Murray? You can tell us."

"Damn it, Sandy," Tristan snapped, taking her arm and pulling her back. "Don't get so close to him. We don't know what he might do."

Murray's head started going back and forth, back and forth in a negative response. "No, no, no. I won't hurt you, Mrs. DuChaud. Not you. I'm so sorry. So sorry."

"Murray, calm down," Sandy continued. "Why don't you tell me what's wrong."

She felt Tristan's glare. "Stop it, San. He's not a hurt dog or an abandoned kitten. Go back into the bedroom and let us handle this."

Who was this man who had come back to her? It wasn't her Tristan. Tristan had never treated her as anything less than equal in their lives. She propped her fists on her hips.

"I will not be sent off to the bedroom like a child. And you could at least untie him," Sandy pushed back at him. "He may not be a puppy or a kitten, but he's not a wild boar, either. But that's how Boudreau has him trussed, as if he's ready for the spit."

Boudreau spoke up. "I watched for him and got him, like you wanted me to, Tristan. But me, I ain't no bounty hunter, and anyhow, this man got no bounty on him. So what you want me to do with him?"

"Murray?" Tristan sighed and turned back to Cho. "Will you talk to me? Tell me what's going on here? And not try anything?"

"Oh, yes, sir," Murray said. "Sure. Sure, I talk."

Tristan nodded to Boudreau, who opened his shotgun and emptied the shells from the barrels, then closed it again, leaving it ready to be cocked if necessary. He set it against the door facing and, with a single snap of his wrist, untied Murray's hands.

In a flash, Murray shoved Boudreau aside and took off as fast as he could, considering Boudreau had hobbled him with rope.

Tristan started after him immediately, but he knew he was doomed to failure. Even hobbled, the fisherman had a distinct advantage over Tristan with his bad leg. Still, Tristan did his best, feeling the excruciating pain in his right leg with every step.

But while Murray was faster, his short legs weren't made for the irregular terrain. He tripped on a mound of dirt that covered a mole tunnel and went down. Tristan stopped, gulping in lungfuls of air, straining for oxygen. Boudreau walked past him and yanked Murray up by the collar. "You try that again, you, and I'll treat you to a butt full of bird shot, *n'est-ce pas?*"

Murray nodded furiously.

Tristan straightened, but he was still gasping for breath. "Take him back to…the house, Boudreau, and tie his hands again," he said haltingly.

"You got no business running, you," Boudreau said to Tristan. "You'll undo all the good we done."

Tristan didn't answer. He just glared at Boudreau for

saying that in front of Murray Cho, because he was now absolutely sure that Murray worked for his enemy.

"Let's go," Boudreau said, jerking Murray in the direction of the house. "March."

Tristan followed at a healthy distance, favoring his leg until he finally caught his breath. He'd never been in such rotten condition in his entire life. Not even the summer he suffered a collapsed lung in a touch football game that turned into a brawl. He was furious with his weakness and terrified that this was the best he was ever going to be.

No! He stopped those thoughts. He *would* get back his strength and agility. He'd do whatever he had to do to be the man he'd been before. But until then, he had to face the truth. He had no way to protect Sandy and their baby except by using his brain, and against enemies with lethal—probably automatic—weapons, his brain, as good as it was, would not be enough.

Chapter Eight

When Tristan limped back into the kitchen, Murray was seated at the table and Boudreau was standing near the French doors with his shotgun pointed at the fisherman. Sandy had just set a glass of cold water in front of Murray and was talking to Boudreau.

"Could you please put the shotgun down?" she asked.

Boudreau shook his head. "No, ma'am, Miss Sandy. And no," he said when she opened her mouth again, "I don't want any water. Ain't changed my mind from ten seconds ago," Boudreau grumbled.

Sandy shot the Cajun an irritated look, then turned the same look on Tristan. When she met his gaze, she frowned.

"I could use some cold water," he said.

"I'm sure you could," she snapped. "Why would you take off running like that? After everything you've been through, and with that leg not even healed yet? What are you trying to do? Kill yourself?"

Tristan felt a hot rage building up inside him, fueled by pain, exhaustion and humiliation. He clenched his jaw, trying to keep from firing a nasty response back at her. He told himself she was worried about him, but he had the sinking feeling this was how it was going to be from now on. Him fighting a losing battle to regain her respect and prove to her that he was not less of a man because of his injury, and her treating him like a fragile invalid.

It occurred to him that he'd stayed with Boudreau longer than absolutely necessary in an effort to hide from this reality, this truth that he would never be the man he'd been before.

Sandy's expression softened. "Sorry. I shouldn't have said that."

Tristan's face felt hot. *Stop. You're making it worse.* Aloud he said, "Never mind that. Can you get me some water?" he asked again.

He knew by her expression that even though she apologized, this was not the end of it. He was going to get an earful once they were alone. He rubbed his forehead and considered trading places with Boudreau. He'd guard Murray and let Boudreau deal with Sandy. But even as the thought entered his head he almost had to smile. Boudreau had more sense than to fall for a deal like that.

And he was wasting time, He needed to find out everything Murray Cho knew and he needed to do it now. He sat down opposite Murray. "Sit if you want, Boudreau."

The Cajun shook his head. "What I want is to get back to the house and check on that pig roast I put on this morning, but I can't do that till you decide what you going to do about this." He angled his head in the general direction of Murray Cho.

"Murray, you know me, right?"

"Yes, sir, Mr. DuChaud. Yes, sir." Murray's command of English was almost back to normal now that he'd calmed down. "I'm glad you're not dead."

"I let you use the DuChaud dock sometimes, right?"

"All the time, Mr. DuChaud. I appreciate it."

"So why were you sneaking around on my land spying on my wife?"

The Vietnamese fisherman's face turned a sickly pale yellow color. "I can't say, Mr. DuChaud. I can't. I can't."

"You don't have to be afraid of me or Boudreau. Just tell us why you're lurking around and who put you up to it and we'll leave you completely alone."

"No, no, no. That will not work. I can't tell you. It will be awful. No, please no. Just let me go. Please."

Sandy was right. The man was terrified of someone, but it wasn't Boudreau and it sure wasn't him.

"And let you get close enough to my wife to hurt her or kill her? Hell no."

Murray shook his head, looking disappointed in Tristan. "Mrs. DuChaud should go away. Take her away for a long time. Then she be safe."

Tristan vaulted up and slapped his palms down on the table. "That's it. *That's it!* I'm not waiting any longer for answers, Murray. I'll put you in the car and we'll go to the sheriff's office right now and you'll be locked up until you decide to tell me what I want to know."

He'd banked on Murray not wanting to go to jail, on him being so scared that he'd blurt out the information he needed, but there was someone who frightened Murray more than Tristan.

"More than me," he said, then realized he'd spoken aloud. "You're scared to death, aren't you?" he asked Murray.

Murray shook his head rapidly, side to side. "No, no," he said. "No."

"You're lying, Murray. I can see it in your face. You're trying to feed me a bald-faced lie. Well, it's not going to work. You're terrified of somebody." Tristan got up to pace, but when he put his weight on his right leg, the horrific pain in his calf changed his mind for him. He sat back down as if he'd just thought of more questions.

"You're Catholic, aren't you?" He didn't wait for an answer because he already knew that Murray went faithfully to mass several times a week as well as to Sunday services. "Do you believe in God?"

Murray frowned, but he nodded. "Yes, of course. I'm Catholic most of my life," he said, pulling a rosary out of his pocket and kissing the small crucifix that dangled from the chain. "Of course I believe."

Tristan eyed him. That meant he didn't fear dying. So that wasn't the threat that had him terrified. There was only one other explanation. "Then it's got to be your son."

Murray's eyes went wide as saucers and his sallow complexion turned greenish white. "What? No, no, no, no, no. Where'd you get that? No." But he hurriedly stuck the rosary back in his pocket and wiped his hands on his pants. "No."

"Yes," Tristan said triumphantly. He'd pocketed the rosary because he didn't want to be holding it while he lied. "That's it. They're threatening to harm your son. Where is Patrick now?"

Suddenly, the fisherman was no longer a threat to Tristan or Sandy or Boudreau. He'd turned into a worried father. Tears streamed from his eyes as he shook his head, back and forth. Back and forth. "They have him. I don't know where. They kill him if I don't do what they say. I can't… I can't do it."

Tristan sighed. Kidnappers had Murray's son and were using him to force Murray to spy on Sandy—and for what? He was sure he knew the answer to that question, too.

"Why, Murray? Why did they want you spying on my wife?" he asked, deadly quiet, but when Murray didn't answer right away, Tristan lost the careful control he'd been holding on to with all his strength. He leaped to his feet and slammed his fists down on the table. *"Why?"*

Murray jumped and held up his hands protectively in front of his face. "I don't know," he said. "They just say do it. See where she go, what she do. See who come see." Murray's English was becoming almost impossible to understand. "They say, if I get a chance, go inside and get computers, flash drives, everything I see that's like computers."

Tristan wanted to slap the man and tell him to snap out of it. He needed Murray to calm down. He needed him to think rationally and talk calmly if he was going to find out anything about the people who wanted him dead so badly.

Tristan straightened, took another deep breath and drank a big swallow of the cold water Sandy had finally set in front of him. After the anger that was burning in him had decreased to a flicker, he spoke to Murray again. "What did they tell you about Sandy or me?"

Murray spread his hands. "Nothing. Just say do what they tell me or they kill Patrick."

"Give me your phone."

"No. Can't. Can't. They kill me I don't bring back picture—" Murray suddenly turned frightfully pale. He looked as though he might pass out.

"Picture?" Tristan repeated. "What picture?"

The fisherman's head started shaking back and forth again. He moaned. "Didn't mean to say that," he wailed.

"So sorry, Mr. DuChaud. So sorry. Shame, shame on me." Murray's entire body seemed to deflate. He hung his head and his voice sounded broken. "I tell them about you. No choice. They have my son." He spread his hands, then clasped them in front of his chest.

"Tell me what you told them," Tristan said, working to keep his voice even.

"I say I see you. Say maybe it Tristan DuChaud. Maybe not. But pretty sure. They give camera. Take picture. Get proof. No more spy on Mrs. DuChaud. Watch to get picture, or they kill Patrick. They kill him."

Get proof. So whoever ordered him dead had learned from Cho that he was still alive and they sent him back here to get proof. He'd be happy, more than happy, to oblige. "It's okay, Murray. You did good. I'll be glad to give them what they want."

Boudreau shot him a look. "What you got in that head of yours, boy?"

Tristan ignored him for the moment. He clasped Murray's shoulder and squeezed. "Murray, will you do what I tell you? If you will, I'll do my best to save your son. I can't promise you that I'll be successful, but I can promise that I'll give it my all. My wife is pregnant. I'm going to have a son—" His throat closed up. He swallowed hard. "A son of my own. So I can understand a little of what you're going through."

Murray studied Tristan a long time. Then he straightened. The frightened little man who wouldn't look him in the eye, who'd tried to run, whose perfect English had deteriorated to the point that he was almost not understandable, had transformed again.

This time, the man who straightened was a father,

still scared and worried, but ready to stand up to anyone for his child's sake. "I'll do anything to save my boy."

Tristan stared at him. Nothing Murray had said so far had affected him as much as watching him gather strength and determination in the face of terror over his son's safety. But all the courage the man was able to gather was not enough to erase the desperation in his eyes—the overwhelming fear for his son's life.

And seeing that, Tristan knew exactly how he felt. When he'd first fallen off the oil rig, he'd been convinced he was going to die. He'd thought about Sandy and their baby. In those moments, he'd known he would never see his wife again or ever get a chance to meet his child.

Was that a part of his hell, he'd wondered? The agony of being separated from Sandy and their child? Then he'd thought of the utter emptiness and desolation his life would become if something happened to her, and he had decided yes. That would be the worst hell imaginable.

An understanding took seed and grew inside him. That's how it had been for Sandy, when she'd found out he was dead. A small inkling of why she had been and still was so angry with him—not for staying away, but for not letting her know.

But she wasn't just angry. He remembered the look on her face, in her eyes, when she'd discovered him in the house. She'd been talking to the baby. Even when she recognized him, her hands had wrapped protectively around her tummy. She was keeping her baby safe—even from him.

There had not been one tiny shred of happiness in her eyes. She hadn't been glad to see him.

Had she started to get over him? The thought hit his heart like a physical blow. He felt the anger building

again. Anger at himself, yes, but also anger at her. She'd
begun to let go. She'd begun to move on. She had begun
to make a family out of herself and her unborn child. The
pain in his heart nearly doubled him over.

"Tristan?" Boudreau said. "The phone?"

Tristan blinked. Boudreau had called his name more
than once. With difficulty, he brought his thoughts back
to the problem at hand, finding out who had threatened
Murray. He looked at the fisherman then at Boudreau.
His Cajun friend held out his hand. He was holding a
cell phone.

"What's this?" Tristan asked.

Murray glanced at Boudreau.

Boudreau's brows raised. "Where you been the past
few seconds?" he asked.

Tristan sent Boudreau an irritated look, then turned
to Murray. "The kidnappers gave this to you?"

He nodded. "To take picture with. They say it better
than my phone."

"What can you tell me about them?"

Murray was close to panicking again. "Big men.
Maybe American, maybe not. I don't know. I press record button on my phone last time they called."

"You recorded them?" Tristan perked up. A recording. "Good for you." Maybe something on there would
reveal who had ordered his death and had masterminded
the smuggling operation. "Play it." He held the phone
out to Murray.

"Not that phone." Murray pulled a phone from his
pocket. "That phone for picture. I recorded them on my
phone, the one they call me on."

"Fine. Just play the recording."

"I don't know how. Patrick handles these electronic

devices. All I did, I saw the record button and hit it. I haven't tried to listen." Murray was calming down again and his English was getting better.

Tristan took Murray's phone and looked at it for a moment, pressed a couple of buttons to access internal settings and help, then pressed a few more. He heard Murray's voice, pleading with someone.

"—but the storm was too bad."

"The storm was too bad for you to perform a simple task to save your son's life? I guess that's it, then. Hey, get the kid ready. Say goodbye to your boy, Mr. Cho."

"No, wait!"

Cho's voice coming through the phone's speaker was agonized and broken. Tristan saw a reflection of that pain and fear etched in Murray's face.

"For what, Murray? Till pigs fly? Because it looks like that's how long it's going to take you to finish your task. Well, we don't have that long. Hey, Farrell? Where's the kid? There he is. Settle back and listen, Murray. You're going to get an earful of what happens when you don't do what you're told."

In the background a young male voice cried out in pain once, twice. It was sudden, awful pain, from the sound of his agonized cries.

Murray moaned as his voice on the phone choked out another plea. *"No. Please. Let me talk to him. I swear, I can do it."*

"We don't have time for this, Mr. Cho. If you can do it, why haven't you done it already?"

"Dad! Da-a-ad." The boy went into a coughing fit. *"Come—get me. Please! I'm scared."*

"Patrick!"

Tristan gritted his teeth. The love and fear were so

evident in their voices. He glanced at Sandy, who was looking down and rubbing her hand across the side of her belly. She looked like a Madonna, her goodness shining like a halo. And he knew what he had to do.

He wanted to watch their baby grow up. He wanted to feel that much love for his son, but not through a cloud of fear. He swore to himself that he would not allow Murray's son—or his own—to end up as a casualty of this mess.

"Patrick! Be brave." Through the phone, Murray sucked in a deep breath. *"Don't hurt my boy. I've got something else. Information you will want, but first you have to let Patrick go."*

The man's laughter echoed through the phone line. *"You're ordering us? That is not how it works. You're a little confused. We give the orders. You follow them. Hey, here's a bargain for you. You tell me what you've got, and if it's good enough, maybe we'll let your son live. That's a sale you can't afford to miss."*

Murray put his hand over his mouth and tried to stifle a sob. "I'm sorry," he whispered, looking up at Tristan. "I had to. He's my son."

Through the phone's speaker, Tristan heard Murray take a deep breath. *"It was so dark, except for lightning."* In his fear, Murray's smooth English was breaking down. *"I get close as I could, but when lightning finally light up long time, I see Mrs. DuChaud, and a man."*

"A visitor?" the man said.

"No, no," Murray replied. *"It was dark, but lightning was bright. I think it was Tristan DuChaud."*

"What? Are you serious? Because if you think you can fool us into letting your kid go—"

"*No. I see what I see. Maybe it's him. Maybe not. But I know Mr. DuChaud. The man look like him. A lot.*"

"*Could have been a relative. Stop wasting our time.*"

"*A relative? You mean like cousin or brother? No, no. You don't get it. Here's the rest of the story. Mrs. DuChaud and him got very close. Closer than cousin. They were kissing—not like relatives.*"

"*Kissing? I'll be a sonofabitch,*" the kidnapper said, then muttered under his breath.

Tristan couldn't understand him. He paused and backed up the recording, then played it again.

"*—not like relatives.*"

"*I'll be a sonofabitch.*"

Tristan held his breath, but he still couldn't quite make out the kidnapper's muttered words. "Do you know what he said right there?"

Murray shrugged. "*'Got to get proof. Lee will want proof.'*"

"Lee? He said Lee?" Excitement coursed through Tristan's blood. Vernon Lee was the owner and CEO of Lee Drilling, the multibillion-dollar corporation that owned a lot of a whole lot of things, including several thousand oil rigs around the world and a large number of land drilling operations. Murray shrugged, and Tristan grabbed his shoulder. "He said *Lee*? Are you sure?"

Murray shrank away from Tristan's hand. "He said it in English. I'm pretty sure."

Lee will want proof. His suspicion had been right all along. He'd known from the start that the man on the satellite phone giving orders to the captain had to be high enough in Lee Drilling, the company that owned the *Pleiades Seagull*, to expect the captain to obey him without argument.

Whether that official was Lee himself, Tristan hadn't known—until now. Now he had some corroboration that who'd ordered Sandy watched and Murray's son kidnapped was the same man who had ordered his death on the *Pleiades Seagull*.

The popular media classified Lee as practically a recluse who fiercely and expensively protected his privacy.

The implications of exposing the multibillionaire were stunning. Even a rumor suggesting that he had masterminded the smuggling of automatic handguns into the United States with the idea of arming criminals and kids with the lethal weapons could destroy him and decimate his multibillion-dollar corporation.

Tristan started the recording back up.

"—want you to do now. You get back over there. Get me proof that the man you saw is Tristan DuChaud. A photo or video. And you'd better not be seen. My boss is smart and thorough and he's got all the money in the world. He'll know a fake within seconds. And trust me, Cho, anything suspicious happens and your kid's dead. Just get me that photo."

"I'll get you the photo. Then what?" Murray's voice was toneless. *"What about my son?"*

"Well, Mr. Cho, you turned out to have something that just might be useful. If you improve how you follow directions and you bring us proof that the man you saw is DuChaud, maybe you can save your son." The man hung up.

Tristan stared at the phone for a moment, reviewing the information he'd just gained. *If* Murray was right and the man had said *Lee*, and if things went perfectly, Tristan just might be able to bring an end to the nightmare of the past two months.

SANDY FELT COMPLETELY at loose ends while Boudreau and Tristan were deciding what to do about Murray, so she decided to cook, if there was enough gas for the portable stove, that was. She checked the can and found that it was over half-full.

She found a couple of cans of chicken stock in the cabinet, along with a small can of cooked chicken. She put the broth and the chicken in a pan. While it was simmering on one burner of the portable stove, she made a roux out of flour and oil on the second burner, then added the South Louisiana holy trinity of cooking—onion, peppers and celery—to it.

Once the vegetables were cooked perfectly, she added them and some sliced andouille sausage from the freezer, a few herbs and some cayenne pepper to the pot. Finally, a can of boiled okra and a can of tomatoes went into the mix.

Tristan came in about the time the pot began simmering. He took a deep breath. "Mmm, gumbo," he said, smiling at her. "When will it be ready?"

Sandy set her mouth and shook her head. "There's not enough for everybody," she said.

"That's okay. Boudreau and Murray have gone to his cabin. I'm headed up there in a few minutes."

"You're going to Boudreau's? Again? Why? He can handle Murray without your help." She sighed. "You are unbelievable."

He frowned. "What? What did I do?"

"What did you do?" She tossed the metal spoon she was holding into the sink, where it clattered against the porcelain. "Are you saying you don't know? You dismissed me with a wave of your hand. You essentially told me to shut up. Then you ignored me. Not to mention you almost killed yourself running after him. Boudreau could have caught him in half the time. And I saw Boudreau's face. He was as worried about you as I was. And you—" She barely stopped for breath.

"I don't know. You're not the same person you were the last time I saw you." She threw down the dishrag she'd tossed over her shoulder while she was cooking. "I'm not sure I know you anymore and I'm not sure I like this new person very much."

Tristan listened to Sandy tick off all the things she was upset about. He'd known she was boiling mad, but he was expecting to be chastised for running, not for failing to take care of himself. Then when he'd smelled the gumbo, he'd had the fleeting fantasy that she wouldn't harangue him at all, that she'd be too worried about him to be angry.

But no such luck. She'd never cut him any slack and she wasn't now. And he knew she was right.

He wasn't the man he had been. He knew that. He had wanted to fully recuperate before he saw her, hoping that she wouldn't notice any difference in him.

But that had been a forlorn hope. She would never have missed the scar on the left side of his head, where the roughneck's bullet had barely missed blowing his brains out, or his deformed right calf, which had only half the muscles it ought to have.

But in his heart, Tristan knew those weren't the things that made him so different.

He'd stared death in the face. He knew what it felt like to be ripped away from everyone and everything he loved. He'd been through the strange and horrible experience of waking up to find himself still alive, in a body that was not the body he remembered, not the body that could do all the things that had been second nature to him.

This body couldn't walk, could barely hold itself upright, it was so weak and clumsy. His whole life, he had defined himself in terms of what he could do. He'd been the best at everything—the best swimmer, the best runner, the best wide receiver. He'd not made the best grades in school, but he'd never had to study to get by.

Then, when his father had been killed on an oil rig and he'd had to give up veterinary school and go to work on the rigs to support his mom and sister and Sandy, his brand-new wife, it had been a huge blow, because it was the first time he'd ever been forced to do something he hadn't wanted to.

From that moment, it had seemed his life had evolved into a dull routine of things he'd never wanted to do.

"Tristan?" Sandy touched his arm.

"What?" he said automatically, then realized he'd been staring into space. He looked at his wife with her T-shirt stretched over her small baby bump and spattered with gumbo and her hair drooping into her eyes.

He'd never seen her when she didn't look adorable and this was no exception. Even spattered with grease and gumbo, with her face bright pink from the heat of the gas stove, she was pretty and cute and glowing. His gaze returned to her tummy. He stepped closer and spread his hand over the rounded shape of their child, growing inside her.

"You're so beautiful," he said.

She lifted her face to his and kissed him. "And you look awful. You need to eat and rest."

"I'll eat later. I have to get to Boudreau's. They're

going to take a photo of me that proves I'm alive. Where's today's newspaper?"

Her face set into the stony expression that told him she disapproved of what he was doing. "Still outside, I'm sure. Tristan, I can take your picture."

He shook his head. "Don't wait on me to eat. It's probably going to take all day to get that picture and get it to the kidnappers. I'll eat some of Boudreau's roast pig."

"Why don't you take the gumbo to Boudreau's, if you don't want—"

"No. Stay inside, Sandy. Just to be safe. I'll be back before dark."

He stalked out and slammed the French doors behind him. He winced at the rattle of glass panes. He hadn't meant to slam the door on her while she was talking, but he couldn't say he was really sorry. He was sick and tired of being sick and tired. He couldn't deal with Sandy right now, because he had no idea how to explain the way he'd been acting toward her.

Besides, if he was going to have a prayer of catching Vernon Lee, and saving Murray's son, he had to get the picture taken and send Murray on his way to turn it over to the kidnappers.

Chapter Nine

"This is a stupid idea," Tristan growled as he shifted his weight off his bad leg while trying to hold the newspaper up so the date was visible. "There's a date and time stamp on the camera. Why isn't that enough?"

"Might be enough, but it ain't dramatic. That man needs to know you know what he's doing, yeah," Boudreau said. "Now stand still." He frowned and squinted at the phone he held in one large hand.

"It's the icon that looks like a camera," Tristan said, unable to keep from chuckling at his friend's efforts to press the minuscule touch screen with his large, bony fingers. He heard the clicking noise that signaled that a photo had been taken.

"Oh, no," he said, the laugh fading. He tossed the newspaper down and reached for the phone. "Give me that. I'm not sending that SOB a photo with me laughing."

But Boudreau held on to it, tapping on the screen. "It's in focus," he said. "Only good one we've gotten, with you fidgeting so much, you."

"It would have been easier if you weren't trying to press the button with those gigantic ham-hands."

Boudreau's face creased into what Tristan knew was

a smile, although someone who didn't know Boudreau might think his expression was murderous.

"Humph," Boudreau huffed, holding up his hands. "These ham-hands saved you in that water. You were caught on a branch so big I almost couldn't break it."

"I was lucky that you were fishing in that inlet that day," Tristan said. He felt a pang in the middle of his chest. Boudreau had been like a father to him all his life, especially after his own dad was gone. And he'd happened to be in just the right place at the right time to save his life. Tristan scowled at the older man.

"What?" Boudreau said grumpily, then turned toward the sink. "I got to make some coffee,"

"Boudreau, what were you doing fishing in that inlet that morning? You don't like it there. You always said it was too close to the rigs. That the discharge from the oil rigs collected there and ruined the fish. You said not even the sharks would eat them."

Boudreau filled the pan with water and put it on the gas stove and lit it. "Probably why you still alive, you."

"You knew, didn't you? Someone told you that night that I'd gone overboard and you figured if the oil from the rigs ended up there, that a dead body might, too."

"That little wife of yours walked up here to tell me. She said I should know. Said I was family." Boudreau's voice faltered at the end.

"So you were looking for me." Now Tristan's voice cracked. It was overwhelming and humbling to think about Sandy and Boudreau, these two people who loved him, who, together, had created the miracle that saved his life.

The gratitude and love that erupted from deep inside him was too much. It filled up his heart and overflowed.

Sandy, in the midst of her grief and pain, had thought about Boudreau. She understood that he needed to know what had happened. He shook his head, trying to stop the stinging behind his eyes. "You went out there to look for me."

Boudreau spent a full minute adjusting the flame under the pan of water, although it appeared to Tristan to be perfect. "I didn't want you getting torn up on the branches and driftwood, or dragged out to sea."

A lump so large he couldn't swallow past it blocked Tristan's throat. He could never repay either his friend or his wife for what they'd done.

He picked the phone up off the table where Boudreau had left it and moved the photo from the phone's memory to the SIM card, then took the card out and placed it in a small manila envelope, which he sealed and set on the table.

"Coffee?" Boudreau asked.

"Only if it can walk over here by itself."

Boudreau chuckled. "It's been boiling awhile. It might do it. Do you want to take some to Murray?"

"Sure." Tristan pushed himself to his feet. His leg was hurting like a sonofabitch after this morning's chase. His body was achy and stiff, as though he hadn't gotten a wink of sleep for days.

"You all right?" Boudreau asked as he handed him two steaming mugs.

Tristan nodded, but he knew he'd groaned when he'd put weight on his leg, and he knew it was going to be painful to walk. "Just a little stove up from this morning."

"Tell Murray he'd better drink up, 'cause as soon as I clean up, we'll be going."

Tristan stopped at the door. "Boudreau…"

"*Mais non.* We have had this talk already, and it's barely past noon. You with that gimpy leg, you'd slow us down. Anyhow, oughtn't you be back home with your wife? What happened to all your worry that she was in danger?"

"Didn't you tell me you thought she was safe?" Tristan muttered.

Boudreau didn't say anything. He just gazed at Tristan.

"Anyhow, Murray said the kidnapper told him to leave her alone. I'm sending Lee proof that I'm alive. He has no reason to go after her now." Boudreau's head bobbed up and down slowly. Was he agreeing or thinking?

Tristan headed outside and found Murray where they'd left him earlier, his hands tied separately and loosely around a tree trunk so he had some range of movement. The fisherman had been working on the knots, but apparently had given up and gone to sleep. He didn't stir until Tristan nudged him with his shoe.

"What? Patrick—" Murray jerked awake. "Oh." He looked around for a few seconds, until he remembered where he was. He lifted his gaze to Tristan's with a carefully blank expression.

"I don't understand why you have to tie me up," he said. "You're going to help me find my son. Why would I run away?"

Tristan shrugged. "You did before. Here's coffee," he said, setting it on the ground between them.

He still didn't trust Murray. For all he knew the fisherman would kick out and try to trip him, and he didn't want to take any risks with his bad leg. "Boudreau says drink up. You two are heading out soon."

Murray reached for the coffee and blew on its surface, then took a cautious sip. "What time is it? Where's my phone? The kidnappers should have called by now."

"Yeah, see," Tristan said, "there's no cell service here. I mean, look around. It's a jungle and a swamp. You'll hear their message when you're on your way to Gulfport."

"They're going to kill Patrick if I'm not there when they get there."

"Don't worry. You'll be back at your trailer in plenty of time. Boudreau will tell you exactly what you're supposed to say and do."

Tristan propped himself against the old rough-hewn bench and drank his hot, strong coffee as he watched Murray until Boudreau came out with a washbasin and tossed the water into the side yard, then set the basin down. He was freshly shaved and he had his shotgun with him.

He did the same trick he had at the house, loosened Murray's bonds with a simple flick of his wrist, leaving the fisherman staring bewilderedly at the ropes he'd tried unsuccessfully to loosen.

"See this gun?" Boudreau asked Murray. "She don't have no compunction about shooting somebody who's not being smart. And she ain't sure how smart you are."

"I'll do just what you say, Mr. Boudreau. I want my boy back. I don't want him hurt. I'm a smart man, Mr. Boudreau. Mr. DuChaud." Murray looked desperate. Given that it had been several days since he'd seen his son, Tristan couldn't blame him.

"Well?" Boudreau said, looking at Tristan, who frowned. "You never did tell me what you're going to do."

"I'd like to go with you."

Boudreau shook his head. "I told you no. You'll slow us down. Go back to your house. Be with your wife."

He gestured to Murray. "Let's go. We got to walk down to the dock and then to the seafood warehouse parking lot to get to Murray's pickup."

Once they were gone, Tristan ducked into Boudreau's cabin and grabbed the automatic handgun that his friend had hidden behind a loose board.

The board covered a hiding place Boudreau had shown Tristan years and years before.

If you ever get in trouble, Boudreau had told him, *behind this board is everything you need.*

And Boudreau had not been exaggerating. Doing a quick inventory, Tristan saw the large magazine for the gun, matches and lighter, a windup flashlight and a battery-operated one, and five hundred dollars in fives and twenties.

Tristan remembered what Boudreau had told him about the stash. *If you're in so much trouble that this ain't enough, then God help you, because I can't.*

"Thanks, Boudreau," Tristan muttered as he pocketed what he needed. The gun for sure, the ammo, the lighter and all the cash. "I'm good for it," he muttered, rising.

He passed the walking stick propped by the door, almost reaching for it but not. He couldn't keep depending on it. Besides, he was probably going to need both hands.

Tristan pocketed everything but the gun. He looked behind the door and found a hunting vest of Boudreau's. With the gun and the large magazine in it, the pockets were a little bulky, but it worked.

He made his way to the dock and across to his garage, where his Jeep was parked. It probably hadn't been driven since he'd gone into the water. Luckily, it started right up.

As he pulled out onto the road, he saw Sandy at the French doors, but he didn't stop. He had to get to Gulfport, where Murray and Boudreau were meeting the kidnappers to hand over the photo.

He and Boudreau had talked about what might happen once the kidnappers got their hands on the card that contained the photo of Tristan holding the newspaper. Both of them were afraid they would kill Murray and his son.

That was why Boudreau was going with Murray and it was part of the reason Tristan was determined to be there, despite Boudreau's objection. Neither Murray nor his son would die if he had anything to do with it.

Tristan caught up to Murray's truck about two miles from the Gulfport commercial pier. He stayed well behind the old vehicle.

Finally, Murray slowed and stopped in front of an RV park across from the pier. Tristan pulled in behind an SUV and watched as Murray got out, unlocked the door of a small recreational vehicle and went inside.

"Go, Boudreau," Tristan said under his breath. "They could be waiting for him inside." But he didn't have to worry. Boudreau waited no more than a few seconds before he got out. He had the shotgun in a seaman's ditty bag.

Tristan slipped out of the Jeep and circled around to the back side of the RV. The small camper was hardly big enough for two people, so he wasn't sure what the kidnappers were going to do.

Truthfully, he didn't know what he was going to do, either, except for one thing. He'd decided a mere picture of him holding a newspaper wasn't good enough to send to the man who'd ordered him killed. He planned to send him a video that proved in no uncertain terms that he was alive.

With Murray's recording of the kidnappers, Tristan

was at least one step closer to finding the man who'd wanted him murdered. If the kidnapper had said *Lee*, then the step was a huge one.

Now he needed to get the flash drive he'd hidden in the nursery, in a shiny blue mobile Sandy had hung over the bed. She'd told him she'd bought blue as good luck, because he'd been sure the baby was a boy.

If the voice on Captain Poirier's satellite phone ordering the commission of traitorous crimes against the United States was proven to be Vernon Lee's, the multibillionaire mogul was about to crash and burn.

He hadn't had a chance to listen to all the conversations he'd captured. With any luck, the captain had called Lee by name at least once.

Tristan wanted to confront Lee in person so he could identify his voice, but if he had to settle for sending the man a video, so be it.

It was around three o'clock and the pier and the RV park were essentially deserted. Murray had told them that most of the slips held fishing boats and fishermen were up and out at sunrise and didn't return until sunset, leaving the dock and the RV park almost empty during midafternoon.

So the kidnappers had chosen the perfect time for their meeting with Murray.

Tristan leaned against the hot metal side of the camper and tried to look casual as he waited to see how the kidnappers were going to contact Murray.

Within moments, he heard a telephone ringing inside, through the obviously thin walls. When Murray answered, Tristan could hear him plainly.

"Hello," Murray said anxiously. "Hello?" After listening for a brief moment, he said, "Wait. Which slip?"

Tristan straightened, hardly daring to breathe so he wouldn't miss a word.

"Forty-two? Did you say forty-two? Oh. Forty-three." Murray paused. "Yes, yes. Of course I have it. I said I would. Is my son there? Hello?"

They'd hung up on Murray, but Tristan had the slip number. He only hoped it was Slip 43 at *this* pier.

He took off at a gimpy run, needing to make it as far away as he could from Murray's RV before he and Boudreau came out.

Boudreau could possibly be angry enough at him to fill his butt full of bird shot if he saw him. By the time he reached the Jeep and dared to take a look back at Murray's camper, Boudreau and Murray were hurrying toward the pickup. Boudreau said something to Murray on the way and Murray responded by pointing east across the rows and rows of slips that made up the docks of the commercial pier.

Tristan climbed into the Jeep and pulled out into traffic. He drove well past the general area that Murray had pointed out and parked in a loading zone. If his Jeep got towed, he'd deal with it after he'd dealt with the kidnappers.

When he got out of the Jeep, his leg nearly gave way. It was throbbing with pain and the little muscle he had left quivered with fatigue and weakness. He probably had only a few seconds' lead on Murray and Boudreau, so he quickly scanned the docks until he saw the row of slips that included number 43. Reaching into the rear seat of the Jeep, he pulled out an old baseball cap and a rag he kept in the backseat to wipe his windshield.

As he walked carefully down the dock toward Slip 43, which held a relatively small fishing boat, he put the cap on, pulling it down to shadow his face, then he shook out the rag and mopped the back and front of his neck and then his face, just about the time he passed the slip. If the kidnappers were waiting for him somewhere nearby, he didn't see them, but then he'd limited his vision greatly by holding the rag over his face as he passed.

Slips 44 and 45 were empty, so Tristan stopped at Slip 46, which held a houseboat. After taking off the bulky hunting vest and hiding it behind a coil of rope, he stepped onto the deck of the houseboat and hid, waiting to see who showed up at Slip 43. He thought Murray and Boudreau would be walking down the pier by now, but maybe Boudreau was checking out the area, too, before he let Murray expose himself.

The houseboat rocked a little and Tristan had to steady himself when his leg protested. Then, at the same instant he realized there was someone behind him, he felt a gun barrel in the middle of his back.

"What the hell are you doing on this boat?" a gruff voice said.

"What?" Tristan said, his voice high-pitched as if he were terrified. "What are you doing? What's that?" He tried to turn around, but the pressure in the middle of his back increased.

"Don't move, bud, if you know what's good for you," the gruff voice said.

"I—I'm not. I mean I won't. I mean—"

"Shut up," the man snapped. "Now, what's going on here? Who sent you?"

"No-nobody sent me," Tristan stammered, trying to sound genuinely afraid. He was, a little. After all, the man had a gun stuck in his back and his weapon was on the other side of the dock. The only thing that would make the situation worse at this moment would be if Murray and Boudreau showed up.

He glanced down the pier, but didn't see anybody— yet.

"I swear. I was just hiding here, waiting for…" He stopped, his mind suddenly blank. What could he say? What would sound reasonable enough and at the same time slightly ridiculous?

He'd like to make the man think he was harmless if he could. Then he had it. Or at least the beginning of it. A story that just might work.

"See," he said breathlessly, "my wife's screwing the guy that owns that boat down there." He pointed vaguely in the direction of Slip 43, then tried to turn around to face the man, as probably anyone would do if they hadn't quite figured out that what was sticking into their back was a gun barrel.

"Don't! Move!" the man said, sounding as though he were gritting his teeth.

"O-okay. Sorry. Anyway, she told me she was going shopping, but I think she's coming over here with who-ever owns that boat. I found a note in her purse that said Slip 43, Gulfport pier. I'm sure this is it."

The man cursed, long and colorfully. "Get the hell off this boat," he ordered Tristan, "and keep going until you're off the pier."

"But they're probably on their way. They might see me. I don't want her to see me. And I sure don't want him to. Not till I'm ready."

Tristan felt the pressure of the gun barrel ease. Had he done it? Had he convinced the man that he was harmless?

"Get off the boat, now!"

"But I need to—" Tristan didn't have to come up with

what he needed to do because the man grabbed his arm and turned him around, right into a big right fist.

Tristan went down like a rock. He was barely conscious and he tasted blood, but the man wasn't done with him. He picked him up bodily by the neck of his shirt and the back belt loop of his jeans and tossed him off the boat. Tristan's shoulder hit the deck hard. He rolled a couple of times, coming to an abrupt stop against the coil of rope where he'd hidden his weapon. His cheek scraped against the rough wood of the deck.

While he lay there, trying to gather enough sense back into his head to figure out which way was up, he heard Murray, about forty feet away, probably at Slip 43, saying he had a SIM card with a photo of Tristan DuChaud on it.

Tristan tried to clear his vision. He blinked and rubbed his eyes, but it didn't help. Meanwhile his tongue was exploring the bloody cut on his lip. He blinked again and this time, he saw something.

He was lying on the pier directly across from the houseboat, and although he was inclined to doubt what he saw, he decided to believe it, because if what he saw was real, then he and Boudreau and Murray might make it away from here alive.

As he watched, Boudreau silently paddled a dinghy up beside the houseboat and reached up to catch one of the tie lines and haul himself up onto the deck, his shotgun slung over his shoulder.

When he saw Tristan he made a face and shook his head. Then he held up the shotgun and pointed to Tristan, looking a question.

Tristan nodded and pulled the vest from behind the rope. Boudreau nodded, then gestured toward Murray. Tristan lifted his head enough to take a look at the odds.

Murray was, at best, half the size of the two men who were towering over him. One of them had to be the man who had coldcocked Tristan.

He looked back at Boudreau and read the Cajun's gestures as clearly as if he were talking. *I'll go first and get the drop on them. You follow. Tell Murray to run, and you and me can tune those two giants up a bit.*

Tristan frowned, pointed in the direction of his leg and shrugged, hoping Boudreau could read his answer in impromptu hand signals. *Maybe you. Probably not me.*

Boudreau stepped onto the pier and cocked his double-barreled shotgun. The two big, strapping blond men froze, then slowly turned and eyed the weapon. One of them held a pistol in his hand.

"Drop it or I'll make a sieve outta you," Boudreau said.

The man looked at the shotgun, then at his handgun.

"Throw the guns in the water," Boudreau added, lifting his weapon.

"What?"

"I don't like killing," Boudreau said. "But when I got to, I make a good job of it. I'll start with your legs, yeah." He pointed the gun at the man's legs and slid his finger across both triggers.

"Okay," the man said quickly. "We don't want no trouble. We got business with Mr. Cho."

Tristan pushed himself to his feet with all the strength he could muster. Just as he pulled the handgun from the vest, he heard something from inside the houseboat. It sounded like a muffled voice crying out. But he didn't have time to check it out because Boudreau needed him.

"Business about a photo?" Tristan said, finding it a little hard to speak around his swelling lip.

The man looked at him. "I knew you weren't quite as dumb as you sounded."

"And I knew you were," Tristan responded. "Murray, take your phone out and hit the video record button. And don't screw up."

Murray frowned, but he did as he was told. He held up the phone and started recording.

But Tristan wasn't nearly as interested in showing off for Lee as he had been. He'd taken an awful chance, following Boudreau and Murray out here, and he knew he'd hear about it from Boudreau later. So he just walked around until he could put his face in the middle of the phone's screen with the two kidnappers in the frame behind him.

"Hello, Mr. Lee. I'm Tristan DuChaud. I'm giving you plenty of footage here, so you have time to get a match for my face. Sorry about the cut on my lip. That shouldn't hinder the face-matching software much. I want you to know that I'm alive and mostly well, and that I'm looking forward to meeting you. I'd like to have the opportunity to shake the hand of the man who tried to kill me."

He smiled. "I won't do it. I wouldn't touch you with a ten- or even a hundred-foot pole. But I do want to stand in the same room with you and choose not to shake your hand. You are the lowest piece of scum on the planet, and another thing I'd love to do is shoot you in cold blood, but I won't do that, either. I'm going to let the international court deal with you, you traitor, you subhuman, you piece of slime under my boot."

He wiped a drop of blood that he could feel trickling down his chin. Then he smiled again. "By the way, if you even think about sending anyone near my wife again, I might just have to change my mind about touching you.

I won't be shaking your hand, though. Have a nice day, Mr. Lee." He made a throat-slicing motion at Murray, who looked down to find the stop-recording key.

"Give it to me," Tristan said, and Murray complied again. Tristan held up the phone. "Here you go, boys. Take that to your boss and tell him Tristan DuChaud says he hopes he enjoys the show." He looked behind them at Boudreau. "You going to shoot them?"

"No!" Murray cried. "They know where my son is. Please!"

Boudreau shook his head. "Shells are pretty expensive these days. Reckon I might opt for a cheaper alternative. Say—" Instead of finishing his sentence, Boudreau took one step forward and shoved one of the men hard into the other one.

Both of them teetered for a second, then tumbled from the pier into the water.

Tristan grinned at him, then looked down to where the two men were splashing about. "Hey, boys, I'm going to put the phone right here. Mr. Lee will be looking for this. You'd better get dried off and get it to him. Once he sees that I'm alive and well, tell him to come and see me. My wife and I are getting reacquainted, so please call first." Tristan made a show of getting ready to walk away, then he remembered the noise he'd heard in the houseboat. He stopped and looked at Murray.

"Murray, I think your son's in the houseboat. Boudreau, you want to keep an eye on these guys while Murray and I check it out?

"Sure," Boudreau said.

"Come on, Murray," Tristan said. "Let's go make sure there are no more muscle heads around and get Patrick out of there."

They made short work of searching the houseboat for another thug. Inside, they found Patrick tied up and strapped to a chair. His face was bruised, but he looked healthy otherwise and he started crying when he saw his dad.

Murray untied his son and got him to his feet, then pulled him close for a long hug. Patrick hugged his father back.

"Patrick, my boy. Are you all right?"

Patrick nodded. "They hit me and kept me tied up," he said brokenly, still crying. "But I'm okay. Oh, Dad, I'm sorry. I forgot to lock the door. I'm sorry."

"Shh," Murray said. "None of this is your fault, son. They'd have broken the door in. I'm just glad they didn't hurt you any…any more than they did." He hugged his son close again.

"Think you can walk?" Tristan asked.

Patrick nodded.

"Let's go. It'll be dark before long and I'd like to get out of here before those guys manage to pull their thousand-dollar suits out of the water."

Tristan led the way back down the dock. The two thugs were wading toward shore, glancing back at Boudreau with every step.

"By the way, guys," Tristan called to them, "tell your boss my number's in the book. Have a nice day." He tipped an imaginary hat.

"Don't get too cocky, son," Boudreau muttered, looking around. "They could have friends."

Tristan smiled at Boudreau. "Not as good a friend as I have."

Chapter Ten

Vernon Lee watched the recording his computer expert had just received and uploaded to the plasma screen. He didn't take his eyes off the screen for the entire one and a half minutes. When it ended with Tristan DuChaud saying, *Have a nice day, Mr. Lee*, Lee growled, "Play it again!"

On the screen, his voice amplified by the state-of-the-art speakers in Lee's media room, Tristan DuChaud said, *Have a nice day, Mr. Lee.*

A shiver of disgust slid through Lee. He didn't like smart-asses, and based on what he'd just seen, DuChaud was definitely a smart-ass. Lee watched the recording a third time.

So this was the man who had overheard him talking to that moron Poirier. The man who, in all likelihood, had copies of those conversations somewhere.

"Back it up to where he says have a nice day," Lee ordered his computer expert. "And freeze it there."

He studied DuChaud. Yep. A smart-ass. "You probably hid it in your house, didn't you?" Lee muttered. "You look like the type to hide it in plain sight." Without taking his eyes off the frozen picture of the man who could bring him crashing down, Lee picked up his phone and dialed a number.

"I'll get rid of that recording and you, smart-ass, with a perfect match." Lee chuckled. "A match. That's a good one."

After giving orders to his employee on the other end of the phone, Lee hung up and watched faces flash by on the screen, too fast to recognize what they were, much less who.

Bored, he stood. "Gartner," he said to his computer expert, "I'll be back in an hour. I'm having dinner with my daughter. Print out the facial matches and have them ready for me to look at."

Charles Gartner turned in his chair.

"Mr. Lee, it will probably take all night for the computer to find every facial match. Your database now contains more than a billion people."

"Did I ask you how long it would take?"

The American blinked, but his gaze didn't waver. "No, sir," he said, his face completely blank of expression.

Lee lifted his chin slightly. "What did I ask you to do?"

"To print out the facial matches for you."

"Do you know why I want that, even though DuChaud told me who he is?"

Gartner swallowed. "Yes, sir. You don't like mistakes or loose ends."

"That's very good, Mr. Gartner. What else don't I like?"

"Smart-asses, sir."

Lee thought he saw, just for an instant, a look of annoyance, maybe even anger, on Gartner's face, but it was gone before he could react to it. "Very good, Mr.

Gartner. Very good. Print them in color, if that's not too much trouble."

"No trouble at all, sir." Gartner turned back to the monitor. He picked up a pen and jotted a note onto his desk calendar.

Lee pushed the door to the penthouse open and went inside, looking forward to having dinner with his daughter.

SANDY WAS TIRED of reading, tired of napping, even tired of eating. She'd heated soup and made herself a grilled cheese sandwich earlier. She glanced at the portable stove and thought about firing it up again and making a cup of tea, but she didn't really want tea that badly.

Pouring a glass of water, she walked over to the French doors, thinking about where Tristan had been going in such a hurry earlier.

She'd heard the Jeep's motor, but by the time she'd gotten to the doors and opened them, he was taking off up the road. It occurred to her that in the past, she'd almost always known exactly where he was and what he was doing. He'd seldom stayed out late with buddies or stopped at the local watering hole for a drink or six.

But today, it had been hours since he'd taken off in the Jeep. He'd promised her he'd be home before dark. Apparently his word wasn't worth squat these days.

The sun was sinking low and the sky was turning pink. It looked as though it was going to be a clear night.

Her restlessness returned. She knew what she wanted to do. She wanted to go for a walk, maybe down to the dock, where she and Tristan had sat on so many evenings like this and watched the sun's reflection in the water until they could no longer see it. But it wasn't the same without him. Nothing was.

Besides, he'd told her to stay inside. Dejected and feeling a little sorry for herself, she watched the sky turn from pink to magenta, then to purple.

It was gloaming, that few minutes right before dark that she disliked so much.

Then, out of the dull palette of dark hues, a bright set of headlights caught her attention. Her stomach flipped, but immediately she recognized the Jeep's headlights and her heart soared like a teenager in the throes of her first crush. She reached for the doorknob to throw the door open and run to him, but as the door swung open, she stopped herself. She actually felt timid about going to him.

Because if he didn't gather her up in his arms, she wasn't sure if she could bear it.

So she waited, her pulse pounding in her ears. She tried to calm her breathing and her heartbeat, but it was no use. She knew she was on the verge of hyperventilating, but she couldn't help it. As he stepped onto the patio the light from the kitchen played on his face and emphasized the deep lines around his mouth and between his brows as he stepped inside.

He looked exhausted and in pain. His face was drawn and pale and his clothes looked two sizes too big. But he was here.

"Tristan," she said softly, the longing inside her reflected in her voice. Then she saw his swollen lip. "What happened?"

His nostrils flared as if he were taking in a deep breath. "Nothing," he muttered, looking down at the floor.

Suddenly, she wanted him so badly her entire body quivered. A desire so deep, so primal that it nearly doubled her over spread through her, and she wanted to grab him and kiss him and mold her body to his and damn the consequences.

But just as she began to lift her arms, his steady, solemn gaze filled with fire and he pulled her to him, so quickly that she lost her footing.

He caught her, wrapping his lean, muscled arms around her and burying his nose in her hair. She could hear and feel his unsteady breaths. He said nothing, just held her, squeezing a little too tightly, which was the perfect amount. She slid her arms around him and hugged him back.

After a long, long time, he lifted his head and kissed her. It was barely a kiss, just a brushing of lips against lips, but it ignited a sweet flame so deep and strong that it disturbed the little bean.

"Oh," she said.

"What?" Tristan whispered hoarsely, his lips still against hers.

"He kicked me. He's getting really good at that."

"Yeah?" His mouth flattened and he glanced down between them.

She took his hand. "Come with me," she said.

"San, I'm tired. This has been a long, long day. I just need to go to bed."

"Lucky for you," she said, "that's where we're going." She tugged on his hand until, with a sigh, he followed her.

In the bedroom, she turned back the covers. "Take off your shirt and sit down. I'll untie your shoes." She crouched down, settling her baby bump onto her lap, untied his sneakers and slid them off, then slid off his socks.

"I ought to take a shower," he said, his voice muffled as he pulled off his shirt.

She looked up at him. "You look clean."

"I bathed at Boudreau's, but still…"

She started to rise and Tristan stood and caught her arms, helping her up.

"I'm not that bad off yet," she said. "I can get up by myself."

He didn't comment as he unbuckled his belt and let his pants drop to the floor.

Sandy went to the other side of the bed and quickly shed her clothes.

"I've got something to show you," she said, climbing under the covers beside him. She lay back against the pillows. "Look." She pushed the covers down to expose her breasts and belly.

Tristan took a swift breath. "Wow," he said.

"I know. I'm huge. The little bean's kicking around in there and making things pretty uncomfortable for me."

Tristan put his hand out, then drew it back.

"It's okay." She caught his hand and placed it, palm down, on her tummy. "Rub right here." She moved his hand to the right side. "The bean likes that."

Tristan's fingers tentatively spread over her skin and she closed her eyes.

The desire was still there, throbbing within her, but her heart was filled with something more now. This was all she'd ever wanted. She and Tristan, together, with their baby. A family, bonded together with such strength of love that nothing could ever tear them apart.

She pressed Tristan's hand against her skin, guiding it back and forth, back and forth, in the spot where the little bean's feet usually were. After a few seconds, she felt a tiny kick from the inside.

"Did you feel that?" she asked.

Tristan turned onto his side. He looked up at her. "That was a kick?"

"Hey, he's not very big yet," she said indignantly.

"How big?"

She held her hands up, about ten inches apart. "And he probably weighs around twelve ounces or so."

"Our little bean," Tristan whispered. "Have you named him already?" He looked up at her.

She shook her head. "I'd wanted us to do that together, and then you— Then I kind of figured that I'd probably name him after you."

Tristan stared at her for a long time, then he pushed up on his elbow and leaned over and kissed her belly. "Hi, little bean," he said softly.

Sandy's breath caught as she watched her husband greeting his child. "You know, the doctor told me he can hear now. He said we should talk to him."

"You've been doing that all along, haven't you?"

Sandy laughed. "Yes."

"Because you talk to everything. The plants, the food, me—even when I'm asleep."

"I cannot deny that I do," she said.

Tristan straightened, still looking at her. "San, I don't know what will happen if I try to make love with you, but I'd like to try."

She touched his face. "I'll do anything you need me to do."

"You may need to be on top. My damn leg won't hold me up very well."

"That won't be a problem," she said.

Tristan pushed himself up until he could reach her mouth and kissed her with all the abandoned ardor of a man who hadn't made love with his wife in more than four months.

She felt him harden against her thigh and thought, as she had the last time they'd almost made love, that if he had trouble it would not be with his virility. Her desire swelled inside her until she ached and pulsed with need. With a moan, she slid down into the bed on her side, facing him.

She leaned over to kiss him and he grimaced. "Oh, you're on your right side," she said. "That's your bad side. Here." She sat up and moved over. "Lie on your back and I'll do the work."

His face turned red. "I don't want it to be like this, San."

"Like what? You're injured so I will take over temporarily, because I do love it when you're above me, my man."

Tristan opened his mouth to protest again, but Sandy bent down and kissed him. She kept on kissing him as she straddled him, feeling his arousal grow harder. She lifted herself onto her knees and let him be the guide as she slowly and carefully lowered herself onto him.

Being filled by her husband was an exquisite pleasure and a pulse-pounding need. Her muscles contracted around him and he groaned and thrust upward, grasping her around the waist and lifting her, his lean, muscled arms straining to hold her suspended while he searched her face for any trace of pain or discomfort.

"I'm wonderful," she said, her voice low and sultry. "Let go. I want to feel you. One hundred percent of you." He did as she asked and she sank down onto him, then began to move.

Tristan made a noise deep in his throat as he took her

by the waist again. She moaned in protest, but it was immediately obvious that he wasn't planning to stop her or slow her down this time.

No, he was controlling the pace, easing them into a deliberately steady rhythm that was not enough for her. She kept trying to rush each thrust, but Tristan held on to her and kept the rhythm steady.

"Tris, let me move," she murmured.

"Don't rush it, San. Keep it slow and steady. In and out. In and out. Feel the sensations. You know how we like it best."

"But it's been so long. I need—"

Tristan leaned up and pulled Sandy to him, until he could reach her breasts with his mouth.

She touched his cheek. "Tris, don't forget about the milk," she said softly.

He took a shaky breath. "I haven't." He closed his mouth over her right breast and ran his tongue across her distended nipple.

"Oh!" she cried, trying to breathe normally, trying to keep it steady and failing. Her back arched to push her breast into his mouth. Then she felt him sucking lightly on the tender tip. She gasped and at the same time, his insistent rhythm sped up, until they were moving together, faster and faster.

His thrusts sent her higher and higher until she was sure she was about to explode into a thousand pieces.

Her jagged flashes of pleasure synced with his thrusts. They breathed in tandem and moved in perfect accord.

Then Tristan thrust harder than he had so far, and he touched something so deep within her that she did explode. Thousands of bright stars burst in front of her vision and thousands more popped and sizzled inside her.

And everywhere they touched, they singed her with another level of pleasure. She had no concept of anything
except the two of them and the culmination of joy they
were sharing.

Much later, Tristan's shoulder moved restlessly under
Sandy's head and she murmured in protest. He turned his
head and pressed a kiss into her hair. "My arm's going
to sleep. Sorry I'm such a wimp."

"You are not," Sandy said, lifting her head enough that
he could slide his arm out. She laid her head back down
on the pillow. "You're injured. You've hardly had time
to recover. That's not a wimp. That's a very brave man."
She stretched and yawned, feeling tiny aftershocks of her
climaxes. She moaned in languid pleasure.

Tristan stretched, too. Sandy watched him, admiring
his lean torso and smooth golden skin. She reached out
to touch his chest, but he suddenly froze for an instant,
then jackknifed, uttering a cry of pain as he reached for
his right leg.

"Tris? What's wrong?" she asked, sitting up to see
what he was doing.

His fingers were gingerly massaging the muscle
that was left on the inside of his calf. His face was distorted into a mask of pain. Sandy reached for him, but he
shrugged away. He was breathing between clenched teeth
and every so often another groan would escape his lips.

She saw the knotted muscles on the inside of his calf.
They were bulging and twisted. This was the first time
she'd seen the damage the sharks had done. The outside
of his calf was horribly disfigured. There was nothing
on there but skin pulled over bone and the scars of ugly,
uneven stitches.

She pressed her lips together to hold back a moan at

what she saw. The muscle that ran along the outside of his right calf had been ripped away by a shark's sharp teeth. There was no imagining the kind of pain he'd endured, and the physical agony had only been part of his suffering. He'd been plunged into dark, murky water filled with sharks. He'd been lucky not to have been sliced in two by the fish's sharp teeth.

"Oh, Tris, how did you stand it?"

He didn't answer her. But she felt a lessening of the tension in his body. The cramps were easing. His fingers relaxed and he leaned back against the pillows. When she dared to peer at his face, it appeared almost relaxed, as well.

"It's stopped hurting?"

He blew out a breath. "It stopped cramping. That's a big deal." He let his head fall back against the pillow. His face was pale, but it was no longer a mask of pain. Within seconds, he was breathing softly and evenly. He was asleep.

Sandy smiled and touched the tip of her finger to the lines in the middle of his forehead. She smoothed them out as lightly and carefully as she could, then she leaned over and kissed him just at the corner of his mouth. He didn't seem to wake up.

She sank down into the bed and settled her head on the pillow. Now that he was no longer in pain, she felt comfortable going to sleep herself.

Tristan was here. She was safe.

Until all hell broke loose.

Chapter Eleven

"What the hell?" Tristan cried, his head filled with what sounded like the howling of the hounds of hell.

"Smoke alarm," she muttered, groaning as she pushed the covers away. "I'll reset it."

"No!" he yelled as he vaulted out of the bed, straightening his right leg carefully. He couldn't have it cramping again. Not now.

"Sandy!" he shouted to be heard over the siren. "Sandy! Get dressed. The house is on fire!"

"What?" She sat up and squinted.

"There." He pointed toward the open door to the hall. Eerie orange and yellow reflections danced on the walls.

She got up and grabbed her jeans. "Oh, my God. I didn't leave the portable stove on, did I?"

"Hurry!" He had his jeans and tennis shoes on. He grabbed his shirt. "Lee did this."

"Lee?" Sandy repeated as she pulled on her jeans and stepped into her Skechers flats.

"The man who tried to have me killed. Stay here. I'm going to see how bad the fire is. And stay away from the windows."

"They're still out there?"

Just as she spoke, a very loud crack split the air, easy to hear above the blaring siren. She screamed.

"Get down!" Tristan yelled.

Sandy immediately dropped to the floor. "Was that a gunshot?" she asked incredulously. "They set fire to the house and now they're *shooting* at us?"

Tristan looked up. The bullet had come in high. It hit just under the crown molding. "Maybe not. That came in really high. Lee may have told them not to kill us."

"Thoughtful of him," Sandy said archly.

Tristan smiled. "I think we'll be okay. The alarm is hooked up to the fire department now, right?"

"No," she said.

"Damn it, I told you to call them and—"

"I did. They couldn't get it to work this far out."

Tristan cursed. "Okay. No problem. *Those guys* don't know it's not hooked up. They're not going to stay around long with the siren blaring like that, *and* I'll bet you Boudreau will open fire any second now."

He heard something, a lower-pitched blast, still loud enough to overcome the siren. "There he is." He walked over to the window.

"Tris? What are you doing? Get away from there."

He didn't answer. He crouched down in front of the window and pulled the automatic pistol out of his jeans. He'd taken off the specially made magazine, so he couldn't use it on automatic, but he could let them know he was armed and dangerous.

He opened fire before he could identify anything to aim at. He aimed low, hoping not to kill anyone. The only person he'd ever killed was the unfortunate roughneck he'd dragged with him into the water on the oil rig. And that had been mostly accidental.

A bullet shattered the upper part of the window and slammed into the wall behind him about a foot above their heads. Maybe they weren't trying to miss them.

"Sandy, lie down on the floor. All the way down." He didn't hear her if she answered him because at that instant a reverberating boom split the air.

It was Boudreau's shotgun. The Cajun had let loose with both barrels. The 12 gauge was an impressive weapon. It's only disadvantages were its weight and how few rounds it held.

Behind him, he heard Sandy say something, but she wasn't talking loud enough.

"What?" he shouted as another slug hit the wall barely a foot above his head. He fired back, still unable to see anything except the darkness and an ever-growing cloud of smoke from the fire. He could smell it now.

"Sandy?" he yelled. "Stay put. Boudreau's out there. This will be over in no time."

She didn't answer.

"San?" he called, just as a slug whistled close to his ear. "Damn it! They are shooting to kill. San? Where are you?"

"I'm right here," she said.

He glanced around and saw her crawling toward the closet.

"Get back behind the bed," he yelled. "What the hell are you doing?"

"I need to get the box with all our photos," she rasped, then coughed. "And all our papers."

"No! You're going to get shot."

"But all our papers will burn up. Our marriage license."

Another slug whizzed past his ear, too close for comfort. "Damn it, Sandy. Get. Down!"

Boudreau's shotgun roared again, its low-pitched boom echoing through the air underneath the squeal of the siren.

Tristan ducked below the edge of the window and looked toward Sandy. She was on the floor, crawling back toward the far side of the bed.

At that instant a barrage of gunfire hit the window, sending shattered glass everywhere.

"Cover your head!" he yelled as he closed his eyes and did the same. Once the gunfire ceased, he eased his head up so he could see out. He saw something fiery red, lighting an arc in the darkness. A flare gun. *God bless Boudreau.*

Tristan heard more gunfire, but it wasn't aimed toward the house this time. They were shooting at Boudreau. Another flare erupted and lit up in the dark.

In the red light, Tristan saw two moving shadows. He opened fire, forgetting his plan to try to avoid killing anyone. These people were shooting at them. They deserved what they got.

He saw the flare stop suddenly and heard a man scream. The flare had hit him square in the torso.

He fired again. "Shoot another one, Boudreau," he muttered. "I need to see." As if he'd heard him, Boudreau fired another flare that lit up the area with eerie red light. Tristan saw a moving shadow bending over, probably checking on his buddy. He aimed and fired and the shadow went down.

Tristan realized he was holding his breath. He blew it out and took a deep breath to replace it. But instead of clean, refreshing air, harsh smoke filled his lungs, throwing him into a painful coughing fit.

By the time he caught his breath, he heard the crunch of footsteps outside the window. He stiffened and aimed his weapon, wondering why he could suddenly hear. Then he realized the siren had stopped. The battery must have run down.

"Tristan!"

It was Boudreau, standing at the window. "Boudreau!" he yelled, triggering another coughing fit. He heard Sandy coughing behind him, too. "Are they down?"

Boudreau nodded. "One dead. One wounded. One running for the truck they came in. Let's go. The house is going up."

"What?"

"You got to get out of there. You're inhaling smoke. Where's your wife?"

"Behind the bed. Sandy?" he called.

"Get her. That fire's out of control."

Tristan turned away from the window. "Sandy, let's go. We've got to climb out the window. Boudreau will help you." He backed toward the door to the hall.

"Where are you going?" Sandy asked.

"Go to the window, San. I'll be right behind you."

He ran out of the bedroom and saw exactly what Boudreau was talking about. The whole front of the house was painted with an odd red-yellow color, swirled about with black. *Fire and smoke.*

He'd been absolutely right when he'd told Sandy there was no time to save belongings. But he had to grab one thing. The flash drive that held the incriminating satellite phone conversations. That was why Lee had resorted to fire. He was determined to destroy any evidence of his involvement.

Shoving the nursery door open, he jerked the blue mobile down from over the bed. As he hurried back to the master bedroom, he felt around on the plastic decoration until he found what he was looking for. A blue rhinestone-studded flash drive in the shape of a baseball glove. He tossed the plastic mobile onto the floor and put the flash drive in his pocket.

Back in the bedroom, Sandy had barely moved. She was trying to get her feet under her, hanging on to a bedpost for balance.

He held out his hand. "Come on. We've got to get out of here. Boudreau's taken care of the bad guys."

She didn't answer. She was almost passed out from the smoke. He pulled her to her feet. "Okay," she wheezed. "I'm fine now." But she was panting for air.

He held out his hand and Sandy took it, squeezing tightly. "Don't be afraid," he said. "I'm right here."

The shallow breaths became coughs. Once she started coughing she couldn't stop, not even long enough to catch her breath.

"Tristan, let's go." Boudreau's head was turned, checking out the area around them. "You got to get her out of there. She's got too much smoke in her lungs."

Tristan took a breath to answer, but all he breathed in was smoke. He started coughing, too.

"*Maintenant.* You both got to be breathing clean air—now!"

Sandy had quit trying. Her limbs were limp. She was exhausted from coughing and from lack of oxygen. He wrapped his arm around her waist to guide her.

"Try to climb up on the windowsill, San. Boudreau, help me. My leg's about to give out on me."

"Sit her up on the sill," Boudreau said.

Tristan managed to lift her by balancing most of his weight on his left leg.

"Do it...myself," she muttered between coughs.

"Okay, Boudreau. Pull her out. She's exhausted."

Boudreau's large hands caught her by the waist and lifted her out through the window.

"Got her!" he called.

Tristan managed to climb through the window, but when he let go and landed on the ground his leg gave way and he fell. His calf muscle cramped and he could do nothing but roll on the grass and massage the knots until the pain eased up.

"Get up, you," Boudreau whispered. "The guy who ran for the truck's coming back. And there's a second man coming behind him."

"Take Sandy and run to my Jeep," Tristan said, massaging the muscle.

"*Non! C'est impossible.* They shot out your tires first thing.

"Sandy's car, then." Tristan pushed himself to his feet.

"They're between us and her car. We'd have a shoot-out in the open and she's in no shape to run." Boudreau kept an eye out for anyone approaching as he talked. "Now get up!" he snapped.

"And do what?" Tristan shot back. "Sounds to me like we're trapped here."

"We've got to find cover. Somebody's gonna notice the smoke and the fire department will come. Meanwhile, we got to hide. Head for the cabin."

Tristan helped Sandy to her feet and held on to her as she had another coughing fit.

"That's a surefire trap. They'll follow us and block the path."

"*Oui*, but, *cher*, we know the swamp. They don't."

A spate of gunfire sounded. Boudreau looked at Tristan and nodded toward the path to the dock, then he headed for the corner of the building. He planned to draw the pursuers' fire while Tristan and Sandy made it into the vines and branches that would hide them from view.

Tristan felt like a coward and a failure, leaving Boudreau to fight alone. But at the same time, his primary goal was to keep Sandy and the baby safe. So he guided her toward the path as quickly as he could, cringing every time he heard a gunshot.

Sandy had finally quit coughing, but fighting the smoke in her lungs had exhausted her. She had more trouble navigating the path than he did. He tried letting go of her, but they were more stable together than apart.

Before they'd been on the path one minute, he heard rifle fire, followed by two shotgun blasts. He stopped, so suddenly that Sandy stumbled. He couldn't bear the thought that he'd left Boudreau back there by himself, fighting men who were probably trained soldiers and who likely had some of the best weaponry available.

But getting Sandy to safety was the most important thing. Wincing at the gunfire, Tristan pulled Sandy close again and headed up the path to Boudreau's house.

"Just a little farther, San."

She nodded doggedly, obviously concentrating on putting one foot in front of the other for long enough to get to the cabin.

He turned her face to his and studied it. Were her lips

turning blue, or was he seeing the combination of soot and the dancing reflections of the fire and smoke? He ran his thumb across her lips, then looked at it. Sure enough, his thumb came away stained with soot.

But the blue tint was still there. Was she that oxygen-deprived? There was no doubt that she was struggling to breathe. If he didn't get some clean air into her lungs and some fresh water for her to drink to wash out the toxins, her lack of oxygen could not only hurt her, it could harm the baby.

He cursed his leg. They should have gotten to the cabin by now. He set his jaw against the pain and tried to increase his speed, hoping Sandy could keep up.

He heard a rustling of the vines and leaves lining the path behind them. He immediately dropped to the ground behind a tree and pulled Sandy down beside him. Retrieving his gun, he waited.

Beside him, Sandy made a small, distressed sound. "Tris, I'm tired—" A strangled cough erupted from her throat. She covered her mouth with both hands, but it didn't help. The coughs kept coming.

"Hang in there, hon," Tristan muttered, wincing at the noise she was making and wondering who—or what—he'd heard moving through the underbrush. "We'll be at Boudreau's in no time. Can you try not to cough?"

She made a guttural sound, a laugh or a groan.

At that instant, the leaves and vines started shaking and someone stepped into the path. Tristan stiffened and tightened his hand on the gun's trigger, but it was Boudreau.

He breathed a sigh of relief and stood. Boudreau looked startled to see them.

"I'm sorry. We're going as fast as we can."

Boudreau's mouth tightened. "Just keep going. I'll stay here, hold 'em back."

"We'll make it. Come on, Sandy." He helped her to her feet and put his arm around her again. He turned them toward Boudreau's house and started walking.

Just then a loud crack followed by a whizzing sound split the air.

"Down!" Boudreau whispered. He remained standing and held the double-barreled shotgun at hip height and fired two shots.

Another rifle shot split the air.

"Mon Dieu," he heard Boudreau mutter. "I let them get too close."

Tristan pushed Sandy down behind a bush. He crouched beside her, listening. From what he could tell from the direction of the gunfire, the men were below his friend on the path, so any shot he took might hit Boudreau.

Within a minute, the men pursuing them loosed a barrage of gunfire. Boudreau threw himself to the ground.

"Boudreau," he called out quietly between rifle shots. "You okay?"

The Cajun waved his hand. His message was *I'm fine.* The fact that he used their sign language sent its own message. *Quiet! They're very close.*

More gunfire erupted from below them. Tristan ducked.

"Sandy?" He looked down at her, but she had her eyes closed. The corners of her mouth were white and pinched.

At that instant Boudreau rose, fired two thunderous rounds, ducked to reload in record time, then rose and fired two more rounds. He half turned and gestured to Tristan to head on to the cabin.

Tristan rose carefully. His leg was practically useless now. He felt as though he were dragging it. "San? Can you stand?"

She nodded. As they rose, two more shots rang out and Boudreau fired back.

He held out his hand for Sandy. She jerked and uttered a small, strangled moan as she straightened.

"I'm sorry, hon. I swear it won't be much longer. Just keep going for me. Can you?" He had no idea where his determination was coming from.

If he were alone, he was sure he'd have collapsed long ago and done the best he could until a bullet took him out. But he wasn't alone, so he couldn't give up. He wouldn't do that. Not to Boudreau, who'd saved his life at least twice already, and certainly not to Sandy and their baby. He had to keep going for them.

"Okay," she said breathlessly.

They set out again for the cabin, trusting Boudreau to fend off their attackers.

Chapter Twelve

By the time they saw Boudreau's cabin, every step for Tristan was a separate, blazing agony and a fool's bet on a losing hand. Odds were that his next step could send him sprawling.

The only reason he hadn't collapsed already was because he'd known Sandy couldn't make it on her own. Her breathing was so shallow that she was panting. For some reason, she wasn't recovering from the smoke as quickly as he was. His cough was almost gone and he was breathing more easily.

He stumbled through the cabin door and finally let go of Sandy. She flopped down onto the bed Boudreau had made for him. "Breathe deeply," he said. "Sandy. Listen to me."

She had her eyes closed, but she obediently tried to pull in a deep lungful of air, but it set off a coughing fit.

Boudreau came in on their heels.

"Miss Sandy," he said. "You got to breathe deep. Got to get all that smoke out of your lungs. Drink water, too. Get rid of the toxins the smoke make."

He pressed his fist into the middle of his chest. "Tristan, press on her diaphragm, gently, like this. Not hard. Just enough to make her blow as much air out of her lungs as possible. Then let go. She'll have to breathe." As he talked, Boudreau grabbed a hunting vest from a nail behind the door.

Tristan nodded. "Got it," he said, pulling the handgun from the vest. "Wait. Are you headed back out? Can't you rest?"

But Boudreau shook his head as he stuffed the pockets of the vest with shotgun shells. "Got to keep an eye out for them. Can't let them get any closer. Long as we can hold them off, we're okay. They got the path from here to the dock blocked. We can't get down and anybody that comes up this way's got to go through them."

"What about the north side, by the artesian spring? Zach and I climbed up that way when we were kids."

Boudreau nodded. "When you weighed less than half what you weigh now. Remember all that rain back a couple months ago, right before you were shoved off the rig? It washed a gully across down below the spring. Weren't really possible to go that way before, the spring had eroded it so much. Now there ain't no way anybody can get through there. It's like a gumbo mud moat around my house."

"So they can't get to us without us seeing them on the path, but we can't get out, either," Tristan said.

Boudreau sighed. "Let me get out there. I got to do some thinking about what we need to do."

"Boudreau," Tristan said as his friend headed back outside. "Be careful."

He was barely out the door when Sandy started coughing again and Tristan kept pressing on her chest.

"Oh," she said, gasping. "You're pushing all…the air out. I can't…breathe."

"I've got to. You've inhaled a lot of smoke. I'll get you

some water." He didn't like how she looked at all. She was pale and her hands were trembling, as were her lips. She sat, limp, with her eyes closed.

From a bucket that sat on a wooden table, Tristan filled a cup with water and brought it to her. "Here. It's water. Take it." He lifted her right hand and pressed the cup into it.

She curled her fingers around it and lifted it to her lips.

He went back to the table and washed his hands, then brought a bowl of clean water over to the bed.

She had drunk about half the water. "That's good, hon, but you need to drink it all."

"I'm fine," she said, but talking made her cough again. She took another sip from the cup.

"Good. Now see if you can breathe deep on your own. You're doing better. We're going to get those lungs cleaned out."

He wrung out a wet cloth and started cleaning her face as she sipped water from the cup.

Then by the time he got her face clean, she started coughing again. She gasped and grimaced.

"Your throat hurting?"

She shook her head. "My tummy."

Tristan emptied the bowl and wrung out the cloth. "Like a stomach cramp?"

She shook her head and looked at him without blinking. "No. It *hurts*. I think something's wrong."

Tristan stopped wiping at a smudge on her cheek and studied her. "What do you mean? With the baby?"

She shook her head. "I don't know." She lifted her shirt above the waist of her jeans and placed her hand on the top of her baby bump. Beneath her fingers, the denim was dark and damp. Too dark.

Blood? His heart thudded against his chest as a sick fear overtook him. Dear God, was she losing the baby?

"Ugh. My jeans are wet." She looked at her hand, which was streaked with blood. "Tristan? Is that blood?" she said, her face turning pale.

"Yeah, there's a little blood," he said matter-of-factly, doing his best to mask his fear. "Do you remember running into anything?"

"I—I'm not sure. Tristan? What is it?"

"Don't worry, San, it's okay," he said, hoping it was. But what could have happened to make her bleed, except... "Lie back. I need to take a look."

Sandy took hold of his hand and pulled herself around so she could lie down. He pushed her shirt up again and immediately saw why she was bleeding.

There was a small hole in the jeans, about two inches to the right of the zipper.

"Oh, God," he whispered. He touched the ragged hole. There was no doubt what it was. It was a bullet hole. She'd been shot.

"Tris? What's wrong?" Sandy asked.

He tried to speak, but his throat had closed up and nothing, not even a squeak of air, could get through. He swallowed and tried again. "Damn jeans are *tight*!" he muttered.

"The little bean is getting bigger," Sandy murmured.

By the time Tristan got her jeans down and off over her feet there was a lot of blood. The tight jeans had apparently served as a compress, keeping the bleeding to a minimum.

Without their pressure, she was bleeding freely—too freely from the small entrance wound. He used a clean cloth to wipe the blood away from her rounded tummy so he could see the wound. It was no bigger than the hole in her jeans, but that was no comfort. She'd been shot—in her tummy—where she was carrying their baby.

He wanted to scream, but he couldn't. She was watching him with wide, frightened eyes, waiting for him to assure her that everything was all right. He had to hold it together for her, because for some reason she still thought he was strong.

"Okay," he said, doing his damnedest to keep his voice steady. "Looks like one of those bullets that were flying around hit you in the tummy, but it's not nearly as bad as all the blood makes it look."

"Bullet?" She lifted her head to try to see. "I was shot? Tristan?" She took one look at his face and started crying. "What about the baby?"

"Shh, everything's going to be okay," he said, hoping she would believe him. "Do you know when it happened?"

"No," she said, her eyes closed and her arms limp at her sides again. "When we stood up from behind that second bush, I thought the jeans zipper pinched me. Maybe it wasn't the zipper. Maybe it was a bullet."

It had to be. There had been a couple of shots fired about the time Boudreau had yelled at them to run.

"Tristan," she cried, grabbing his arm. "What about the baby!"

"Hey. I'm right here. I promise you, he's going to be fine." He mentally crossed himself and asked forgiveness for whatever kind of lie it was that spared a terrified, wounded young woman a horrible possibility.

"How can you know? You can't know. Bean!" she shrieked, wrapping her hands around her baby bump.

"Little bean?" Those two words were so low he barely heard them.

Boudreau appeared at the door. "Tristan, she's got to stay quiet." He looked at her belly. "Oh." He muttered a French curse word and propped his shotgun against the door facing.

Tristan met his gaze and saw the worry on his face. "Is there an exit wound?" he asked.

"I don't know," Tristan said. "I don't think so."

Boudreau's brows drew down. "Move over," he ordered.

Tristan moved.

Boudreau sat in his place. "Miss Sandy, I've got to look at your back for a minute. Okay? I'm going to lift you up. I hope it don't hurt too much. But I've got to do it. Okay?"

Sandy's eyes lifted to Tristan's, and he nodded. So she nodded at Boudreau.

He lifted her with his big hands and turned her toward him, onto her side. She sucked in a quick breath when he lifted her, but then she was quiet.

Boudreau examined her from her buttocks all the way up to her hairline. Then he looked at Tristan and shook his head.

Tristan felt a combination of relief and dismay. Relief that the bullet hadn't exited her body, leaving a much larger and more damaging wound than the entrance one.

But no exit wound could be worse. That meant that the bullet was still inside her. And if it had bounced off a bone, a bullet could do immeasurable damage to internal organs. The fog in Tristan's brain turned to a sharp, sheer panic.

That bullet was in there, inside his wife. She could be

hemorrhaging internally. If it had ripped into the womb, it could have hit the baby.

"Tris? What is it? Is it bad?" Sandy asked, her voice rising in pitch again. Tristan needed to say something comforting to her. He tried. But his voice wouldn't work.

His gaze met Boudreau's and he read the message in the old man's eyes loud and clear. *Do not upset your little wife.*

Substituting determination for truth, he turned to his wife. "No. Luckily your back's not bleeding, and that's a good thing," he said with a small smile.

Boudreau stood. "I got to go. I think they're pretty close. Can't give them a minute or they might be on top of us."

Tristan could see that Boudreau was past exhaustion. In his tired eyes and in the droop of his sinewy shoulders, Tristan could count how many hours it had been since he'd slept.

He looked back at Sandy and found her watching him with that same wide-eyed, frightened expression on her face.

"Are you still hurting?" he asked.

She nodded without taking her eyes off him.

Boudreau pointed to a box sitting on the rough-hewn table under the window. "There's salve and potion in there. The same potion I gave you. Don't give her much. And look in that trunk at the end of my bed. You might find a nightshirt she can wear. Tie a couple of cloths together to make a bandage to wrap around the wound. Miss Sandy, you hold pressure with your hand until he gets the cloth wrapped around. Okay?"

Her head moved infinitesimally.

Boudreau went back outside.

When Tristan brought the potion to Sandy with a chaser of water, she asked him, "Is it safe for the baby?" she asked.

Tristan nodded as he poured some of the milky liquid from the brown jug into a tin cup. "Boudreau wouldn't give it to you if it wasn't okay. But it'll probably make you sleepy," he said, brushing her hair back from her face again. "That's okay. Just go ahead and take a nap. I'll get you a nightshirt in a little while. Okay?"

"Tris?" she said softly. "I haven't felt him kick." Her eyes were shining with tears. "And I know that's a bad sign."

He smiled at her and touched her lips with his fingers. "No worries, okay? That baby's fine. He's tired, just like the rest of us." He touched her chin and leaned down and gave her a quick kiss on the corner of her mouth, but she didn't smile back at him. She closed her eyes and a lone tear slid down her cheek.

"I'm going to see what it looks like outside. I'll be close by," he said, then stood and stepped outside.

The first thing he saw in the dark sky was the fire. The yellow and orange flames licked at the sky. It was obviously out of control. The house had been his father's and his grandfather's before that. Now it and everything inside it was gone.

"Our friends do that?" he asked Boudreau.

"Yep," Boudreau said, walking up to stand beside him. "I'm pretty sure they used gasoline."

"It's going to burn to the ground."

"Yep."

Tristan watched the fire for a moment, then realized that besides the flickering light of the fire he saw red blinking lights.

"Fire trucks," he muttered. "They finally saw the smoke and fire from town. We didn't call them and God knows we don't have any neighbors out here."

Boudreau nodded. "I think that blue light's the sheriff. Reckon the fire department notified him."

"He'll be looking for us—well, Sandy and you."

"And he'll see the spent shells and the shot-out tires."

"Think he'll try to find you?"

"Wouldn't be surprised," Boudreau said, "but he can't do any good coming up here by himself. Sure do hope he'll call in the Coast Guard or some help from up in Houma."

Tristan understood what Boudreau was saying. If the sheriff tried to take the path to Boudreau's house, the assassins could pick him off like a trapped rabbit.

Boudreau shifted and lifted his head, as if he'd heard something. "Now, son, listen to me," he said quietly. "There's a crate buried in the ground in back. It's under the woodpile. Move the three logs on the far left, then pry the top off the crate. Inside there's another flare gun, more ammunition and a few small mines."

"Mines?" Tristan echoed. "You mean land mines? Where did you get mines?"

"Army surplus," Boudreau answered coolly, letting Tristan know by his tone that he wasn't referring to the neighborhood store that sold camouflage clothing and old ammo boxes. We're going to need some leverage to stay ahead of them, so I need you to pull out three of those mines for me, grab a bucketful of shells and load a flare gun. I'll be back to pick them up. I need it inside, ready to go, because I might not have much time."

After another few seconds of silence, Tristan said, "Boudreau, she hasn't felt the baby kick."

Boudreau didn't move, but his head bowed a fraction of an inch. "Can't do a thing but wait, son. A woman's body is a powerful thing when it's protecting a child. Have faith."

But Tristan heard a worried tone in the other man's voice. "What's the matter?" he asked.

"There's two of them varmints, at least. Maybe three. I don't know where they are. Like I said, I heard something a while back. Could have been them, but they never showed themselves, neither did they shoot."

"Two? Maybe three? You mean including the two you shot at the house? Because I only saw three total."

"Nope. Remember, I saw another guy get out of their truck. And there could have been another one still. I thought I saw a shadow, but I was intent on aiming at the one I did see, not checking shadows."

"Are you sure they're still following you? Maybe they turned back, or—" He'd almost said, *Or went another way*, but Boudreau had already told him there was only one way out. They were surrounded by swamp water that covered gumbo mud.

"They ain't turning around," Boudreau said. "Not with the firefighters and the sheriff down there. And if the sheriff tries to pursue them up here, he'll be like a sitting duck on that path."

"So they're lying in wait on the path for us to go down or the sheriff to come up."

"I suspect that's right. They might not have sense enough to know what the land around here is like, but I'll bet either them or their boss know how to read a topo map. He won't know about the log bridges to the hideout, though. All he can see on those maps is swampland."

Tristan nodded. For the first time in his life he found

himself hating the gumbo mud and murky waters of the bayou. Right now they weren't beautiful and mysterious— they were the reason he couldn't get Sandy to a doctor.

"God, Boudreau. We shouldn't have come up here. We're stranded now. We should have run for the car."

"I told you earlier, son. They shot your tires out."

"Then we should have—hell, I don't know—grabbed one of their trucks or run up the road toward town or called the sheriff. Something other than coming here to be trapped. Boudreau, she could die."

"Keep your voice down."

"Maybe we should go to the hideout." But as soon as Tristan said it, he knew he couldn't do it. He cursed. "I can't walk the log bridges. They were slippery and wobbly back when I was a kid, and this damn leg's already quitting on me."

Boudreau sent him a sidelong glance. "Then you'll crawl across if you want to live—and save your wife and that baby."

Tristan took a deep breath. Boudreau was right. He was acting like a spoiled kid. He straightened and looked Boudreau full in the eye. "Then I'll crawl across."

"Okay, then. Get her up and go. It's going to be dawn in a couple of hours and those varmints will probably think they can do things in the daylight they can't in the dark."

"You can't stay here by yourself. You're exhausted, too. I'll take her, then I'll come back."

"Nope. No, you won't, son. You come back here and I'll feed you to 'em and leave that bad leg for last, just so it'll hurt you longer."

"Yes, sir," Tristan said, too tired and worried to react to Boudreau's attempt at humor. "But what about the sheriff? What do you think is going to happen when he comes upon those guys? He'll figure they set the fire."

"Maybe," Boudreau said. "But he's not going to be expecting hostiles. If he tries to walk over here, he'll be thinking he'll see me and maybe your little wife. And that's all."

"We can't let them kill him."

Boudreau laid his hand on Tristan's arm. "Son, if you can think of something we can do, I swear I'll do it. But it's up to you. I'm all out of ideas. The only thing I got left is hide till they find us and try to pick them off, wait for the sheriff to bring in reinforcements, or attack them, although I'd rather not risk that. I don't know."

Tristan stared at him. For his entire life he'd looked up to Boudreau. He'd thought the old Cajun was the smartest man he'd ever known. He'd never heard him say the words *I don't know.*

In the silence, a bird sang out. Boudreau lifted his head, then he lifted his rifle. "Mockingbirds don't sing at night. That's them. Why don't you get inside there and find your little wife something to wear while I make sure those varmints aren't getting any closer."

Tristan fetched the mines and flares and brought them inside, along with some nylon rope he found back there. He pushed them underneath Boudreau's bed, then went to the old trunk. When he opened it and dug beneath the winter coat and a couple of blankets, he found something that surprised him. It was a gown. Not a nightshirt. A woman's nightgown, made of cotton with a lace collar.

He hesitated a second, then decided that Boudreau meant for him to find it and use it. But even as he tried to imagine the woman who had worn it here in this cabin, he vowed that if Boudreau didn't bring it up he never would.

He set the gown on the bed and fetched some rags, which he tore into long strips then tied together. He hated to wake her. She was sleeping peacefully. Her breathing was almost normal and she wasn't coughing every few breaths.

She woke up with little effort and he got the bandages around her and anchored the cloth without too much trouble. She was obedient and raised her arms so he could slip the gown over her head and down.

He wanted to hold her and kiss her and tell her how much he loved her, but there was no time for that. Sadly, there might never be if he didn't hurry up.

"Everything okay?" he asked as he pushed her gently down to sit on the bed so he could slip her shoes on.

Then he took her hands and urged her to stand. She did, leaning against him, the heat of her body reaching him through the gown and his shirt. Her cheek against the side of his neck felt hot. For a brief moment, he stood there, letting her heat warm him.

But then it occurred to him that she might be too hot. He put his palm against her forehead, but he couldn't decide if she was giving off the comforting yet sexy warmth of sleep or if she had a fever.

"Is it far?" she asked, her head lolling a bit. "I need to go back to sleep."

"It's not far, I promise," he said, squeezing her tight and kissing the top of her head. "Okay, hon, ready?" He guided her and supported her on his left side while he used a walking stick that Boudreau kept by the cabin door to steady his right side.

When they came out of the cabin, he didn't see Boudreau, but he wasn't worried. There hadn't been any gunfire and he knew if Boudreau felt he needed to know where he was, he'd have told him.

"Okay, Sandy. We're off," he said with more spirit in his voice than was in his heart. He didn't know how much longer his leg was going to work. He knew that for the sake of avoiding damage, he should have stopped hours ago. But that was under normal circumstances, when he was not trying to save his wife and unborn child.

He looked in the direction of the hideout. There was no path visible. In fact, there was no indication that there was anything but dense, thick groves of cypress and mangrove along the entire perimeter of Boudreau's little clearing. But he knew there was a narrow strip of dry land there somewhere. Not exactly a path, but a way to get to Boudreau's hideout. He just had to find it.

He'd been to the hideout several times in the past—twenty years before. Praying for enough sense to find the hideout and enough strength to get that far, he trudged on, supporting Sandy.

"Tris," Sandy said, her voice slurred. "Where we going?"

"We're going to have a spend-the-night party in Boudreau's hideout."

"Spend-the-night party?"

"Yep. At his hideout. It's a great place to play cowboys and outlaws. And it's comfortable, too. Like camping out."

"Tris? Don't patronize me," she said, her voice still soft and sleepy-sounding, but her tone was imperious. Tristan's heart ached at the familiar warning tone in her voice. She was still weighted down by the fog of sleep. If she were fully awake this would be the beginning of an all-too-familiar argument. So familiar that he could quote it. It would be a lot like the last argument they'd had.

"Why won't you tell me the truth? I've got sense enough to know that there's something wrong."

"I am telling you the truth. I do enjoy working on the rig. I like the computer work."

"I see you, Tristan. Every time you come home, you're more worried. You don't talk to me. You don't touch me."

"I'm talking to you right now."

"No. This is not you. You've changed. This person standing in front of me is not the man I've loved all my life."

"Well, I don't know who you think I am, but I can assure you, I'm me."

"See, this is what I mean. I just can't talk to you."

"Sorry," he said to his sleepy wife. "I didn't mean to patronize you. We're going to Boudreau's hideout for a day or two."

"Because of those men who set fire to the house?"

So she was awake enough to remember the fire. He felt her straighten. "They're looking for us, but they won't find us there."

"How long till we get there?"

"Not long. Just a few minutes more. I know you're sleepy."

She put her free hand on her baby bump. "My tummy hurts. Little bean, what are you doing to me?" she said, then stumbled a bit.

"Whoa," Tristan said, struggling to keep his balance and hold on to her at the same time. He shuddered as pain shot through his calf. "I know you're hurting. But you've got to be aware of everything, okay? We're going to have to walk over a log bridge, and every step counts. Try to wake up."

He hoped she wasn't bleeding again. He had no idea if there were bandages in the hideout. Knowing Boudreau, there probably were. He hoped his friend had stashed some medication there, too.

"Bridge?" Sandy roused a bit. "Not those log bridges you and Zach used to play on? They were so slippery."

"We'll be fine. The logs are sturdy. And they'll keep us from having to walk in the swamp water. It's not deep, but you know how the mud is, and there could be snakes or alligators. And besides, these are the only clothes we have, so we've got to stay dry and that means no matter how tired we are or how much we hurt, we've got to stay on the bridge."

"You'll be right beside me, won't you?"

Dismay and fear roiled through him. Would he make it better or worse for her if he walked with her across the narrow logs Boudreau had put between the tiny islands of dry land deep in the swamp? "I will. I'll be right beside you. I'm sorry your tummy hurts, but it'll be all right. It's just the bean, jumping around."

"Jumping bean," she said sleepily. Tristan's eyes stung and his throat wanted to close up. He had no idea what kind of damage the bullet had done to her or to the baby. If she was bleeding internally, he didn't know if she would live long enough to have the baby or if the baby was even alive.

What he did know was that it was his fault she'd been shot. He hadn't taken good enough care of her. He should have been between her and the shooters the entire time.

She was looking at him with a frown on her face. He started to say something, but she spoke first. "Don't worry, Tris. I'll be fine. You always take good care of me. I know I'm safe with you."

He nodded at her, then put his arm around her so she couldn't look up into his face. He shook his head disgustedly. She thought she'd be safe with him. Well, he'd made a major mess out of that. Not only had he abandoned her for two months, as soon as he came back to her, he'd brought nothing but trouble following in his wake.

Sandy's left hand rested on her baby bump, her fingers curled as if she was afraid to let go. He wanted to ask her if the baby had moved, but he was sure that if the bean had kicked or wiggled, she'd have told him. What if their child was dead?

"What's the matter, Tris? You got a cold? You're sniffing so much."

"Yeah, hon," he said, gritting his teeth and blinking against the wetness in his eyes. "I must have caught a cold."

Chapter Thirteen

It was a slow and pain-filled walk to the first log bridge, during which Tristan heard several faint rounds of gunfire that he couldn't identify. He thought he heard rifles and Boudreau's shotgun and a third, different sound that might have been the echo of the flare gun. It was hard to tell, what with the distance and the muffling effect of the trees and underbrush.

About the time Tristan thought that sawing his leg off with a nail file couldn't hurt any worse than continuing to walk on it, he came upon a familiar and welcome sight. It was a large pile of dried foliage, vines, branches, twigs and leaves.

It looked as though a small whirlwind had blown it into the shade of a big cypress tree. But Tristan could see Boudreau's hand in the carefully disarranged pile. He knew the back of the deceptive pile of underbrush and leaves was woven together to create a mat that fit over the opening to the hideout. The other three sides were a wall built of mud and vines and brush that had been there for who knew how many years and completely hid the rough-hewn lean-to from even the most suspicious eyes.

He pushed aside the cover of woven vines and branches. The inside was as clean and carefully main-tained as it had always been. For a marginal shelter, it contained some surprising and clever amenities.

The lean-to was made out of scrap lumber and sturdy branches with a tarp draped over them. Over the years the wood had weathered and rotted and been replaced, as had the tarp. So the inside walls were an abstract patchwork of blue, silver and brown.

The largest item inside was a long, shallow wooden crate turned on its side. It was deep and wide enough to sleep one person easily or two if they were very close. The way it was positioned, it was always dry. The floor of the shelter was covered with thick sisal mats. They wicked water easily and kept the shelter floor feeling relatively dry.

Tristan got Sandy inside and laid her down in the makeshift bed. He found two thin wool blankets wrapped in plastic and took them outside to shake them. They looked clean and whole and the plastic hadn't been chewed through. So he covered Sandy with them. By the time he got her tucked in, he was shivering with exhaustion.

"I'm sorry, Tris," she murmured as she pulled the covers up to her chin. "You need to rest, too."

He shook his head. He didn't have the strength to answer her or tell her that she had nothing—*nothing*—to apologize for.

"What's in all the boxes?" Sandy asked, pushing a wad of blanket under her head as a makeshift pillow.

Tristan shot her a sidelong glance. "I thought you'd gone to sleep. You need to conserve your energy."

Sandy looked at her husband. The small scar on the side of his head where the roughneck's bullet had grazed him stood out against his dark hair. He sat with his back against the lean-to wall and his right leg carefully extended. He leaned his head back and closed his eyes.

"You're the one who needs to rest," she said. "You look like you're about to pass out. I haven't been up for two days."

"Actually, I don't think you've had much more sleep than I have," he said without moving.

"Well, I'm not down to one leg to walk on."

"No. You've just—" He stopped, but she knew what he'd been about to say. *You've just been shot in the stomach.*

He grimaced. "I'm going to watch for Boudreau."

"You are a stubborn, stubborn man," she muttered, then louder, she said, "I'm exhausted, but I'm not sleepy. What's Boudreau got in here?"

His shoulders rose a little, then relaxed. "Survival stuff. Canned food, coffee, water and tools like a can opener, a screwdriver, hammer. You know. Things you might need in an emergency."

"So this is a storm shelter?"

"Storm house, hideout, maybe even guesthouse."

"What?" Sandy lifted her head and stared at his profile. He grinned and her heart skipped a beat. She loved him so much. On the heels of that thought came the memory of her mother's words. *Don't fall in love if you can help it. By the time it's over, he'll own every tiny sliver of your broken heart.* Sandy smiled sadly, her gaze still on her husband. "Every sliver," she whispered.

"Hmm?" Tristan asked.

"Provisions and some tools? Is that all? This looks like a lot of crates."

"He's probably got some clothes in here. Maybe a couple of sleeping bags. He had one he'd let Zach and me use."

"That's what's in these big ones?"

"No. Actually that's his weapons stockpile."

"Weapons?" She wasn't sure if she liked sleeping in a weapons stockpile. "Not loaded, I hope. What kind?"

He sat up and wiped his face, rubbing his eyes wearily. "I remember a revolver and a few boxes of ammunition. Oh, and a gun-cleaning kit."

"A revolver. That's like a six-gun, isn't it?"

He nodded. "Maybe some shotgun shells, too, for his big gun."

"What about the other big crate?"

He shrugged. "I don't know. Boudreau caught me looking in that first one and nearly skinned my hide."

"Really? When was that?"

"Years ago. I wasn't thirteen yet. Maybe not even twelve. He got madder than I've ever seen him. He said, 'You never touch those crates. *Mais non.* You do not come here without me from now on. Understand, you?'"

Sandy chuckled softly. "You do a pretty good impression of him. Wow…" Her voice trailed off. After several seconds, she spoke again. "Tris?"

"Yeah, hon?"

"Are we going to be okay?"

He scooted closer to her and leaned over and kissed her on the temple. "We're going to be fine. The sheriff has to know that these guys are up here. He's probably got the Coast Guard on their way in helicopters, or at least standing by." Tristan had little hope that his words were true. He prayed that Sandy, who knew him so well, didn't notice.

"How long will they take?" she murmured, almost forgetting what she was asking about.

"Not long," Tristan whispered.

She yawned. "Probably going…sleep now."

Tristan sat down and carefully stretched out his legs. He hadn't meant for her to know how badly he was doing. But she knew him too well.

He stretched, trying to get the aches and knots out of his arms and neck. Everything hurt and quivered with fatigue. His calf muscle was on the verge of a cramp and so he flexed his foot, but his effort was too little too late. In spite of his care, the overworked muscle seized.

He clenched his jaw and massaged it, holding his breath against the pain. He tried to keep quiet, but once in a while a quiet moan or grunt would escape. Luckily, they didn't wake Sandy, who was snoring softly by the time the muscle settled down.

Watching her sleep was relaxing to him and he began to get drowsy. With a quiet curse, he straightened, stretched and looked at his watch. It was ten minutes after three. The sky was clear, but with the thick overhang of branches in this dense part of the swamp, there were lots of shadowy places. The sun wouldn't go down until after seven o'clock, but the bayou would be dark long before that.

He was worried about Boudreau. Tristan had been able to sleep a few hours, but his friend had been awake for as long, if not longer, than he had. He wasn't even sure if Boudreau had taken a nap in all that time.

It was frustrating to sit and do nothing, knowing Boudreau was out there, exhausted and sleep-deprived, defending them all alone. Still, it was Tristan's job to protect Sandy. And Boudreau knew the bayou better than anyone.

He shifted and felt something in his pocket. He pulled out the small rhinestone-encrusted baseball glove that hid a flash drive. He smiled as he turned it in his hand. He'd chosen the baseball glove on a whim, hoping it might portend a boy. The fact that it matched the mobile closely enough that he could hide it in plain sight was a happy accident.

Thank goodness he'd grabbed it. The tiny, sparkly flash drive held the recordings that he hoped would match Vernon Lee's voice. He wanted to see the evil man's multibillion-dollar empire fall.

A shot rang out and he jumped. The report sounded like a rifle, so it was one of Lee's men. He waited, listening for Boudreau to return fire with his shotgun, but heard nothing.

Boudreau must not want to give away his position by firing back. At least, Tristan hoped that was why he was quiet.

Still, just in case, Tristan crawled inside the lean-to and grabbed one of the large magazines for his handgun. He inserted the magazine, then hefted the gun to feel how the extra weight was distributed. Not bad. He positioned himself in the opening of the lean-to, where he could see and hear.

"Tris." Sandy's sleep-softened voice floated over him.

"Hey," he said. "Go back to sleep."

"What's going on?" she asked.

"It's okay. I heard something."

"A gunshot," she said matter-of-factly. "What's that blue thing you're holding? Is that part of the mobile over the baby's crib?"

He looked at it. "It's—" He was momentarily stumped. Did he tell her what it was and explain that this was the proof that Vernon Lee had tried to kill him? Or did he make up something?

"Wait. Shh. I think I hear something again."

She lifted herself up on one elbow. "No, you don't. What's the deal about the baseball glove?" She stared at it. "Oh, I see. It's a flash drive. That's your evidence, isn't it? You hid it in the nursery? In the mobile?"

Tristan let it dangle from his fingers. "I was going to transfer the files to Homeland Security the next time I was home," he said quietly.

"But you never came home," she said, her voice breaking. "You should have told me. I could have sent it to Maddy."

He nodded. "I thought there was time. I won't make that mistake again,"

Her eyes filled with tears. "I won't, either," she said.

Tristan looked away. He was afraid if their gazes held very long Sandy would see the worry in his eyes.

"Tris?"

He winced at her tone. "Sandy—"

"No, wait. What's going to happen? It looks to me like there's a standoff. I'm afraid two injured people and one exhausted man are no match for those men."

He had a reassuring answer all planned, but a noise interrupted him. He held up a hand.

"Shh!" he said.

He heard the sound of footsteps tromping through the woods toward them. He slid inside the lean-to and pulled the cover across in front of him, leaving a small slit. Carefully, he thumbed the toggle switch on the side of the weapon to Auto.

When Boudreau appeared from the tangled woods,

relief cascaded through Tristan's veins. His friend was all right.

The first thing the Cajun said was "Cover's not all the way over the opening."

"I left myself room to see and shoot. Sandy was asleep on her feet, so I got her tucked in as quickly as I could," Tristan said defensively, knowing that wasn't the whole truth. He was too tired and so he was making mistakes and Boudreau knew it.

"Going too fast can slow you down a lot, yeah," Boudreau said as he looked around 360 degrees, then stared at nothing, listening.

While Boudreau checked out the area, Tristan checked him out. His sun-browned face had a greenish-gray tint to it, and his mouth was drawn down and pinched looking. His eyes looked weak and his shoulders were slumped even more than they'd been a couple of hours ago at the cabin. "You're about dead on your feet. Climb in there and take a nap. I'll keep watch."

"*Non.* Something to eat and some water and I'll be fine."

Tristan reached back into the lean-to and pulled out one of the small food crates.

Boudreau pried the wooden lid open with the big knife he always carried. There were two glass jugs inside and what looked like jerky and some kind of fruit and nut bars in a glass jar. Boudreau grabbed a jug and drank about a pint of liquid out of it.

"That's water?" Tristan asked.

Boudreau nodded and handed the jug to Tristan, who took a long drink, then stuck his head inside. "San? Want some water?"

She opened her eyes to a small slit. "Please," she said. Tristan left the bottle with her.

Boudreau grabbed a handful of jerky and closed the glass jar. "She doing okay?" he asked softly.

"I don't know. I don't think she's bleeding anymore, but she felt hot. I think she has a fever."

"Could be," Boudreau said. "I reckon it's time to fight."

Tristan flung his head back and sighed deeply. "I guess we can hope they're as tired as we are."

"Probably are. Plus, although they got good weapons, they're slow and they don't know the swamp."

"They don't, but hell, Boudreau, you're so exhausted you probably can't lift your gun, and I'm not even half a man with this leg."

Boudreau lifted the shotgun to his shoulder and aimed at the path. "This look like I can't lift my gun?"

Tristan didn't bother answering his question. "How close are they?"

"Probably as close as they can get without running into the mines."

"The mines?" Tristan said, "What did you do? Are they going to step on them?"

"*Non.* I don't want to kill them. I want them to turn tail and run right smack into the sheriff. I chopped down all but one log on the longest bridge and I wired a mine in full view on either end of the log."

Tristan tried to picture what Boudreau was describing. Each mine was about fourteen inches in diameter. It might fit across the log. "Can't they jump over them or remove the wires?"

"Son, how long you known me? Did you ever see me do something halfway?" Boudreau didn't wait for Tristan to answer. "They can try to do something with the mines, but it wouldn't be a good idea. I wrapped the wire that I used to fasten 'em to the trigger. If they try to cut the wires or unwrap them they're liable to blow themselves up." He chewed on the jerky. "And the way I've got the wire strung, they can't jump high enough from that wobbly log over the mine without catching their feet on the wire. They should know they can't touch them. And if they try to walk through the swamp—"

"The gumbo mud'll get them." Tristan studied him. "Sounds like you covered every base."

Boudreau shrugged and bit off another piece of jerky. "Not every one." He paused for a beat. "There's one thing they could do. It's chancy, for them and us. It could work, but it could also—"

His words were interrupted by a huge explosion. Actually two explosions right on top of each other. Boudreau tossed the last bite of jerky down in disgust. "—blow up the log bridge," he finished. "Push that biggest crate out here."

Boudreau pried the lid off with his knife, then cursed in Cajun French. "I was counting on these grenades, but they're corroded."

"So they're duds?"

Boudreau shook his head. "*Non.* Worse than duds. Duds are dead. These, you don't know if they'll explode on time or if they'll go off in your hand before you can even pull the pin."

Tristan shuddered at that thought. Looking into the crate, he saw the white crystals that covered the grenades. "What should we do with them?" he asked.

"They been fine here for fifteen years. They'll probably stay fine, long as nobody bothers them."

"So if we don't have grenades, what are we going to use?"

Boudreau pushed himself to his feet, grunting at the effort. "Our heads, son. We're going to have to use our heads. Now let's go. We've got to disarm some bad guys. Let's hope they ain't too smart to get stuck in the mud."

SANDY HEARD PEOPLE TALKING, she thought. She couldn't be sure because her ears were ringing from the explosion that had shocked her out of a restless doze.

"Tristan?" Her voice echoed in her ears. She yawned, trying to get rid of the ringing.

Tristan stuck his head into the lean-to. "Hey," he said. "Did the explosion wake you?"

His voice was distorted, too. She rolled her eyes at him as she moved to get up. When she did, a sharp, stinging pain hit her stomach. Her hand flew to her tummy. "Oh!" she cried. "Oh, no!"

"What's wrong?" Tristan asked.

"I think I tore the cloth away from the wound." She looked up at him and felt tears start in her eyes. "I forgot," she muttered, wrapping her hands around her tummy protectively.

Tristan crawled over to sit beside her and pulled her close. "Let me see." He checked the bandage on her tummy. "I think you're okay. I don't feel or see any blood and the bandage is still in place."

She shook her head. "You don't understand. I wasn't careful. I went to sleep and forgot about the baby," she said, sniffling. "I forgot him. And not only that. I forgot I'd been shot. I forgot that he…he might not be okay." Now she was crying in earnest.

She pressed one hand to her heart and the other to the

spot on the right side of her tummy where the little bean liked to kick. "Oh, Tristan, I for...got—" She sobbed.

Tristan pulled her close and held her, his face pressed into her hair, his hand still on her baby bump. "It's not your fault. I gave you something to help you sleep. You probably were dreaming—"

"Stop." She laid her hand over his. "It's because he's not moving—" Her words were cut off by a sob.

"Wait," Tristan said. "Be still."

"What if he's—"

"Shh." He pressed harder.

Then she felt it and her fingers curled against the back of his hand. Had she really felt a tiny kick?

"San?" Tristan's voice was unsteady. "Did I just feel something?"

She looked down at her baby bump, then up at him. "He kicked," she murmured, almost overcome by relief.

"I know," he said, his voice unsteady with awe.

"He kicked! Oh, Tris, he's alive!"

"Tristan!" Boudreau's gruff voice called from outside the lean-to. "We got to go. Even an idiot can figure out how to move through the mud, if you give him enough time."

Tristan closed his eyes and sat still. She could feel the fine trembling of his hand against her skin, even through the bandage and the nightgown.

"Tristan!" Boudreau sounded irritated.

"Coming!" Tristan called, then he leaned over and kissed her. She was still crying, but now it was with joy. Her baby was alive. She kissed Tristan back, feeling the same thrill and the same growing flame that she felt every time, whether it was a kiss of passion during lovemaking or a sweet, tender kiss, like this one right now.

He pulled away reluctantly. "Got to go help Boudreau take care of those guys," he told her as he pulled a long, curved magazine and three normal ones from Boudreau's weapons crate.

Once he'd stored the ammunition in the hunting vest, he kissed her once more. "Stay here and stay hidden. You'll be fine. I'll be right back," he said.

Sandy knew he was lying. He and Boudreau were exhausted. Neither of them had the strength or stamina to stand up to the men chasing them.

She watched him as he crawled awkwardly out of the lean-to, wincing as every movement hurt his leg.

Despite her determination, the tears started again. "You lying liar," she whispered, too quietly for Tristan to hear. "You'd better come back. I don't want to lose you again."

Tristan pulled the camouflaged mat over the lean-to's opening while Boudreau talked about the best way to approach the log bridge. After a few minutes Sandy heard their footsteps crunching on the forest floor and fading as they got farther and farther away, until she could no longer hear anything.

She sat there for a few moments, willing him to turn around and come back, but knowing in her heart that he would never do that.

She'd felt betrayed and heartbroken when she'd found out he'd been recuperating less than a mile from their home. But now she understood that he hadn't left her alone. He had done everything he could to protect her.

"Bean, your daddy's crazy if he thinks I'm going to sit here and do nothing while he's in danger," she whispered. She looked around at the crates. Tristan hadn't known what was in most of them. They were worth exploring. She might find something that they could use.

"But first, we've got to find that revolver he mentioned. I don't know anything about guns, but I'll bet I can handle a six-shooter." She patted her tummy. "I heard them say there were at least two of those *varmints* out there, little bean. That gives me three shots each."

Chapter Fourteen

Boudreau was at least two hundred yards ahead of Tristan. Before he could catch up, rifle shots rang out. Tristan listened but didn't hear the bass roar of Boudreau's shotgun.

"Bastards," he muttered, doing his best to run. "You'd better not hurt him."

The first thing he saw as the tangle of vines, branches and brush began to thin were the two small craters left by the exploded mines. The craters were shallow, but the force of the blast had knocked the log that connected the two islands of dry land into the swamp.

The next thing he saw was a man hip deep in the swamp, holding a rifle up over his head with one hand and trying to grasp a wet, slippery cypress knee with the other.

Tristan knew exactly what had happened. The man had jumped in, fooled by the deceptively calm surface, figuring he could walk across the firm bottom and climb up onto the dry knoll on the other side.

Instead, he'd found himself ankle deep in what the folks in South Louisiana called gumbo mud. It stuck to everything—skin, boots, tires and itself.

The other man was on dry ground, on the knoll behind

his partner. He was yelling at his buddy to stop struggling, because he was only making things worse.

Tristan gave the man on dry ground a second look. He was one of the kidnappers. The one who'd held a gun on him and had tossed him across the pier.

Finally, Tristan spotted Boudreau. The Cajun was crouched down behind a lantana bush. There was blood staining the left sleeve of his shirt. A hollow dread washed over Tristan. He'd never seen Boudreau hurt or ill. His friend had always been invincible, larger than life.

It took all Tristan's willpower not to rush over to him. Boudreau's head angled slightly in his direction, signaling that he knew Tristan was there. Then he moved it back and forth in a negative shake. Tristan read him loud and clear.

Stay back. Let them dig their own graves.

He could live with that. Carefully and silently, he shifted his weight to his left foot and got as comfortable as he could. He gripped the automatic handgun and waited to see what the two men were going to do. As he relaxed, the men's yelling began to coalesce into words and phrases.

"Stop thrashing around!" the kidnapper yelled. "If you fall over you'll never get up."

He was right. The more the man in the water struggled, the more the mud sucked him down.

"You got anything that might actually *help*, Echols?" the man in the mud shouted.

"Maybe stand still and see what happens. And careful with that rifle. I need you to be able to shoot."

Boudreau's head lifted about a quarter inch. Tristan was barely a second behind him in realizing that the man was beginning to figure out how to handle the mud.

Boudreau pushed himself up onto his knees and raised his shotgun. Tristan held his breath. Was he going to shoot one of them? That wasn't like him, but then Tristan wouldn't have thought it was like Boudreau to shoot the *Pleiades Seagull*'s captain without hesitation, either, for ordering Tristan killed.

"Bonjour, varmints," Boudreau said and shot the ground around three feet in front of Echols's feet. Echols jumped backward and nearly tripped. Boudreau emptied the second barrel two feet in front of his toes.

"What the hell?" Echols yelled and raised his rifle again.

"Why don't you explain what you doing chasing us?" Boudreau yelled. "'Cause I'm tired, me. I'm ready to go to the house."

"We want Tristan DuChaud. My boss wants to talk to him."

Tristan stepped far enough forward to be seen, but not so far that he couldn't take cover if either of the men started shooting.

"Hi there. Remember me?" he shouted.

The kidnapper Echols threw his hands out in a frustrated gesture. "You. Still cocky as ever."

"Oh, I'm not cocky," Tristan said. "Just confident. So how you been?"

"Tristan," Boudreau said. "Don't get too cocky."

Tristan felt his face grow warm. Boudreau was right. This was serious business. He had no business acting as though it was not. "Well, Echols, here I am. What's Vernon Lee got to say to me?" he asked, watching Echols closely, waiting to see his reaction to the name of the owner of Lee Drilling.

It was the man in the water who reacted. He tried to

lower his rifle to his shoulder, but the movement nearly toppled him into the water. Quickly he raised his arms again, waving them like a tightrope walker trying not to fall.

"How'd he figure out—"

"Shut up!" Echols yelled, then aimed his weapon at Tristan.

Tristan didn't react. He just kept his gaze on the man's hands and continued talking. "You're just going to shoot me? Here's an idea. Have your buddy record it on his phone so you can prove to Vernon Lee that I'm dead—this time.

"Oh, wait." Tristan gestured toward the man in the water. "He's sinking already. If he drops the phone, you'll have nothing. Legend says that the gumbo mud'll suck you all the way to the center of the earth."

"What?" the man in the mud screeched. "I'm sinking? How deep is this—" He looked down. "Echols? Get me out of here."

"Shut the hell up and throw that rifle over here."

"What? Oh, hell no!"

"Do it. We need that gun and without it, you can move much easier. Plus, if you drop it in the mud it'll be ruined."

Tristan saw Boudreau turn to look over his shoulder at him. "You okay?" Tristan called.

"Yeah. They just winged me."

"Look out!" Tristan cried suddenly as he saw Echols swing his rifle in Boudreau's direction. The Cajun dropped to the ground just as the rifle's loud crack split the air. The bullet tore through the brush above Boudreau's head. Then without hesitating, Echols whirled and fired off two rounds at Tristan.

Tristan hit the dirt where he stood as the bullets whistled by his ear. He waited a beat, then peered over the tangle of vines. Dappled sunlight glimmered off the steel barrel of the rifle as the man swung it back and forth between him and Boudreau, gauging how low to aim to send a bullet through the underbrush and directly into their bodies.

There was no time to check on Boudreau. Tristan lifted the automatic handgun and pressed the trigger. A burst of about six or eight shots spewed out of the gun, much faster than Tristan could count.

He dropped again at the very instant that his hand flew upward from the recoil. A squeal told him his wild volley had hit at least one man, probably the one in the mud. He doubted Echols was a squealer.

"I'm hit!" the man cried.

"Throw that gun over here before you drop it!" his partner yelled.

But the man stuck in the gumbo mud ignored him. He scooted sideways enough to steady himself against the cypress knee. He'd finally stopped struggling. There was blood on the left side of his shirt, but not much. The wound probably was a graze. As Tristan watched, he lifted the rifle and fired off a couple of wild rounds one-handed.

Then Echols joined the fray, and bullets spattered the leaves and branches all around Tristan. He had to stop them somehow. He didn't want to kill them, nor did he want Boudreau to have another death on his conscience, but what he wanted took a backseat to his determination to do whatever it took to get Sandy out of there and to a doctor.

"Tristan." Boudreau's voice was a little breathless.

"Get on back there. I'll take care of these two. You need to take care of yours."

Tristan fired again another volley. More rifle slugs bursting all around them. "You go," he called to Boudreau. "I'll take care of these guys. They can't have much more ammunition."

"Neither one of you are going anywhere," Echols said. Tristan rose up and took a look. Echols had been hit, too. Blood was staining the front of his shirt. But he had the rifle up and aimed again.

Then Tristan heard a sound that nearly stopped his heart. It was footsteps, treading lightly on the path behind him. There was only one person in the world it could be. He prayed he was wrong, even though he knew he wasn't.

"Sandy," he whispered through gritted teeth, when he heard the footsteps stop a few feet behind him. "Get the hell back to the hideout *now* or I swear to you I will shoot you myself."

"Tristan," Sandy whispered. "I found some grenades."

"What? Sandy!" Shock and gut-wrenching fear sent Tristan's pulse skyrocketing. "Damn it. Didn't you hear Boudreau? Those things are corroded and unstable. They could go off in your hands!" He shimmied backward until he was deep enough into the foliage that hopefully Echols couldn't see him. He pushed himself to his feet.

"Corroded? No, they're not. Look." She was holding a small metal box. She started to lift the lid.

"Where did you get that?" he demanded. He hadn't seen any metal containers in the lean-to.

"Inside a big crate. They were the only thing in there."

Behind them a rifle shot cracked, then another and another. "Get down!" he yelled. He grabbed her and pulled her down with him. She pushed the metal box into his hands. He opened it carefully. But instead of white crystals, he saw four perfectly good grenades, with shiny pins intact. "Boudreau," he called. "Metal box in the hideout? Can't be very old."

"Metal box?" Boudreau repeated. "Ooh-la-la. I put that in there the day before I pull you out of the water. I guarantee I plumb forgot."

Tristan kissed Sandy briefly. "I love you. Get back to the lean-to."

She glared at him. "I've got the revolver. I'm going to help."

"The hell you are."

"Tristan, you know what to do with those?" Boudreau called.

But Tristan didn't answer him. "You have to go back," he said to Sandy. "I mean it. You've probably saved our lives by finding these grenades. But I'm not letting you get shot again."

"I'm not going to sit in that lean-to and wait to see who shows up, you or them." The glare that Sandy aimed at him was nothing short of a laser, drilling straight into his heart. "I will never sit back and wait for you again, you stubborn lying liar."

He closed his eyes, hoping the stinging behind them would not turn into vision-blurring tears. "Sandy, I love you. I will never lie to you for your own good. I will never ever leave you. But please stay back. Please keep you and the little bean safe so I can get you both out of here."

She opened her mouth, then closed it. The laser glare dimmed as her mouth thinned grudgingly. "Fine. Okay. For the baby."

Tristan breathed a sigh of relief, then scooted back

to his shooting position. "Boudreau? We've got four," he said.

"Shh!" Boudreau whispered. "Listen."

Tristan froze, listening. Echols was talking. Not yelling. Talking. Tristan took a quick peek. "He's got a satellite phone," he whispered to Boudreau. "If we can get our hands on that, we can call the sheriff and he can get a position on us."

"We're stuck back in the swamp," Echols was saying. He hadn't even tried to lower his voice. The tiny knoll he was on wasn't big enough for him to have a private conversation. He knew that Tristan and Boudreau could hear every word. "In a standoff, facing each other on two islands surrounded by a sticky mud that sucks you down into it and won't let go. Farrell is stuck in it."

He stopped talking and listened. "You did! Yes, sir! Thank you, sir. I'll be listening for it. Tell them they can't land here. Not enough solid ground. They'll have to hover and send down a harness to pull us up."

He paused, listening. The relief on his face turned to terror. "But—but, Mr. Lee, you can't do that. We're right here, not fifty yards away. That won't work. The strafing will hit us, too. We've done our jobs, sir! Please. You have to get us out! Mr. Lee, no! Mr. Lee? Sir?"

Farrell, who had been listening, forgot what he'd learned in the past few moments and started struggling again. "Strafing? Oh, my God! That rat bastard Lee is going to kill us, isn't he? Damn it, Echols, I told you we'd never get out of this alive." He tried to pick up his right leg, then his left. "I can't move," he shouted. "Help me!"

Tristan's pulse was hammering again, this time because of what he'd heard. Both of the men had used the name Lee for the man who had just called them on the satellite phone and told them he wasn't going to rescue them. From Echols's side of the conversation, it sounded as if Lee was sending a helicopter. The bird could probably pinpoint their location from the satellite phone and Tristan had little doubt about its orders.

Lee apparently wanted no loose ends. So he'd ordered the helicopter to strafe the entire area, thereby killing Tristan, Boudreau and Sandy and Lee's own men in one pass of the helicopter.

"Hey, Echols," he called out. "Things don't sound good for you and your buddy there. What do you say we team up to stay alive? I'll help you if you'll help me. Call the sheriff on that phone. I'll give you his number."

Echols set the phone down and lifted his rifle. "Call the sheriff so he can shoot us or arrest us or try us for treason?"

"He won't shoot you, I'm pretty sure. And arrested for treason? It's better than being strafed alongside your enemy, right?"

Echols glared at him. "Why should I believe you'd even think about keeping your word?"

Tristan pushed himself to his feet and took another step out of the foliage. "Maybe you shouldn't. But I'll tell you this. I'm one of the good guys. I want to get out of here. My friend is wounded." They probably knew that Sandy was with him, but he wasn't going to mention her. "I'm no more interested in being strafed by Lee's helicopter than you are."

Echols stared at him for a long time.

A vague sound reached Tristan's ears. Farrell heard it at the same time Tristan did.

"Oh, my God!" he screamed. "That's a helicopter! For the love of heaven call the damn sheriff! I don't want to die here." He turned and tried to make his way to the knoll where his partner waited, but he slipped and sank to his armpits.

"Echols!" he yelled, in full panic mode now. "Call him, man! You've got kids, just like me."

"Call the sheriff," Tristan pleaded. "You know Lee's got a copter on the way. You've got to know the sheriff is searching for us, too. He mentioned the Coast Guard. We all heard the fire trucks. I'm sure the sheriff was right behind them."

"I'm sinking, Echols! Help me! Make the call!"

Echols made a shushing gesture, then asked Tristan, "How do I know you won't shoot me?"

Tristan shrugged. "You don't. But I haven't shot you yet and you and your buddy both are wide-open. Not to mention you could shoot me, too. Come on. You're trading certain death for a trial and a possible prison sentence."

"And if I decide to take my chances with my boss?"

"It's your funeral." Tristan shrugged. "Oh, wait a minute. I forgot to mention one thing. Lee won't have the pleasure of blowing you up after all." He reached into the box and grabbed one of the grenades. "See what I've got?" He held it up high so Echols couldn't help but see it.

"What the hell?"

"This? It's a good ol' US-military-grade grenade. You know what a grenade is, don't you?"

"You won't detonate that so close to you."

"That could be a smart bet, but the stakes are pretty high, I guarantee. We've got a lot more room over here. We can run. Besides, I can throw it way on the other side of you. Of course, if you call the sheriff for me, I won't have to waste these."

Echols was silent. Farrell talked almost the entire time, his tone varying from pleading to screeching to rationalizing.

Finally Echols switched the rifle to his left hand and picked up the satellite phone. "Give me the number."

"And one last little thing," Tristan said. "Thanks to you guys, the sheriff thinks I'm dead. You might have to do a little explaining to convince him that I'm alive."

"What? How am I supposed to explain that?"

"You could tell him about your boss, Vernon Lee."

Farrell was still pushing himself toward the knoll. He'd figured out that lifting each leg high enough and shaking it could help the water melt the sticky mud. It was excruciatingly slow, but it worked.

Tristan made a show of setting down the metal box of grenades and the automatic pistol. Empty-handed, he called out to Echols. "Come closer to the edge and hold the phone up so I can talk to him."

Echols started forward, but Tristan held up his hand. "First, drop your weapons. I did."

"Nope. I'm keeping my handgun," Echols said emphatically. "And I'm not talking to the sheriff. You can do your own explaining. You'll have to yell at the phone."

He could do that, but he did not really want to leave his cover and walk over to the edge of the dry land in order to be heard. That was probably stupid. Either of the men would have an easy shot.

"What are you doing?" his wife's voice whispered from behind him. "You can't go out there."

Tristan's heart jumped. "Damn it, Sandy. What are you doing here? I told you to go back to the hideout. I should have known you weren't going to listen to me. When have you ever?" He shook his head as he started forward.

"You know that this is the best chance we've got to get out of here. I've got to let the sheriff know that I'm alive. The only way he'll believe it is if he hears me himself."

"They will shoot you. Then they can call Lee and tell him you're dead and they'll be safe."

She was right. That was a possibility. But he'd heard Echols's voice on the phone. Echols knew that Lee was going to kill them. "It's a chance I've got to take," he told her, then looked at Echols. "Okay," he called to Echols. "I'll trust you."

"Tristan!" Sandy snapped. "That's like telling a hornet on your leg you'll trust him not to sting you while you're trying to get him off. So what if they trust you. You cannot trust them."

"Give me the number," Echols shouted.

Tristan gave him the number. He keyed it in and waited, the bulky phone held to his ear. Within a few seconds, his face changed from trepidation to a vague relief. But then how relieved could he feel about the certainty of being imprisoned for treason, kidnapping, assault with intent, arson and whatever else the government might want to charge him with. Of course, one difference was that when he faced a United States court, he could be relatively sure he'd come out alive. From how he'd responded to Vernon Lee earlier, it sounded as if Lee's plan was to wipe the slate clean. Get rid of not only Tristan, but the assassins he'd sent.

"Is this the sheriff?" Echols asked. Then he went on, "I'm calling regarding Tristan DuChaud." There was a long pause, then, "You don't need to know my name. Not yet. But I've got news for you. DuChaud is not dead." He listened for a moment, his gaze on Tristan.

"I'm standing here looking at him. Where? Hell, I don't know. Somewhere in the swamp."

The sheriff talked again and Echols looked at Tristan, frowning. "I don't know about his wife. She was in the house?"

Tristan shook his head.

"DuChaud is telling me she wasn't in the house." He listened, then sighed. "Yes. Fine. Fine. I set the fire. Yes, that was us, too. We shot at you when you tried to take the path to the dock." Echols listened some more, then looked at Tristan again. "He wants to talk to you."

"Sheriff!" Tristan shouted. "Can you hear me?"

"Hello?" the sheriff said. "I was about to hang up. Who the hell is this?"

"Sheriff Nehigh," Tristan yelled. "It's Tristan DuChaud."

"What? DuChaud's deceased. What's going on here? I warn you, I've got helicopters on the way. You guys are in big trouble and this is not funny. I'm having your phone traced."

"Barley," he yelled desperately, hoping that using the sheriff's nickname would convince him. "I'm Tristan DuChaud. You dated my sister in high school. We're on a satellite phone. I'm *not* dead. Boudreau, tell him."

Boudreau sat up and bellowed, "Sheriff, it's Boudreau here. Tristan tells the truth. He is alive."

"Boudreau? DuChaud?" Sheriff Nehigh said. "I just got word from the Coast Guard that their helicopters have picked up your signal. They'll be on top of you in no time." The sheriff cleared his throat. "Now, we got some time. Tell me this. What the hell is going on?"

Chapter Fifteen

When Sandy opened her eyes, everything was glowing an odd, ugly sea-green color. She blinked and looked around. It was a hospital room and she was in a hospital bed.

Her first thought was that she'd lost the baby and her pulse leaped in fear, but then he kicked.

"Ow, bean," she whispered. "That was a good one."

When she took a breath the harsh smell of antiseptic stung her nostrils and made her sneeze.

Sneezing made her hurt, deep in her stomach. She moaned a little, then lifted her head to look around. She wanted to shift her position, but when she tried to put her hands down on the mattress, she felt a pull and a small sting on the back of her right hand. IV solution. Bandage. Soreness.

On the wall in front of the bed was a whiteboard and a plastic box. It was too dim in the room to read what was written in green marker on the white board, but the box was labeled *Biohazard, Warning: Risk of Contamination* and *Dispose of Properly* in red letters.

Of course. She was in a hospital room.

She tried to remember how she got here, but her brain was hazy and the memories were more like dreams that always fluttered away on butterflies wings when she tried to catch them.

A vision of Tristan yelling across the swamp came to her. Was that the last thing she remembered?

She closed her eyes and explored her memory as well as she could. What had happened between that snippet of time and now was in there. She knew it was, if she could just access it.

Within seconds of closing her eyes, she began to drift off to sleep. While sleeping some more seemed like a great idea, she wanted to remember, so she flexed her right hand and the pain from the IV cannula stung her again, pushing away her drowsiness.

A memory of the prick of a needle and a voice promising that she'd relax soon came to her.

Well, she'd relaxed, all right. She could barely hold her eyes open. She glanced at her left wrist. Her watch was gone.

That made sense. They didn't let anyone wear jewelry into surgery.

Surgery? She'd had surgery? From somewhere came a faint recollection of a male voice telling her she wouldn't remember a thing, then lots of painfully bright lights hurting her eyes.

She wondered what time it was. She squinted at the clock on the wall above the whiteboard, but the green glow in the room was too dark to see the time.

Suddenly, she had to know the time. She felt along the edge of the hospital bed, looking for the buzzer. And she was thirsty.

When she turned her head as she felt for the buzzer, she was startled to see a figure in a chair beside the bed.

She pressed her left palm against her chest, where her heart pounded.

The sight of the shadowed figure triggered more memories, this time of endless questions.

Suddenly, it all came rushing back. The hammering interrogations had started with the EMTs on the helicopter and continued with the emergency-room staff downstairs.

But they were nothing compared to the grilling she'd gotten from the sheriff, a Homeland Security Agent, a member of the Governor of Louisiana's staff and a rather handsome, if uptight, young man who had never explained who he was.

And now here was *another* stranger, waiting for her to wake up? No. She pressed her lips together tightly.

"No," she muttered. "No more questions." Not until she got to ask a few of her own.

She reached for the buzzer again, so she could tell the nurse to get rid of this man, whoever he was, but she couldn't find its cord.

Suddenly tired, she laid her head back on the pillow. "Well?" she said, letting her eyes drift closed. "What do you want?"

The man didn't answer. She glanced sideways at him, then lifted her head to look more closely. He was sitting awkwardly, his head bowed.

He'd fallen asleep. She leaned as far to the left as she could and squinted, trying to make out his features in the early-morning sea-green light. As soon as her eyes focused on his face, her heart skipped a beat.

"Oh," she breathed. "Tristan."

He stirred and lifted his head.

She reached out to him.

"Hey, San," he murmured, reaching out to take her hand. "Are you all right? The nurses wouldn't tell me anything except that you were *resting comfortably*."

"Oh, Tris." Her voice broke. He was really here. "Oh, my Tristan."

And then her brain was awash with everything that had happened, from the fire to the running and hiding in the swamp to listening to the doctors talking about the miracle that was her baby.

The images and words rushed past her like fast-flowing river water. After a moment, she tried to verbalize some of it.

"I remember waking up in the ER and thought the past few days were a dream. I thought I was back in that world where you were dead."

He took her hand and wrapped his around it, then kissed her fingers. "I'm not dead," he whispered. "Feel this?" He pressed a trail of kisses onto her skin, from the back of her hand to her forearm to her shoulder, all the way up to her cheek. Then he said softly, "Tell me what the doctors said? Did they get the bullet out? Is the baby okay?"

Sandy smiled. "The doctor said we were very lucky. The baby's fine." A delicious warmth spread through her when Tristan gently pressed his forehead against hers. She closed her eyes as he pulled away just enough to kiss her.

But behind her lids, new images appeared, of bullets flying and blood spattering. She frowned at him.

"What about you?" she asked, looking him over. He was dressed in scrubs. His face was scratched, probably by branches, and his eyes were sunken with fatigue, but he was here. He was alive.

He nodded. His hand tightened on hers. "I'm fine."

"Are you really okay? And what about Boudreau?"

"He's here. We're in Houma. Terrebonne Parish Hospital. They're releasing Boudreau this afternoon. One of the rifle bullets parted his hair, on the wrong side, no less," he said, the frown fading a little as the corner of his mouth turned up. "They admitted him because the slug that hit him in the forearm kind of pulverized the bone."

"Oh, no," Sandy said. "He won't be able to get along with one arm."

"Okay, *pulverized* is probably the wrong word. They put several pins in it and they think it's going to heal okay. It'll hurt him when it rains, though."

"I hope it does. Heal, not hurt."

"He's been asking about you. He wants to come see you as soon as it's okay with the doctors."

"Really? I'd have thought he'd be chomping at the bit to get back home."

"Well, that, too."

She paused to look at him. The light in the room was getting brighter as the sun rose outside. "Tristan, please tell me. You're really okay? Have you been here the whole time?"

He shook his head. "I had to be debriefed. They flew me to DC. I guess they wanted to see for themselves that I was alive."

She frowned at him. "Really?"

He gave her a crooked smile. "Just kidding. It's standard procedure to be transported in for a debriefing after a…situation."

"You look exhausted," Sandy said. "How are you? Have you been able to rest? Did the doctors look at your leg?"

He angled his head. "I'm fine, really."

"Fine? That's all you have to say after everything that's happened?"

Tristan lowered the guardrail and leaned forward. He rested his palm on top of her head and stroked her forehead with his thumb.

"Homeland Security had me thoroughly checked out, mentally and physically. I must have talked with every acronym in the city. FBI, CIA, NSA. But they also sent me to Walter Reed for a complete physical. I might have to have surgery, but it can wait awhile."

"Surgery. On your leg? Oh, Tristan, maybe they can fix it," she said, squeezing his hand.

He frowned. "We'll see. Anyhow, I've been back here since yesterday evening. Spent about three hours talking with the sheriff, then I came to see you about eight-thirty, but you were asleep. They let me stay in here, a booby prize, I guess, since they wouldn't tell me anything specific except that you and the baby were resting comfortably." He stood and bent over to kiss her on the lips.

For a moment, Sandy floated in the blissful knowledge that Tristan was real, he was alive and nothing could change that.

When she opened her eyes and took her first good look at him, she saw that his face was drawn and pale. He looked worried and—as she'd told him—exhausted. More than anything in the world, she wanted him to kiss her again. She wanted to feel the vibrancy of his skin, the warmth of his lips. She wanted to soak in everything about him that proved to her that he was alive and real and here.

But because of the way he looked, all she said was, "They got them, didn't they? The bad guys?"

The frown returned to Tristan's face. "Oh, you surely remember that. Lee had told Echols, the guy on dry land, that he was sending a helicopter to strafe the whole area and kill us and them. That's the reason he finally decided to call the sheriff for me.

"The sheriff managed to get the Coast Guard to send two helicopters to intercept Lee's bird and send it running back to where it came from. Then one copter airlifted you and Boudreau here, and the other one picked up our two friends and me."

"I remember floating really high up but I thought that was a dream."

"Nope. No dream."

Sandy stared at him, openmouthed. *Butterfly wings.* "Not butterfly wings, helicopter propellers," she muttered.

"What?"

"Nothing. And they put you and those two killers in one basket? Tristan. They could have killed you."

He shook his head. "They were too happy not to be killed by Lee. I understand they're in DC now, singing their little hearts out to Homeland Security and the FBI about Vernon Lee and his plot to bring down the US from the inside by supplying automatic handguns to kids on the street and organized crime."

"Have they caught Lee?"

Tristan shook his head. "They can't find him. I was told there was evidence that he'd been shot, or had shot himself. But all that was found in his penthouse office in the Lee Building in San Francisco was a gun with his fingerprints on it and a fair amount of his blood. I don't think anybody connected with this case is going to make an assumption about whether he's dead. Not after they all assumed that I was."

"So he could still be out there?"

Tristan didn't answer for a beat. "He could be," he finally said.

"You don't think he is? Do you think he's dead?" she asked on a yawn.

Tristan frowned and was silent for a long time. "I don't. I think I'd have to say show me the body."

"Tristan," she said. "I have to tell you something. Lee Drilling sent a really nice condolence letter and they have set up a trust fund for the little bean."

"A trust fund? Screw that."

Sandy shivered. "I know. It kind of makes me nauseated to think about it." She lay quietly for a moment. "I might be sleepy," she murmured.

Tristan smiled at her. "You'd better sleep while you can. Everybody from the sheriff to the media to the government's going to want to talk to you, too, now that you're awake."

"I've already talked to them," she protested.

"Apparently not enough. I was given the times by my boss at Homeland Security and told that the alphabet agencies would like me to be at the interrogation, too."

He brought her fingers to his lips and kissed them. "I'm afraid all this will go on for a long time. I'm sorry." He sat there, pressing her hand to his cheek, that frown back on his face.

"What's wrong?" she asked.

He shook his head. "Nothing."

She pulled her hand away and took a long breath to try to push through the drowsiness. "Oh, no. No," she said sternly. "You are not going to keep on doing that. I won't stand for it."

Tristan lifted his gaze to his wife's eyes, which were blazing. But he couldn't hold it. Anger and fear shone from their depths. He stood and walked over to the window, where the sun was just coming up.

What could he do, if anything, to repair their broken hearts? They'd grown so far apart during the past few years. And then all this had happened and he'd let her down so completely that he was sure she could never forgive him.

He'd done it for her and their baby, and to try to stop a murderous terrorist, but had he lost everything important to him in the process? "Sandy," he said without turning around. "I'm sorry."

"What?"

He turned awkwardly, favoring his bad leg. "I let you down in so many ways. I hope you can forgive me."

"For-forgive you?" she stammered. "Are you kidding me?"

He closed his eyes, pain wrenching his sore heart. "I know. It's not enough, but I swear to you, I'll do everything I can to make it up to you if you'll let me."

"Tristan, there's only one thing I want you to do."

He nodded. "Of course. Anything."

"Come here and turn on the overhead light."

Baffled, he did as she said. When he looked at her, her face was glowing as it had when she'd first found out she was pregnant. He almost gasped aloud. From the time they were nine years old, he'd always thought she was the prettiest thing he'd ever seen. She still was.

"Unless I dreamed it, too, there should be a big manila folder around here somewhere. Do you see it? I'm pretty sure the doctor left it here." She looked around.

He saw it lying near the sink. He picked it up. "Is this it?"

"Yes. It's my sonogram. They printed it out so I could show you. They made a DVD for us, too."

"Of what?" he asked, still confused about what she was doing and saying.

When he looked at her, her eyes were wet with tears. Fear clawed at his insides. "Sandy? You said everything was fine. Is something wrong with the baby?"

"Just look at it." Her voice was tight with emotion.

He took out the glossy photograph and looked at it, his hand shaking with the force of his pounding pulse. "This is the bean?" he asked, angling his head one way and then the other. "Sandy, what is it? What am I looking at?"

A sniffle made him glance at her. "Are you crying? God, Sandy. Just tell me. What's wrong with him?"

"Can you see him?" She traced a shape on the photo with her finger. "His head, his back, his little legs?"

Tristan did. He traced the tiny head, the curve of the little back. The perfect arms and legs. "Oh," he said. "He looks perfect. Please tell me he's okay." His voice broke and his eyes stung. "Please."

Sandy didn't say anything. She just kept her gaze on the sonogram. Tristan turned back to study it. Then he noticed something odd. He frowned. "What's that?" he asked, pointing.

"Hmm?" Sandy murmured innocently.

"That." He pointed to a small opaque object that appeared to be clutched by the bean's impossibly tiny hand. "It looks like—" He stopped. He bent to look closer.

"Like what, Tris?" she whispered.

"It looks like a—" He shook his head. If he thought his pulse was pounding before, now it was slamming against his breastbone like a battering ram. "But that's impossible," he muttered.

Sandy chuckled softly. "You'd think so, but there it is."

"How— What—"

"I don't know how, but that is the bullet that shot me."

"But that's his little hand. He's *holding* it." Tristan looked up. "What—what do the doctors say?"

"They can't explain it. They say that it should have still been going fast enough to go right through me. They said they'd have expected it to do a lot of damage to—" she swallowed and gestured vaguely "—you know."

"I don't understand," Tristan said as much to give his brain time to catch up with what she was telling him as because it was the truth. How had a lethal bullet penetrated Sandy's skin and come to rest in their unborn baby's hand? "It looks like he caught it—"

"—to stop it from ripping through my kidney. A few people are calling it a miracle."

He shook his head in wonder. "It looks miraculous to me."

Sandy smiled at him through her tears. "That would be a total of two."

"Two?"

"Two miracles," she said, pushing up into a sitting position and reaching for him. "The first one was you coming back to me."

Tristan sat down on the edge of the bed and pulled her into his arms and kissed her, gently, then more deeply, until when they finally stopped, both of them were breathless.

"Hmm. Actually," Tristan murmured, "I'd have to say it makes for three miracles."

"Three?" Sandy stared at him. "What's the third one?"

Tristan pressed a sweet kiss to her temple. "That the three of us are here together. I love you, San. With all my stubborn, stubborn heart. And that's no lying lie."

Sandy laughed through her tears and kissed her husband. Her heart soared and the little bean kicked.

Epilogue

Several weeks later

"But you promised to bring your wedding dress," Sandy said to Maddy. She was sitting in an overstuffed chair in the cramped living room of the mobile home Tristan had gotten set up on the site of his family home that had burned. When the windows were open, there was still a charcoal smell in the air. "I wanted to see you in it since I couldn't go to the wedding."

"Honey," Maddy said, "that dress would have taken its own oversize suitcase. It would have cost a fortune to bring it and I didn't want to drag it around on our honeymoon."

"Okay, fine. But I want to see all your photos. We'll tell Tristan to put them up on the TV screen."

Maddy sat down in a kitchen chair and looked assessingly at Sandy. "You look good. Are you really doing okay?"

"You mean except for being confined to bed for my entire pregnancy? Sure. I'm fine."

Maddy picked up the sonogram photo off the table and looked at it again. "This is unbelievable. So they don't want you moving around too much because he might let go of the bullet?"

"Yes. Apparently it could be dangerous, and they don't want to have to go into the uterus prior to his birth."

"Well, your sonogram went viral. Your baby is famous before he's even born."

"I know. That's disgusting. If I can help it, he'll never know."

"You're not going to tell him?"

"Well, not until he's twenty-five or so."

Maddy smiled at her. "Sandy, I'm so glad nobody was hurt any worse than they were. What an ordeal you had."

"No more than you being kidnapped and Zach being shot."

"Oh, honey, if I'd had to go through losing Zach like you had to live through losing Tristan, I'd have died."

Sandy rubbed her very large tummy. "I might have, if not for the bean here."

"You're so brave," Maddy said.

"No. It's Tristan who's brave."

Maddy glanced toward the door. "He looks pretty good."

"He's doing better. He almost ruined the muscle tissue he has left on that right calf, with all the running we had to do. And he still hasn't gained back his weight. He's had to spend hours every week in hearings, interrogations and interviews, but they have finally proven that the voice on the recordings is Vernon Lee's."

"Right. I see summaries of what's going on, since I was involved in the case at the beginning."

"It's eating Tristan up, though, that there's no proof that Lee is actually dead. I don't know if he can rest until he can view the man's body."

Maddy shook her head. "The prevailing opinion is that he's alive. There was a lot of blood, but there have been cases in the past where people have bled themselves and saved up their blood so they could be declared dead by exsanguination."

"Ugh. Where are Zach and Tristan? I'm hungry."

"I know, right? How long does it take to grill some burgers."

"And bacon!"

Maddy laughed. "You've done a 180 on bacon, I see. Even the word made you nauseous when you were first pregnant."

At that moment, Tristan and Zach came in, laughing. Sandy noticed that Tristan was not limping as much as he sometimes did. And he looked happy. He and Zach had been best friends practically all their lives. Male friendships were odd and interesting. The two of them were acting as though they saw each other every day.

"If you'd been there, Boudreau and I would have had to carry you kicking and screaming across that bridge," Tristan said, laughing.

Zach scowled as he set a plate of grilled burgers on the kitchen counter. "I'm not that afraid of heights. You have to get me a little above sea level before I start panicking."

"Lunch is served," Tristan said, walking over and bending to plant a kiss on top of Sandy's head.

"Oh, Tris, come on. No buns? No mayonnaise? No cheese? And where's my bacon?"

Zach was already headed toward the refrigerator. He pulled out a tray that contained everything, even the bacon. "Right here."

Zach and Tristan fought over the biggest burger while

Sandy and Maddy sat and watched them act like six-year-olds.

"Zach," Maddy said. "You two are like bulls in a china shop. You're going to break the whole kitchen if you keep scuffling." Finally she got up and forced her way between them.

"My turn," she said.

Tristan emerged victorious, with the giant burger captured in a bun. He squirted mayonnaise on it and added cheese and bacon and brought it over to Sandy.

"Here you go, Ms. I'm-Eating-for-Two." He handed her the plate, then sat on the arm of her chair with his hand on her tummy.

"I can't eat all that," she protested as she prepared to take a huge bite.

She looked up at him and caught him watching Maddy and Zach.

"You've missed Zach, haven't you?"

Typical for him, he didn't answer.

"You might get to see him more if you take that position in DC." She felt him stiffen, but she went on. "I'd be perfectly happy there. Anywhere, actually, as long as I've got you there with me."

He looked down at her, his expression soft with a mixture of sadness and humor. "You like me," he said teasingly.

"I cannot deny that I do," she responded.

"What if I didn't go to DC?" he said, looking back at Maddy and Zach. "Those two were born to be government agents. Look at them. They're totally in sync. I was never good at it."

"No. You have an honest face and an honest and romantic heart."

"I was going to say I didn't like it. Anyhow, I happened to overhear a conversation and I almost got killed for it. I'm not interested in a steady diet of danger."

Sandy took a deep breath as a profound relief settled on her, dissolving the heavy cloud of worry she'd been carrying around for months. Carefully she said, "What are you thinking you might want to do?"

"I've talked to a guy who's a large-animal veterinarian in Houma. He could use an assistant a few days a week. I think I'll try that. The rest of the time I plan to start working on a house."

She couldn't stop the grin that spread on her face or the love that swelled in her heart. "You're going to build it here, where your home was?"

Tristan nodded. "Is that all right with you?"

Sandy smiled as the bean kicked the side of her growing baby bump. She took a bite of her huge burger without answering him.

Everything was all right with her world, because Tristan DuChaud loved her.

* * * * *

MILLS & BOON®

Regency Vows Collection!

If you enjoyed this book, get the full Regency Vows Collection today and receive two free books.

Order your complete collection today at
www.millsandboon.co.uk/regencyvows

MILLS & BOON®

The Chatsfield Collection!

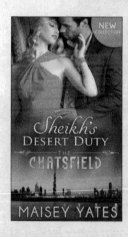

Style, spectacle, scandal…!

With the eight Chatsfield siblings happily married and settling down, it's time for a new generation of Chatsfields to shine, in this brand-new 8-book collection! The prospect of a merger with the Harrington family's boutique hotels will shape the future forever. But who will come out on top?

Find out at
www.millsandboon.co.uk/TheChatsfield2

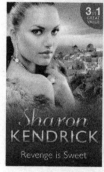  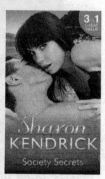

MILLS & BOON®
INTRIGUE
Romantic Suspense

A SEDUCTIVE COMBINATION OF DANGER AND DESIRE

A sneak peek at next month's titles...

In stores from 19th June 2015:

- **Surrendering to the Sheriff** – Delores Fossen *and*
  The Detective – Adrienne Giordano

- **Under Fire** – Carol Ericson *and*
  Leverage – Janie Crouch

- **Sheltered** – HelenKay Dimon *and*
  Lawman Protection – Cindi Myers

Romantic Suspense

- **How to Seduce a Cavanaugh** – Marie Ferrarella
- **Colton's Cowboy Code** – Melissa Cutler

Available at WHSmith, Tesco, Asda, Eason, Amazon and Apple

Just can't wait?
Buy our books online a month before they hit the shops!
visit www.millsandboon.co.uk

These books are also available in eBook format!